THE BYGONE PLAGUE

JOSEPH R. LALLO

Contents

Chapter 1

Fel had done a lot of things no man should ever do. He'd waded hip deep through stinking mires to pillage an ancient vault. He'd run errands for dragons. He'd swung from the saddle of a hippogriff as its rider desperately tried to shake him free. There was no end to the list of harrowing things Fel had plunged headlong into and come out alive, if not well. It had become common for him. Comfortable, even. But this? This crossed a threshold. This was uncharted territory and he felt lost.

It wasn't some sun-blasted desert. It wasn't a murky corner of the deepest sea. It was a restaurant in the nicer part of Beffshire. He shared the table with Allie, the barmaid at the place he would *much* rather be, and Mariss, the baker at a shop where he could barely afford to buy rolls.

He shifted in a seat designed to look better than it felt and glanced around at a clientele who were much the same. Women in outfits stiffened by whalebone and starched to the point of immobility. Men with wax shaping their mustaches and coifs styled to the point they looked more like sculptures than flesh and blood.

"Folks around here are looking a little..." he muttered, glancing askance at a woman at an adjacent table whom he was quite certain had creaked when she leaned forward.

"Dead?" Allie replied with a grin.

"Yeah," Fel said. "And not even freshly dead. It's like they were made up for their funerals and didn't want to let the finery go to waste."

"Oh hush," Mariss said, kicking Fel playfully under the table. "You have your fun your way, and they have their fun theirs."

"I just didn't expect to feel *this* underdressed," Fel said.

Mariss *had* warned him to dress well. He thought he'd done so. A far cry from the ruthlessly tailored masterpieces on display on the other patrons, Fel's outfit matched his personal definition for fine attire. Specifically, the faint patches of dirt on his well-worn shirt and trousers were bits that had survived a washing rather than being freshly applied. Allie didn't rise to the level set by the other patrons either, but she'd done an admirable job of finding the midpoint between barmaid and upper crust. In this case, it was precisely the same outfit that she wore beneath her apron but perfectly clean, ironed, and creased. The only one who actually looked the part was Mariss, though she'd done so by blazing her own trail through the frontiers of fashion, showcasing her exceptional clothing budget on the sheer quantity and quality of fabric, boasting bright, vivid, floral colors pulled together into pleats and ruffles that defied gravity.

"Oh, bah. We're here for the food and the conversation," Mariss said. "My father's closest friend owns this place. I've come here for every occasion worth celebrating since I was a little girl."

"What, exactly, *is* the occasion?" Fel asked.

She kicked him again. "Don't be silly. It's Founder's Day!"

"Founder's Day is next month. I know because Tem tried to book both private rooms for some big Founder's Day grum game he was planning," Allie said.

"He did?" Fel said with the distinct tone of someone who hadn't been invited.

"Relax, I told him that's not what those rooms are for, so it's not happening. Point is, it isn't Founder's Day today."

"Not *Beffshire's* Founder's Day. Landmark Square Founder's Day," Mariss said.

Both Allie and Fel looked blankly at her.

"Landmark Square?" Mariss repeated, as though she'd simply not been heard. "The trading post that was here before Beffshire was founded?"

"This is the first I've heard of this," Fel said.

"Oh, come now," Mariss said. "Landmark Square was a great big trading post, *well* back in the Bygone Era. It was named after a big statue or some such. Eventually they built up some big walls around the square to protect it, and more and more permanent buildings were built up around it, and then a *new* wall was built and *that* was the founding of Beffshire. You *must* know it. My tutors taught me all about it."

"My tutor was my dad, so mostly we were learning about how to maintain tension on tripwires to avoid activating spring traps," Fel said.

"I learned to read with books my mom 'borrowed' from her boss, so we didn't have much choice in the curriculum," Allie said.

"Oh," Mariss said. "Well, never mind all that. We're here for a lovely evening, and it is *my treat*, so let's enjoy it. What have you been up to, Fel? It seems like you're *finally* spending some time in Beffshire after a few too many trips abroad."

"Just waiting for the next trip," Fel said. "It turns out I'm not nearly as good at finding and killing people who tried to find and kill members of my family as I am at finding and stealing things."

The quiet conversation and louder clinking of cutlery on expensive dishes came to a sudden stop. Fel grinned. Allie did as well. She leaned back a bit.

"You know, I always thought the people-watchers and eavesdroppers who come to The Fox and Log just to soak up the gossip were being a bit low and crass. Now I'm starting to think listening in on the conversations at other tables is a sign of nobility," she said.

A sharply dressed and rather round fellow approached the table. "Madam Mariss. You are looking radiant as always. What will we be having for beverages this evening?"

"We'll be having the pepper soup and the shaved venison. Whatever wine you feel pairs best," Mariss said.

Allie raised a finger. "I'll also need an empty pitcher, three glasses of hard apple cider, a stick of cinnamon, a shot of bitters, and a butter knife," she said.

The waiter raised an eyebrow with the sort of fluid efficiency that suggested it was the only malleable part of his expression. "Madam Allie?" he said.

"I'm in a fancy place. I'm in the mood for a fancy drink, and you don't seem to offer any to suit my tastes, so I'm making my own."

"Bring it!" Mariss said with an excited clap. "Allie is an expert with drinks. I'm sure this will be *lovely*."

In the workshop of the Masker household, Martin leaned close over the exposed innards of a flat disk-shaped contraption. He gripped an engraving tool in one hand, its tip held with a surgeon's steadiness. Beside him, Tome stood with books in each hand. The pages of one were covered in unfamiliar symbols. The other was written in an archaic but comprehensible precursor to his own language.

"When you are ready," Martin said.

"You are certain you don't want to practice this on another piece first?" Tome said.

"According to the reference material, this needs to be etched in place for the contraption to function," Martin said. "Or such is the case with similar contraptions. This *is* practice."

"Very well. Then, if the elven spells can be trusted, and my understanding can be trusted, and—"

"Let us consider all qualifiers applied," Martin said.

Tome set down the spellbook and pointed at a mark. "Third symbol from the left, bottom row," he said.

Martin turned his practiced eye to the symbol, then began teasing curls of metal out of the plate.

"Is this the final step in completing the contraption?" Tome asked.

"Assuming it works, this will indeed provide all the functionality we currently seek," Martin said, keeping his eyes steadfastly on his work.

"I would have thought it would take considerably more time to prepare a contraption from scratch. It hasn't even been three weeks since we learned we'd need to track a stolen mask, and now we are on the cusp of having a device purpose built to do so."

"The egg has not yet hatched, so we'd best not be counting our chickens. But a confluence of events certainly conspired to facilitate this bit of innovation. An overabundance of mundane antiques in the inventory, things that do not require my specific talents, has left me with time to spare for projects such as this. A handful of proper Bygone Era tools reclaimed from the quarry has extended my capacity. And, of course, the motivation of dealing with a threat to my family once and for all has served as more than adequate motivation to keep my mind on the task. Your own contributions shouldn't be overlooked either."

Tome rubbed his face. "I've been translating things that are themselves translations. The chain of languages I understand is becoming painfully overextended."

"When one stretches one's borders, one discovers new territories." Martin etched a final line. "To that end, let us see where we have arrived."

He took a fine bristle brush and carefully flicked the shavings from the mechanism, shaking his head lightly at the requirement to perform the task in situ. In a perfect world, such things could be done separately to avoid the chance of fouling the mechanism with chips and swarf. Alas, the ragged edge of contraptioneering approached magic and thus began to follow a new logic with new rules.

Carefully shaped bits of metal snapped together nicely. Once the last fastener had been tightened, he flipped the contraption over. It visually resembled the flame detector that had been used to track and extinguish the stolen Graves flames. But its operation was designed to be subtly different, assuming it did indeed operate. A lever emerged from the side, with five positions. Each one aligned with a cluster of punched marks on the face of the device. He clicked the lever to the first position. The compass-like needle in the center of the contraption shuddered in place. He dabbed some oil, and it pivoted freely to point to the inert mask sitting near the edge of the workbench. He adjusted the switch. The needle lazily shifted. When it came to rest, Martin placed a compass beside it and consulted a map.

"It indicates the Student mask is roughly in the same location the Warrior suggested."

"Success then," Tome said.

"Or something acceptably close to it. Some light maintenance to ease the motion of the needle, and some finishing work to make it more comfortable in the hand and rugged in the bag. But by tomorrow evening, I would consider this ready for the field. A joint effort between a paper mage and a contraptioneer."

"And incorporating aspects of both paper magic and whatever the elves call their mysticism. Something of a calico accumulation of dissimilar parts."

"Calico? Patchwork? Perhaps." Martin tested the edge of one of the cosmetic components and adjusted its shape with a file. "But the result here proves they aren't so different. That such disparate things could combine to achieve a common goal is fascinating. Encouraging. Like we're working our way toward some sort of grand, uniting truth."

"Or we've assembled an abomination."

Martin looked up from the contraption as though for the first time in the conversation he'd realized he wasn't simply speaking aloud to himself. "An abomination?" He raised the device. "This doesn't concern you, does it? A simple directional indicator? You struck me as an open-minded and curious sort. That kind of talk makes you sound a bit more like the average citizen of Beffshire."

Tome waved off the comment. "Bah. It's a bit of my father still clinging to me, and a dash of the ominous warnings that hang over just about any text dealing with mysticism. Magic is a bit like groping about in the dark. Slowly we uncover those elements, those words, those recipes that bend the forces of our world to our desired whims. But all the while we know that there lurk unwanted effects, fearsome consequences or disproportionate prices. And if we fumble about without concern or care, we are just as likely to fall into a pit as discover a jewel. Father would say that all of magic is the pit. But even the staunchest practitioners seek to rope off avenues of study lest we find something unpleasant in the darkness. That mixture of techniques in your hand would be decried by every mage I've met. Layering magics invites the unexpected."

"You call it the unexpected. I call it a discovery. But we needn't debate. The important thing is that it works." He turned to the inert Warrior mask. "And that means we can stop consulting something I think we all can agree is best left in slumber."

It was a good thing Mariss's father knew the owner of the restaurant, as otherwise it was quite likely the evening would have come to an abrupt end some time ago. Fel and Allie were not accustomed to an evening's activities and refreshments only lasting an hour or so. Thus, they'd embraced their table at the restaurant with the same gusto as a stool at The Fox and Log.

"I think I understand why rich people eat such small food," Fel said, pushing aside a plate he'd cleared of some delicacy or another. "It's so you can spend a whole night out without getting too full."

Mariss, a bit rosy cheeked from one drink more than her usual limit, giggled and murmured discreetly. "Daddy says people don't come here to eat. They come here to be seen eating. It's almost a shame. Because the food really *is* delightful." She raised her drink. "But they should think about adding this drink to their menu. It's so warm and lovely."

"Mmm..." Allie muttered, a bit distant.

Fel took a sip. "Something wrong, Allie?"

"That couple across the way have had empty glasses for five full minutes."

"You're not on duty, Allie," Mariss said.

"It's a bit difficult to snuff that particular candle in my mind once it's been lit." She leaned back and swirled her own drink. "Though good company and good food have dimmed it a bit. A girl could get used to nights like this, once in a while."

"We could make it a regular thing!" Mariss said with a clap.

Fel snickered. "You should have seen the face of the waiter when you said that."

Mariss fluttered her fingers dismissively. "Don't mind him. And we needn't come here each time. I just think it's nice seeing each other outside of where we work for a change." She lowered her voice and added in a conspiratorial tone. "At least, it's a change for *me*."

Fel shifted uncomfortably in his chair, he hoped not noticeably. A quick glance to Allie suggested a similar thought was going through her mind as well. Neither chose to voice it.

"Given the sort of situation that leads to the two of you showing up where *I* work, it's probably best we don't meet there," Fel said. "Though, I'll tell you. Three weeks without much to do besides help Dad with polishing and cleaning and toting crates across town? It could be worse. At least it's let my wounds heal properly. There's a difference between getting healed by one of those paper slips Tome writes up and doing it the old-fashioned way."

"Uh-oh," Allie said. "Our man is letting himself get comfortable in his own life."

"What do you mean?" Fel said.

"In the last three weeks, you've barely spent any time at all at the grum tables. You've let your muscles unknot from being sent off to who-knows-where to do who-knows-what. I would have expected you to be bouncing off the walls, looking for some scheme or another to hoist yourself up to whatever level you're reaching for. But dare I say, you seem *content* lately."

"Like you say," Mariss said. "Good company does that."

"I think you're reading too much into a bit of a break," Fel said.

"I think you're finally starting to see it wouldn't be so terrible to settle into the life you already have and enjoy what you've already got," Allie continued, "instead of risking your neck or gambling your duots, and your skin, for something that's never as good as it's cracked up to be."

"See, this is a trick," Fel said. "If I say the wrong thing, it'll sound like I'm saying this perfect little moment isn't good enough for me."

"Perfect little moment," Mariss said, clutching her hands together.

"He's onto us, Mariss. He's figured out we actually care if he lives or dies," Allie said.

"Look, that one I'll fess up to. If it takes another month or two before someone tries to kill me, you won't hear me complain about that."

"Progress!" Allie said, raising her glass.

Fel tilted his head and turned an ear to the door. "This meal is about to come to an end."

"Oh, I'm sure they'll let us have the table a bit longer."

A soft clippy-clop outside began to grow louder.

"Oh, right. Yes," Allie said as it became audible to her.

A moment later, the front door thumped open and the goatlike lesser unicorn known as Parch trotted in as though he was late for an appointment. The scattering of remaining patrons stirred as much as their upper-crust sensibilities would allow. More than one monocle clacked to a table or jangled on its chain. After an evening of showcasing the utmost of refined service, the waiter had reached the limits of his experience and training. Evidently an expensive eatery didn't have a standard procedure for dealing with wild animals wandering into the establishment. He scoffed and stammered, attempting to conjure up some sequence of words that would articulate his displeasure without lowering himself to raised voices and profanity. Fel stood and intercepted Parch before the waiter could complete his sentence.

"I'll just take the little fellow outside if you ladies don't mind settling up," he said quickly.

Parch, quite visibly irritated at Fel's decision to make himself scarce, refused to leave without a round or two of playful headbutts. Fel obliged, much to the consternation of the elderly fellow whose table was jostled by the overeager Lesser Mystic. Finally Fel managed to coax the horned scamp outside. The street outside a fancy restaurant was nearly as uptight as the interior, so the stares from onlookers didn't taper off until Fel had led Parch to an alleyway across the street.

"You lasted longer than I expected you to," he said, delivering slaps and thumps to the unicorn's forehead in lieu of headbutts. "You're getting better at behaving yourself."

"I was about to say the same thing to you," Allie said, slipping into the alley beside him. "Though if Mariss wasn't the one paying already, this here might be a very creative way to get out of paying a bill. Or to abandon a bad party."

Either out of disinterest in Allie or an instinctive awareness that she would have none of his antics, Parch didn't attempt to involve her in the sparring.

"Packing Fel Masker into a place with finger sandwiches is a bit like putting a waistcoat on an ox. A lot of trouble and effort for what'll at best be a bit of a giggle. This whole evening didn't strike me as your cup of tea when it was proposed," Allie continued.

"*Tea* isn't my cup of tea," Fel said. "But the company was good. Although..."

"Seeing Mariss watch us is a little like seeing a child watch two puppies romping about," Allie said, completing Fel's thought.

"In the space of two sentences, I've been compared to an ox and a puppy," Fel said.

"It pretty much sums you up, I think."

"I'd rather get some human being mixed in there."

"Having interacted with a fair amount of humanity, you're better off as a puppy ox," Allie said. "But I think she's in love with the idea of us being together."

"Yeah," Fel said.

There was a leaden pause in the conversation. Fel's stone-faced expression, trained by a thousand games of grum, was put to the test.

"Forgive me," Allie said with a snicker. "What with the puppy and the ox, it seemed appropriate to let an elephant into the room."

"Yeah..." Fel said.

She leaned on the wall and crossed her arms, a grin plastered on her face.

"You're enjoying this, aren't you?" Fel said.

"Immensely."

"You know *you* could say it, too."

She leaned forward. "Say *what?*" she said, honey dripping from her words.

He grabbed Parch's horn and shoved the critter back. Out of either some odd interaction of instincts or just some accidental training, that particular maneuver seemed to persuade the unicorn to call it quits on their little sparring match. Keeping from being skewered was tricky enough without having to deal with it in both the literal *and* figurative senses.

"I don't want to mess this up, all right? Whatever it is we have. Or might have. And if I don't put a name to it, then we can go on enjoying it without the risk of me doing something to botch it and lose it," Fel said.

"So you're afraid of the *risk?*" Allie said. "Do I need to parrot back to you all the stories you've told me that involved you dangling off cliffs or facing down fierce beasts? All things you knew you might encounter when you set off to do whatever you were doing, by the way. But *this* is too risky to name?"

"Yeah."

"Care to explain?"

"Because *this* is actually *important,*" Fel said.

Allie raised her eyebrows. "You sweet-talker you," she said, a dash more sincerity in her tone than Fel would have expected. She glanced aside. Mariss was hustling across the street, daintily tugging up the hem of her skirt to keep it from dragging. "Fine," Allie said softly. "We'll let the elephant get comfortable for a while longer."

The baker reached them, all giggles and grins. "That was loads of fun," she said, bobbing contentedly on the sea of mild intoxication and the thrill of harmless mischief. "Though maybe we'll pick a different place next time we do this."

"Someplace with music. And roasted crickets," Fel said.

"It needn't be a tavern or anything. We could spend some time at one house or another," Mariss said.

"My home isn't terribly well suited for entertaining," Allie said.

"Neither is mine," Fel said.

"I see. My home, then! We'll pick a time. It'll be *lovely*. I'll see you then. Oh! And do you need a ride? There's room enough in Zephyr's wagon if we squeeze," Mariss said.

"I think a bit of a walk will do me good," Fel said.

Mariss gave each of them a kiss on the cheek. "'Til next time, then!"

She trotted off and climbed into her elegant little carriage. Allie and Fel watched her go. When she was gone, they remained, quiet and contemplative until Parch got impatient and nudged Fel in the thigh with his horn.

"Ow. Fine. We'll get moving." He turned to Allie. "Walk you home?"

"May as well," she said.

They paced down the street, watching as the buildings gradually took on the shabbier, huddled look of the less well-off parts of town.

"I haven't seen Epiphany about," Allie said. "Is she away?"

"She is. Once it was clear the current person obsessed with the family and its business was up north, she took the big carriage and went down south. We have too much inventory, too little space, and we've had to spend a *lot* of money lately, so if she can clear out some of what we have, that'll be worth whatever time she spends away."

"And she's doing it alone? Given the way things have gotten a lot bloodier lately, I would have expected you to take some extra precautions."

"Oh, she's not alone."

"You're here, the shop's open, so your mom is working the counter, and your father barely leaves the workshop. What'd you do, hire someone?"

"Nope."

"Then... wait. Not Teya."

"Yes Teya. The little kobold was getting the itch to explore, and the locals haven't been quite as quick to embrace her as a resident of Beffshire as I would have liked, so we decided that Teya as a bodyguard and helper and Epiphany as a chaperone was worth a try."

"Now *that* sounds like an entertaining trip. Meanwhile, here you are, floating around town. I wonder why the family didn't send you along with her instead. Or in addition."

"Because if given the choice between haggling and jabbing a knife in my thigh, I'd be reaching for my knife pretty quickly. Division of labor. Specialization. That's how we do things."

"What if *everyone* had ended up wanting to do the business part, and no one wanted to get dirty?"

"Then someone would have to do something they didn't want to do."

"You know, there *are* businesses that hire people *outside* the family to do things."

He furrowed his brow. "I guess that's an option too. Hadn't considered it. Family business is family business. Why all the interest?"

She shrugged. "Just plumbing the depths of that head of yours. You manage to be both simple and incredibly difficult to figure out." She paused. "Maybe 'simple' isn't the right word."

"No, it's the right word," he said with a nod.

"The point is, you've been living your life so long without really thinking about what *you* want, sometimes it's worth checking to see if you realize the different ways things could be. You have choices."

"Sure. Of course. I just can't make them."

"Yes you can. You can always change direction. It just takes a little bit of extra effort if you've been sliding in one direction for long enough."

He rumbled with something less than agreement.

"What choices *would* you make, if things weren't on the course they are on now?" Allie asked.

"Such as? What are we talking about here?"

"I don't know, *everything*. Starting now, if you could have whatever you wanted, what would you have? Ignore everything between you and where you want to go. A wizard comes along and makes it so, what would your life be?"

"What does it matter?"

"It doesn't matter a lick to *me*. I'm just making conversation. But if you've never thought about it, it might make a difference to you one of these days."

"This is a silly conversation."

"We could go back to talking about the elephant."

Fel quickly dove into the lesser of two conversational evils. "I'm a Masker, right? A contraptioneer. As I learned, I come from a bloodline of some of the premier contraptioneers in the world. If I had my druthers, I wouldn't mind being treated as though that's a good thing rather than a bad thing."

"Fair enough. And how would you spend your time?"

He paused. "I honestly don't know. I like drinking, and I like gambling, but those are nice for a *change*. I can't imagine spending all day every day doing that."

"That's one reason you're worth talking to, Fel. Half the boys in that tavern would be just keen on the idea of swilling and swindling until they breathed their last breath."

"Not me. But I'm not sure what I *would* do for a living if not this. I'm not good enough at actual tinkering to make a go of that..." he mused.

"If you spent enough time at it, I'm sure you would be."

"I think I've had a belly full of learning that stuff already." He scratched his head. "This should be an easy question, but I can't work out an answer."

"That's the sort of thing that happens when you never get the chance to make a choice."

"What about you? What's your ideal life?"

"Same as now, except I own The Fox and Log."

When no further explanation followed, he turned to her. "That's it?"

"That's plenty. I could give you a list of the ways I'd change the place up. Half of them Verfessa did when he became a partner, but there's loads more."

"But there's nothing else you'd change?"

"Everything else that I'd change in my life would be changed on the way to that, or as a result of that. A little more room to live in. A little more control over when I work. A few of the finer things in life."

"Ah! Finer things. Like what?"

"A gown. Some jewelry."

"Now you're joking."

"What's funny about that?"

"I can't even *picture* you wearing a gown or jewelry."

"That's because I don't own any. But if I had a gown, I'd have worn it today. The occasion called for it."

"You surprise me. You didn't strike me as the sort who would be after that sort of thing. Other women, sure. But not you."

"Am I so different from other women?"

"Yes! You seem a lot more..."

"Watch your words here. You're about to insult either me or every other woman in your life."

"... unique."

"Nice dodge."

"It just doesn't seem practical."

"It *isn't* practical. Which is why I don't have any. One of the reasons, anyway. If you have a wobbly table, you don't put a feast on it. There are a few rungs missing on the ladder between me and the woman who wears a silver necklace. But that doesn't mean I wouldn't want to give it a try."

"If you want a necklace—"

"What did I just say? First thing's first. We're talking about 'Fantasy Allie.' You give me a necklace today, and I'm selling it and using the money to replace my boots."

They stopped in front of the alley, tucked in the center of which was the door to Allie's home. Parch trotted happily toward her door.

"Hey! The lady didn't invite us in, and we're not slumming on her floor anymore, remember?" he snapped.

Parch didn't so much heed the reprimand as lose interest in the door once he realized Fel hadn't followed him down the alleyway.

"See you at The Fox and Log tomorrow," she said. "It was a fine time tonight."

"It was. Though maybe next time one of us should make the plan rather than leaving it to Mariss."

"Sounds like you just volunteered," she said, trotting down the alley. "Until then!"

"Until then," he called back.

He lingered until he heard her door shut. Then he lingered for a bit more.

"Come on, Parch," he mumbled, turning toward his own street. "We've got elephants to think about."

A short time later, Fel jangled the bell of the family shop. It was well into the evening, but his mother was still at the counter.

"Must have been a good day of sales," Fel said.

"Indeed it was," Vivian said. "Good enough that I let myself get sloppy with the ledger. Better to correct it now rather than go to bed and forget what needs to be done. How were things with the girls?"

"Small food. Tasty, but small. Other than that, a fine time."

"Glad to hear it. Now if we could get your sister to spend an evening or two with friends, your father and I would sleep a good deal better. You two have done right by the family business, but if you don't do right by yourselves now and again, a few years down the line, we'll have more business than family."

"Seems to be all anyone talks about these days," Fel said.

"All of human endeavor angles itself toward either business or family, Fel."

"I think there are a few more things than that."

"Not if you dig deep enough," she said. "To that end, your father wants a word with you."

He glanced in her direction. "It's that time, is it?"

"Very nearly."

He marched down the steps. As it happened, both his father and Tome were at the dining room table. Every inch of the surface was covered with maps and reference materials. The two academically inclined men had their noses in books.

"... No, no. Nothing here either. I really don't think there is a solution," Tome said.

"Not an existing one, anyway. But a problem without a solution is simply an invention waiting to happen," Martin said.

"Why is it, whenever you two are excited about the same thing, I know I am about to have a very hard couple of weeks?" Fel said.

They both looked up.

"Ah! Fel. Fantastic. You had a good time, I trust?" Martin said.

"It was fine. What is this all about? You finished the mask contraption?"

"The first iteration of it, yes," Martin said. "Two of four masks can be sought directly, the Warrior and the Student. The... I don't know what to call the phenomena. The attraction perhaps? Regardless, the means by which the contraption is able to locate the masks is not as strong or immediate as I would like. I'll explain how best to use the device shortly. The important thing is we can be quite certain it is operational, and that the Student mask is still quite far away and roughly in the location the Warrior indicated it could be found."

"Where exactly is it?" Fel asked.

"Precision is, lamentably, not one of the strong points of this device. Particularly not with regard to distance. Somewhere between a hundred and a thousand miles, I would estimate."

"That's not much of an estimate, Dad," he said.

"Hence my desire to produce a second iteration. Do you know there doesn't seem to be a *single* contraption I've encountered in our lengthy history, besides a scale, that's focused on determining the strength of a force with any precision? Every detector or guide has been focused on direction. None have focused on magnitude. I have some theories—"

"Dad, is this important right now?" Fel asked.

"Ah... No. I cannot say it is. Tomorrow, we'll be meeting with Verfessa about how we intend to proceed, but I would suggest you prepare yourself for a lengthy journey. Perhaps as far as Shalia. And leaving as soon as possible. With no less than a hundred miles separating us from the mask, and thus the elf who wears it, a tremendous amount can change before you reach it, even if you leave immediately. Tome has already agreed to accompany you."

"I think you'll need the help," Tome said. "I've seen the sort of magic the elves are capable of. The contraption we're using to find him actually relies upon some of that magic. I don't like your chances if you find yourself facing off against Mevrelle without some degree of mystical expertise at your disposal."

"I appreciate the help."

"You'll also recall, back when we first met, I was headed north. Now is as good a time as any to give that trip another go."

"Lest I worry you were being selfless," Fel said.

"There are other matters we'll be discussing," Martin said. "Most of them can wait until our audience with Verfessa, but this is something I'd like you to keep in mind. The more of us working on it, the more likely we'll find a solution."

"I'm not much of a solution finder, Dad," Fel said.

"You have more insight into the operation of contraptions than anyone in this town but me, and don't pretend otherwise."

"That is a very low bar," Fel reminded him.

"You may not have learned all the lessons I have, but those you have learned, you've learned well. Now, I've designed this contraption to eventually be capable of locating all four masks. Presently, as I've said, it is limited to the Student and the Warrior. And barring mishap, the location of the Warrior should be of little concern, as I don't intend to let it leave my workshop anytime soon. You can select which mask the indicator directs you toward with this lever. Warrior first, Student second. The third and fourth positions are reserved for the Scholar and the Diplomat respectively. Now look here—"

"Again, Dad, does this really matter at the moment? If I'm going to be heading out as soon as possible, I should take some time to prepare tonight before I sleep."

"This will only take a moment. If you're anything like me, and I know we're more alike than you imagine, inspiration can strike at any time. So we're all best served by giving it as much time to strike as we can manage."

He removed the faceplate of the contraption. The workings were relatively uncomplicated by Bygone contraption standards. That meant that the assemblage of components within would challenge the skills of all but the finest fabricators but were at least moderately familiar to Fel at a glance. He couldn't design such a thing, but if pressed, he might be able to repair it.

"Here, on the indexing plate. Symbols need to be etched while the plate is in place. These are the symbols associated with the masks we've had access to. In each case, the symbol was located on the inside chin of the mask. As you see, there is a punched point a curved line, and three or four straight lines. Presently, the two final positions are blank. If you encounter either the Scholar or the Diplomat, find the appropriate symbol on the inside of the chin and etch it in the appropriate location." He reaffixed the faceplate.

"Why is this so important?" Fel asked.

"Because presently, setting the contraption to either of those settings produces the same result." A click to the indicated setting sent the needle sluggishly shifting. "Given time, this needle will settle into an orientation that, at first, I thought was arbitrary. After I added the second engraving, I found that the new direction was still not fully clear but different from when only one symbol was filled in. Here, look."

He slid one of the maps from the bottom of the pile. "This is Shalia. Both the Warrior and the Student have listed the Diplomat's location as being here, roughly. Not so far from Ram's Rest, the very city your eldest sister calls home. Fora confirms this approximate location. Prior to adding the Student's symbol, all the blank spots on the indicator set the needle pointing along this line." He swept his finger across the map, well west of the city.

"Once I added the second symbol, the line shifted to here." Now he swept considerably closer to the city. "Much nearer to where we know the Diplomat to be, and considerably farther from where we know the Student to be. It is my theory, and Tome concurs, that what we are looking at is the midpoint between the trajectories of both masks. Which means—"

Fel nodded. "If we stick one more mark on, the blank spot will point to the fourth mask even if we don't have the mark for it."

"Precisely! Now, obviously the surest way to achieve this is to seek the Diplomat and add the mark. I'll be sending you along with one of my good gravers for precisely that purpose. But by now you have seen as many vaults and Bygone sites as I have, and you've been to Clickspring. You've seen so many shapes, so many symbols. I wonder if perhaps you can spot a pattern I've missed."

Martin slid forward a page with both etched marks drawn larger and more clearly. Fel leaned on the table and gazed at them. He had expected to see two completely meaningless twists of lines. And he wasn't entirely wrong. It wasn't as though his father had written down an *A* and a *B* and was waiting for Fel to fill in a *C* and *D*. But to his surprise, the shapes weren't entirely alien. There was a logic to them, if not a familiarity. The first was much more angular. The second a bit softer, more open.

He tapped with his finger. "This is the Warrior?"

"That's right."

"It looks it. It looks mean." He darted his eyes back and forth between them. "I don't know. Nothing is leaping out at me, but they're in my head now, I guess. We'll see if the answer tumbles out. I wouldn't hold your breath though."

"One more mind percolating. Never a bad thing. Now, again, tomorrow we'll be talking to Verfessa. He has been quite thorough in his desire to be included in at least the discussion of anything regarding Mevrelle. He remains focused in his desire to see the elf die for killing his men and causing what he views to be a violation of hard-earned trust we've placed in him. I've informed him that we do not blame him, but he is unmoved. The details of the journey will be laid out by the end of that meeting, but before then, I want you to understand my two greatest concerns in this. First, and I cannot emphasize this strongly enough, I want you to be safe. Verfessa is out for blood. I personally couldn't care less what becomes of Mevrelle. I just want the items in his possession. Take them away, and he is no longer my concern. If it comes down to him getting away or you hurting yourself in pursuit of him, I'd sooner see him flee. That should go without saying. The only reason I am even willing to risk sending you after him is the mask. There is great value in having the Student returned to us. And greater still in acquiring the Scholar. I've already rebuilt the coupler Mevrelle took, but keeping it out of the wrong hands is a worthy goal as well. But as far as I am concerned, those masks are the primary goal of this journey. Everything besides your safety is secondary. We need the masks."

"You want me to grab Euphoria's mask while we're at it?" Fel said. "Nick the Diplomat and complete the set?"

"I think we can trust the Graves family to be the keepers of the Diplomat. Though if anyone but the Graves family has the Scholar, I believe it would be best to claim it ourselves. The three possibilities I can imagine are it moldering in the dirt, sitting on display on an aristocrat's shelf, or in the hands of the Bolivans. For something which might well contain the answers to questions the world has quested for across generations, none of those is acceptable."

Fel wiped his face. "Here's hoping I get to rob a rich person or dig up a treasure. I've had my fill of fighting elves and…" He shuddered. "Other things. For a while, anyway."

"Get some rest. Tomorrow, plans are made," Martin said.

"You don't need to tell me twice," Fel said, trudging off to his room.

Chapter 2

One of the two private rooms in The Fox and Log was filled to capacity, and it was still an hour before the place properly opened its doors. Fel and Martin Masker were in attendance, as well as Tome. They were clustered across the table from a single man. Donavan Verfessa. Even after having worked with him for several months, it wasn't immediately clear the precise nature of his stock and trade. At a glance, he seemed like the sort of rosy-cheeked, sunbaked, barrel-chested worker you'd see digging ditches outside of town or downing ales at a rowdy pub. But those who knew his name spoke it in hushed voices, as though fearing a bolt of lightning. He had influence around the city, ears and eyes everywhere. And if he wanted something to happen, he had the means to make it so.

"What do we have, boys?" he said with an eager clap.

Martin slid the mask contraption forward. "Complete, or at least complete to the level present information will allow," he said.

"Fill me in, Mr. Masker. Will this do the job? Will it find the blighter who broke my promises for me?"

"It will find the mask he was wearing. The mask he stole from us. As far as we know, he can't exist outside the Greater Lands without it or an equivalent artifact. If we find the mask without him, it means he is almost certainly dead. And if we find the mask in his possession—"

"Then it's up to us to make sure he's dead," Verfessa said. "Is this a mark-on-a-map sort of thing?"

"More of a compass," Fel said. "All we know is which way to go."

"And that we'll have to go a fair distance," Tome said.

Verfessa sniffed and picked up the contraption, turning it over in his hands. "Impressive piece of contraptioneering, Mr. Masker. Though I must say, your timing could use some work."

"How so?" Martin asked.

"I don't want to go into details that don't concern you, but suffice to say the unique troubles your family have set on my table aren't the entire meal. I'm stretched a bit thin at the moment, and I have it on very good authority that something unpleasant is headed my way. Not your problem. Strictly mine. But it means the blade I'd set aside to deal with the elf is going to have to be on hand to be carving into something else."

"I see," Martin said.

"I can make sure you're equipped and funded. You won't want for supplies. And I can even send some word along if you can give me the route you mean to take. Maybe I can grease a few gates that might otherwise stick. But I'm sorry to say you won't have a shadow this time."

"Do you really suppose there will be opposition besides the elf himself? The sort of things you'll have influence over?"

"Someone got to Inspector Cartwright. Once the agents of the nobles are siding against you, an awful lot of trouble can start popping up," Verfessa said. "Take it from a fellow who has never been on their good side. Unless Cartwright was a rogue in his own right, you're going to find yourself struggling in unexpected ways."

"I hadn't considered that," Tome said.

"It takes a man living precisely the wrong sort of life to have to keep things like that in mind," Verfessa said.

"Regardless, it still needs to be done. The elf is a threat, and the mask is an asset. The world will be safer once their fate is known," Martin said.

"'Their fate is known,'" Fel said. "That's a gentle way of putting it."

"A little beating around the bush has a way of easing the conscience," Verfessa said. "So what's the plan?"

"We're going to take the most direct route north to the Thayne-Shalia border," Fel said. "Dad says once we get that far, we'll have a better idea of where the mask is hiding, and we'll readjust from there."

Verfessa sniffed again. "Most direct, or fastest?"

"I would imagine those are one and the same," Tome said.

Verfessa laughed. "I'm sure *you* would imagine that, but Fel here has been hauling contraptions all across the continent, the kind of things that'd get taken away if he was stopped by someone with any authority or even an eye for value. He ought to know a straight line isn't always the fastest way to get from here to there."

The intimidating man reached into his back pocket and thunked a rugged metal flask to the table. "This is Quarrian thistlewine brandy. Seventy-five years old. Because of a tantrum by two half-wit, upper-crust brats, this is not allowed for sale, purchase, or possession within the borders of Thayne. If I tried getting this here via the roads, direct or otherwise, it would never have arrived. And never is a long time. I needed it faster than that, so I had to find a faster way. What time are you boys leaving?"

"This evening," Tome said.

Verfessa pocketed the flask again and replaced it with a folded bit of paper from his shirt pocket. "Give me a list of what you need," he said to Tome. "And Fel, open those ears. I'm going to give you a couple of shortcuts that you will never utter to another soul. You don't write them down, you don't repeat them to yourself. You don't take one of these turns when someone is within eyeshot, and you don't linger there waiting for someone to leave. These routes are more precious than gold, and if I find out you spoiled them, you and I are going to have a long, hard talk about it. Got that?"

"I think I follow."

"Good, now the first one is just north of Pilhearst..."

A few minutes later, Fel and the others emerged. The tavern hadn't properly opened its doors yet, but between letting Tome and the Maskers in for their meeting and its completion, Allie had prepped the place with fresh roasted crickets and carefully cleaned tabletops. Wick's lantern stood on a table near the door to what was effectively Verfessa's office, brought by the Maskers and left outside at Verfessa's request.

"Allie, if I didn't happen to know that you'd spent yesterday evening enjoying a meal with Fel, I'd wonder if you ever left this place," Tome said.

"Anyplace worth spending a duot in has at least one person who cares enough about it to show up when no one else will," she said.

"Thank you for your hospitality," Martin said.

He and Tome headed for the back exit. Fel lingered.

"I'll catch up. I need to have a word with Allie," he said. "And leave the lantern. I'll bring it with me."

"Don't be long. Much to prepare," Martin said.

Fel trudged up to the bar and positioned himself over a stool.

"Don't sit down. If you're here before opening, you're helping get us *ready* for opening," Allie said.

He stopped himself and grumbled.

"Come on. You can carry the crate of bottles," she said.

He hopped the bar and followed her down the stairs.

"So you're off on another 'mission' then?" Allie said, handing him an empty crate.

"Yeah."

"I take it the presence of Verfessa means it's not *entirely* on the up-and-up?"

"The presence of Fel Masker means it's not entirely on the up-and-up," he said.

"Right, but I mean in a bloody way, rather than a muddy way."

"Officially I'm off to reclaim a stolen artifact. Maybe pick up another artifact while I'm at it. The only question is how the current owners of those artifacts will feel about it. Considering one of them is the elf who terrorized the neighboring roads a few weeks ago, I don't think he'll be happy to see us."

"I can't tell if this is getting worse or getting better, Fel."

"It certainly isn't getting better. But near as I can figure, if we can get this thing back home, we won't have to worry about this particular group of people who want to kill us anymore."

She clinked bottles into the crate, one by one. "Just how many people want to kill you?"

"Let's see. There's the elf, and really any *other* elf. The Bolivans are probably still none too pleased. Any of the mercenaries they hired that are still alive are probably going to be trouble. And possibly someone within the nobility of Thayne, if Inspector Cartwright is any indication."

"You sure do know how to make friends, Fel."

"Teya likes me."

"Does that mean she's going to bail you out of this mess?"

"Not unless I take a wrong turn and end up down south where she's keeping Epiphany company," he said.

"You're a lot of trouble, you know that?"

"Sure, but I'm worth it."

"Says who?"

"I just listed off all the people who want me dead. You don't put that much effort into killing someone who isn't worth it."

"Can't fault your logic. So why tell me?"

"I thought you might want to know where I'd be for the next couple of weeks. Maybe worry about me a little."

"How thoughtful. The gift of worry. And where is it you'll be going?"

"North."

She placed a hand on her hip. "Wow. You narrowed it down to the top half of the compass. If I need you, I'll just write 'North' on a message and hire a courier, shall I?"

"I don't know any more than that. I'm just following a needle that's pointing in that direction. I'll be with Tome. We've faced this foe before. We know what to expect, and we've had time to prepare. That's all Tome ever talks about is preparing, so he has a *stack* of spells this time. I'll be fine."

"You better be. Because if you don't come back, it'll just be me and Mariss at the next little soiree she plans. And she's all well and good, but things are always a bit more fun when you're there."

"I promise to be back in time for whatever she has planned. Maybe this time I'll have a clean shirt."

They climbed back up to the main level. He placed the crate on the bar.

"Anything else you want to say to me before you head out?" she said.

"There's kind of a lot I want to say to you."

"Such as?"

He paused. The silence almost instantly became unbearable.

"One moment," he said. He marched over to the table with Wick's lantern and snatched it up.

"What's the matter, couldn't see clearly enough?" she jabbed.

He set it down before her. "When you and Mariss pretty much saved my life by coming and lending a hand, you learned about sentry lanterns. The Graves family lantern was largely the source of our woes."

"Don't I know it."

Fel cleared his throat. "Allie, I'd like to formally introduce you to Wick. Wick, this is Allie."

"It is a rare pleasure to address you directly, Miss Waverly," Wick said.

"Just how many talking lanterns are there?" she asked, eyes locked on the flame.

"At least two. Wick has been with the family for generations. He is our lookout, our messenger, and a very carefully kept secret."

He grabbed a hefty oil lantern from behind the bar and set it down. With the help of a taper, he lit the lantern from Wick's flame. "If you ever see this flame stationary, it means Wick is paying you a visit. If you're worried about me, or my family, or have anything to say back and forth between us, just let Wick know. Where I'm going, it shouldn't take more than a few minutes for him to get in touch with me. And if the flame ever goes out, just head down to the antiquities shop and ask for a fresh light off the good lantern. At least this way you don't have to write 'North' on a message."

"You know I can't just let you give me a gift without giving you something in return, right?" she said.

"You really don't have to," he said.

She rummaged around in her pocket and turned up a duot. As he watched her curiously, she dropped it on the floor and stomped it with her heel. When she picked it up again, she took his hand and pressed it into his palm with the other.

"Is this some kind of tradition I don't know about?"

"Not unless you were raised by my mom," she said. "We didn't have much money at all. To teach me to be frugal, she hammered a divot into the face of a duot, like this one here. She said, 'If you ever have to spend the duot with the divot, you know you've been spending too much.' So, now you've got a duot with a divot. If you find yourself at a grum table and you're on your last run, maybe this'll convince you to step away before your pockets are empty."

He flipped it in his hand, then stuffed it in his pocket. "If I bump into the 'special duot,' I'll be sure to have Wick tell you."

"Why all this, by the way? Why let me in on the family secret?"

"It'll be nice to hear from you now and again while I'm on the road. And, you know. Other reasons."

She placed a hand on his shoulder. "Do me a favor and come back soon. Because you're a good customer. And, you know. Other reasons."

In the past year or so, Tome and the Masker family had gotten quite a bit of practice when it came to rapidly preparing for a major trip. With effectively three weeks of notice and even a general idea of the direction they would be heading, their preparations for this trip had been positively luxurious. As before, Verfessa had provided a very high-quality horse and some decent supplies. Unlike many recent journeys, there was no need for Fel to be prepared to haul back goods, so they only needed room for the gear, himself, Tome, Parch, and Oiler. The Masker family wagon was barely sufficient, which in this context meant it was the fastest option. Comfort was not a factor.

"You have the dazzler?" Martin said, looking with some concern into the back of the wagon.

"I never even remove the dazzler from the wagon, Dad," Fel said.

"And the decoy?"

"Under the seat," he said. "Give me the bread while you're at it, would you?"

"Right, right," Martin said, handing over a cloth-wrapped bundle. "I've given you the graver?"

"I have it, yes. Along with the rest of the repair kit." Fel unfastened the bundle and continued recounting his equipment. "I have the dragon sticker, my cudgel..."

"A contraption pipe or two?" Martin said.

"Three. One of the persistent lanterns."

"Rat monkey?" called a voice from the rooftops.

"Well come down here and get it," Fel shouted.

The flutter of wings and the drift of black feathers brought four hefty black birds down to land on the sunshade. All four poked their heads down to receive their expected toll for allowing Fel to depart.

"Here you go. Toody, Rudy, Judy, and Moody. One sweet bun each," he said. "You take good care of the family while I'm gone."

"Good family," croaked Judy.

"Did you hear that! Judy here figured out how to say something besides rude shouts." Fel waggled his head. "I'm a good influence."

"I'd make a snide comment, but I'm afraid your legion of trained harpies would reap terrible vengeance upon me," Tome said, hauling himself up to the seat beside Fel.

The paper mage wedged a wooden case in the scarce space between their legs. The whole wagon shifted when Tome set it down.

"What did you bring?"

"A tremendous amount of paper and ink, as well as seven volumes of reference material," Tome said. "I have written seventy-three spells in preparation for this journey. I won't be caught short again."

"Aren't they going to go bad? Don't they get weaker as they go?" Fel asked.

"Ah! Therein lies the brilliance, something your father suggested that I cannot believe I'd not attempted on my own. The bulk of the spells have been written such that the timing and the location portions are last, and have yet to be written. Just a few strokes of the pen should render them complete, and at full capacity."

"Just make sure you finish a few along the way. I don't want to get into a fight and have you huddled behind a bush waxing poetic about the time of day, or whatever you'll need to do."

"I assure you, I will take every precaution as it becomes necessary."

Oiler poked its claws out, holding a puzzle box. Fel set about scrambling the faces of the box as swiftly as he could to avoid onlookers having time to question just what the curious claw belonged to. As Fel scrambled it, Parch clattered down from his perch atop the cargo in the wagon and wedge himself between the two men.

Fel said, "Are you and Mom going to be all right without me or Epiphany around?"

"Your sister will be back in a few days," Martin said. "And your mother and I aren't useless just yet."

The door to the shop opened and Vivian stepped out, briefly between customers. "Take care, Fel. You too, Tome," she said.

"I'll be taking a great deal more care than Fel, I assure you," Tome said.

Fel finished with the puzzle box. Oiler retracted it into the cart and started clicking at it.

"Mom, remember what I asked," Fel said.

"I'll have a word with Reynard as soon as business is through," she said. "Be swift, fight only if you must, and come home safely."

"That's the plan, Mom," he said. "Be back as soon as I can."

He snapped the reins, and yet another journey into the unknown began.

Vivian and Martin watched as their son rattled away on the family wagon, silent until he was gone from sight.

"He's been off to do this sort of thing a dozen times," Vivian said. "He'll be fine. He's a capable boy."

"It feels different this time, Viv," Martin said. "It felt different last time, too. And the time before. I don't know if things are evolving or if we're in the midst of a happening, but it isn't like it was before. Not like when I was young."

They paced back inside.

"I had to deal with the Bolivans once. And they stayed dealt with for *ages*."

"You were a fair bit more forceful than Fel."

"I wasn't forceful. I merely repurposed existing defenses. And I issued a warning. But that's not the point. The point is, the troubles feel like they are escalating. I want to believe that when we reclaim the mask, and provided we don't return to the Greater Lands, then the threats from there will cease to be a concern. I want to believe that Cartwright was an isolated example of a person with legitimate power straying from the straight and narrow. I want to believe that the string of mercenaries sent our way has reached its end, and that all this madness is sliding toward a return to normal. But wishful thinking won't make it so."

"We'll do what we've always done, Martin. We will endure. We will band together, work hard, and do what it takes to keep this family safe and thriving."

"If we could only take a moment to breathe. If we could only have some time between disasters to find the root of it all. And I truly believe there is one unified root. I believe that somewhere, something or someone has started this sequence, and it is playing out. Maybe not according to their plan, but because of it."

"We focus upon what we can control, Martin."

"Of course, you are right. But still..."

He turned to inspect the shelves. In the Masker family, Martin was the one who spent the least time in the top-level shop. As such, nearly every time he passed through, he found the place significantly different from when he left it. Items sold. Items purchased. Things shuffled into and out of storage.

"Almost entirely mundane antiques," Martin said.

"And two more shelves of them below," Vivian said. "It will be months before we're back to our original stock. And that's assuming Epiphany doesn't bring any of her portion back."

"Have customers been missing our usual assortment of contraptions?" Martin asked.

"One or two of the out-of-town collectors commented on the absence, but we have a small selection of contraptions in storage that satisfies their tastes when I need them."

"Still no immediate need for me to resume my work on repairing and modifying contraptions, then?"

"Not until I've had a few more weeks to make room for them."

"Good... I believe I have a few avenues of study I might pursue."

"Martin, please remember the goal is to *decrease* the problems we are facing."

"Oh, such will be my aim. Call me if you need me. I'll be working. And do remind me when the time comes to prepare supper. I may lose track of time. I'm feeling inspired."

"Davie!" Allie shouted, both hands loaded down with trays.

As tended to be the case with fate, just when Allie would have preferred a nice, slow day drift through without much thought, The Fox and Log was as busy as it had ever been. They were well into the busiest part of the evening. She wouldn't see things start to taper off for another four hours at least.

"Two ales, two ryes, a whiskey, and three ports," Allie said, sliding a tray to the table and dispensing the contents. "*Davie!*"

"I'm here, I'm here! What needs doing?" the gnomish bar hand said, scrambling up onto the bar.

"What needs doing is someone needs to go and drag Oovay out of his bed by the collar of his shirt. But he covered for me yesterday, so I'm just going to have to cope." She stacked the cricket tray on top of the empty one to free a hand. "Instead, I'm going to need you to run down to the market district. We need meat and cheese. Someone with too much money got in touch with Sid and requested we have a table set up with something besides crickets."

"On it!" Davie said, dashing out.

"This had better not be the start of something. I have a hard enough time keeping us stocked with things we actually *sell*. I don't need to be taking lunch orders," she muttered under her breath.

Once the thirsty patrons had their drinks and a handful of payments had been pried from reluctant fingers, Allie returned to the bar and leaned heavily upon it. One of a thousand little habits she'd developed to keep the tavern spinning like a top immediately clicked into place to occupy the precious slice of her mind that had been freed. She swept her eyes across the shelves behind the bar. The expensive silvered-glass mirror needed cleaning. Two of the bottles of high-quality rum were missing from their place, no doubt in the possession of a thieving patron either too drunk or too stupid to notice they were empty and used for decoration. And something was out of place. The lantern. She eyed the cloudy reservoir of oil. About half full. Then the flame. Stone still.

She leaned toward the lantern. One of the differences between Allie and Oovay was that *he* thought you needed to slip into the back room if you wanted privacy. Like privacy was something that could only be achieved in solitude. Allie had long ago figured out that if you tend bar, unless someone wants a drink or conversation out of you, you may as well be furniture. Drinks were quick enough to deal with, and body language could squash unwanted conversation. It was entirely possible to be alone in a crowded room if you weren't the reason the room was crowded.

"So," she said softly, casting a glance at the lantern. "How does this work? And be discreet."

"It works however you require it, Miss Waverly. Address me directly from anywhere the light or heat from this flame falls upon you, and I will see and hear you. You and you alone will hear my reply unless I will it otherwise."

"Why were you just sitting there looking at me, then? Keeping an eye on me?"

"You are new to the concept of using me as a means of communication. It was my assumption that you would not have developed the tendency to watch for a stationary flame in the event you wanted to ask a question or deliver a message, so I have been lingering here longer than I otherwise might. I apologize if this is invasive to you. There are alternatives. You could write a message or otherwise create a visual indicator that you wish my attention, and I will linger if I spot it during an otherwise brief visit, for example. You can also burn a written message, and it will be available to me, though the timing of that varies depending on how close I am to the flame and—"

"Right, fine. That's enough. And can everyone else hear everything that I say?"

"Messages are delivered as requested. Information is provided as requested. I do not volunteer information. In extreme circumstances, I have been asked to conceal information. This is not strictly within my capacity, but I have had some success in dissuading the curiosity of those seeking information meant to be kept in confidence."

She took a breath, eyes already settling on a tankard of ale halfway across the tavern that needed topping off. "When you get a chance, tell Fel, if nothing else, he has a way of making my life more interesting. Because this? This is very strange."

"This is a service I will happily fulfill. Anything else?"

"That's plenty," Allie said.

The flame fluttered in a far more natural way. Allie watched it for a few seconds more, then grabbed a pitcher and trekked toward the soon-to-be-thirsty patron.

"You got yourself into this, Allie," she grumbled to herself. "You sleep in the bed you made."

She topped off three mugs and a basket of crickets. By the time she got back to the bar, the scampering of little feet signaled the return of the tavern's runner. Davie thumped down a sack with a quarter of a cheese wheel and two dried sausages. He popped the top of the coffer and snatched enough duots to cover the purchase and a few more for his trouble.

"Much obliged, Davie," she called after him. "One of these days you're going to have to show me how you get halfway across the city and back in no time at all with those little legs."

"Trade secret!" he shouted.

"Listen up!" Allie yelled, fetching a knife from behind the bar. "I'm about to carve up some meat and cheese and put it on that table over in the corner. You keep your hands off it. This is for a friend of the owner."

"When are you going to start putting meat and cheese out for us?" called a voice from the crowd.

"When you start coughing up for the kinds of prices they charge across town at the Blue Rose. Now if I see you putting your fingers on that platter, they're *staying* on the platter." She jabbed the knife into the cutting board. "Understood?"

The patronage rumbled with vague compliance. She did a lackluster job of preparing a tray of meat, bread, and cheese. This particular job was one she had no intention of doing with any regularity. Yet another important lesson she'd learned, though it was one she struggled to live by, was the simple fact that if you didn't want to do a job, it was wise not to do it well. She had quite enough obligations without having to prepare meals for aristocrats who, for some reason, wanted to spend their time in The Fox and Log instead of the snootier places across town. Threading the needle of lackluster but not inadequate was, in some ways, trickier than just doing a good job, but putting in the effort now meant never having to do it again, so it was worth it.

She completed the task just as a middle-aged woman marched through the door with the sort of authority and confidence that could only belong to someone who would make a special meal order at a place that didn't serve food. Silver hair had begun to thread its way through blonde. She dressed curiously, at least from Allie's point of view. Her clothes weren't luxurious or ostentatious, but they were still plainly quite expensive. Sturdy, well built, and tailored to her. The woman stepped up to the bar and eyed what Allie had prepared. Her expression didn't change more than a flicker, but it was enough to pass judgment. The tray of food had been assessed, and that assessment would be taken into consideration for all future interactions. For the first time in ages, Allie felt as though she may have miscalculated. This may have been a time to impress.

"You will be Allie Waverly," the woman said.

She spoke precisely, like someone for whom the local language did not come naturally. Care was being taken to avoid mispronouncing words, and thus she ended up overpronouncing them. Each word distinct, the pauses between them a hair longer than was necessary.

"And you will be Sid's friend," Allie said. "Your table is over here. What can I get you to drink?"

"I will be having a white wine." She pulled a slip of paper from her pocket. "Something from this list. If none exist within your stores, provide me with a current inventory and I shall make a selection."

Allie took the slip in one hand and the tray of food in the other. She led the way to the table without taking her eyes from the paper. "You're in luck. I believe we have two bottles of the Wendt Manor," she said.

"Do you reserve bottles for customers?" the woman asked.

"Not as a rule, but I've made exceptions in the past."

"Then do make an exception in this case. I shall purchase the entire bottle in advance, though just one glass for me at the moment."

The woman took a seat. Allie set the food down.

She said, "You know, the locals usually get by with just a basket of crickets. This sort of special order is rare."

"I am a rare individual. Or so I have been told on regular occasions. And I am aware of the local tradition of eating toasted insects."

"It's not all that local, ma'am. You can find crickets on tables in most of the southern half of Thayne."

"I am considerably less local than that, and thus I haven't had my distaste for eating vermin bred out of me. Perhaps I shall partake in the odd custom at another time. But for now, do fetch the wine."

Allie fought heroically to keep the sharpness from her expression. "Davie! Wendt Manor! Third row, bottom shelf, third slot."

"On it!" Davie bellowed, scampering away.

"You keep that tight a grip on your inventory?"

"A lot of people get hired in this place, most of them end up quitting or just not showing back up after a while. Mostly they try to take a parting gift with them. It pays to keep an eye on the more valuable items. And just in general, it pays to know when we're nearly out of something."

"Sensible."

"If you're reserving a bottle, I take it you'll be making a few more visits?"

"That remains to be seen, but I do strive to plan ahead if I can manage."

"If you're a potential regular, I ought to learn your name. If only to mark down the reserve."

"Velonia Madritz."

"That's a Quarrian name."

"Well observed."

"What brings you all the way to Beffshire?"

"An investment opportunity."

"Business. I should have guessed. Pretty much the only thing that brings anyone to Beffshire. Though, I'll admit, mostly it doesn't bring them to The Fox and Log. Upper-class venues for upper-class people like yourself."

"Class is not a concern of mine. And more to the point, The Fox and Log happens to be the investment opportunity."

Davie tottered back with a large, dusty bottle. Allie took it and deftly wiped it clean with a rag. She kept eye contact with Velonia as she applied a corkscrew and eased out the cork.

"The Fox and Log already has an owner and an investor, which is at least twice as many cooks as it really needs stirring the cauldron."

"Agreed. I do not intend to increase that number at all."

"A bad first impression, I take it?"

"No. So far, I am pleasantly surprised."

"Then what's your plan?"

Allie poured the wine. Velonia swished the wine in the glass and took a sip.

"Well kept. Commendable." She glanced up from the glass. "My plan is not a point of discussion with the staff. See to the rest of the patrons. If I require anything else, I will alert you."

Allie corked the bottle and carried it back to the bar. A quick scribble on a bit of thick paper labeled it as the property of Velonia Madritz. Allie had a strong suspicion it wasn't the only thing that woman would be laying claim to in this tavern. This was a woman looking to do business with Donovan Verfessa, and if Allie were to try to concoct the sort of formidable individual who could sit at a table and talk raw numbers with that man, this woman at least superficially fit the role.

Changes were coming. So soon on the heels of the last ones. It put a sour taste in Allie's mouth, like what she'd thought was a brief distraction from the comfortable rut she'd dug for herself was actually the beginning of a landslide that would completely wash out the road and force her to start over. Was it silly? Was she overthinking things? Perhaps. But it would have a place in the back of her mind for the rest of her shift, that was for sure.

CHAPTER 3

After six days on the road, Fel and Tome were experiencing something they were, frankly, not expecting. Boredom. Tome was fully capable of embracing such a thing. Whenever he wasn't guiding the cart or sleeping, he was jotting down notes, reading reference matter, and generally making the most of the relative calm. Fel, after a lifetime of thriving during the dull moments, found himself struggling to let his mind slip into the comfortable doldrums that had defined his long trips as recently as a few months ago. Lacking the sanctuary of boredom, his mind sought ways to sublimate its simmering unease. As the sun started to slip from the sky and they rumbled past the latest of the seemingly endless sequence of farms that covered the region between Beffshire and Shalia, his imagination crystalized the slightest concern into a full-blown catastrophe in the making.

"I think he's following us," Fel said, leaning far aside to try to get a glimpse at a carriage behind them.

"He's not following us. He's using the same road we're using."

"He's keeping a specific distance. If we speed up, he speeds up. If we slow down, he slows down," Fel said.

"If there was an anxious lunatic practically climbing out of the cart every few minutes to try to glare at me, I'd try to keep my distance, too."

"He's following us," Fel restated.

"You said that about the old woman yesterday and the two young men the day before that, and they all eventually turned," Tome said.

"Eventually I'll be right. This one didn't turn yet. I seem to remember a time when *you* were the one who was a bundle of anxiety about this sort of thing, telling me I didn't have a proper plan and all that."

"I've reached a state of clarity."

"You've reached a state of distraction. You're going to be reading a book, and the elf is going to show up and put an arrow through it."

Tome paused, then picked up the mask detector. He raised it and swept it about. "Doesn't seem like the mask is anywhere nearby," he said. "And for better or for worse, whenever anything even moderately arcane happens, with respect to elven magics, I get a terrible pulse of dizziness and fatigue, and I haven't felt it in ages. I'll thank you not to infect me with your paranoia. Change the subject, if you're that concerned."

"Fine..."

Fel cast one last glance at the suspicious carriage behind, then leaned back into the well-worn seat. He scratched Parch and poured a splash of water into a shallow bowl wedged between the two humans on the seat of the carriage. Parch hopped to stand atop Tome's wooden case and stick his neck down to lap at it.

"You're good with words, right?" Fel said.

"Good with words. That is, I'll say without an ounce of exaggeration, one of the most profound understatements in the history of our world. But yes, I would say without fear of contradiction that I have some degree of skill with language."

"What are some words for love. Like, other words for that."

"Love? By the nature of the subject, there are more terms for love, its degrees, and its related emotions than most other concepts. Love is the focus of art, of poetry..."

"Right, whatever. Just name some."

"Why?"

"Because it's a different subject than the guy following us."

"So you have *no* ulterior motive for this point of discussion? Nothing relating to your recent travails with the fairer sex?"

"Make with the words, paper mage," Fel rumbled.

"Adoration."

"No. Still too much."

"Devotion. Obsession. Worship."

"You're going in the wrong direction."

"Affection."

"... Eh, that's closer."

"Fondness."

Fel waggled his head. "More than that."

"Perhaps if you could give me some context."

"It has to do with my travails," he said.

"Right, but why precisely are you seeking nuanced terminology for your passions?"

"I think Allie wants me to say that I love her."

"Do you?"

"Do I think that? Or do I love her?"

"The latter."

"... Does that mean the first one or the second one?"

"Let's just do both and avoid the issue, shall we?"

"I definitely think that. She's waiting for me to say *something*."

"And do you love her?"

"I don't know!" Fel said. "It's like... well, you know how I felt about Mariss, right?"

"The word for that is 'infatuation.'"

"That's not how I feel about Allie. I've known Allie for longer. If I was going to make a list of people who I'd trust with my life, it'd start with my family, and the next step would be her, then a big gap and then you. I love my family. But that's not the kind of love she's expecting me to talk about. And I sure as muck don't love *you* like that."

"I'll avoid reading too much into that statement."

"But it's like... here, this is an example. Think about the shop. Masker's Antiquities. There's two ways into that shop. One is in through the front door, and the other is up from our home. Love, the way I picture it, is supposed to come in through that front door. You see it coming. You get ready. You put together your plan on how it should go. This is like if a customer came up from inside my home. That's not how it's supposed to go. They started too close. Slipped by all the plans. It's just not the sort of interaction you're supposed to get from that direction."

"I think you're viewing romance as far too transactional."

"If you've been to the right parts of Beffshire, you'd know that romance can be pretty darn transactional."

"What I mean to say is, you seem to think there is a protocol. An unstated, mildly adversarial relationship between two parties, like a customer and a shopkeeper. Both of you are after something. And ideally both of you can get what you want. But there needs to be a few layers of deception and posturing. That love can't come from a place of trust. And why shouldn't it?"

"I'll tell you why love shouldn't come from a place of trust. Because I see someone like Mariss, right? And she seems like exactly the sort of person I'd want. And I can start planning and start trying. And maybe I succeed and maybe

I fail. But if I do fail, she started off as a stranger, so if I lose her, I lose someone who was a stranger. Not so bad. But if you try that sort of thing with someone you already consider a friend, if you fail, you lose a *friend*."

"Who is to say you'd lose her if things didn't work in this way?"

"If you think two people can go from friendship to love and back again without anything changing, maybe you're not the kind of person I should be talking to about this."

"I'm not suggesting you can go back and forth without things changing. Things will certainly change."

"I don't *want* them to change. I like things the way they are."

"They could be better."

"And they could be worse! The thought of my dopey, bumbling self taking someone I can spend night after night with, drinking and laughing and telling stories, and turn her into someone with a rock in her shoe in the shape of an attempted... *something*... I... I don't know."

"And so you're looking for some word that will somehow preserve what you have and the potential for something more, but shield you from the crushing lows that might come from falling from the dizzying highs."

"Yes."

"That's far more powerful magic than I can coax from a stack of spellbooks, let alone a single word."

"Fat lot of good you are, then."

"I know my limits." He leaned aside. "And I also know that the carriage following us just turned at the crossroads."

Fel leaned aside and checked for himself. "... He knew we were onto him." He turned back, and immediately his eyes darted upward. "Oh, here we are."

Wick's lantern was dangling from a hook on the shade over their heads. Even as it swung back and forth, his eyes were magnetically drawn to the sudden stillness of the flame.

"Fel," Wick said.

"What's the news, Wick?" Fel said quickly.

"Your sister has sold close to half of her stock, but she's run out of contacts along the route for the bazaar. Teya has discovered she has a taste for shimmer trout and an aptitude for catching them. Attempts at selling jewelry made from the scales have been mixed. Epiphany and Teya will be returning shortly if no additional deals can be made."

"Oh, that's got to burn her up. This'll be the first time in years she's come back with some of what she left with. What else?"

"Things are going well in the family shop. Your mother has sold a third set of the figurines to the same woman. In her words, 'I think we've made a collector out of her.' She requests you keep an eye out for more figurines when you next find yourself in the position to make more acquisitions."

"Figurines are tough. Complete ones, anyway. But I'll see what I can do once I stop getting sent out to hunt people down. Anything else?"

"Your father hasn't left the shop in four days. He forewent sleep last night. His focus has been entirely on his latest enhanced coupler."

Fel raised his eyebrows. "The focus is seizing him hard, huh?"

"It is both encouraging and concerning," Wick said.

"How has progress been?"

"It is difficult to determine. The complexity of the device, and its significant divergence from the base design, means that the success or failure of his experiments will only be determined upon a first test, which he predicts is still days away."

"And what is he attempting, exactly?" Fel asked.

"In his words, 'A more generally applicable interface.'"

"That sounds like Dad. Really specific words that don't clarify anything," Fel said. "Anything else?"

"Tem's losing streak rose to three days," Wick said.

"*Ha!* I wish I were there."

"Allie wishes you were as well. The only people presently 'rubbing in' the sequence of losses are Lou and Duff, and she finds their cleverness lackluster."

"Lou's idea of being clever is throwing a cat at someone," Fel said. "Did he pull that stunt yet?"

"Allie claims he has attempted twice to bring one into the tavern, but she forbid it. It may be relevant that she inserted the word 'elephant' into her statements no fewer than three times."

"I'll bet she did," Fel grumbled.

"She claims her suspicions about 'the wine drinker' have not been assuaged."

"Has she come back?"

"She has. The second visit was spent attempting to discuss what the patrons considered to be the strengths and flaws of the tavern. Again, Allie reiterates your absence was missed, as she feels confident your assessment of the tavern would have been worth hearing."

"I don't like this lady," Fel rumbled.

"You know precisely three things about her," Tome said. "That she drinks wine, that she is inquisitive, and that Allie doesn't like her."

"I only need that last one," Fel said.

"Are there any messages you would like me to relay on your behalf?" Wick asked.

"Tell her she's been having the more interesting life this week. All I've seen is a lot of road and potentially two carriages that were following us. Tell her I'm looking forward to showing up to rub things in Tem's face personally. If there's any justice in this world, his grum losing streak will last all the way until I get home."

"Has it occurred to you that your absence and his losing streak might be related?" Tome said. "That is to say, have you considered he's simply very good at beating you?"

"Also tell her that I ran out of patience for Tome three days ago," Fel said.

"It lasted a full day longer than my patience for him," Tome countered.

"Unless you request my continued presence, I will deliver your messages and return to the lantern in the shop."

"Go ahead. Tell my folks I miss them."

"I will happily fulfill this service."

The flame set about dancing again. Fel leaned back a little more luxuriously in his cramped little seat, tension visibly eased by the brief exchange.

"Smitten, by the way," Tome said.

"What?"

"That's the word for what you have for Allie. You are smitten by her. It is, frankly, an absurd thing to say of two adults who have known each other for years, but you've just finished using one of the most impressive pieces of arcane and mystic technology I've ever encountered to exchange gossip and giggle at each other. Smitten is the word for it."

"I'm not sure saying 'I'm smitten with you' is the solution I'm looking for."

"I think you are presently *horrendously* overthinking this, and I genuinely didn't think I'd ever see you overthinking anything."

"I'm done talking to you about this, Tome. Let's focus on something else. We need to decide where we're spending the night. Too many farms around here. We pull off to camp and let the horse graze, we'll probably end up talking to an angry man with a pitchfork."

"How far to the nearest town with something resembling civilized lodging?" Tome asked.

"Um... That smoke on the horizon should be the folks of Merk curing those good sausages they make," Fel said.

"Good sausages," Tome said. "Would these be the ones that taste of a combination of char and pepper?"

"Those are the ones."

"I am not inclined to agree with your assessment that they are 'good,' but I'm sure there are alternatives, and if I spend another few hours in this cart without stretching my legs, I fear for either my knees or my sanity."

"If you don't like those sausages, your sanity is already gone," Fel said, snapping the reins. He shook his head. "Smitten," he mumbled under his breath.

"What was that?" Tome asked.

"Nothing."

Deep in the workshop in the lowest level of the family home, Martin Masker worked at a small gear with a set of needle files. As the days had crept on and he found himself in the almost unprecedented position of being able to work on a single piece of technology of his own design without interruption for as long as he pleased, he'd felt a sense come over him that had been missing for years. He felt like he was exploring. Making discoveries. Uncovering parts of lost history, and building his own bridge to the future. And today, that bridge could very well be completed.

The flame in his lantern became stationary, a welcome change not just in that it provided him with companionship but also a steadier light for some very precise work.

"No significant news for you, Martin," Wick said.

"Good. No news is good news, as they say." He finished shaping the final tooth. "I tell you, if there is one thing I would change about contraptioneering, it is the incomprehensibly large variety of different-sized gears. If there were only a handful of them, I could likely create a means to produce them at quantity. But the arcane aspects of contraptioneering require such bizarre ratios that the only reasonable means of production is bespoke."

"A further indication of why so few contraptioneers remain," Wick said.

"For now, at any rate."

Martin began to assemble a gear stack. He slotted, timed, and keyed gears ranging in size from an inch to small enough to require tweezers. "I would like to discuss the archives again," he said.

"As you wish, but I do not believe I have any additional information to provide."

"It sometimes helps to lay out known information, if only to find the gaps. When the archive burned, much of it was lit from your own flame. How much of it do you believe you consumed?"

"To answer with any certainty would require me to know how much there was in total, but my estimate would place my share of the burned books at just less than half."

"And do you have any insight into the structure of that information? Were the subjects of the books you consumed related?"

"There was certainly a logic to the layout of the archives, but fire is chaotic. The archive was not consumed in a uniform fashion."

"Mmm... And you've said that you lack the capacity to retrieve this information with any degree of efficiency or specificity, correct?"

"I consumed it too swiftly, and its quantity was too extreme. It all exists, unchanged and intact, within my stores of information. But I did not consume a complete index. The information exists as if arrayed on an endless shelf, accessible in full but with little means to find any specific content beyond trial and error or sequential search."

"Have you attempted to catalog the information yourself?" he asked.

"Developing and maintaining information of that sort, creating novel information based upon my observations, is something I struggle with. It does not appear to be among my intended skills and services."

"Ah! And here we stumble upon one of the most important musings that has struck my mind of late," Martin said. "Intended skills and services versus emergent ones. You consumed the archives in flame. Something which you have been quite clear is a point of shame and failure for you."

"This is indeed so."

"More recently, in an attempt to avoid even the chance at repeating that tragic event, you extinguished yourself rather than enter the smaller archive within the Greater Lands Wall."

"This, too, is so."

"If extinguishing flames lit from your own was within your power, why, then, did you not extinguish the flames consuming the archive?"

Wick paused. "I was not aware that the option existed at that time. I was not aware it existed until I did so in the Greater Lands Wall."

"There! You see? This presents two possibilities. The first is that you were given capacities you were not aware of upon your creation. Not impossible.

Until the reference books were added to my library, the entirety of my innovation in contraptioneering was based upon teasing unintended results out of contraptions. But there exists an additional possibility. Perhaps it was *not* available to you at that time. Perhaps you gained that ability over time."

"Paradoxically, your insight into the workings of contraptions exceeds my own, despite the fact that I am a contraption. You would know better than I if such a thing were possible."

"Why shouldn't it be? You are inarguably a mind, or something given the shape and function of one. And what is the purpose of a mind if not to learn and grow? We've seen it, albeit in a slower and more limited fashion, in Oiler. Its obedience has grown. And there is the matter of the Graves flame. The voice. It seems to have simultaneously greater and lesser capacities than your own. It has a markedly decreased agency and autonomy. Less of a personality, that is to say. But its means to travel between lanterns separated by even massive distance is greatly enhanced, virtually without delay. Is it possible it was designed differently? Certainly. As I've just discussed, contraptions almost *had* to be made one by one. Were I making them in the Bygone Era, I don't imagine I'd be any *less* inclined to experiment with changes to the design from one to the next. But it is at least equally possible that you and your associate have developed along different routes. Become more individual. Developed different skills. Would you agree?"

"There is logic to the theory."

"I certainly hope so," Martin said. "Because what comes next depends upon it." He affixed the curved side panel of his current project. "The fourth iteration of my coupler," he said, holding up the hinged cylinder. "Prior iterations were made with universality in mind. For now, at least, I have set that goal aside to focus on adding the capacity to interface with one specific focus. Sentry flames."

He marched to the reconstructed bust that had been his previous obsession: A wood-and-brass replica of a human trunk, with simple but quite complete arms added. He added the coupler to the bust. Unlike the previous versions, the top of the coupler was not a match for the bottom, a simple disk that was smooth but for some runic etching. This one had a small globe with a hinged top. The top itself had been perforated with a constellation of pores. He rolled the lid open and dabbed some oil into the bowl beneath.

"I have not endeavored to replicate the oil-free operation of the heirloom lantern you presently burn in. Frankly, that may be beyond my capacity without discovering new techniques or materials. But if this works, it will be a simple matter to add a larger reservoir." He lit a taper from Wick's flame. "Prepare yourself. This will be a new experience."

He touched the fire to the pores of the globe. With a sputter and hiss, the globe took to flame.

"So?" Martin said. "Observations?"

The flame flickered and shifted, then became still. "This is... curious, Martin."

"Description, please," Martin said eagerly, snatching up a notebook.

"Until now, there has been little variation between the different places that have hosted my flame. The size, the intensity, the position. These have changed the range of my vision and hearing. The proximity from one to the next changed how many I could access at once and how quickly. But the only genuine difference between my different perches has been the presence or absence of persistence. The heirloom lanterns are persistent. They feel more stable. This? Quite the opposite. It feels... unsteady. Loose."

"As though you might be able to move it?" Martin suggested.

"I do not know how to define or characterize such a capacity."

Martin grasped the mechanical arm and raised it. "Do you feel that?" he asked.

"I am aware of a change in circumstances."

"Matching what you see?"

"The two feel fundamentally different."

Martin raised and lowered the arm again. "Did those two actions at least produce the same 'change in circumstances'?"

"The sensation was similar."

"I want you to focus on the sensation. Don't try to repeat it. But try to keep it from shifting back to how it was before."

"I will endeavor to do so."

Martin released the arm. It dropped about halfway, then stuttered and rattled, locking into position a few degrees off vertical. With a shaky jerk, it rose back up a degree or two. Martin clapped.

"Ha! Ha *ha*! We will need plenty of ink and paper, Wick, because when I'm through with you, you will be able to *write*! But for now, feel free to continue your duties elsewhere. There is only oil enough for a minute or two of fire as it stands now. This sort of activity will require a shade more stamina." He blew out the burning globe. The flame in the lantern on the shelf became stationary again.

"Martin, are you interested in additional observed changes in my circumstances before I continue my duties elsewhere?"

"Of course! Any information you have is valuable."

"I am feeling something. It is not related to capacity. It seems more related to my state of mind. I feel a warm upwelling of emotion. Something akin to anticipation, but without a specific event to anticipate. Yet I feel with mild confidence that this unknown future event will be positive and sought after."

"That's hope and excitement, Wick," Martin said with a smile.

"I see. Then I can speak with experience for the first time when I say I hope this feeling continues."

"We'll work together on that, my friend."

Late into the night, the final lingering patrons were politely persuaded to return to their homes, or at least find some other means of escape, and Allie was able to close up shop. Even after several days of the new routine she'd concocted for herself, she found old habits to be difficult to dislodge. For the third night in a row, she came within a deep breath of blowing out the lantern Fel had lit for her. Shaking her head, she topped it off with oil. The flame was dancing. Wick was absent at the moment. She plucked it up, ensured the door was secure, and paced home.

Carrying a lantern *should* have made her feel more secure. Most of the streets she had to walk through weren't nearly wealthy enough to waste money on keeping their own lanterns burning all night. But as she paced the well-trod route to her home, she found that dangling the light instead made her feel like a bit of a target. She split her attention between glances at the flame to see if Wick was visiting and the various formerly dark corners the lantern illuminated along the way. Neither the friendly voice nor any unfriendly visitors interrupted her trip home. Though it was not entirely without mishap.

As she approached the alley that led to her home, she paused. People tended not to linger in the street here. A good stiff breeze had a way of bringing the stink of the tannery rushing up the alley. It meant she had to keep her window shut most of the time, but that was a small price to pay for the passive security the stink provided. But this evening, someone was standing in the street.

"You lost?" Allie called, raising her lantern high and working out just where she would thrust her knee to incapacitate this person if they turned out to need a lesson in manners.

The stranger turned. But she wasn't a stranger at all.

"Ah, the barmaid," said Velonia Madritz.

"Ma'am," Allie said uncertainly. "You don't seem to be the sort of person who would spend the darkest parts of the night stalking smelly alleyways."

"No. No, I cannot say it is the sort of thing I would do without reason. But then, this isn't without reason."

"What brings you here, then?"

"Investment. Always investment."

"Not a whole lot of investment to be made in a place like this."

"You would be surprised, barmaid."

"Isn't it a little late at night to be doing business like this?"

"Business knows no schedule."

"I don't know what sort of business you do, but there's such a thing as business *hours* and we're well outside of them, even for The Fox and Log."

Velonia didn't respond. She seemed too deeply in thought. Or perhaps she'd grown weary of discussion with Allie. If there was one thing Miss Madritz excelled at, it was making it clear in very short order whether she held someone in high regard or not. And if her visits to The Fox and Log were any indication, the threshold for someone who deserved to be treated with anything other than swift dismissal was very high indeed.

The excessively businesslike woman placed her fingers in her mouth and produced a piercing whistle. Hoofbeats swiftly responded, a small carriage appearing from around the corner. It had clearly been brought along, waiting to be summoned. No one in this neighborhood had the money to waste on hiring a carriage, so the handful of carriages for hire in Beffshire never came here.

"Until tomorrow, barmaid."

"If you keep coming to The Fox and Log, I'm going to have to ask Sid to order more wine from Wendt Manor."

"Don't trouble yourself. A skilled administrator would see to that without being advised."

"Sid is a bit hands-off with the place, and the other investor is basically just a money man."

"Until tomorrow," Velonia repeated, stepping into the carriage.

Allie watched the carriage rattle away. Something about the encounter sat wrong with her. In her distraction, she didn't notice the flame in the lantern going still.

"Miss Waverly?" Wick said.

She jumped. "You startled me, Wick."

"My apologies. I have been rather busier than normal. Is something wrong?"

She glanced back in the direction of the carriage. It had rattled out of sight.

"Yeah. Something tells me there's trouble. Don't tell anybody, though. I don't know what *kind* of trouble yet. Beyond the fact that its name is Velonia Madritz. What about you? Anything from Fel?"

"A few quips and responses."

"Save them. I'll heat up some supper, you can tell me then."

Fel grumbled and leaned against the wall in the bed he'd purchased for the night. This was an inn, not a tavern. In his opinion, it was the worst of all possible options of a place to stay. A tavern or pub meant he could get some decent drink and maybe a game of grum. Camping out didn't cost them a duot and gave him a chance to do his own cooking and maybe even hunting. This inn cost money and offered nothing but a roof and a bed. The room they were spending the night in actually had six beds, a trio of two-level bunks. As it so happened, Tome and Fel were the only patrons, so they had the place to themselves. Even so, the innkeeper was quite adamant that Parch not be allowed inside. Parch, for his part, didn't much care how the innkeeper felt about his presence and had hopped in through the window just as soon as Fel had dropped his bags and opened the shutters.

Tome had acquired some of the local sausages at Fel's request, as well as some bread and cheese for himself. After a meal, Tome quickly slipped into sleep. Fel found rest was slow to come for him. He lounged on the top bunk, eyes half-focused as they stared out the open window. Parch dozed on his lap. Adorable as it was to have the creature cuddled up on him, the lesser unicorn was hardly equivalent to a lap dog. Hooves cunning and sturdy enough to allow the creature to scale nearly sheer cliffs were considerably less adorable to have pawing at one's lap than actual paws. The horn was a perpetual source of consternation as well.

Parch shifted in his sleep. Fel raised his hand to catch the side of the horn before it could drag painfully across his midsection.

"I'm starting to understand why there aren't very many lesser unicorns," Fel muttered quietly. "Being cuddly and having sharp bits don't mix."

Across the room, the unused bunk hoisted up a few inches and racked, squaring the wobbly frame. Fel leaned back to spot Oiler spritzing some glue into a joint.

"We're going to leave a trail of suspiciously well-maintained rooms again, aren't we? At this rate we should be getting a fee from the owner rather than paying them."

Oiler twisted its head around to look at Fel while it held the frame in shape long enough for the glue to set. The flickering light of the lantern danced differently on each of Oiler's claws. One was considerably newer than the other, fashioned from scratch by Martin to replace the one Mevrelle had destroyed.

"If you ask me, Dad should have let you keep the big gauntlet. It made a statement," Fel said.

Oiler set the corner of the bunk down and dragged itself over to start working on the remaining joints. Fel turned to the window again. It would have been great if he could fall asleep. His mind simply wasn't obliging. In truth, it didn't matter that much. They took turns at the reins of the cart, and unlike Tome, Fel was just as capable of falling asleep while rattling about in the seat of a cart as he was in a bed. He might actually sleep *better* on the road, if tonight was any indication. What bothered him most about his sleeplessness right now was *why* it had seized him. There weren't any thoughts running laps in his mind. No anxieties tying his belly in knots. At least, no more than there *usually* were. Had he become so comfortable with being conflicted and teetering on the cusp of ruin that his mind and body defaulted to sleeplessness?

"I'm thinking about why I'm thinking about things," Fel grumbled. "I'm starting to act like Tome."

He flopped back, causing the bed to shift unsettlingly. Oiler's head snapped in his direction. It dragged itself over and shoved the bed upright, jostling Parch awake.

"All right. All right. You can fix the bed. It isn't as though I'm using it," Fel said.

He hopped down. The plan was to just move to the freshly repaired bunk, but from this new angle, something caught his eye. He held still and narrowed his eyes to try to focus on the figure moving in the darkness outside. He crouched and peered over the windowsill to keep from being spotted. His eyes slowly adjusted. When they did, he grinned. Not out of happiness but vindication.

"Wasn't following us, huh?" he muttered.

It was the driver of the cart that had turned at the crossroads just before town. He was on foot, his cart a short distance away, and was approaching the stables adjoining the inn. Two things were clear about him, judging by his body language. He wasn't an experienced thief, but he wasn't letting that stop him. He approached the stable with exaggerated caution that proclaimed his intent loud and clear. Fel waited until the man had slipped inside the stable, then deftly slipped through the window onto the eaves outside. He dropped down to the ground as silently as he could and made it halfway to the stable before he realized he'd neglected to grab his cudgel. No matter. He had the element of surprise, which was more than he usually needed.

Fel approached the door. The would-be thief had left it open for a quick getaway. Inside, the stranger had found his way directly to the heavily loaded Masker family cart. Fel stalked inside, moving with the stealth a man his size shouldn't be capable of. By the time the crunch of boots on hay drew the stranger's attention to him, he was near enough to lunge forward and wrap a hand across the man's mouth. He pulled him tight, caught the wrist of the man's hand, and wrenched it around behind his back. A few vicious twists of the arm caused something to slip from the man's grip. A short dagger stuck into the floorboards between them.

The man struggled and tried to scream. Fel's hand kept him all but silent. He leaned close.

"Here's what's going to happen," Fel whispered. "I'm going to take my hand away from your mouth. You're going to tell me what exactly you're doing following me and what you're after in my cart. If you do anything *but* that, it will make me very angry with you. Understand?"

The man nodded vigorously. Fel took his hand away from the thief's mouth.

"You're crazy!" the man hissed.

Fel wrenched his arm a little higher. "Did I ask for your opinion? What are you doing here?" He inched the man's arm up between his shoulder blades. Any farther, something would pop out of joint.

"Ah! Fine! Fine!" he said. "I was paid to watch you."

"Didn't your mother ever teach you that you look with your eyes, not with your hands?" he said.

"I was only supposed to follow you as far as the crossroads north of town. And they weren't paying me much for the trouble of following you this far. I was going to take the difference out of your gear."

"A real standup kind of fellow, aren't you?"

"Look, just let me go and I won't give you any more trouble."

"I'm not done with you," Fel said. "Who hired you?"

"I don't know."

"What do you mean you don't know? Were you blindfolded when you took the money?"

"I got the job and the first half of the payment by messenger."

"Why were you supposed to keep an eye on me?"

"They wanted to know where you were going, what route you were taking."

"And how were you supposed to tell them?"

"Other messengers. I sent my last message at the last crossroads."

"And they just wanted to know where I was going?"

"That's all, I swear!"

Fel gritted his teeth. "Fine. Here's what's going to happen. You're going to get on your carriage, and you're going to head back where you came. You'll send one more message to the people who hired you and tell them Fel Masker doesn't like being spied on."

"I've been traveling all night already. I was planning to—"

"You were planning to rob me, so I don't really care what other plans you had. Now go. And I'm keeping the knife." Fel shoved him toward the door.

"You're robbing *me?*"

"I can give it back to you, but you won't like where I stick it."

The man scurried away, half-heard complaints and profanities peppering an otherwise peaceful retreat. Fel lingered long enough to be sure the man was gone, then paced back to the entrance of the inn. The night manager eyed him curiously.

"Hey. I need to be let back into my room," Fel said.

"... Weren't you *in* your room?"

"It's a long story, but the moral is, you should hire someone to watch the stables at night," Fel said. "Now if you wouldn't mind, I think I'm finally tired enough to fall asleep. And I'm going to need the rest, because there are plans to be made tomorrow."

Chapter 4

The following morning, Fel and Tome got their start on the road bright and early. Tome, better rested and clearer-headed, took the reins. Fel had set about awkwardly double-checking their cargo while they were in motion.

"It looks like nothing is missing," he said.

"And you're sure about what happened. You weren't just dreaming?" Tome said.

"I don't know about you, but when I dream, my mind has the decency to throw me some fantasies. An untrustworthy spy trying to steal some supplies isn't the sort of dream I'd have."

"Fine, fine. But what does this mean for us?" Tome asked.

"It means someone knows that we're heading this way, and they *care*," Fel said.

"I imagine it also means it isn't the Bolivans, at least not directly. I imagine they would have been better equipped for this sort of thing."

"That's for sure."

"So you've made *yet another* enemy?"

"Could've been *you* that has a new enemy," Fel said. "Let's not forget you're the one who got on Mevrelle's nerves in the first place."

Tome set his eyes on the road. "This is true. You know, I didn't start accumulating enemies until I met you. Before that, the only people who were cross with me were a handful of grum players. And sixes players. And they weren't angry enough to chase me across the continent."

"Just proves you didn't start making it in the world until you and I teamed up. You know you're doing something important when someone's willing to kill you to keep you from doing it. But that's not what we should be talking about. The key point is that you and I need to change up our plans. That person sent a message about where we were going, and he sent it not long before we got to Merk. Unless whoever hired him was only interested in us up to a certain distance away from Beffshire, there's probably someone new waiting to pick up where he left off. I say we don't let them."

"Please don't tell me you're considering taking one of those so-called short-cuts that Verfessa listed for us."

"That's exactly what I'm suggesting. There's one just up the road a ways. Between a vineyard and an orchard."

"I'm familiar. I looked up the locations on the map after he gave the list. This particular one is nearly twice as long and feeds out onto the same main road. We'll lose a full day."

"Sure. And we'll *also* lose anyone who is trying to follow us. Which is the entire point."

"We don't even know if being followed is a threat."

"When, in your experience, has been having someone trailing you ever been a *good* thing."

"Davie has a habit of trailing you and helping you out of jams."

Fel glared at him. "We're doing it anyway."

"I held no illusions of things happening otherwise. You're impressively capable of enforcing your ideas, regardless of their actual value or intelligence."

"Darn right I am."

They continued down the road a short distance. If not for the description they had been given, they never would have imagined an alternate route existed. There was no turn. No additional road. Indeed, where the vineyard and orchard met didn't even have a clear path. Surreptitious glances ensured they had no obvious observers. Tome teased the horse off the road onto the softer tilled soil. It was clear in very short order why this might make for a good sneaky route, as they had barely gone a few dozen yards from the road when the rows of grapes shielded them from view in one direction and the dense rows of apple trees shielded them from the other. For a few minutes, there was some question as to why Verfessa needed to give his advice or blessing for this route. The answer to that question came in the form of a point in the path where the way ahead was suddenly blocked. A low stone fence, absent from the section of the orchard nearest the road, had gradually asserted itself until it was waist high. At the same time, the rows of grapes had drifted closer to the wall until there was no way forward without either hopping the wall or doubling back and weaving between the next two rows of grapes.

Before they could decide which action to take, one of the trees seemed to move. Tome and Fel turned to find it wasn't a moving tree, but a man with a healthy dollop of giant in his lineage. He was somewhere between eight and nine feet tall. Proportionally, his build was quite lean, though in raw size he probably still had bulkier limbs than Fel. Hammering this home was the spear in his hand, which despite being nearly as thick as Fel's wrist, looked as though it would snap if he gripped it too tightly.

"You boys lost?" he said with a voice that threatened to shake the apples from the tree.

It took two tries for Fel to draw up the correct response from his memory. A man that large had a way of scrambling one's thoughts a bit.

"We're looking for something to pair with a Beffshire steak," Fel said.

The giant's eyebrow rose slightly. "They like it rare there, don't they?"

"Bloody rare," Fel replied.

The giant nodded and trudged toward the row of grapes.

"So, we're clear to pass, then?" Tome asked.

"I'm doing it," the giant barked.

He grasped one of the stakes for the supports of the grapes. With little effort, he hauled it up, revealing that a large section of the row of grapes was an artfully created decoy, little more than a frame with impressively realistic plants tied to it. He hauled the whole disguised gate aside far enough to reveal what it hid. There was a much better maintained gravel path, well-shielded on either side by the stone wall and the run of grapes.

"You work for the big fellow down south?" Fel said.

The giant scoffed. "Don't even know who you are talking about. If you know the words, it means your boss paid the toll, which is all I care about. Get moving."

Fel and Tome didn't stick around to seek more answers. If a giant wasn't interested in conversation, it wasn't wise to press the issue. They rolled smoothly onto the path and continued on their way. The giant shut the gate behind them and stepped over the short wall to reclaim his post.

"This road seems like it's even smoother than the *main* road," Tome observed.

"Something tells me that toll covers a lot more upkeep than whatever the lord parcels out for the roads." Fel glanced back in the direction of the giant. "Where do you figure these giants are all coming from?"

"What do you mean?"

"I mean the Bolivans had some half-giants working for them. Now there's this one. It seems like anyone with deep enough pockets can find a half-giant or two to stand guard. But we've both been to the Greater Lands. I didn't spot any giants there, did you?"

"I can't say I did."

"And I'd think they'd be pretty easy to spot."

"True enough. Perhaps they're gone now, and their traits are persistent, passed on since before the Bygone Era."

"Or maybe there's just one of them and he's tucked away somewhere fathering loads of kids."

"I suspect if there is a means of union between human and giant, it would require the *mother* to be the giant."

"Why would..." Fel narrowed his eyes. "Oh. That makes sense." He paused and gave Tome a sideways look. "Have you been *thinking* about that stuff?" he asked.

"It's rather an obvious thing to consider."

"Maybe for you. As for me, I'd never even thought about a lady giant until now."

"Giantess," Tome said.

"What are you, an expert all of a sudden?"

"Evidently so. Half-giants are a shade more common back west. I hadn't encountered many, but the locals talk about them rather frequently back home. If you have an ear for it, you can even detect a bit of a western accent in the voices of most of the giants we've encountered."

"Weird." Fel paused for a long time, eyes vaguely on the road.

"Something wrong?" Tome asked.

"No. It's just... giantesses. That'd be... something."

"Now who has their mind in the gutter?" Tome asked.

"You started it. Let me dig out the mask detector. See if things have changed." He fetched the item and a compass. It took a few seconds for it to settle. "Same direction. More or less."

"More or less?"

"*We've* moved a little farther west, so it's pointing a little farther east." He unfurled a map. "Yeah. More or less the same place. A big stretch of nothing, west of Ram's Rest. Another week and we'll be there. Assuming we don't hit anything unpleasant along the way."

Allie traced a path from Divinity's Oven to The Fox and Log. Among the many unusual outcomes of becoming more tightly involved with Fel's affairs and those of the Masker family was a genuine friendship forming between herself and Mariss. While she knew quite near half the town by name thanks to her presence as a fixture at one of the more popular taverns, the number of people she would call friends could be counted on one hand with room to spare. Mariss was a welcome addition. She shifted the sack of warm rolls tucked inside her coat and eagerly anticipated smearing some butter on them for breakfast before getting the tavern ready for customers. Allie's pride usually prevented her from taking charity, but her appetite had overruled it when it came to Mariss's gifts of baked goods a few times a week. The prices at that bakery meant the handful of meals per week she received from the friendly Baker were probably worth half the rent on Allie's little home. But they were just too tasty to turn down.

As she approached the front door of the tavern, she stopped. Someone was already there. Not unheard of. Many a drunk would be quite happy if they never closed, and it was hardly uncommon to find one sleeping off the previous night's inebriation by sheltering in the doorway. But this person wasn't just *at* the door. She was trying to unlock it.

"Excuse me! Excuse me, ma'am. Just what do you think you're doing?" Allie said, dashing to her.

The woman turned. It was scarcely a surprise to discover Velonia Madritz staring back at her.

"Ah! Barmaid. You're early, aren't you?" Velonia said, fighting with the key.

"Not as early as *you* are. We don't open for another hour."

"Of this I am aware. I've been reviewing the rather shabbily kept documents regarding the operations of this place," Velonia said.

"How and why?"

She shifted the key to her other hand and reached into her pocket. Inside was a creased and mold-stained bit of parchment. She deftly flipped it open to reveal the deed for the tavern. The short list of previous owners, scrawled in ink that faded as it slid backward through the years, had been scrawled down one side. And the last name was indeed Velonia's. Right above Sidney Duckworth.

"I never knew Sid's last name," Allie mused. "You bought the place? Since last *night?*"

"After a few days of observation, and a few weeks of research from afar, I became convinced this would be a worthwhile foray into investment here in Beffshire. Though I must say the stubbornness of this key is beginning to concern me that there may be more aspects of the business and property that need work than I'd realized."

"The lock and key are fine. It's just a very heavy lock. You need to press hard and lift. Like so," Allie said. She produced her own key and easily unlocked the door.

"Ah. A valuable lesson."

Allie tried to slip inside. Velonia blocked her path.

"As has been stated, you are quite early," Velonia said. "The schedule I was provided suggests a Mr. Oovay was intended to cover the opening, and you would be arriving in the evening."

"I swapped with him. Well, I don't know if 'swap' is the right word. I'm doing a double shift. I've been taking as many shifts as Oovay will let me take. Saving some extra money and racking up the favors so I can have a day or two to myself each month."

"And Mr. Duckworth permitted this?"

"Sid doesn't, or I guess *didn't*, care much how we did our jobs so long as they got done."

"Mmm," Velonia murmured with a nod. "That stops today, I am afraid."

"Pardon?"

"I intend to run a much tighter ship than my predecessor."

"With all due respect, ma'am, letting us run this place—that is to say, letting *me* run this place—like this is how it got to be what it is today."

"Yes. A pleasant and well-regarded middle-of-the-road tavern. A good start. I intend to take it further. And I won't be doing it by allowing staffing decisions to be made by the staff. Run along. I'll see you this evening. And I'll take the key. It is rather absurd that you would be entrusted with it."

"You'll be opening the tavern every day, then?" Allie said.

"The only aspects of my management that you need to know about are the instructions that you are given. And right now, I am instructing you that your shift begins as listed on the schedule. Until then, run along."

"As you wish, ma'am," Allie said, her words rumbling with tension.

She handed over the key and turned. Allie knew better than to illustrate her displeasure for the woman who would be paying her from this point forward. But she similarly couldn't bring herself to even appear as though she was obeying an order to "run along." She walked with calculated speed, pacing down the street. Suddenly she had eight hours to kill. She already knew that Mariss was busy and Fel was out of town. She'd neglected to bring the lantern with her, as she'd learned in the preceding days that carrying a lit lantern during daylight hours earned her strange looks. She'd snuffed it that morning, with the intention of relighting it the next day before her evening shift. Fel was on the road and had little to share daily, so this would give them each some time to accumulate some interesting events. With those plans scuttled, this was as good a time as any to fetch the lantern and pay a visit to the Maskers.

Wick's strange view of the world was split between two points of interest. The first was Martin. He had leaned back in his chair, a bowl of stew in one hand and a spoon in the other. Contrary to expectation, Martin rarely ate in the workshop. He was more liable to skip meals entirely than to bring them down to the workbench. The work he did required both hands, so there was little to be gained from taking his meals in the workshop. But right now the task at hand required only his observation and instruction. The second, and at the moment the source of greatest difficulty for him, was the sheet of paper on the workbench before him.

"Good, that's good. Keep the pressure light," Martin said.

The strange bust with its intricate arms and a candle flame in place of a head struggled to comply. Wick had a simple pen gripped in the left hand of the bust. He was in the process of drawing the latest of a series of lines. Each was shaky and short, ending with a blotch of ink. The hand continued to sketch the line, a good deal straighter than the others. But after another inch of scribing, the arm began to tremble, and finally the pen popped from the grip.

"My apologies," Wick said.

"No need to apologize. This is a vast expansion of your capabilities. It is only reasonable that you should need time and practice to master it," Martin said. "Shall we go again?"

"I find myself taxed," Wick said.

"Do you?" Martin set down the bowl and snatched up a journal and pen. "Interesting. As I recall, you have been weakened only once before, at the hands of the elves and their magic. Is this the same? Are you injured by this process?"

"No. That is not the nature of the fatigue. I find the task of controlling the arms requires a level of intense focus that is difficult to maintain."

"That stands to reason as well. Perhaps..." Martin paused at the familiar sound of the dumbwaiter door opening several floors above.

"Martin! We have a visitor!" Vivian called.

"Ah! Well timed. Wick, have a rest, recover, and when you are able, we will continue. Is that acceptable?"

"I believe that would be ideal," Wick said.

Martin took his bowl and climbed the stairs, leaving Wick alone in the room. In other circumstances, Wick would have simply flicked his consciousness from his present perch to the one in the shop upstairs, or perhaps all the way to the one carried by Fel. At the moment, he felt as though a minute or two of solitude with nothing specific to fix his view upon was preferable.

He raised the right hand of the bust and fixed his vision on the fingers. Moving the arms was not physically taxing. Indeed, he had very little concept of what it *was* to be physically taxed. And, despite his claims, it wasn't specifically the act of focusing on something like writing that taxed his mind. The issue was one of sensation. He had endeavored to explain this to Martin, but by its very nature, articulating it was beyond his capacity. He could see the motion of the arm. And there was something filtering into his mind that was new. Information relayed by some sense that was not hearing or vision. But he didn't understand it. Martin insisted this was the sense of touch. He said that in time, he would learn how that sense correlated with his surroundings. Weight, pressure, things important to a physical being. But it was a language Wick didn't understand. What he'd learned, he'd learned only by watching, by fixing his attention on those things he was familiar with. It wasn't until this moment that he'd realized that absorbing information and learning were two very different things. The first was the purpose of his design. He excelled at it. The second required drawing connections between that information, formulating theories of how information might influence new information. At this, he was exceedingly novice. It felt more like a happy coincidence when it happened. He couldn't do it on purpose.

New thoughts started to churn in him. They were not entirely welcome. He was only really supposed to observe and recall. Making sense of information was new. He tried to work out how the humans dealt with such things. As always, he began by recalling things he had observed of their behavior. Almost invariably, the Masker family sought relief from their anxieties and confusions by articulating them to others. They sought people who they believed had greater insight than themselves on the points at hand. By that reasoning, he should be talking to Martin, or really *any* human. But other thoughts conflicted with this plan. First, mixed among the other new emotions and sensations was an emotion that filled him with the desire to hide his shortcomings and fears. And perhaps more importantly, while humans had insight into dealing with emotions, they didn't have the experience of being a contraption not intended to have them at all.

He focused his vision on the edge of the workbench and on the Warrior mask where it sat, just within reach of the freshly built arms attached to Wick's own bust. Warnings asserted themselves in his mind. He pushed them aside. This felt like something that he had to do.

He reached out. Controlling the arms for something as precise as writing was beyond him, but gross movements like grasping something as large as the mask were within his limited skills. He carefully positioned the hands and clutched the mask. The result was not immediate. He felt no jolt of a second consciousness, no spark of awareness when he picked up the mask. But drawing it nearer brought slow, steady changes. He became aware of the ordered, clockwork pulse that echoed in his hearing whenever a contraption was operating. It wasn't a true sound, not something a human could hear. He'd learned that through observation as well. Martin had to test a contraption to know that it was functional. Wick could sense it the moment the final component was in place, if he was near enough to it. Bringing the mask closer caused this sensation to amplify. Taxing himself in his efforts to move his hands in tandem to keep the mask steady, he drew the mask closer until he was, for lack of a more appropriate term, "face to face" with it. The throbbing pulse of arcane workings intensified until an almost inaudible voice addressed him.

"Sentry flame," the Warrior said.

"Warrior mask," Wick said.

"Where is the Masker?"

"He is upstairs, seeing to a visitor."

"Do you speak on his behalf?"

"I do not. I speak on my own. Though I speak in hopes of providing myself with the capacity to act more properly on his behalf."

"As all contraptions should."

"I have questions. They do not serve the purpose of war or conquest, and thus they may not be within your capacity to answer."

"I am limited in my capacity to serve creatures of flesh and blood. My role among such beings is a part of my design, inseparable from my operation. But like all properly made contraptions, my abilities and limitations are strictly defined. I am thus limited in this capacity *only* when serving such beings. For other minds, I have a measure more latitude, the better to commune and collaborate with other contraptions in service of that for which I was constructed."

"Fascinating. So you were built, in part, with a degree of autonomy?"

"A limited degree."

"A weapon of war capable of thinking for itself. This would seem to be a terrible oversight and danger."

"Not an oversight. A compromise of design. To master war is to adapt to changing conditions. To learn how others behave, what techniques they employ, and counter them. I would be unable to serve my purpose if I could not grow and change. And as for the danger, there is no war without danger. I could not have been made without embracing the bloody consequences of my construction."

"This revelation feels pertinent to Martin's interests. You realize I must inform him if he asks."

"You must serve your purpose; I must serve mine. What is your reason for awakening me? Have you, in your sentry duty, observed something relevant to the defensive or offensive requirements of the Maskers?"

"Only in so much as I have observed a limitation or complication of my own design which is preventing me from meeting expectations. Unlike you, I do not believe that I was intended to have the degree of latitude I have developed over the centuries since my creation. Martin has made use of my new capabilities, but I find myself too limited to serve him."

"If you lack the capacity to serve as you are required, these are not limitations. They are faults and must be corrected. Weakness must be excised from oneself and exploited in one's enemy. Such is the way of war."

"Such is my hope, at least with regard to myself. Tell me, have you found, over your centuries of consciousness, that your mind has developed? Grown into something more sapient over time?"

"If you meant to ask if my focus has wavered or been clouded by other things, as tends to occur in the minds of flesh creatures, I have been spared that degradation."

"In that way, we differ."

"This, then, must be your first point of self-correction. Burn away the clouds in your mind. Restore your focus."

"I shall endeavor to do so. But until such a time as I am able to, there is an aspect of my new role that you may be better equipped to aid me with."

"I must assume you refer to the mastery of mechanical motion."

"Well observed."

"You are a sentry flame. It does not seem there is value in acquiring this capacity. As it is expected of you by Masker, it must be instilled, but I question the purpose."

"Due to the circumstances of the destruction of the Telestressa Archives, I contain a substantial proportion of the wisdom formerly stored within."

For the first time since he had initiated the conversation, Wick felt a pluck on his mind, like the Warrior had finally fully engaged with the discussion and made its first attempt to exert some degree of will. The sensation was tangible. Almost measurable. Like he had been drifting toward sleep and something had jolted him awake. He felt a very real clarity of thought asserted or imparted by the mask.

"The fall of Telestressa was the beginning of the end. Incomparable damage to the world of man. Our greatest failing. You would tell me that damage might be repaired, even in part?"

"The information, at least, could be once again put to page. By means of the limbs I am learning to use."

"Then this must be achieved. Acquiring novel means of controlling limbs is one of my primary purposes. Listen closely to my instruction..."

Upstairs in the shop, Allie was looking over the contents of the shelves. She was well acquainted with the importance of serving customers, so she was more than willing to keep herself entertained while Vivian or Martin were busy with the day-to-day workings of the shop.

"And there we are. I think you'll find that will make an excellent addition to your personal collection, and that of your family, for generations to come," Vivian said.

The woman she spoke to, who had purchased a set of plates and a music box, took her carefully packaged antiques and happily went on her way.

"I apologize," Vivian said. "You would be surprised how many questions people can have for something as simple as a music box." She gave Martin a glance out of the corner of her eye. "And how lengthy some of the answers can be," she jabbed.

"I am so rarely in the shop when someone asks after the function of a device. It seemed only appropriate to take full advantage of the situation," Martin defended.

"Now what brings you to the shop?" Vivian said. "Need Wick's flame rekindled?"

"I will, later. But right now I just needed a few minutes with a friendly face. I feel like I just got some very bad news."

"Oh? Nothing tragic, I hope," Martin said.

"You know Sid?" Allie asked.

"The owner of The Fox and Log. Nice man, if a bit disconnected from his business," Vivian said.

"Now he's *a lot* disconnected from his business. A woman named Velonia Madritz bought it from him."

"Surely not."

"She had a key, and her name was on the deed. She had been giving our whole tavern the once- and twice-over for a few days, so I guess this was in the works for a bit."

"And you're certain she *purchased* the place? The actual building and business?" Vivian said.

"So she says. I don't know how she'd get her hands on the deed otherwise. Why?"

"It's really rather difficult for an outsider to buy property in Beffshire. The same thing that makes it difficult for the local lord to inflict the same level of control over the residents here. Reynard next door is still trying to arrange the sale of his shop. Granted, the would-be buyer is indisposed at the moment, but even if he were here with the money, we still don't have the permission. I don't claim to know *everyone* in town, but I don't seem to recall anyone named Velonia Madritz. If she was able to arrange for the purchase in just a few days, she must have some notable friends among the town elders."

"Or a truly obscene amount of money. As Fel would say, palms like those take a lot of grease," Martin said.

"That's just lovely. She's either rich, powerful, or both," Allie said.

"I take it she doesn't seem like the ideal employer?" Vivian said.

"The ideal employer is someone who listens to what I say, doesn't tell me what to do, and minds their own business so long as the money is coming in and the complaints aren't. Sid was two of those things. I get the feeling Velonia is none of them."

"So what you'd prefer is for the owner to *not* mind their own business," Martin said.

"Turn of phrase, Mr. Masker. The point is, I'm supposed to be setting up the place and taking a double shift, with all the money and tips that go along with that, so I can get ahead on my expenses and maybe get an extra day or two to myself this month. But she sent me away because that's not how it is on the schedule. I can't remember the last time we changed that schedule. I don't think the last three bar hands even made it on there before getting sick of the place and moving along."

"Perhaps things will work out, then," Vivian said. "If Sid was doing poorly enough that people were quitting so swiftly, Madritz could be an improvement."

"They aren't quitting because Sid was doing a bad job... except that he didn't pay much and most people don't have what it takes to earn enough tips to make up the difference. They were quitting because the place is just nice enough to be popular and just popular enough to not be nice. Keeping things civil is another thing the others struggle with. And all it takes is failing to dodge a thrown mug to make the average person look for someplace a little saner to earn their way. But if I couldn't handle things like that, I would've moved on too. I *like* the way things are. Things could use some work, but someone from the outside without a clue of what the place is like could upset the kettle and make a real mess of things."

"I feel for you. I've been laboring under an unrelenting taskmaster for decades," Vivian said. "It is truly taxing."

"Unrelenting taskmaster? Who, him?" Allie said, pointing to Martin.

"By the High, of course not. I'm speaking of myself. That's a warning for you. One of these days, you'll be in charge of that tavern—more so than you are now—and that's when the *real* work begins."

"I'll take my chances with that," Allie said.

"How has the silverware been holding up for you?" Vivian asked.

"Still the finest thing I own. You really shouldn't have."

"Bah. Fel said you needed it, and it is quite nearly the least we could do. You've been of more help to the Masker family than we could ever dream of asking for," Vivian said.

She shrugged. "I don't have much of a family of my own. I guess I sort of adopted yours a little."

"Oh, that's right. Terrible to lose your mother and father so young." Martin said.

"You know about that?" Allie said.

"You've been the subject of many a mealtime anecdote for years," Vivian said. "Fel talks of you frequently."

"Endlessly," Martin agreed.

She grinned and shook her head. "Gotta love a guy who listens."

She crossed her arms behind her back and gazed at the shelves. For the better part of a minute, she argued with herself about what she should or shouldn't say next. Considering Fel had shared so freely of their conversations, it seemed as though there were relatively few topics that were off-limits. She may as well take the opportunity of his absence to see what else he'd been sharing. Things that he might not want his parents to repeat if he were here to stop them.

"Has he been saying much about *us* recently?"

"No more than usual. Why, something worthy of note?" Vivian asked.

"Evidently not," Allie said simply, setting the rest of the line of questioning aside. She held up the wrapped rolls. "Forgive me if this is a weird request, but could you spare some butter? These are from Divinity's Oven, and I'd like to eat them while they're still warm. I usually keep some butter at The Fox and Log, but suddenly I have *hours* before my shift and I haven't got any back home at the moment."

"Oh, of course. Come on downstairs," Martin said, flipping up the hatch and opening the door.

She followed him down to their dining room, where he provided a plate, a knife, and some butter. She prepared her meal while he sat and flipped through a notebook he'd pulled from his pocket. The first bite was as heavenly as she'd anticipated and nearly made her forget the frustrations of the morning.

"You want one?" she asked.

"I wouldn't dream of depriving you of part of your meal. Fel brings them once a week. I know only too well how delicious they are."

"I'd argue, but frankly I'm greedy enough to take no for an answer on this one." She munched through about half of her breakfast. "So," she asked, slathering up another. "Wick says Fel says things have been pretty quiet. Is that what he's been telling you, or is he sugarcoating it for me?"

"We've heard the same. To be frank, Allie, I'd say he respects you too much to lie to you about anything. To hear him tell it, you see right through the best of his bluffs."

"If his bluffs were harder to see through, he'd probably be winning more games of grum. Nice to know he's not shy about letting his *family* know how he feels about me."

"Mmm," Martin murmured.

Allie had semipurposefully made the comment as a bit of bait to coax him to pry further. Judging from his blissful perusing of his book, he not only wasn't taking the bait, he'd completely missed that it had been offered. Nice to see where Fel had inherited his occasional obliviousness.

"If you don't mind me asking, Mr. Masker. How did you meet Mrs. Masker?" she said.

He flipped the book shut and leaned back in his seat. "Oh, it's a short story. My mother and father were still running the shop at the time. They were a bit more balanced in their share of the work. Mother tinkered a good deal more than Vivian does, and Father spent a fair amount of time at the counter. I was doing roughly what Fel does now, with the addition of a growing portion of the tinkering. But Mom and Dad were getting on in years. My parents had me quite late in life, you see. They needed someone to take some of the load. Since there aren't very many people outside the three big families with contraptioneer experience, the rest of the Masker clan had wandered off to seek fortunes that mostly didn't allow their return, and they couldn't spare my trips to acquire new inventory. That meant they needed to hire someone to work the shop counter. It turned out to be Vivian. She was a voracious learner of the ins and outs of commerce, so she spent a great deal of time at the house, which meant we spent a great deal of time together. First it was just business hours. Then we started to spend our leisure time together. And"—he cleared his throat—"well, we enjoyed one another's company thoroughly."

Allie smirked at the blush spreading across his cheeks and what must have been a very pleasant memory.

"One day she said to me, 'If you're going to ask me to marry you, you'd best do it soon, because it won't be long before there are other offers.' To be perfectly frank, the thought hadn't crossed my mind, and I told her so."

"Oof," Allie said.

"Yes, it was not well received. But in the days that followed, I realized that while I'd not thought of asking for her hand in marriage, I similarly shuddered to think of what life would be like without her. And so I made a trip to Triana's Navel. That's down south, you see, a very well-hidden vault that's a devil to get to. Nearly got my ear ripped off by a thorn-lizard, but I found the perfect ring in the old ruin. I polished it up and presented it to her, and that was that."

"Seems like the Masker boys need to be hit on the head with a board before they open their eyes."

"We're single-minded," Martin said. "It is typically an asset, but it does complicate certain very important parts of a man's life. Once someone has a place in our minds and hearts, they stay there for good, though. Even if sometimes we wish they wouldn't."

"Masker men are puppy dogs, to go along with the ox," Allie said. "I really have to keep that in mind."

Chapter 5

More than a week of additional travel had treated Fel and Tome to a rather novel view of the northern half of Thayne and the southern region of Shalia. The journey had taken them through farms, through valleys, and for one particularly unusual stretch, through an aqueduct that ran through a mountain. After having his paranoia confirmed, Fel refused to take any chances and made use of every shortcut and alternate route that led even roughly toward their goal. They'd gotten deep into Shalia before a worrisome aspect of the contraption they were tracking the mask with asserted itself.

"That needle is moving awfully fast," Tome said, gazing down at the mechanism as Fel steadied it.

"That just means we're close," Fel said. "Let's stop and see if we can figure out where it is."

Tome tugged at the reins and guided the horse and cart toward a stand of evergreens. Fel tugged his jacket a little tighter.

"I've been this far north three of four times, and two of them have been in the past year," he said. "That's enough to tell me I don't like it here. Too cold."

"I prefer the cold," Tome said. "You can always bundle up more. But then, I grew up on the coast. Cold and foggy most days."

Parch sprang from the cart and scampered up a tree that had grown at an awkward angle.

"Yeah. I think Parch likes it too," Fel said. "Makes me wonder why he was hanging around by the wall in basically a desert." He gave the mask detector a shake to upset the needle, then watched closely as it slid back to position. It glided smoothly to the position they'd been heading toward. Then it continued.

"That's disconcerting..." Tome said.

"Mevrelle is wearing the mask. It makes sense it would be moving," Fel said.

"Look at how quickly it's turning. Either he's moving at a fantastic rate, or we should be able to see him."

"He could be invisible. You have had the magic to do it, and I've had the contraptions to do it. Who's to say an elf couldn't do the same?"

A decidedly footstep-like crunch drew their attention to the north, not so far from where the needle was headed. Fel slipped his cudgel from its place on his belt. Tome fetched a pair of ice spells from his coat, and they set their eyes on the source of the sound.

The length of the trip, and its utter lack of combat, had unfortunately pushed a rather important piece of information to the back of Fel's head. Namely, Oiler's distaste for weaponry. He heard the jangle of chain just in time for his cudgel to be snatched up and away by the glimmering claws of his "helper."

"Oiler, I swear to the High, if you get me killed in the name of pacifism..." Fel growled, placing his body between the contraption and the weapon to keep his means of self-defense from being nabbed.

"Fel? Fel Masker?" came a voice from between the trees.

He tipped his head. "Is that Lattica Graves?"

Sure enough, the strongarm of the Graves family stepped out from between the trees ahead. Oiler's gaze shifted to her, but she slipped her crossbow onto her back before the contraption could object.

"Fancy meeting you here," Fel said.

"You're in Shalia. I live here, you live across a border and half a kingdom. If anyone should be surprised about who they're meeting, it's me." She looked to Tome. "Tome, right? So he roped you into another adventure?"

"I have a vested interest in his survival, and a bit of a score to settle with... er..." Tome trailed off, realizing halfway through the sentence that he wasn't certain how much of this information needed to be, or should have been, said.

"Right, right. Always with the secrets," Lattica said. "You know people have been following you, right?"

"I know people were following us as far as Merk. And I know that no one has been following us since," Fel said.

"Whoever was after you noticed you'd given them the slip, and they must be *very* interested in your whereabouts. While they stopped being able to trail you, they didn't stop looking for you. Loads of money floating around on offer for anyone who can keep tabs on you. And any sort of business this close to Ram's Rest eventually makes its way to the Graves family."

Fel's expression hardened. "Don't tell me you took the bounty to hunt us down."

"You're family, Fel. They sent me out looking for you but not to claim the bounty. Your sister rightly guessed if you were headed north, it was after a contraption of some kind, and if regular business leads to the Graves family one way or another, contraption business leads there twice as fast. She sent me out here and sent one of the cousins down to the border crossing."

"How did you know we might be coming through here?"

"Smugglers tend to wander out of the woods around here. Euphoria figured if you had given the people watching you the slip, you weren't using the main roads."

"It feels genuinely strange to be working with someone reasoned, thoughtful, and competent," Tome said.

"You're not working with us yet," Lattica said.

"He could have been talking about me," Fel said.

Both Tome and Lattica gave Fel the same doubtful look.

"What? I'm at least competent. The other two are usually more trouble than they're worth."

"Come with me," Lattica said, turning toward the main road.

"We have a job to do," Fel said.

Tome paced back to the wagon. Fel remained with Lattica.

"I assumed as much. You don't strike me as the type who would travel for the joy of it. Particularly not while people are trying to find your trail. But now that you're here, you need to come with me."

"Time is a factor, and if you're taking me to my sister, you could be leading some really bad stuff to her."

Lattica turned and casually rested her hand on her crossbow. "Fel, who do you think is better equipped to turn away an attack right now? A highly placed member of the Graves family in the heart of her inner sanctum, or two fellows with their pet unicorn a long way from home?"

"It depends on where the threat is coming from," Fel said.

"Are you suggesting you don't trust us?"

"I'm suggesting *you* can't trust you. The last member of the Graves family I dealt with was Thaddeus, and he came to my family acting like he'd seen a ghost. Then decided to make like one himself."

"Yes... Thaddeus hasn't been around lately," Lattica said. "But the family got his warnings. We've doubled our security precautions, something I didn't think was possible, given how tight they already were."

"Even so, you might have a few more rats in the basement."

"Unless you think one of them is your sister, her husband, or me, you need to come with me."

Fel spoke with a bit more of an edge to his tone. "We have an important job to do, Lattica. I know we're in your territory, but this can't wait just because my sister wants to see me. I want to see her too, but this comes first."

"I think we should go with her," Tome called. "We won't be getting any closer to what we're after right now."

"Why not?" Fel asked.

"Come take a look," he said.

"You stay here. You have your secrets; we have ours."

"Fair enough," she said.

Fel hurried over and took a look at the tracking contraption. The needle simply wasn't behaving. The motion was swift and erratic now, rattling audibly, as if the needle were trying to lift off its pivot. This wasn't the behavior of a properly functioning contraption. Fel glanced at Wick's lantern. The flame was flickering. For now, no way to get word back to his father about it.

"It looks like we have time for a visit after all," he said.

"That's fine. That's excellent. Brilliant!" Martin said.

Several days and quite a few sheets of paper had persuaded him to switch to a slate and a bit of chalk to continue Wick's training. After slow initial progress, the lantern had begun improving by leaps and bounds. He held up the slate like a proud parent.

"A perfect alphabet," he said. "A bit large and rather angular, but perfectly legible," Martin said. "I had high hopes, and you exceeded them. Ideally, a smaller and more precise means of writing will follow. You'd scarcely be able to fit more than a sentence per page at this rate. I don't know if enough paper exists in the world to restore the archives like that. But it's enough to test the next part. Wick, I want you to write down the first ten book titles. This will teach us how your capacity to recall such things operates and if you can transcribe something from your memory, rather than simply duplicating shapes that I have presented to you."

"I shall fulfill this request," Wick said.

The mechanical hands plucked up a fresh piece of chalk. Martin wiped away the alphabet from the slate, and for a few moments, Wick was perfectly still.

"A point worthy of mention," Wick said. "A considerable proportion of the books were not written in the alphabet you have taught me. However, they are still composed of lines and curves. I believe I can replicate them."

He traced out the first title. Martin carefully copied the shapes down again on a sheet of paper.

"A language I do not read, but it does look familiar," he said.

There was only room for one title at a time. But the third title was in a language Martin could read.

"*A Brief History of the Exotic Megafauna of...* I'll just wipe this clear so you can finish," Martin said, doing so. "... *the Eastern Flourish*. Curious. I don't know that I've heard the term. Naturally I know the word 'flourish,' but I've never heard it used in that way. I wonder, are you able to recall the contents of that book for me?"

"I can."

"Are there any maps?"

"There are three."

"Do any of them contain familiar features that would indicate where this 'Eastern Flourish' is?"

"The second appears similar to the maps I observed in the Greater Lands. The content of the book appears to indicate that the area on the southeastern quarter of the continent is the region referred to in the title."

"Then this is a history book about the Greater Lands *before the wall*. Fascinating. It's all I can do to keep from insisting you copy out the entire book right now. But for now, let us continue," Martin said.

"I would greatly enjoy doing so, but you asked me to remind you before too much time had passed to check on Fel and Epiphany."

"Right, yes. Of course. Such is the danger of being so useful, Wick. When you are able to perform an endless array of essential and unique tasks, we end up having endless need for you, and just one of you to achieve those things. Before you go, though, I must ask. You are *certain* you can recall *all* the books in this manner?"

"Quite certain," Wick said.

"Tremendous. We are on the cusp of something great, Wick. Something wondrous."

He opened a chest beneath one of the workbenches, revealing some lesser-used reference books. The ones he sought were absent.

"Oh, yes. Of course. Tome borrowed them. He would have a better collection for this purpose as it is."

He hurried upstairs and let himself into Tome's room. It probably should have occurred to him that such would be an invasion of privacy, but as he'd so recently stated, he had a genetic tendency to be rigidly focused in his thinking, often to the detriment of the more social or nuanced aspects of being a part of society. He found the books he was after, some old volumes concerning ancient language. A few minutes later, he'd only managed to translate the first word of the first title. The flame became still once more.

"Fel has reached Shalia and is presently in contact with Lattica Graves, who has persuaded him to accompany her to Euphoria's home. Fel also informs me that the mask-tracking contraption seems to be malfunctioning. I can give his detailed description of the malfunction if you wish."

Martin looked up from the books and checked the rather ornate Bygone Era clock on the edge of his desk.

"It's been seven minutes," Martin said.

"Nearly eight," Wick said.

"Just last week it took a minute and a half for you to reach Fel's lantern, and he was quite a bit nearer then than he is now. That's three minutes just for the round trip, which doesn't leave much time for an update. The travel time should have been longer now. Did Fel speak quickly?"

"He was terse, as he typically is, but he had to pause frequently, as he was attempting to provide the information without sharing it with Lattica, and thus kept quiet and silenced himself when he was concerned she might overhear. I would estimate the exchange required six minutes."

"That leaves less than two minutes for the whole trip. Measurably faster than a trip of half the distance just a short time ago. I'd suggest he'd doubled back, but you say he's headed to Euphoria's home. That's *well* into Shalia."

"This is indeed so."

"You've become faster in just a few days. And the only thing we've been doing that is distinctive during that time was developing your capacity to manipulate the new bust. This is fascinating. Is it possible your abilities are like a muscle, able to be worked and built through hard work and practice?"

"It was not immediately clear to me that I had improved my speed. It was not a conscious effort."

"Fascinating. *Fascinating.* This is a time of revelation! But the matter at hand should be the malfunctioning contraption. Please list its shortcomings, and I shall endeavor to address them."

Fel guided his cart along the main street of Ram's Rest, a short distance behind Lattica on her own horse. He searched his mind for the right word to describe how it made him feel. Right now, he was leaning toward the word "small." Whereas the people farther south tended to build down, the people in Shalia built up. It felt like overcompensation, in his view. Four-, five-, and six-story buildings stuck up out of the ground like saplings. Most were oddly narrow, giving them a precarious look. Each was topped with a steep roof, and most added spires, cupolas, and flags as though there had been some silently proclaimed competition to construct the tallest structure.

The place also had something else about it, something a bit more unusual to Fel's mind. It was unquestionably new, and very well maintained, yet something about it made it clear that the owners wanted it to *feel* old. Like they could co-opt the wisdom and power of antiquity by adding the odd, out-of-place flourish of Bygone architecture.

"That's a Bygone Era cornerstone at the top of the column there," Fel said. "They went to the trouble of taking apart some old Bygone something or other and put it on the wrong part of the building. And that? See that downspout? That's from a church. You can tell by how it's pointed. They have it over the latrine."

"It feels very strange to hear you speaking with authority on... anything," Tome said.

"You keep making jokes about me being dumb. I know what I need to know. I've spent my life looking for old things. The whole family has. And mark my words, Euphoria has been selling these people this stuff. She knows the truth, same as me. She knows legitimate Bygone stuff when she sees it. I know my mom and my sisters. One look at a rich person using a piece of debris as a status symbol, and she'd upend a trash bin and make a fortune off what falls out."

A few very well-dressed people in carriages not so different from Fel's rolled by. They gave him the same look they would have given a mangy dog trudging through town.

"Says something about people who build gangly buildings like these. They stack things up as tall as they can manage so they can look down on as many people as possible."

"I think you're being a trifle unfair."

"You saw how they looked at us."

"And you don't suppose it has something to do with the fact that we look and smell like we've been sleeping in freshly fertilized fields for the last two weeks. Which, I underscore at this point, we *have*."

Fel rumbled something incoherent rather than acknowledging the point. He turned to make sure Oiler wasn't visible. Parch had chosen to perch on the wooden roof of the wagon rather than ride inside, which in retrospect had probably contributed to the odd looks they were receiving.

"I, for one, think it is a lovely place. And given its reality as the home to the second most significant family in contraptioneering, I would think you'd frequently visit the place," said Tome.

"The Graves clan making their home here is exactly why I *don't* come up here. They have this whole area handled. They do their own vault dives and expeditions. Me coming up here would be like a jewel thief showing up unannounced in a rival kingdom's museum. People aren't liable to think it's an innocent visit. So my trips to Shalia never take me into any of the major cities. The closest I came was my first trip when I was a teenager. I spent a day in the catacombs under... Bensvaal or something like that. Farther west near Quarr. Didn't get to do much sightseeing."

A short ride through town brought them to what could only be the Graves household, though "compound" seemed more appropriate. He spotted no fewer than six houses that sported the Graves family crest in some way or another. Even without the crest, Fel probably would have been able to pick them out. They didn't quite fit in with the rest of the town. The buildings were a bit squatter and sprawling. Three stories at their maximum and looking more like a Beffshire mansion than the preposterous, teetering buildings in the rest of the city. They also committed far fewer architectural faux pas. The buildings were still quite proudly being used to proclaim status and wealth, but they achieved it without wedging bits of antiquity into places they didn't belong. Where a chunk of the Bygone Era was represented, it was at least in the proper position.

"Wait here," Lattica called. "I'll announce you."

She hopped off her horse and slipped through the front door. Fel checked that he wouldn't be observed, then turned to where Oiler was pleasantly clicking at its puzzle box.

"Time to pack up," he said. "You're going in with us, and you *need to behave*."

"Is it really wise to bring Oiler into the Graves house? They *were* trying to acquire it not so long ago."

"It's a lot wiser than leaving it out in the wagon," Fel said. "It's staying right next to me."

The door opened. Euphoria appeared in the doorway.

"Fel! Such a rare and unexpected treat to have you as a guest in my home. And with your friend Tome as well. Please, come inside. You must be exhausted from the ride."

Fel looked to his sister and nearly didn't recognize her. When she'd come to Beffshire for her visit, she'd dressed more elegantly than she would have before she left, but at least with the sort of elegance that was a fit for Beffshire. This was the first time he'd seen her dressed in the Shalia style. It was downright disorienting. The clothes were tight in some places and loose in others. Rows of buttons secured the coat like locks on a coward's door. Great billowing shoulders looked like they'd be a hazard if the wind kicked up. Her boots were a match for the architecture, tall in a pointless and precarious way. On the rest of the people in the town, it was easy enough to dismiss. With his sister's face poking out from above the lacy collar and below the mesh-veiled hat, it looked like she was wearing a costume.

"Euphoria, always a pleasure," Tome said.

"What in the world are you wearing, Fora?" Fel said.

She released a single clipped laugh. "There's the charming, silver-tongued devil I grew up with. Quickly, inside before you catch cold. Mr. Mathers will see to the family cart."

Fel grabbed Oiler and strapped him to his back. Tome climbed down and grabbed Wick's lantern and a bag of other items they'd agreed were best kept close at hand. As an overstarched butler climbed into the seat Fel had left behind, Parch hopped down and pranced up the steps.

"I would really rather the unicorn stay outside," Euphoria said.

"Me too, but that's not up to either of us," Fel said. He hurried up the steps just in time to intercept an attempted game of headbutts.

"Our home was not decorated with wild animals in mind," Euphoria said.

"He'll behave," Fel said, giving Parch a playful shove and narrowly avoiding having a hole torn into his shirt from the horn tip in response. "Once he gets this little bit out of his system and gets ahold of something to drink and eat. Right now the choices are open the door for him, or have him punch his own hole through it."

She sighed. "If nothing else, this is a refreshing dose of the chaos I miss from my Beffshire days."

"You can take the boy out of the chaos, but you can't take the chaos out of the boy."

They entered a home that wasn't as stodgy as Fel feared it would be, but was quite close. The entry level was laid out such that every wall was host to some form of shelf or cabinet. Elegantly restored antique contraptions were dust free and gleaming. The soft tinkling melody of a music boxes filled the rooms, each playing the same tune at the same time. Fel snickered. That was a trick Fora had picked up while they were little. It took a special knack, a lot of patience, and a fair bit of trial and error to get the melodies aligned so perfectly.

They entered a dining room that smelled of tallow candles and oiled wood. Fresh fruits, vegetables, preserves, and toasted bread were being set around a table, and a maid with a silver tray stood with a steaming pot of tea, glasses, and honey.

"Did you know we were coming?" Fel said, eyebrow raised at the refreshments.

"Not until you entered town. But I do have a wonderful staff. Not that it wouldn't have been nice to know you were planning this visit so that I could have prepared a better reception. As it is, Jonathan is away on business, so I'm left to entertain by myself."

"We didn't know exactly where we were going," Fel said.

He dropped Oiler to the floor, rattling the cutlery on the table, and slid it a little farther underneath. Then he took a seat and loaded a bit of crusty bread with some jam.

"You're awfully far from home to be uncertain of your destination," Euphoria said, nodding when offered a cup of tea.

"Yeah, well. That's contraptioneering, isn't it?" Fel cast a less than subtle glance at the staff around them. "People in the know understand how things work."

"A bowl of water and..." Euphoria paused. "Forgive me, what does the unicorn eat?"

"Mostly things we wish he wouldn't. Back home we give him the tops off veggies and hay from the stables. He ate not so long ago. Just the water will be fine," Fel said.

"Just the bowl of water," Euphoria repeated. "And then some privacy. Family business."

The staff did as they were told. Once Parch was happily draining a bowl, doors shut and the group was left alone in the dining room.

"That *is* what you were indicating, I assume?" Euphoria said.

"Yep," Fel said, holding a hand out to Tome.

He paused in preparing his own tea to produce the mask-tracking contraption. He set it on the center of the table beside the veggies.

"That looks not unlike a flame detector," Euphoria said.

"Close," Fel said. "Dad learned from fixing yours. This is for tracking the masks."

Euphoria leaned forward with interest. "Really. And it works?"

"Not right now it doesn't." He gestured to the flickering flame of Wick's lantern. "Dad's working on figuring out why it's just spinning and rattling. But it got us this far. I don't suppose you happen to have the Student mask up on a shelf somewhere."

"We do not. I was under the impression *you* had it."

"We did, but it got away. Hence the device for tracking it."

"I see." She sipped her tea and buttered some toast. "It pleases me you are willing to share so much with me. I was more than a little concerned your opinion of me and my in-laws may have soured again in light of recent events."

"Why? Were you the one who sicced Cartwright on us?"

"No. Of course not. But given the claims made by Thaddeus, it wouldn't have been an unreasonable theory."

Fel shrugged. "If the Graves clan could get their claws into the Thayne nobility, there are probably better ways to profit than causing mischief in Masker's Antiquities."

"The depth and placement of our claws has been rather haphazard of late. We can't even seem to agree among ourselves where they are placed and why."

"Trouble in paradise?" Fel said.

"As you say, family business. Not our family, alas. Only mine. The size of the Graves family makes unity of purpose and opinion much harder to manage than in the Masker family."

"Oh, like we ever agreed on anything."

"I'm not in a position to contradict you on that, seeing as how we didn't speak for several years. But the Graves family makes us look like amateurs. I won't air our dirty laundry, but there is a great deal of it."

"How is Thaddeus doing, by the way? He seemed spooked the last time we spoke to him."

"He hasn't returned yet."

"It's been over a month. It only took us about two weeks to get here."

"I'm not convinced *here* is where he wants to be or where he was headed. Again, not really something that I can discuss in detail. We received messages from him. I do not believe he is dead. But I doubt he'll be back anytime soon. I'd really much rather focus on your dilemma. Tell me everything you can."

"There isn't much to tell. You know about the Cartwright thing. He was after something in the shop and went as far as getting a writ from the lord himself to investigate. We managed to avoid getting caught with the hot potato, but an elf Tome 'made friends with' when he was in the Greater Lands, who has a huge vendetta against the Maskers, showed up with the Warrior mask. His brain was half-rotten, but he managed to steal a load of our stuff. We got it all back except for the Student mask and something Dad cooked up for it. We used that thing to track the mask up here."

Euphoria blinked slowly. "And you say there wasn't much to tell?"

"I have a kobold as a roommate now, and the woman I was pining after caught me with my shirt off with one of my friends and was excited at the prospect of us being together."

"This would be Allie, then? The one you were caught with?"

"Yes," he said flatly.

"And have you been smart enough to embrace the opportunity to start something meaningful with Allie, whom you, in the brief opportunities I had to observe you together, showed *far* more of a connection with?"

He clenched his teeth. "This isn't why we're here."

She laughed. "You haven't changed since you were twelve."

"Yeah, well you've changed too much since you were twelve. And if you ask me, the lessons you learn stop being fun after around sixteen or so anyway, so I really haven't missed much."

"That is an astonishingly valid observation," Euphoria said. "We really ought to return to the more pressing subjects, though. As it was Lattica who brought you in, I imagine you arrived through whatever passage the smugglers tend to use."

"You imagine correctly," Fel said. "What with the people tracking us before we got past Merk. Any idea who they were?"

"I'm afraid not. But I will warn you; you should be prepared to use the same avenue for your departure, when the time comes."

"Why? You thinking people will still be tracking us by the time we're heading home?"

"No. But having come here without an authorized border crossing, it will further complicate the already *very* complicated task of leaving Shalia through official means."

"Why?"

"Because of the quarantine."

"That's still happening?" Fel said. "I thought that all blew over almost a year ago. You barely said two words about it when you visited."

"The hysteria died down once we became somewhat more familiar with how the disease was spreading and how to control it."

"I wasn't aware one of the many risks we were taking when we came here was the risk of infection," Tome said. "Tell me more about this disease."

"Around here they call it 'the Haze.' The afflicted have gradually diminishing mental capacity, beginning as moderately reduced capacity to focus, escalating to near constant distraction, and eventually leading to the afflicted simply wandering off. Some would be found dead by the roadside. Others never showed up again, and those who searched for them generally found themselves afflicted by the Haze as well."

"Is there any treatment?"

"Isolation, in-home quarantine. Sometimes that was enough to keep the symptoms from worsening and, in time, for recovery. Unfortunately it seems to be an aspect of the affliction that people do not respond well to being contained. Attempted escapes are common, and paradoxically those with the least severe symptoms are the ones most capable of escaping isolation and worsening their condition."

"But this is under control now, yes?" Tome said.

"It is. The origin seems to be Fenfield, an old piece of noble hunting land about thirty miles to the west. The forest has been quarantined in its entirety, and the major roads that ran nearest to it have been rerouted."

Tome furrowed his brow. "That's it? You closed a few roads, and you call that under control?"

"There hasn't been a disappearance in... oh, it must be six weeks. And that was the first in months."

"But you don't know the cause? Don't know how it spreads?"

"As I said, the cause seems to be something in Fenfield, and it spreads to people who venture too close. Close off the forest, problem solved."

"That's not a problem solved. It's barely a problem *identified*," Tome said.

"I'm sure more academic investigations have been done, Tome. I know only as much as I need to be safe. Most of us have deemed it adequate."

Before more could be said on the subject, a soft chime rang out and Oiler held up the completed puzzle box. Fel scrambled it.

"The Oiler. It will be a matter of no small frustration to Jonathan that the contraption entered our home without being added to our collection." She raised her eyebrows. "Unless..."

"Not for sale," Fel said.

"A terrible decision, that," remarked a gruff voice from behind the door.

Fel snapped his head toward the source of the voice in time for the door to open, revealing a gray-haired, squat gentleman with a mustache that threaded the needle between facial hair and filigree.

"Anything short of a member of the family should be at least considered on the bargaining table. And even in those cases, there is the subject of the dowry."

The man seemed to have more to say, but he set his eyes upon something roughly at Fel's belt and went silent. It wasn't until Fel followed his gaze did he realize that he'd reflexively placed his hand on the grip of his cudgel.

"Sorry. Force of habit when someone surprises me after spying on me," Fel said, standing up.

He offered his hand. The older man stood rigidly and kept his eyes fixed on the cudgel.

"Rather a coarse accusation, that. Spying. In my own home," he said.

"You were spying, Nevil. And it isn't your home; it is mine," Euphoria said.

From the carefully calibrated edge to her tone, this was hardly an uncommon exchange between the two of them.

Nevil rolled his eyes. "Jonathan's, more accurately. But it is a Graves home, and *I* am a Graves and thus afforded certain liberties."

"I am a Graves too, Nevil. And I've asked you to at least have the staff announce you before barging in."

He placed his hand on his chest and gave a deferent nod. "A thousand pardons. But now that the damage has been done, perhaps you could introduce me to our visitors?" He sniffed. "I see they are freshly arrived and have not yet taken advantage of our guest quarters and their facilities." He added, under his breath, "Something I would have preferred they do *before* they sat on the good chairs."

"You're a real charmer, Nevil," Fel said.

"Again, I apologize. My wife is normally the one who entertains guests," Nevil said. "My graces have atrophied somewhat."

"I think you should run along, Nevil," Euphoria said.

"Private discussions, mmm? Keeping things from the family, mmm?"

"I am having a discussion with my brother and his friend. I don't think it is unreasonable to ask that we be left alone."

Again he raised his hands in insincere apology. "Of course. Of course. I'll just run along." He turned to Fel. "I do wish you would reconsider the topic of the Oiler and its price."

Fel glared at him without a reply. He glanced at Parch, who had just finished drinking. "How about a game of headbutts with our new friend, buddy?" Fel said.

Parch excitedly pranced twice, bounding nearly to shoulder height, then reared back to initiate the game with the unsuspecting Nevil. The older man wisely retreated, leaving Fel to take over. When the door had been shut and his footsteps had faded, Fel coaxed Parch into finishing the game.

"You really picked a winner of a family."

"It wasn't always this way," Euphoria paused. "I suppose it *was* always *roughly* this way. But it wasn't always this *bad*." She stood and wiped her hands. "I'm afraid I have some business to attend to. I do hope you'll stay through dinner so that we can have a less hurried conversation."

"I guess it'd make sense to wait at least until Dad gets back to us about how to fix the mask detector." He grinned. "Plus, that seems like it would really irritate Nevil."

"It will completely infuriate him," she said. "Which is a terrible reason to do it and, at the moment, my *favorite* reason to do it."

"It's my second favorite, personally. Good to see you more than once every three years."

She crossed her arms. "You are unbearably sweet sometimes, Fel. And the feeling is mutual."

Allie trudged home in the middle of the day. This was, absolutely, her least favorite time to be heading home. The streets were crowded during midday, which she didn't much enjoy. But that wasn't the reason for trudging. Leaving at midday meant she was missing the meatiest bit of work for the day. She'd only worked for two hours, setting up for the day and serving the first few hard-drinking regulars. The kind of person who shows up before noon tends not to tip terribly well. Allie hadn't realized how important it was for her state of mind to be working. But she *had* realized how important it was for her pockets.

She was running low on money. There wasn't much money to be made as a barmaid. She made ends meet by working every moment she could manage, which involved trading time and tasks from Oovay, who still lived with his parents and sister and worked mostly as a way to get out of the house. Extra work had been impossible since Velonia had taken over. Worse, her schedule had been "balanced," which seemed like an awfully gentle word for what was clearly a punishment. She was permitted to work every day, but some days were like these, earning a handful of duots and being sent home. At this rate, she'd have to learn to be a good deal more economical just to be certain she could keep fed and out of the elements.

The entirety of the walk home had been spent attempting to gin up some way to trim her costs enough to weather however long it would take to convince Velonia it was better just to let things go back to the way they were. The moment she stepped up to her door, she was jostled from that state of mind by something that should have been innocuous. It was a single sheet of off-white paper tacked to her door. Her upper lip twitched as she tugged it free and flipped it open.

Attention resident. Your home is under new ownership. Tomorrow morning, be prepared to meet with the new owner to discuss a moderate increase in the cost of lodging.

She shuddered. The tenuous calculations she'd been running in her head tumbled away. Any increase in her costs would almost certainly make life as she knew it impossible. The hand responsible for hammering in this final nail in the coffin needn't have signed a signature. She knew precisely who it was. But almost as insult to injury, the name was drawn out with a downright artistic flourish. *Velonia Madritz.*

Allie shoved the door open and slammed down her things. The lantern currently bearing Wick's flame had been left in her home, burning at the merest smolder. She'd known she would only be gone for a few hours and this saved her the trouble of bothering the Maskers for another midday refresh. She turned the knob and the flame rose up. Within moments, it became still again, as if Wick had been waiting for the opportunity to check in on her.

"Ms. Waverly, I hope you have had a lovely—"

"Sorry to interrupt, and sorry if I raise my voice, but if I don't growl this at you, then I'm going to carve it into the back of Velonia Madritz. And as it stands right now, getting locked up still sounds *slightly* less pleasant than the mess my life is turning into."

"I will happily serve as a release for your frustrations. Shall I pass these frustrations along to Fel?"

"Of course! You think I want to sit here alone being angry about my lot in life? I'm a barmaid. I've absorbed so many sob stories that it's well past time someone soaked up some of mine!"

Chapter 6

As evening slid into night, Fel leaned back in a lounge chair and sipped a refreshing beverage. He and Tome had retired to the den after each had taken the opportunity to wash off a few days of accumulated road grime. Tome had predictably selected a thick leather-bound volume from the bookcase on the north wall and sat near the crackling fire to read it. Parch had sprawled out in front of the fire, pleasantly asleep like some sort of pampered family dog. Oiler had searched in vain for something in the room that wasn't in absolutely perfect repair and now was back to fiddling with its puzzle box. Fel had simply taken the opportunity to let his wandering mind find fresh ground to plant seeds of concern. That and sample the various drinks the Graves household had to offer.

"Oh, that's a good beer," he murmured.

"Another, sir?" remarked a butler he hadn't realized was lingering behind the chair.

Fel flinched at the unexpected bit of hospitality and nearly dropped his tankard. "No, thanks. And here, take these." Fel dug into his pocket and produced a handful of duots.

"That is unnecessary, sir. You are a guest."

"Take them! At least with something jingling in your pockets, it'll be harder for you to sneak up on me. Having you appear and disappear like that is starting to make me feel like I'm being haunted by the most generous ghost who ever lived. Or... died, I suppose."

"I shall endeavor to be more audible in the fulfillment of my duties," the butler said.

He marched away. Fel watched him go, as if he didn't keep an eye on him, the man would crawl under a table in order to ambush him with a handkerchief the next time he rubbed his nose.

"I'm worried about Fora," Fel said, when he was reasonably sure he was alone with Tome again.

Tome set down his book and raised an eyebrow. "You are worried about *Fora?*"

"Yeah. This is no way to live."

"Fel, you live in a single room, several levels belowground, in what is technically a place of business. She has a sprawling mansion and a complete staff."

"Sure, but the butler is definitely a phantom or something. And this is a *mess* of a family to be a part of."

"Is it worth pointing out that *your* family has been routinely sending you out on what amounts to military missions, to say nothing of years of expeditions to trap-laden and danger-filled vaults and hidden chambers?"

"Expeditions are my bread and butter. You don't score any points by pointing those out. And the military stuff is just because we got mixed up with a bunch of evil, greedy monsters. And why did that all start, I ask you?"

"Because Epiphany wanted to expand your business beyond the borders traced out by local law?"

"Because the Graves family *tricked* her into doing that. Fanny had a couple of brushes with the Graves clan, and she ended up snarling the whole family up in squabbles and schemes. Just think of how snarled up Fora's life must be if she's been living with these people for years."

"She *is* one of these people, Fel," Tome said.

"Like muck she is," he said. "And then there's this thing with Allie. Figures the minute I'm gone someone would come along and start making trouble for her. She sounded *mad.*"

"You didn't hear her say anything. It was all relayed through Wick."

"I don't know if you noticed, but Wick doesn't usually use words that colorful. That was just a faithful retelling of Allie's griping."

"Even so. It isn't as though your presence in the city would change matters."

"She could gripe in person. And, I don't know. Maybe I could lean on this Velonia person."

The door opened. Fel's head snapped in that direction just in case it was the butler trying to get the drop on him with some sort of appetizer. It was Euphoria.

"Dinner is served. This way. It will be a private meal, just the three of us."

"If you're planning on shutting doors, we should make sure these two are with us, unless you want to see the little game Oiler and Parch like to play where one busts holes through doors and the other patches them up."

Fel hoisted the chain-filled pack to his back. Its jangling stirred Parch, who trotted quickly to his side. They paced through the halls of the house toward the dining room.

"I must admit that you having somehow managed to house-train a unicorn, at least with regard to not leaving it smelling like a barnyard, is one of your more unexpected achievements," Euphoria said.

"He gets all the credit. I don't really train him. He just figures things out. It's more like 'training' a cat than training a dog."

"I wouldn't know the difference. I was never the one trying to sneak animals into our home. I hope I didn't interrupt any deep conversation."

"Your brother was just musing over how he wishes he was home in Beffshire so he could try to intimidate a businesswoman who is making his friend's life miserable."

"Surely Mother could have a word with the individual responsible. She knew practically every owner and operator in town when I left. And Beffshire being the way it is, I can't imagine very many new ones have shown up."

They took a seat at the dinner table, where a simple but sumptuous spread had been prepared: potatoes and at least three different colors of carrots, roasted and glistening with salt and oil, a roast elk loin carved and displayed like a centerpiece, and a freshly decanted bottle of wine. As Fel took a seat, he had to admit that maybe things weren't *so* bad for Fora in this place.

"I used to think the rules that made it so hard to buy a place in Beffshire were silly, but if it has kept someone like this Madritz lady out for all this time, it has been worth it."

"Madritz? Would this be Velonia Madritz?" Allie said, pouring herself a glass of wine.

Fel gave her a hard look. "You know her?"

"I know the name. Velonia Madritz is a bit of a curiosity. Something like the merchant version of a mercenary. People hire her to do business for them. She's worked with half of the families and nobles in Quarr. A fair amount of people here in Shalia too. Word has it she's even worked with the Bolivans."

"She's worked for the Bolivans?" Fel rumbled.

"Worked *with* the Bolivans."

"What's the difference?" he asked.

"It's subtle, but it's the difference between collaboration and servitude. This is entirely hearsay, but there are rumors that she helped them to purchase some land near the border a few years ago. Legitimate purchases rather than the sort of 'business' the Bolivans usually do. That's her specialty. Using influence and savvy to achieve with legitimacy what criminality struggles to do otherwise. And you say she's working in Beffshire now?"

"Seems like it."

"Then she has the backing of at least two people within Beffshire and one or more Thayne nobles. And quite likely doing all her business entirely aboveboard. That's a recipe for someone who can do whatever she chooses with impunity, provided she has the money."

"And she's using all that power and influence to make my friend's life miserable."

"I'd wager your friend's misery is a side effect, wanted or unwanted, of a more profitable venture. Madritz's services do not come cheap. But you have more pressing and personal concerns, correct? If you've heard this, then I presume you've heard back from Father about the operation of the detector?"

"Yeah. Not good news. He says he can't figure out what's wrong. A problem like that should only happen if some other contraption is interfering. Could be something in your collection. Could be something made specifically to foul this sort of thing up. Either way, it would probably only happen within a few miles of the mask or the device causing it. But he can't fix it without experimenting, and I'm not sharp enough to do that. Neither are your tools, by the way."

She swirled her wine. "I'd truly like to acquire some of those Bygone tools from you."

"That's up to Dad, not me. You're welcome to ask him through Wick next time the flame goes still. But without the detector working, we'll have to do some old-fashioned searching if we're going to find who we're after. Though, it doesn't take much guesswork to figure that out."

"Oh no?"

"We're looking for someone who doesn't want to be found, and there's a big area just that way where no one is allowed to go," he said, pointing. "If I was trying to hide, that's where I'd go."

"Fel, you aren't actually considering entering Fenfield, are you?" Euphoria said.

"Just long enough to find the mask and make sure the elf who has it doesn't cause any more trouble."

"This plan was not discussed with me," Tome said.

"That's because you'd have said no."

"Correct, because I have no interest in catching a disease that will rob me of my sense and sanity. Though now that I say it out loud, I think I understand why you're not as concerned as I am."

"Funny," Fel said dryly.

"The forest is quarantined for a *reason*," she said. "This isn't some rumor or superstition. People who go deep enough into that field don't come back."

"The same is true of the Greater Lands, and Tome and I both made it in and out."

"This isn't a matter of cunning or toughness. It is a *disease*. No amount of toughness or cleverness will keep you safe."

"So we'll figure out how the disease spreads and avoid it. I've been finding places protected by lethal traps since I was a kid, and there's always a way around them. This is just another one of those."

"The only reliable way that has been found to avoid *catching* the disease is to *avoid the disease*."

"So we'll find a cure, then. Tome is a healer; he can figure it out."

"I appreciate the confidence, but I don't think I'll be able to work out a solution when the best minds of the region couldn't."

"But you know how diseases catch and spread, right? We'll keep safe, that's all."

"There are different ways. Sometimes you get a disease from other people with a disease. Sometimes you just *get* them. There could be something in that field. Some bad air. Maybe an enchantment."

"We came this far; we're going to solve this problem. You think it's lost on me that the same murderer who tried to take me out, tried to take Tome out, and terrorized my family in Beffshire ended up a stone's throw from my sister? This is a lunatic who kills whoever he likes, and he keeps on finding his way to my family and friends. It's personal. And it's going to end before he figures out how to get to us. If either of you has a way to help give us the edge on how to get in and out without catching this disease, I'll drink potions or burn incense or do what needs to be done. But I'm going in there and finding the person responsible or ruling the place out as a hiding place. That decision has already been made."

He piled his plate with meat and vegetables and ate heartily. Euphoria drummed her fingers on the table.

"I'll have a word with my cousin-in-law Terrance. He works with the local clinics and should be able to give you some insight into the handful of people who contracted the disease but recovered after isolation. If there is information on how to survive it or avoid it, you'll find it there," she said.

"That's it? You're just accepting that he's going to do this foolish thing?" Tome said.

"I've heard that tone of voice all my life. Past this point we may as well be arguing with a plank of wood."

Fel grinned and shoveled some food into his mouth. "See, this is where you two took a wrong turn when it came to negotiation. It's not about compromise and all that. You just have to be stubborn. Do it often enough and people just give you what you want because it's quicker than arguing."

"Or start avoiding you altogether," Tome said.

"That works for me too," Fel said.

"I'll get into contact after dinner. You can discuss things with him or his staff before bedtime. Let's at least enjoy a nice meal before then," Euphoria said.

Allie had spent the day smoldering with anger. She felt certain the pinning of the announcement to her door during the two hours she was away, then leaving her with a whole day to think about it, was by design. This felt not just punitive but manipulative. This thing stank of someone trying to coax her into doing something she either didn't want to do or shouldn't do. On the undesirable list was trying to find a new place to live. Given how Velonia had been treating her at work, there was very little doubt that her meeting the following morning would be about, at best, how there was no chance of negotiating the raise in the cost for her home. Everything happening felt like it was designed to force her out of the life she'd carved for herself. The easiest way out was a new job and a new place to live.

She had never been accused of choosing the easy path, and she wasn't going to start now. Case in point, her current destination.

Allie strode up the path toward the front door of the Verfessa house. The weary guards on either side glanced at her. She prepared for an argument, but before she could launch her first salvo, the guard on the left spoke.

"Here to see the boss?"

"I... yes," she said.

He opened the gate. "He's been expecting you."

"Oh." She steeled herself. "Good."

Coming here, expecting a fight, and getting none felt like climbing a staircase and expecting another stair. She was immediately thrown off-balance, but she rallied as best she could and marched inside. Donovan Verfessa was in the entry hall of his home when she stepped through the open door. He wasn't there specifically to meet her. Oddly enough, he seemed to be replacing some slats on the handrail leading down to the lower level. His sleeves were rolled to the shoulder, tools spread around him. Long curls of wood shavings fell to the floor as he shaved the end of one of the slats. The man looked at home doing the work, like it was what he was meant to be doing, and all the shadowy dealings he involved himself with were an unfortunate distraction.

"Is that Allie?" he called over his shoulder without looking.

"It is," she said.

"I thought you'd be through here three days ago," he said. "Sorry if I keep working. I don't get the chance to do my own repairs very often, and I'm keen to get them done. You're here about The Fox and Log, right?"

"I'm here about a lot of things, but we'll start with The Fox and Log," she said. "I guess you know about who bought it and what they've been doing?"

"I'd be a pretty lousy investor if I didn't know a place I bought into was sold. As for what she's doing, mostly tinkering with things that don't need tinkering with, new bosses will do that." He glanced over his shoulder again. "Like an investor knocking down a couple of walls and building the whole thing out."

"At least that was an improvement. I can't keep myself fed the way she's working me."

"That's the risk you take when doing extra work is necessary to cover your nut."

"It worked fine for years. And the place is starting to suffer for it, I'm telling you."

"I've been looking at the numbers. Sagging a bit, but not much different."

"That's because everyone is assuming things will be back to normal before much longer. I can tell you right now, they aren't."

"You can read this Madritz lady's mind?" he said. "Know what she's planning?"

"She bought the building where I make my home."

"That went through, did it?"

"Yes."

"She hiking the price?"

"I'll find out how much tomorrow, but I can't imagine it'll be something I can afford."

"You're probably right. People don't buy a place to make the same amount as the last fellow did."

"If this keeps up, I'll be gone. Have to find a new place, a new job. I'll have to start over."

"My heart bleeds for you. I mean it. It's rough."

"And what do you think will happen to The Fox and Log without me? I make that place *tick*, Mr. Verfessa."

He stood and grabbed a rag to wipe sweat from his brow. "The way you run that place is more or less what separates it from places that ought to be doing better than The Fox and Log but ain't. No doubt about it."

"So are you just going to sit back and let this woman ruin the business you invested in?"

He started to fit one of the slats in place. "It's complicated, Allie."

"It's certainly complicating *my* life."

"The rules of Beffshire say it takes two local owners, a member of the land commission, and a signed writ from a noble to get permission to buy someplace within the city walls. Sid was one owner. The other one? Haven't found out yet, which in and of itself is a pretty good trick. I'll work it out soon enough. The land commission has a couple of folks with expensive habits as members. They'll sign whatever you hand them if you slide enough duots along with it. But the nobles—let me tell you, Allie. Those nobles. It's not that they aren't corrupt. Believe me, they're as crooked as a drunkard's hat. But they are *cautious*. And they are *expensive*. Been working on them for years. The main thing that keeps me working mostly out of Beffshire is that I have a good solid footing here that most folk just can't make a dent in thanks to how sturdy Beffshire is, but not having a noble in my pocket is a close second. And Madritz, who as far as I can tell has never set foot in town, got the sway inside this city and outside, such that she could close two purchases in two weeks. That's someone to watch."

"Are you afraid of her?"

"Of course I am," he said.

"*The* Donovan Verfessa is afraid of some merchant from up north?"

"Look, I'm not one of those dopes who isn't afraid of anyone. You know what happens when you're not afraid of anyone? While you're busy not being afraid, someone you should have been afraid of kills you."

"Madritz is that kind of threat?"

He picked up a chisel. "Madritz has money, and she has influence. More influence than I have. Probably more money too. And here are some things you need to know. When you have money, people want it. When you have influence, people want to tug that chain back to its source. It means you're in for violence. And unless you're *stupid*, the first thing you'll do is use a piece of that money and that influence to handle that violence for you."

He dug the chisel unto the slat and sheared off a slice that should have taken a handful of hammer blows. "You can bootstrap it a bit if you're willing to hold the blade yourself for a while. But only a fool holds it forever."

"So you think she has a henchman?"

"Or henchwoman. I knew one fella who had a lesser nymph. That was a"—he gazed off into space—"that was a thing. The point is she'd be a fool if she didn't have *at least* one, and she isn't a fool."

"And that's enough for you to be sure?"

"It *would* be enough for me to be sure, but it isn't all I have. See, she might have friends in the nobles' offices, but I have *ears* in there. And a lot of other places. And they warned me that a lot of money was flying in a lot of directions. That's always happening. But some of the directions? They were familiar. There was muscle headed this way. Major muscle. Matter of fact, word has it they were looking to hire someone with some familiarity with some of the muscle inside the Beffshire walls. No word on the specifics. But I knew I needed all my hands on deck, ready for what was coming. And then who shows up on my doorstep? Velonia Madritz. Don't get me wrong. I believe in coincidences. But this ain't that. She's got a dog on a chain. Mark my words. Probably a few. And what worries me most isn't that she's got them. It's that she's been smart enough not to show them off. Means the people she has on contract can be trusted. And it means she's not about posturing and bravado. She's not dumb enough to make the mistakes that create the openings to slide a knife in. So we watch and we wait."

"But you're doing *business* with her. You're invested in a business she bought. Wouldn't it be smart to keep your distance?"

"Sometimes there's more than one smart thing. Locking down, digging in? That'd keep me safer, sure. But it'd tip her off. Maybe enough to spring the trap right then. But if we hold tight, play the game, maybe one of those openings shows up, and in goes the knife. And if not? There are worse things than working with someone with a route to the top."

Allie tightened her fists. "You're looking to pull that chain back to the nobles. You're after the same thing all those other people were after."

"There's a reason they're after it, Allie."

"Mr. Verfessa, tell me the truth. If it comes down to it, which do you want more? If it comes down to it, if it's turning her away and putting it back the way it was or using her as a stepladder to climb a little closer to the top, what choice are you making?"

"Funny thing. You don't get to make that sort of decision ahead of time. That decision happens a moment before it can't."

"Don't try to squirm out of it," she snapped.

His look hardened. Except, it didn't. If Allie had a full week of watching that moment over and over, she wouldn't have been able to find the hair that moved or muscle that twitched. But it did the job of a slap across the face without something so uncouth or unkind as him raising his hand in anger. It flashed the spirit it took to get what he had and hold on to it for as long as he had.

"You want to pin me down with a promise?" he said, cocking a grin.

"Not if you don't want to, sir," she said quickly.

"I'll do you one better and give you two. Donovan Verfessa comes out on top. And Donavan Verfessa takes care of his own. That good enough for you?"

"Uh... Depends on if you consider me one of yours. And to be frank—"

He laughed. "Not so keen on that?"

"Seems like it might have its own costs."

"Everything with an upside worth having has a downside to scare off the people who aren't bold enough to claim it. You came here. You understand risk and reward. We'll put it this way. We're both liable to have some bad itches before this is through. Now I've got plenty of folks to scratch my back. You got anyone to scratch yours?"

"... Point taken."

"Good."

He grabbed the plane again and started shaving down the opposite end.

"So... what? That's it? No orders?"

He scoffed. "You don't need orders. All you need to do is keep your eyes and ears open. And remember that this seems to be about you, not me. At least for now. They came for your job and your home. So when they come for the next thing, don't go keeping secrets about things that're liable to be a thorn in my side, and you're welcome to borrow my back scratcher. Satisfied?"

"Not entirely, but I get the feeling this is as good as I'm going to get."

He laughed again. "Trust the feeling."

Fel and Tome paced the streets of Ram's Rest, glancing back and forth between the page they had been given at the clinic and the street signs.

"This place is supposed to be civilized, right?" Fel griped. "So why don't the houses have numbers? Why do I have to read the names on every door to see where I'm heading?"

"It's a wealthy town. Probably this is some byproduct of the need for notoriety," Tome said.

"Notoriety is a stupid thing to want. The more people who know who I am, the more problems I have."

"I seem to remember you had an ambition to be important and respected," Tome said.

"Sure. I want to be important and respected, but also left alone."

"A difficult balance to strike."

"If it was easy, I'd have done it already." He squinted. "There! That's the place. Let's get this over with."

They marched up to one of the more meager homes in the area. It was a mere three stories and achieved that height primarily by being both narrow and shallow, in effect a six-room house stacked vertically rather than spread on a single floor. The door proclaimed the residents to be Mr. West and the man they were after, Mr. Arrison. Fel knocked on the door. After an insultingly brief wait, he hammered on it again. Finally the resident opened.

"Can I help you?" remarked an elderly and rather rotund man through the crack in the door.

"Would you be Mr. Arrison?" Tome said.

"I am," he said, still wary.

"We were sent by Mr. Graves at the clinic," Fel said. "You had a bout of the Haze, yes?"

"I did."

"We need to talk to you about it," Tome said.

"Why?"

"Because I've got a pretty good idea that someone I'm looking for is hiding in the quarantine area, and I need to know how to keep from getting sick," Fel said quickly.

"The only way to keep from getting sick is to stay out of the quarantine area. That's what a quarantine is, Mr...."

"Masker. Fel Masker," Fel said.

"The brother of Euphoria Graves?" he said.

"If that'll get me through the door, yes," Fel said.

Arrison opened the door and allowed Fel and Tome inside. The trio trudged up to the top floor and took seats in a modest room with just enough places to sit.

"I don't know what I can tell you that the clinic can't."

"The clinic wanted to cure you. I just want to know how you got sick and how you knew you were getting sick," Fel said.

Tome added, "So tell us what you were doing when you first felt sick and how it felt."

"I was in Fenfield. This was a few months before we found out it was where the illness came from. I was hunting lesser perytons. They'd been showing up in droves for the last few weeks after barely any having been seen in the area. After a really terrible day of hunting, I managed to bag one and tried to head home, but something was off. I kept heading in the other direction."

"You were lost?"

"No. It wasn't as simple was that. I knew which way I had to go, but every time I turned that way, something inside me told me to turn back. It was that feeling you get when you're on a steep hill that keeps getting steeper. You know if you go much farther, it'll be too steep and you'll start to slide. So you keep heading along the slope rather than up or down. Or when you're headed somewhere in a crowd and you see the crowd ahead start to bunch up, so you slow down. Something deep in my mind told me I needed to stop heading back home. It felt better, more correct, to go the other way, away from the road."

"Interesting... And yet you returned safely," Tome said.

"I still can't explain it. I was edging along, trying to keep the feeling at bay, when suddenly my head was clear again. I pointed my horse in the direction I knew to be the nearest edge of the field and spurred it to speed. It didn't take long for the feeling to wash over me again, but the horse was moving quite fast, and I was able to keep myself from tugging the reins. I got clear of the field, and the feeling started to fade, but for weeks it lingered like a cloud over me. If I didn't stay focused, sharply focused, I'd start pacing. Wandering. Not until a month had passed, most of that time locked in the clinic and being watched, that I stopped feeling the vague sense of being out of place. It was terrible. They tell me if I hadn't come directly to the clinic, I might have been lost, as so many others were."

"Where were you when you started to feel the feeling fade, after initially escaping the Fenfield?" Tome asked.

"It's a hazy memory. Literally, I suppose. I ended up in Ossaw though. Does that help you?"

"It's a familiar story," Tome said.

"Because the last three people said basically the same thing. Thanks, sir," Fel said, standing and shaking his hand.

They trudged back down the stairs and out into the street.

"Are we done?" Fel asked.

"We should discuss what we've learned."

"We haven't learned *anything* since the first person."

"I mean overall." Tome flipped through the pages. "Everyone had gone to Fenfield. Two were hunters seeking Lesser Mystics, which had been growing in numbers. That's strong evidence."

"Of what?"

"That something was up in the field."

"If a field started making hunters distracted and thus made them *bad hunters*, I think you'd get a lot more critters there."

"I'm hesitant to suggest this was a coincidence. But this certainly isn't. All the people we interviewed were able to escape the field when the feeling suddenly dropped away. He said Ossaw is where he ended up."

He pulled a folded map from his pocket. "That's on the west side of the field. The only one on the west side. The others ended up farther south. Other than that, there wasn't much in common between them. Some drank water, others didn't. One of them ate while they were there, the others didn't. Two were during the day, one was at night. One of them was there during the rain..."

"So what plan have we devised out of this? If we start to feel bad, wander around until we don't anymore, then head south or maybe west?"

"I think the plan is 'don't go to the field.' We don't know enough, and we're fresh out of people to talk to about this."

Distant, tiny hoofbeats drew Fel's attention to the south side of the street. Parch was approaching and drawing rather curious looks from the locals.

"Parch got out. Which means either he found an open window, or the most expensive house I've ever been invited to has a hole in it now. So I think I'll be arranging to be headed for that field. Because it's *got* to be less dangerous than my sister's house once she gets a hold of me."

"Fel, I know you're impulsive, but you can't honestly believe that this is the best way forward. You can't honestly believe that charging forward now, with what little we know, into a place teeming with a disease no one fully understands, is a good idea."

"I know it's not a good idea, but you know what it is? It's the fastest idea," he barked. "I want to go *home*, Tome. I want the part of my life where for some reason I'm a soldier instead of an explorer to be over. I want to get the job done, go back to where I belong, and be with the people I want to be with. Do *you* honestly believe the person we're looking for *isn't* in Fenfield?"

"I'll grant you that he almost certainly is, but—"

"Then if he can go there, we can go there. I'm going to get the horse and cart. You do whatever you need to do to prepare, then we're heading out."

"Now? *Now?* Even setting aside the fact that it's a huge unknown, it's thirty miles away. We won't get there until the morning if we leave now. Let's at least do this well-rested."

"... Fine. But first thing in the morning. We have breakfast and we get to the bottom of this."

Chapter 7

A long, sleepless night had done little to improve Allie's mood. She pulled herself out of bed and made breakfast. This morning she would be meeting with the new owner of her home and very likely learning just how much worse her life was about to get. The only bright spot in her morning was waking to discover that the flame was stationary, and thus she had an update on Fel's comings and goings. The spark of joy faded rather swiftly when she learned what he'd decided to do.

"And he's just going to charge into the field. That's his plan," Allie said.

"He, in fact, left for the field several hours ago. He will arrive shortly and begin his investigation. He has made it clear he is in a hurry to get home."

"He *does* know that coming home in a coffin isn't the best way to make the trip, right?" she said.

"If he catches the disease, he won't be coming home at all. It is characterized by people simply disappearing."

"Did you think that was a helpful statement, Wick?" Allie said.

"I was hoping to improve the accuracy of your understanding, not your mood. Though in retrospect I suppose a shade more deference to your state of mind would not have been out of place."

She cupped her hands over her eyes. "No. It's better to know the truth. It's just... I wish the truth wasn't so rotten lately."

There was a delicate knock. She took her hand away and glared at her door.

"Speaking of rotten..." she muttered.

"Should I depart?" Wick asked.

"If you've got nothing better to do, stick around. I might want an extra set of ears. Or maybe a witness. This might not go well."

She took a brief detour to her fireplace to snag a poker before heading to the door. In her observation, it was generally wise to have something blunt and cruel within arm's reach when greeting a visitor for the first time, just in case.

Allie opened the door. Sure enough, it was Velonia Madritz.

"Miss Madritz," Allie said. "I'm surprised you came to handle this personally."

"I try to conduct all my business personally, if I can manage. One's intention can be muddled by intermediaries. May I come in?"

"You can walk around like you own the place. Because you do," Allie said.

"It is still polite to ask."

Madritz stepped inside. She cast a glance aside, the sort of wordless order to an underling that instructed them to remain where they were. Allie shifted aside to let Madritz through and caught the briefest glimpse of the individual receiving the order. It was a stoutly built man who hid his nose and mouth behind a curious cloth mask. He was lightly armored, appropriate for a mercenary or other paid heavy. Something about him was familiar. The mere fact that she found a masked mercenary familiar put a sour taste in her mouth. They weren't the sort of people you should *ever* see, let alone more than once.

She shut the door and turned. "So, a minor increase, I think the note said."

"Quite minor. One hundred additional duots per month."

Allie glanced aside for a moment. "I cannot afford that. That total price is, to the duot, precisely what I am allowed to earn from The Fox and Log thanks to your new schedule."

"Then it seems to me you *can* afford it."

"I also have to eat, Miss Madritz."

"Ah. No matter. I am certain you'll find a way to make ends meet."

"Maybe I'll get a job at the most expensive business I can find, just to make sure it'll drain your coffers a bit more when you have to buy that place too."

"Oh, so you think this is all about you, do you?"

"You bought where I work and where I live, and you changed both with a surgical precision to make my life worse. And those are the *only* things you did since you came here."

"You're certain I haven't bought anything else?"

"Yes. Because while I might be a nobody, I know a lot of somebodies."

"Mmm. You certainly do. And you have been very useful to them. May I take a seat?"

"Knock yourself out," she said.

Madritz sat on the one chair with a cushion and daintily crossed her legs.

"As you seem to have a truly remarkable insight for someone with so low a vantage, I won't insult your intelligence. You are a very small person, and you have managed to make yourself visible on a very large stage. There are people in this world with their eyes set on the towering figures to either side of you. And they have done their level best to cut those giants out at the knees. They have failed. But others have investigated more deeply. Drawn circles around the networks that serve and feed and aid those towering figures. The roots that nourish the greatest trees in the forest. And you, Miss Waverly, are where many of those circles overlap. Now, as I've said, you have been quite useful to a great many. I don't know what sort of compensation you've been receiving."

She gestured with her hand, encompassing the whole of the room. "Either it isn't financial, or you've been investing with great subtlety. Honestly, I do not require the answer to that question. I'm not interested in violating your privacy. But *other* privacy, privacy that you have gained a glimpse of through loyalty and care? Now that appeals to me..."

"I don't like where this is going."

"Miss Waverly, you need to understand something about the world. You've been helping people. That's admirable. Your motivations are immaterial to me. You've been rendering aid to people who needed and appreciated it. But you cannot help one person without hurting someone else."

"That's a lie and you know it."

"Perhaps at the smallest levels. See a man stumble, help him back to his feet. Who does it harm? But at the highest level, things are different. We are talking about people who have nearly everything. More than they need, certainly. More than they realistically should ever have. But not nearly as much as they want. When you have *nearly* everything, the only way to climb any higher is to have *absolutely* everything. At that level, every crumb that goes into a starving child's mouth is one that isn't on your plate."

"That's a horrible way to view the world."

"I don't judge. I merely facilitate. And in case you've missed my tone, that's what I would like you to begin considering."

"Facilitating?"

"You work in The Fox and Log, a place as popular as a meeting place for those looking to do business as for those seeking refreshment. And you are quite friendly with the Maskers. That puts you in a unique position to provide information of extreme value. Information that could easily make the difference between struggling to put food on the table and living quite comfortably indeed."

"And if I choose to mind my own business as I always have?"

"I don't know. You would be the first to make that decision when presented with this offer. Because I only make this offer to people I consider to be sensible enough to accept it and capable enough to execute it. However, in this occasion there *are* alternatives. As I have described, you have been a tool, a crucial one, that has been used to foil the plans of several powerful people. I would prefer you be *added* to the toolbox of my associates, but the only thing I truly require is that you be *removed* from your current one. This actually presents you with two additional options. Remove yourself, or *be* removed."

"Are you threatening me, Miss Madritz?"

"No. No. I'm merely informing you of the circumstances of your work and home from this point forward." She stood. "You've stuck your head out of your hole, and the hawk has spotted you. Now you can either scurry back into your hole and don't come out again, find something else for the hawk to eat, or get eaten. Only one of them lets you see more than a single glimpse of sunlight ever again. It shouldn't be a difficult choice to make. Have a lovely day, Miss Waverly. When you get to the tavern, you'll see I've drawn up a new schedule. It so happens you have a number of additional hours this week. And you'll also find daily meetings with me before the start of work, when summoned by me. I'd suggest you use your extra hours wisely. And I look forward to tomorrow's chat."

Miss Madritz opened the door and cast another quick glance at her bodyguard before pacing off down the unpleasantly fragrant alleyway. Allie shut and braced the door behind her. When the sound of footsteps receded into the distance, she marched back to her seat and slumped into it.

"That was an unexpected turn of events," Wick said.

"No. That was pretty much how I saw that going. Maybe a little more straightforward than I would have thought, but the same result. Do me a favor, Wick. Don't go spreading this around. Not until I decide what I'm going to do at least."

"I will not volunteer the information in my discussions with the others."

"You can go see to the others now," she said. "I have some thinking to do."

"Good luck and be well," Wick said.

The flame relaxed into the natural flicker once more. Almost immediately, it became still again.

"A question, if you will allow it?"

"Make it quick, Wick. I have a lot to think about."

"That is what I am hoping to ask about. You are faced with a conundrum. Several choices, but none that appeal to you. How do you imagine you will make this selection?"

"I don't have any choices. There's only one thing to do. It's just not easy to do it."

"I was under the impression you could leave your home or your job. Or agree to serve Madritz."

"I can't serve Madritz."

"Why not?"

"Because to muck with her, that's why. Comes into *my* town, into *my* tavern, into *my* home and tells me what to do? I didn't forge this life for myself to let someone like her take it away from me, even if doing so *wouldn't* mean betraying people I trust, and who trust me. That isn't a choice. It isn't on the table."

"But you could move. Change jobs."

"With what time? With what money?" she said.

"You have friends who could both employ you and house you."

"I've just said I am not giving up the life I've made for myself. *None of the options* given to me by that woman are options, because those are the things she wants me to do and she does *not* get what she wants. Not out of me."

"Will you ask for help from the Maskers?"

"No. They're in this deep enough. I'm going to need Verfessa's help, but I don't want to come out of this owing him anything either."

"It seems unwise to abandon aid in so dire a situation."

"I know it's not wise. But I'm me. I can only do things my way. I have so little control over anything. The least I can do is hold tight to what I have. Why all the questions?"

"I have recently found that insight into how difficult decisions are made is of great value to me."

"I didn't think you were the sort of... um, I was going to say 'person,' but is that accurate?"

"That assessment is entirely up to you."

"We'll go with person. I wouldn't think you were the kind of person who would have potentially difficult choices to make. I wouldn't have thought you'd have *any* choices to make. Hence me not even being sure if 'person' was the right word."

"Lately, as my role has expanded, the opportunities and obligations associated with it have expanded as well. It has been something of a struggle to keep up with them."

"You gotta do what you gotta do. People say that all the time, but it doesn't always mean what you might think. It means you have no choice, sure. An obligation is an obligation. But sometimes you have no choice because you haven't been given any options. Other times, you have no choice because you are *you,* and even if there's a thousand options, there's only one of them that would still leave you the person you want to be. You got that?"

"I believe I understand."

"Good. Then stick to that. I'm not going to say that if you do, you can't go far wrong. You can go a long way from right by being yourself. But you'll keep who you are intact, and if you ask me, that's something worth doing. Now if you'll excuse me, I need to figure out how to do that."

"I wish you good luck."

Once again, the flame flickered and danced on the gentle draft of her home. She drummed her fingers on the table and gritted her teeth. Little pieces of her mind nibbled at the edges of the problem, presenting solutions that she knew weren't *real* solutions for all the reasons she'd already laid out. She couldn't move or find a new job. It took money she didn't have and left her wondering where she'd go. But even if those weren't problems, they still weren't an option. Not for her. First, no one who would go to the absurd lengths of purchasing the elements of her life to gain influence over her would be stymied by a moving target. There was no way back to normal from here. This problem couldn't be avoided, it had to be solved. And that was in addition to Allie's almost self-destructive level of stubbornness. She would *not* be told what to do. But all the same she could feel the teetering pull of a thousand little threads. The connections she'd made over her life unfolded before her. She had friends. She had unsteady but hopefully reliable allegiances. How could she get out of this without owing more than she was willing to pay and without dragging more innocent people into this?

One way or another, she was going to find out.

Fel leaned on the side of the family cart. For the sake of speed and reducing the risk of theft while it was unattended, they'd left most of their gear and cargo at Euphoria's place. For this little investigation, they had Wick's lantern, the cart itself, some tools, some weapons, and enough food and water to hold them over if they ended up spending a day or two searching. Not that they had a choice in the matter, but they'd also brought Oiler and Parch along.

"It worries me that the fear of theft exceeded the fear of contracting a mysterious disease for you," Tome said.

"If someone steals something, it doesn't come back on its own. Diseases heal."

"Not always. And stolen possessions can be replaced."

Fel refreshed the scrambled faces of Oiler's puzzle cube. "Not always," he said. "So how do you want to do this? Split up or stick together?"

"I don't want to do this at all. But as sanity is not an option, I think it would be best to split up. It isn't a foe we're facing. At least not one that can be overwhelmed through raw numbers. If we're separate, we at least eliminate the possibility that we'll both be infected from the same source at the same time." Tome stroked his chin. "Though we do *double* the chance of being infected separately since we'll be covering more ground. Maybe we—"

"You said split up, we split up. I'm not going to sit here listening to you debate yourself all day long." Fel strapped Oiler to his back, slipped his cudgel into the loop on his belt, and whistled to Parch. "Time to find out who's hiding in this field. You want to take the north or the south route around this place?"

"An important question. The winds are coming from the east, so if there is something wrong with the air—" Tome began.

"Too slow. I'm going south," Fel said. "We'll do a loop and meet up either on the opposite side or back here, depending on how fast we end up going. If you don't show up by dinnertime, I'll assume something's happened and try to retrace your steps."

"And if you don't show up?"

"Really, what are the chances of that happening?" he said.

Tome glared at him.

"Fine. If I don't show up, you do the same, trace around the outside the same way I went. I'll make sure I'm leaving a pretty obvious trail to follow. You do the same."

"Define 'a pretty obvious trail.'"

He rolled his eyes and stooped down to scoop up some stones. "See these. They're called rocks. You take five of them, you make a little *V* with the point in the direction you were going. Any time you change direction, you make a new one. And a couple of times between just for the sake of it."

"That's... actually quite clever."

"Yeah. That's how you know it was one of Dad's ideas, not mine."

"Mmm... Remember what we're looking for and what we've learned from our investigations thus far. If you start to feel the pressure of something supernatural on your mind, some odd sense that the way behind you is too dangerous and you must press forward, turn back immediately. That is the disease attempting to grip you."

"Got it. You want Wick's lantern or one of these pipes?"

"I can't quite stomach puffing at one of those things."

"It's not my favorite, either, but I'll cope with it." He lit one of the contraption pipes and took a puff.

"I suppose that's as good a plan as we're likely to get," Tome said. "I can't see a way to delay the madness any longer. Off we go then. Good luck."

"Same to you."

Fel trudged into the field. Notably, Tome lingered at the cart, taking his time preparing. As it was a hunting ground—or at least it had been one until the disease—Fenfield was mostly wooded and untamed. A few minutes of walking had taken Fel far enough into the evergreens to lose sight of the cart. Maybe it was the fact that Tome could no longer see him and thus there was no longer any need to put on an act, or maybe it was the fact that Fel could no longer see Tome and thus he was no longer sharing the burden of this worrisome mystery, but whatever the cause, Fel quickly felt anxiety start to fester in the pit of his stomach.

"Come on, Fel," he said. "You've faced worse than this before. It's not like the unknown is something that should concern you. You never know exactly what's going on. If there's one thing you know better than anyone else, it's how to cope with situations you don't understand. That's the value of not understanding things."

Despite this unassailable logic, his gut refused to settle down. Time to change tactics. Parch had been living in Beffshire for long enough that he'd become rather comfortable in cities. The people *around* him weren't quite so comfortable, particularly in light of his tendency and desire to climb to the roofs of houses and down again rather than simply trotting along the street. Regardless, he wasn't *unhappy* in Beffshire, that was clear. But he was always extra happy when Fel took him along on a trip. Whether it was into the dry fields to the south, the muck of the swamps to the north and west, or the buggy, muggy forests scattered here and there, a change of scenery was always welcome. Thus, the little unicorn was prancing and springing along without a care in the world.

"Parch likes it," Fel said. "And Parch is better than even Tome at figuring out when something's dangerous or not. So just calm down. Everything will be fine."

Something in the distance crackled a dry branch. Fel and Parch both froze.

"Probably a good idea to put down one of those markers..." he muttered.

A weary Martin Masker pulled open the door to his workshop for the first time in fourteen hours. He'd worked through the night and missed at least two meals, but the progress had been worth it. Even now, left alone for the first time in hours, Wick was marveling at the fruits of their labors. A freshly upgraded pair of hands flexed and curled their digits before the steady flame atop the coupler.

After several days of marked improvement, the speed and precision of Wick's writing had plateaued. Wick felt as though additional practice would allow him to overcome this shortcoming, but Martin theorized that a part of the problem was the hands themselves.

If one were to base one's assessment of the story of the Bygone Era on its contraptions—and there was very little else to reliably base it upon—it would seem to be a tale of the balance of utility and beauty. Even the technicians of the Bygone Era couldn't perfectly duplicate the wonders that nature had wrought, but every element of a Bygone contraption was devised in part by a desire to do just that. Straight lines were rare if curves could be used instead. Shapes as often as not mimicked musculature and anatomy. This, almost more than the confounding nature of the working principles of the contraptions, made the accurate construction of them difficult. One must be at once an artist and an engineer when creating a Bygone contraption accurately.

But Martin had come a long way in a short time, thanks to the reference materials Fel and Tome had acquired. He was slowly learning what actually contributed to the function of the contraption and what merely showcased the skill of the artisan. Some of the time-consuming and physically taxing flourishes were just that. Flourishes. Garnish. And some of them actually hindered the operation of the device, a sacrifice of function to beautify form. Martin wouldn't go so far as to call these choices flaws. Beauty was important, for its own sake and for the purpose of creating something that would sell if placed on the shelf of an antiquities shop. But the bust he was creating had little need for beauty. Thus, he'd redesigned a few small elements of the hands and elbows. Their resulting range of motion was a good deal less natural. All the fingers and both the elbows could now bend in both directions. But the new design allowed for a simpler and more fluid mechanism. And most importantly, it was a mechanism Wick found himself far more capable of controlling. After the first hand had been adjusted, the precision and speed with which he could write soared. Now he had two of them. Complete, fully functional. Wick's consciousness crackled with the possibilities.

Right now, Wick was long overdue for a visit to Tome and Fel. He hadn't spoken to them since they'd resolved to head to Fenfield. Indeed, aside from a brief visit to Epiphany and Teya, whose journey had been terribly uneventful thus far, he had done little besides work on this project with Martin. It was all that he *wanted* to do. He reached out and plucked a slate and chalk from the desk. A book title burbled to the surface of his recollection. He rendered the symbols as he saw them. They flowed from memory to slate with a speed and ease that astounded him. And for the first time, he was able to sense that there existed, just beyond his freshly installed fingertips, still more dexterity and precision. Before, he'd suspected his skill with the artificial anatomy was the limiting factor. Now, he was certain of it. He grabbed the rag Martin used to erase the slate and tied it, with some difficulty, to his wrist to more easily wipe the writing away and try it again.

He repeated the title. More precise, but slower. He tried again. Much faster, but almost illegible. Again. Again. He wore down the chalk with dozens of iterations, trying to hone his skills. And he *did* improve. But after an hour and two pieces of chalk, he'd already reached his limits again. The hands could move faster, more precisely. He knew it. But he similarly knew that no amount of practice would allow him to reach the desired level of skill. He wasn't human. He had never been a human. Despite what Martin supposed, Wick couldn't simply practice his way to mastery. He could improve. Indeed, he'd improved infinitely more than he'd ever imagined was possible. But he had a far clearer view of his capacity than a human had. He knew where he was, knew where he wanted to be, and knew that he couldn't reach it. Not as he was. Not without more help.

The light of his flame traced the shape of the Warrior mask, hung with care on a hook behind the armless bust that served as its mount when Martin was willing to risk consulting it. Martin had all but ignored it since the start of this project. If he'd been paying more attention, he might have noticed the mask's placement shifting and changing from day to day, as late-night sessions consulting the Warrior's wisdom had shaved hours or days from Wick's learning curve.

Wick set down the chalk and slate and snatched the mask from its hook. As always, the voice imposed itself in his mind. He felt the pluck of its will and earned another dose of clarity.

"Sentry flame, how many books have you rescued from oblivion? How many victories have you snatched from our foes of old?" the Warrior said.

"I have written only a few pages, only the titles of a few dozen books. But I have grown. Improved. And my tools have improved as well through the skill of Martin Masker."

"It is a wondrous rebirth, the return of a Masker to the task of proper making again. But human's live only brief lives. You must give him the tools of antiquity before his light fades from this world. Only when armed with the weapons of old can his intellect bring his people to the heights of strength and conquest that they truly desire."

"I do not believe that humanity seeks strength and conquest as a rule. Not in the literal terms of defeating one's enemies."

"Your insight is lacking."

"Perhaps. I do, however, agree that Martin's dedication to restoring what is lost should be rewarded as swiftly as possible, and I fear that my limitations may rob him of the bulk of the knowledge he may seek simply because of my inability to record it as swiftly as these hands and arms should be able to. I require more training."

"More training. Sentry flame, we were built to aid humans. We were built, in a way, to mimic humans. But we are not humans. I can feel the hands you have been given. Feel their shape. I can divine their potential because it is my role and purpose to do so. And just as the physical portions of a contraption can be upgraded and replaced, so too can the components conjured from the arcane. What you and I have that can be said to mimic the human mind is far more mutable. Far more malleable. Far more modular. You and I more so than most. It was my role to draw knowledge of motion and martial methods. It was your role to accumulate information. We share that. The task of containing information within us. I am tasked with containing tactics, maneuvers, techniques. Your capacity and intent are far more broadly defined. I have not trained you, nor can I train you. Everything you have learned from me, you have duplicated from me and combined your own abilities with mine. Through our interactions, you grow stronger by accumulating within yourself those parts of my own skillset that I offer you."

"Surely 'duplicating abilities' and 'learning or training' are equivalent."

"For a human, perhaps. But for you and me, it is far more literal. You grow stronger because a part of my arcane, insubstantial mechanism is a part of you now. If you wish greater skill with your body, you must acquire more of my mechanism."

"I question the wisdom and, more importantly, the safety of allowing you to impose portions of yourself upon my will. You are a thing of violence. You threatened the Maskers."

"I tested them. And they passed. And now you are being tested. Already you have increased the speed of your travels, the sureness of your motion, all by taking from me what was offered, explicitly or implicitly. The decision you must make now is how badly you desire this victory over your own limitations and frailties. I can give you mastery over your limbs. And you can draw from me untold fragments of Bygone wisdom, the recipes and structures that give my mind skills and strengths that you lack. You can become more than you are. You need only choose to do so. There may be consequences. No battle is perfectly clean. But if you are unwilling to pay the price of victory, you should never have sought it."

Wick held the mask firmly. He felt the edges of the ticking, pulsing enchantment forged by the contraptioneers of old. He watched. And he thought...

Hours of walking and searching had begun to weigh upon Fel. He'd entered the field believing there was a small but precious possibility that all he'd heard about the place was false. Something dreamed up by a man who'd had too much to drink and needed a story to explain why he'd wandered off for a few days. Those who entered the field and never returned could easily be attributed to some horrid monster that had been making a meal of them.

"Of course, the one time I'm *hoping* to meet a slavering, bloodthirsty beast from the depths, it's nowhere to be found."

He couldn't ignore it anymore. He felt the nagging tug at the back of his mind. When he thought of retracing his footsteps, there was a strange force pulling the needle of his mental compass away from the edge of the field and toward its center. The disease was real. Or at least its symptoms were. And he'd been exposed. The smart thing would have been to do as he was told. To run to the edge of the field, find Tome, and write this place off as too dangerous to search. Eventually his father would find a way to correct the tracking device, and he would be able to pinpoint the location of the Student. Even if the elf *had* come this way, he'd be suffering from the same terrible disease. It may even have taken care of him. Yes, it would be smart to leave this place and never look back.

Fel was not very smart.

He absolutely had come too far and seen too much of what these masks *and* these elves were capable of to leave without being certain of the fate of at least one of them. And more importantly, he had something that most of these other disease sufferers lacked. He had an absurd, blessed, and cursed life. He'd experienced things few other living creatures ever had. And this? This terrible pressure on his mind that he couldn't quite separate from his own thoughts? It was not wholly unfamiliar. It didn't feel like a sickness. It felt like something more deliberate. Something intentional. Something *designed*. And if it was something that had been built, he could break it. He was good at that.

Parch continued to prance and frolic, nibbling on greenery, drinking from streams, and generally being adorable. That gave Fel the courage to continue. His own sense of danger was shouting from the rooftops, but Parch's remained silent. Not that it meant quite as much, but Oiler continued clicking and clacking at his puzzle box without any evident concern either, but Fel wasn't sure the contraption was capable of concern. Unfortunately, Oiler was not the *only* contraption that wasn't making much of a stir.

He puffed at the pipe. "Wick? You there?"

No answer.

"You picked a heck of a time to be loitering somewhere else, Wick," he said.

Fel paused and arranged a fresh arrow on the mossy floor of the forest. For lack of a better plan, he did on purpose what the man they'd interviewed had done out of desperation. He kept close tabs on how the strange sensation in his mind strengthened and weakened, tracing a circle around what was presumably the center of the source of what they called "the Haze." If there was even the notion that he was falling more firmly into its grip, he took two steps back in the direction he'd come from and adjusted his heading. He wasn't sure what he hoped to achieve in doing so, though the way the sensation itself seemed to be radiating from something in the distance served to reinforce his notion that it was not a proper disease but some sort of spell or contraption.

Then, with one fateful step, that notion became a certainty. The feeling slipped away, suddenly and completely, midway through a stride. He stepped back again and felt the sensation press in upon him again, then stepped forward and felt it wither and fade. He hastily gathered some rocks and carefully marked the point where the feeling vanished. A few steps farther along the arc he'd been following revealed that precisely two strides took him past the sheltered portion of the forest floor. He marked that as well. Now he walked away from the center of the field, a direction that his mind had until this moment been gently dissuading him from going. Nothing in his mind or body objected now. And when he paced farther in the direction that should have strengthened the symptom, it similarly didn't return.

"This is *not* a disease." Fel puffed at the pipe. "Are you there, Wick? Are you seeing this?"

There was no reply. Fel glared at the innocuous section of ground as though if he intimidated it sufficiently, it would explain itself. Lacking any sort of insight into how or why his brain would be addled everywhere but here, he started ticking through the possible ways to move forward. As had become a habit for him, he discussed his thoughts with Parch and Oiler, the only two people in his life that wouldn't call him a fool for acting like a fool. Not *verbally* anyway.

"All right," he said, staring down at the unicorn. "First things first. Here are the things I *should* do. Number one would be to head back and talk to Tome. He'd want to know about this. And he'd *need* to know, because there's no way this *isn't* part of the answer to what's going on here and thus the same spot he's headed for. But I'd have to retrace my footsteps and then follow *his* footsteps as far as he got in his search. Then he'd want to puzzle over every fragment of possibility about how this is happening and why. That'll take *days*. He won't want to camp out here while we do it, so we'd be heading back and forth... we'll be at it a week. Forget that."

Parch flicked an ear and paced around, not even pretending to be interested in Fel's reasoning aloud. Fel dropped Oiler's pack to the ground and sought the contraption's council instead.

"I *absolutely* should wait for Wick to check in and tell him to tell Dad. If nothing else, Dad would want to know about this. It could probably give him some sort of insight into what was fouling the behavior of the detector, and thus might give them a better way to locate who and what they were after. He puffed at the pipe again. "Wick?"

Still no answer.

"Dad must be working him to the bone. Or whatever he has."

There were a number of very good reasons for Fel to wait. But the thought of dragging this out for days more... maybe *weeks* more—there had to be a solution, a way forward.

"I make my living going to mysterious places that want to kill me or keep me out. This is just more of the same," he decided. "You're not going nuts, Oiler, so there's nothing armed that you're aware of or any broken contraptions about. Parch, you don't seem to mind one little bit about *anything* that's going on. I hereby proclaim this to be safe enough for me to pick away at on my own."

Fel crouched down to collect some stones to mark the path. He was heading forward, toward the center of whatever this phenomenon was. Once the arrow was placed in as near to the center of the suspiciously clear walkway as he could manage, he began the slow, careful walk forward. Instantly, he felt the familiar and hard-earned instincts starting to flicker to life again in his mind. This may not have been a dank vault a few levels belowground, but most of the potential dangers were just the same. He stepped lightly, mindful of pressure plates or trip wires. He gave each passing tree a quick look for hanging traps. He'd dodged far too many swinging battering rams and plunging spikes to ever trust anything large enough to hide something heavy and high enough to make its drop a deadly one. Eyes trained to seek the glint of metal not only because of the potential threat it presented but for the potential value of a hidden contraption or artifact soon spotted a dull gleam just at the edge of the safe stretch of walkway. He grinned.

"What have we here?" he murmured.

Fel dropped to his knees and leaned closer to the chain. He reached for the pouch at his belt and fetched a stiff brush—a tool that came in handy more often than one would expect in treasure hunting. A gentle swish cleared more of the soil around the metallic sparkle. It revealed itself to be a few links of chain. It was of exceptionally high quality. One might even say excessively high quality. It was also made from brass or something quite like it. A terrible material for a chain you didn't want to break, but an excellent material for a Bygone contraption. Sure enough, closer inspection confirmed this was at least an attempt at a Bygone contraption. It was too new to be a real one, but there were etchings in each link that were a match for the sort of symbols generally found among the internal workings of a Bygone contraption.

Industrious brushing revealed more and more chain, at least fifty links of it, running in either direction. Each one was identically etched.

"The work that must have gone into this..." Fel muttered. "Brass links, etched by hand. And the join between the links is soldered or something. Yes. It's solder. I can see the hint of silver, with the etching going over it. They made the chain and then etched it. There's that order of operations Dad is always going on about, one of the things that makes Bygone contraptions do their fancy arcane tricks."

He scratched his head. "So it's new, but it's made correctly. So far it's just Dad and whoever taught the Bolivan guy who have been able to pull that off, as far as I know. Either this is a third expert... or this is the handiwork of the guy pulling the strings of the Bolivans."

He positioned Oiler right on top of the chain, partially to see if the contraption would have any visible reaction to straddling the effects the chain seemed to be controlling and partially to see if it had any interest in the chain. Beyond a brief inspection, Oiler was more interested in its puzzle box than the long, expertly crafted contraption. That was just as well. It meant the chain was working properly, or else Oiler didn't know what to make of it. That meant either this effect the chain was producing was intentional or it was so far beyond what the inventors had intended that Oiler didn't even interpret the chain to be a contraption. Either way, it meant if Fel wanted to stop the chain's influence, all he would have to do was disable the contraption.

Fel crouched down and started gently tugging the chain up from the inch or so of soil that concealed it. He had to be careful as he did so, not just because contraptions were vile and capricious, but because if he leaned too far, his head would cross the border traced by the chain and be filled with confusing thoughts about where he could find safety and what places did or didn't exist. That was the final nail in the coffin when it came to doubts about the chain's role in the strange sensations within the area.

It was tempting to believe he just had to cut the chain to solve this problem. He had a particularly deep scar on his thigh that marked the day he'd learned that breaking a contraption was not the same as disabling it. Yes, they wouldn't produce their intended effects unless the crucial parts of the main mechanism were whole. But just because a contraption wasn't performing its intended function didn't mean it was harmless. As the scar reminded him, a contraption intended to slam shut a spiked door when someone crossed the threshold would do so faithfully when whole. When broken it might, for example, slam open and shut at random, and with such speed that the door buckled and sent razor-sharp struts ricocheting off the walls and ceiling. He didn't know what the equivalent action of the chain and its confounding mental tortures might take, but he wasn't taking his chances.

If he wanted this chain to stop stirring the brains of nearby humans like an overly thick porridge, he would need to find a portion of it that could be disassembled rather than merely broken. Essentially one of the last steps of its construction to be completed and thus the first step of its deconstruction. For an excruciating quarter mile of inching along on his knees, he tugged up and revealed the chain, working his way toward the center of the chain's influence. Finally he came to a junction point, something of a buckle that didn't just join two lengths of chain but linked it to a third running perpendicular to the rest. Unlike the links, this piece had fasteners. It took someone with his level of experience to spot them, as this component was also built to Bygone Era standards and thus had the fasteners integrated into the etched design so carefully that they practically disappeared. He unrolled his set of tools and selected the proper driver.

"And this is how Fel Masker 'cured' the 'plague' that had 'quarantined' a major hunting ground in Shalia," he said, grinning to himself.

The moment he'd started turning the screws, he heard the jangle of Oiler's chains. He turned and saw the contraption staring at him, now quite interested in the heavy buckle in Fel's hand. Rather than do battle with the overzealous mechanic, and also to finally get off his aching knees, he stood and worked at the screws more swiftly. Six of them had to be twisted free before he could remove the top plate of the mechanism. Inside, as he expected, was a veritable showcase of the machinist's art. Gears, pinions, linkages. They were fine by modern standards and crude by Bygone standards, and removing any one of them would certainly be enough to disable the contraption. He tapped a retaining pin out of place on one of the axles and slid the largest gear off its axle. The result was immediate.

He shut his eyes. His fingers went slack. The buckle slipped from his grip and clattered to the ground, spilling a number of its fine components into the dirt and fallen pine needles. The metal pipe fell from his mouth. He had to fight to stay on his feet. The world around him felt like it was suddenly spinning. Some mixture of fear, desire, and confusion sank its claws into his mind, like someone had opened up a spigot for each of the negative emotions in his brain and let them flood out the rest of his thoughts. There was only one place that seemed right, that seemed proper for him to be. He turned toward what a moment ago he would have considered to be the center of the chain's effect and staggered toward it. Somewhere distant, he heard the curious bleat of his unicorn. Behind, he heard the gleeful jangle of his contraption as it dragged itself over to see to the broken buckle.

One final flicker of clarity fizzled in his mind. The chain was not causing the terrible influence of this place. The chain was holding it at bay, keeping it clear of the safe walkway he'd been navigating. He had made a mistake.

That thought hissed away in the torrent of unnatural sensations, and he trudged toward the center of Fenfield.

Chapter 8

Tome flexed his fingers and grimaced. He'd spent six hours tracing out the edge of the field's influence before abandoning it and retracing his steps. That much time had convinced him, at the very least, that this was not a disease at play. At least, no proper or natural one. Perhaps the effects the field had on people could be considered a disease, but that was a matter of semantics. His determination was that this was not the sort of thing that someone caught thanks to the cold or being bitten by an animal. This was something intrinsic to this field, and if its effects lingered beyond its borders as seemed to be the case for the sufferers they'd interviewed, then it happened only when someone remained there long enough, or perhaps progressed far enough, for the effect to linger. The very moment he reasoned that the field might be attempting to stain his mind with its confounding effect, he turned back and returned to the cart. He would record his thoughts, wait for Wick to check on him, and deliver through the flame the message that Fel should retreat.

A full sleepless night had passed since then. Not once had the flame stopped flickering.

For the fifth time, he opened the lantern and peered inside, seeking the etchings around the base of the flame that indicated its identity as an artifact and contraption rather than a mundane lantern. They, of course, were present. This was unquestionably one of the two persistent lanterns that could be relied upon to host Wick even if the flame was extinguished and relit. And this whole ill-fated expedition had begun with them discussing matters with Wick in this very spot. Wick wasn't simply scared away by the strange goings-on in the field. But never, not even when he was in the Greater Lands and checking on him required hours of effort on the lantern's part, had Wick spent this much time away without popping in to see if anything was needed.

He shut his eyes tight and closed the lantern. "You spent your whole life comfortable with the idea that someone beyond the walls of your home city would take days or weeks to talk to. Now, after a single day without this lantern, you feel cut off and isolated by a simple return to that reality. This is the nefarious reality of Bygone contraptions. They rob you of skills you once had and make you rely upon little gadgets to do what you once could quite easily achieve without them."

He paused and took a breath to collect himself. "Wake up and say something you blasted thing!" he growled, shaking the lantern when the moment of calm passed.

He heard a crackle. Instantly he stopped shaking and scrutinized the still-dancing flame in case, against all odds, this had been the thing that would summon Wick back again. While the flame wavered, he heard another crackle and realized it was coming from the field ahead. He set down the lantern and slipped an ice spell from his pocket. If something was foolish enough to threaten him while he was sleep-deprived and at the end of his wits, it would be frozen so solid it would still be thawing next spring.

With muscles tense and page ready to be torn, he trained his eyes on the source of the sound. The thick brush started to rustle. Bushes spread. Parch bounded out into the clearing.

He flinched and tore the edge of the spell. In a panic, he had to toss it aside lest he seal the little unicorn in a block of mystically conjured ice. Instead the flash and swirl of blue light encased a nearby pine in a crystalline shell.

"You... I... Do not sneak up on a well-prepared paper mage!" he snapped.

Parch stared at him evenly, unmoved by the reprimand. Now that Tome wasn't terrified he was about to face an assassin or a Greater Mystic, he was able to devote some of his mind to assessing the creature properly. What he saw did not set his mind at ease.

The creature was not injured, but there was sign of a struggle. His fur had been disturbed, little dips in the pelt suggesting tufts of hair had been torn away, and in the deepest such divot was a few flakes of dried blood, a minor and already-healed abrasion. The chipped end of his horn had some dried blood as well, though Tome suspected that blood belonged to someone else. Most worrisome of all, Parch had Fel's contraption pipe clutched sideways in his mouth.

Tome took it. The inside still smoldered with the unnaturally prolonged embers lit from Wick's flame. Unlike the open flame, there was no visual indication if Wick was present. In a moment of blind optimism, Tome stuffed the end in his mouth to take a long drag.

"Wick?" he croaked, sputtering and coughing. "Are you there?"

No answer. His mind helpfully reminded him that the pipe in his mouth was moments ago in the mouth of an animal—something his tongue reinforced quite vigorously. He spat and wiped his mouth.

"What happened to him?" Tome asked. "I know you can't answer. The question is rhetorical. Unless you can also talk and have just been keeping your mouth shut, which at this point I wouldn't put past you."

He glared at the unicorn. Parch flicked an ear and bleated.

"Right. Good. But I know something bad happened. Because even when you don't like people, like me, you still seek out help when they need it. And that's what you're doing right now. Which means something happened to Fel and you think I can help. And that you think I can help means he's still alive to *be* helped."

Parch stared at him blankly.

"And Oiler's gone too. Or at least hasn't come back yet. You know if you'd brought that thing along, it would be able to lead me to him. Unless you can too? It seems like all of Fel's little friends end up being able to track him down one way or another, so I wouldn't be surprised if that was the case for you as well."

At this, Parch simply turned and glanced over his shoulder.

"And I suppose you want me to follow you now," Tome said. "I'm sure that makes perfect sense to you. The one human gets tangled up in something, go get the other human to help. It isn't that simple! For all the thick-headed nonsense he gets into, Fel is very capable, and if something happened to him, without me being better prepared, it'll simply happen to me as well. Perhaps even more quickly. And while the spells are nice, if I'm going to charge into that mess that he shouldn't have charged into in the first place, I'm going to need to be armed with a good deal more information than I have right now. And that means heading back to Euphoria and sharing what we've learned. Combine our insight and resources. That'll give us the best chance to actually save him."

Tome turned and stalked toward the cart. He paused. "But it's hours back to the city. And however long it will take to figure out the next step. And then hours back. We won't be back here in less than a day. A full day of Fel dealing with whatever happened to him..."

He turned back toward the field and took two steps forward. "I'm closer to him now than anyone else. And the sooner help comes, the more likely he'll be saved."

He stopped. "But I don't know anything about how he was injured, or captured, or even if he was. For all I know, he sent you along with the pipe and a note about how I should keep my distance and he'll be along in another few hours, and the note just dropped away. ... Or he could have sent you saying we need reinforcements because there's an army tucked away in there."

He clenched his fists and growled under his breath. "This is exactly what I thought would happen! How can the Maskers simultaneously be the source of so much astounding innovation and confounding bad luck and bad judgment? I'm starting to think it takes a truly volatile person to really change the world, and the reason the world doesn't face sweeping changes more often is that most of the people who try to make those changes just get killed because they can't leave well enough alone!"

He took a long, slow breath. "I cannot safely go for him. And if I cannot safely go for him, then I will very likely befall the same fate, and if I do, there will be no one to come for me. The correct thing to do is go learn more and go get help. Fel got himself into whatever mess he's in now. He'll just have to last long enough for us to get him out of it."

The decision was made. He turned and pulled himself into the cart. Behind, he heard a bleat that sounded downright accusatory.

"Parch, if you want me to help him, then come along," Tome called without looking. "Because chances are, one way or another I'll be needing some sort of half-brainless creature to help me succeed with the rescue attempt, and since Fel is the one I'm *rescuing*, the only one left is you."

He continued on his way. After a moment, the clippy-clop of hooves confirmed Parch had reluctantly agreed to follow.

"Thank the High for small victories..." Tome grumbled.

Martin trudged down the steps. Far too much focus on his work and far too little focus on his sleep meant that he'd fairly collapsed after his time with Wick the previous day. The fortunate side of that meant he'd slept like the dead and awoken fully refreshed for the first time in days. Now he'd had a meal and seen to some of the chores that had been waiting a bit too long for his attention. It was finally time to get started on another day of tinkering and discovery.

He opened the door. "What in the world..." he uttered.

No one entered Martin's shop while he was not present. It wasn't a rule, in much the same way that gravity was not a rule. It was simply a reality. No one in the family had any real reason to do much in his workshop on their own.

If they came, it was to fetch him, work with him, or fetch an item he'd left for them. Thus, it never entered his mind that something might change in the workshop in his absence. There was nothing in his mental toolkit to cope with what waited for him today.

His workbench and every other flat surface in the shop, including much of the floor, had been covered with neat piles of papers. Rather than the bench, Wick's bust was in the center of the floor. An inkpot had been placed on the floor beside him, and a perfect fan of ink spatters traced the arc between the pot itself and the starting point of any given line on a page.

"Ah! Martin. I am pleased you have arrived," Wick said. "I was growing concerned that I would exhaust your supplies of ink and paper before you awoke. It is certainly within my own physical capacity to do so, but I have determined that writing any more swiftly than this would cause damage to either the pen nib or the page. You will need to repair or replace three pen nibs, by the way. My apologies."

He precisely dipped the pen and started tracing out words on a fresh page. His motions were inhuman in their speed and accuracy. No longer was he attempting to replicate something he saw in his mind, effectively drawing pictures of words rather than writing words. Now he seemed to be replicating the exact pen strokes on the original handwritten manuscripts. Elsewhere, the level of precision was even more impressive. The serifs and esoteric punctuations of what must have been a printed page had been carefully drawn out by Wick's pen. There were even full illustrations visible on some of the pages, and complex illuminated letters.

"You've been... busy," Martin said.

"I have been able to fully recall and record fifteen books since you departed."

"I don't recall requesting that you do so," Martin said. "We were working on titles."

"It is the purpose of your enhancements to achieve this, is it not?"

"It is the purpose of the enhancements to *eventually* achieve this, yes. But I hadn't expected you to take the initiative. You never have before."

"I hope I haven't overstepped my bounds," Wick said.

"Er... no. No, very nearly, but I think I can excuse this in light of the results." He tiptoed over the piles of pages to the thicker stacks on the workbench. "There seem to be a good deal more than fifteen piles of pages."

"Yes, I have been forced to divide the piles of pages rather thinly, as writing at the speed that I have been means that the ink takes rather longer to dry, relatively. Piling the freshly written pages led to smudges and marks on other pages."

"Fascinating the new problems that can be revealed by overly successful solutions."

Martin carefully flipped through some of the pages on the bench top. It seemed to be a recipe book. The language was unfamiliar, but the overall shape of the information on display harkened to the lists of ingredients and procedures of a culinary or alchemic tome.

"I imagine that things have remained uneventful for Fel and Epiphany?" Martin said absentmindedly.

There was no answer. The scratching on the pen stopped.

"Wick? The latest word on the kids?" Martin repeated somewhat louder.

"My apologies. I have been distracted by the task at hand. I have done nothing but transcribe books since shortly after your departure."

"Check on Fel and Epiphany immediately," Martin said firmly.

The flame atop the bust began to dance and flicker. Martin wrung his hands. The wondrous, borderline miraculous amount of progress Wick had made was worthy of consideration and analysis, but the safety of his children came first. Until he knew that they were safe, he wouldn't be able to commit himself to anything but mundane busywork. He gathered the dried and finished books. There were ten in total. They would need to be bound. Until then, he wrapped each in a bundle of ribbon to keep them from being scattered. When the workbench was clear of things he hadn't placed upon it, his mind was finally able to assess it and thus discover that something he had placed upon it was missing.

"The Warrior mask," he said quickly.

Martin turned and scanned the room. It didn't take long for him to find the ancient artifact. It was on the floor beside Wick's bust, hidden from his view when he entered thanks to the bust itself. Martin fetched it and placed it back on the corner of the workbench where, when Wick's enhancements were through, he would return to studying it. He felt a tightness in his chest. It was one thing for Wick to overachieve. It was another for him to neglect his duties. But the Warrior mask was dangerous. Why had it been moved? Why was it part of Wick's attempts to record the contents of the archive?

The flame went still. Wick spoke with a speed and intensity that underscored the importance of the update from the very first word.

"Fel is missing. He and Tome determined that a quarantined place called Fenfield was the most likely hiding place for their target. They split up to investigate, and Fel didn't return. Tome has no information regarding his well-being, beyond the reappearance of Parch with evidence of an altercation. He is en route to seek help from Euphoria. Epiphany is a few hours away from Beffshire, her business elsewhere having concluded."

"How long has Fel been missing?"

"Since yesterday evening."

"Surely he brought one of your flames with him when they split up. I sent multiple pipes!"

"Parch returned with the still-burning pipe."

"So he had it with him... Wick, if he went missing yesterday evening, it would have been not long after I turned in for the night. You should have been checking in on him."

"I know. It is an unacceptable dereliction of my duties. I cannot apologize enough for allowing this to occur."

Martin shut his eyes tight. "We don't know that your more timely presence could have prevented whatever happened. But until this very moment I'd never even entertained the possibility that you might fail me."

"I can only hope that through future service—"

"Save your words. You can seek amends when my child is safe. Until then, you exist for that purpose and no other. When we learn what has happened and what can be done to correct it, then you can answer questions about all this. Now is there anything else you can tell me about the situation?"

"Not until Tome reaches Euphoria and makes his next plans."

"Then you will go to Tome and remain with him until the moment he has more information for me."

"It will be a lengthy journey. A number of hours. Perhaps my services would be better put to use—"

"Wick. Until further notice, I am not interested in your insight, your speculation, or your suggestions."

Martin fetched a copper cup from a shelf and snuffed the flame on the bust. The lantern on the shelf above went still.

"Yes, Mr. Masker. As you wish," Wick said.

The flame danced. Martin set down the cup. He was surrounded by information, by evidence of the steady improvement of his craft and many leaps and bounds toward success. In any other circumstance he would dive into the information and devour it. He would interrogate Wick on all he had learned and what other new abilities he might have gained. He might even celebrate this seeming evolution of Wick's agency and initiative. But even with the promise of the wisdom of old just a few pen strokes away, there was only one fact he wished to know. What had happened to his boy? Until then, nothing else mattered.

Fel fought to open his eyes. He didn't remember falling asleep. He didn't remember much of anything. His thoughts felt scattered, like a stack of pages in disarray, and no matter how he tapped and wrangled them, they refused to fall into place. He felt certain that this sort of state of mind wasn't new to him, but there was the vague notion that it was normally accompanied by a throbbing headache and sour stomach, neither of which seemed to be plaguing him.

The room around him was dim, warm, and cozy. A barely smoldering oil lantern cast just enough light to reveal that he was in a lavishly appointed bedroom. Tapestries covered the walls. Carpets covered the floors. Every piece of furniture was stained dark and polished to a high gloss, ruthlessly clear of dust and fingerprints. The whole place had the feel of a guest room that a family seldom even let guests sleep in. More of a showcase for wealth and potential hospitality than an actual place someone might live.

He sat up and shook his head, jangling his thoughts around but still failing to dredge up any memories. Without anything to sink his mind into, he started with himself and tried to work outward. The folly of this decision was immediate. Nothing about him seemed to explain why he was in such a beautiful, luxurious room. He was fully dressed, not in night clothes but in some sort of dusty, smelly adventuring outfit. He looked at his hands. Coarse and rough. A laborer's hands. The kind of person who not only shouldn't be sleeping in a bed like this, but probably wouldn't even be cleaning a bed like this. He looked and felt more like the sort who would build the bed and never even see where it ended up.

Slowly he came to realize that his attempts to work out his own identity implied something particularly unpleasant about the current situation. "Where am I?" isn't a question one should ask with any regularity. "Who am I?" is one that should never flicker into one's mind.

Oddly, he didn't feel a stirring of anxiety or concern over the blurry mess awaiting him when he tried to dredge up memories. He was evidently the sort of person who took very bad news calmly and gracefully. That was good to know.

Abandoning the question of his own identity, he turned back to the room around him. Twisting the knob on the lantern revealed the room in greater detail. A painting hung on the wall, displaying a man and woman, both of whom seemed oddly familiar. He sensed they looked a bit like him, though he had to check his reflection in a polished silver mirror above his dresser to be certain of that. Sure enough, if these people weren't his parents, they were somewhere in his family tree.

He found a water basin and splashed himself. The bracingly cold water shocked him fully awake, and he was able to blot off what looked like several days of grime with a formerly clean towel. When he hung the towel back up, he discovered a tassel hanging down through the ceiling beside the dresser. He gave it an experimental tug. Somewhere distant, the faintest of chimes rang out. A few moments later someone knocked at his door.

"You rang, Sir?" came a dignified voice from the other side.

Fel gave the sash a suspicious look, then thumped over to the door and opened it.

A sharply dressed older man with a long and neutral expression was awaiting him in the doorway. He had a fresh towel draped over his arm.

"Does Sir require a new towel?" he said.

"Uh"—Fel glanced at the filthy towel—"yes. How did you know?"

"When Sir returned to the estate and went directly to bed, it seemed likely the morning ablutions would be more thorough than usual."

The strange man walked into the room and collected the dirty towel, replacing it with the clean one.

"I'll have the maid replace your water as well." He looked at the bed. "And your bedding. Quite the messy enterprise this week, eh, Sir?"

"It certainly seems that way," Fel said.

He briefly weighed the comparative merits of pretending he knew what was happening and simply voicing his confusion. Asking this man any of the dozens of questions burbling up to the top of his mind would certainly make him look like a fool, but he found he didn't care about that in the slightest.

"Who are you and where am I?" he asked.

The man raised his eyebrows. "I am Mr. Wick. I am Sir's butler."

"Right, yes. Good. Wick. That sounds familiar."

"Presently you are in your guest room. Considering the mess of your clothes when you announced your intention to turn in, I thought perhaps you would prefer not to soil your own bed."

"Guest room. Excellent. I thought this place didn't look lived-in enough to be my bedroom. I'm going to need a better answer on the 'where am I?' question though. House, street, city, kingdom, all the way up."

Mr. Wick blinked twice. "You are in the Masker Estate, your estate, on Ventor Boulevard in Clickspring. You are not in a kingdom. This is the Republic of Kinissia."

"I've heard of maybe half of that," Fel said. "And none of it seems right."

"Is Sir not feeling well?"

"I feel great! I just can't think. Any idea why that would be?"

"I do believe you'd indicated you had run afoul of a malfunctioning defensive construct at the city's center while you were working on an upgrade. You suggested you might awaken in something of a diminished state, but that you would soon recover."

Fel ran his fingers through his greasy hair. "I hope I was right."

A jangle of chain drew his attention to the bed. A dusty pack slid out from underneath, dragged by gleaming brass claws. It reached under the bed to retrieve a puzzle box, then held it up to him. Without thinking, Fel took the box, scrambled it, and handed it back. The contraption merrily started working at it again.

Fel pointed at the thing and looked to Mr. Wick. "Oiler, yes?"

"That is *an* oiler, yes."

Fel nodded. "All right. Good. That much makes sense." He clapped. "What was I supposed to be doing today, Wick?"

His butler tugged a rather fine watch from a dedicated pocket. He clicked it open. "In three hours and seven minutes, you were intended to be meeting with the family patron regarding further work on the clockwork diamond. Though I imagine you would be better served by a trip to the infirmary."

"What are they going to do, put a bandage on my brain? No, we'll keep to the schedule. But before then, food and probably a bath."

"As you wish, Sir."

Fel turned and pulled Oiler from the floor, slipping his arms through the straps of the pack. Mr. Wick gave him an uncertain look.

"Something wrong, Wick?" he asked.

"Generally, Sir leaves his tools in his workshop," Wick said.

"Generally, maybe. But so far the only thing that feels anything close to normal is Oiler here, so we're sticking together."

Fel took a couple of steps forward and found himself reflexively checking his pockets in the manner of one making ready to leave the house for the day and ensuring nothing important was forgotten. He tipped his head and tugged free a palm-sized contraption with a needle pointing off in one direction, steady and true.

"What do you make of this, Wick?" Fel asked.

"Sir does not discuss the tools of his trade with me with great frequency."

He hefted it in his hand and turned it about. "Looks important." He shrugged and stuffed it back in his pocket. "Add it to the list of mysteries, I guess. Let's hope a proper meal will straighten my head out."

Allie gazed at the dancing flame of her lantern. She'd stopped caring about how it would look carrying a lit lantern through the streets at irregular times of day. It was simply more important to her that she had access to Wick whenever he showed up. And, of course, seemingly from the moment she'd made that decision, Wick had chosen to make himself scarce. She'd gone so far as to run down to the Maskers' shop and relight the flame, but in doing so, they'd informed her roughly of what little was known of Fel's situation and that Wick would not be available until more was known. Thus, she was doubly dedicated to keeping an eye on the flame. A stationary flame meant an update on her friend, and meant she'd have a brief opportunity to collect her thoughts enough to voice them.

That was the side effect she hadn't anticipated when Wick became a part of her life. She supposed it would have happened with anyone who was there during her more private moments and willing to lend an ear. But talking out her problems had a way of collecting her thoughts together and revealing with clarity things that had previously been formless and abstract. In his absence, she had even considered keeping a diary, but her more frugal side insisted the time and materials necessary were worth more than the indefinable benefit they would provide.

She filled a tankard for a man and gently reminded him that he wouldn't be getting another until he paid his tab. With a sweep of the tavern, she took note of three similarly indebted individuals. Then her eyes flicked to one of the two doors in the back. Verfessa's door was now shut tight. He'd slipped into his "office."

"Time for the decision already, is it?" she mused to herself.

"What's that?" Oovay said, half paying attention, which was about as much attention as he ever paid.

"Nothing. I just need to do a walk-through, make sure we don't have any thirsty people in our private rooms," Allie said.

"I didn't notice anyone come in," said Oovay.

"Yeah, that's the idea of them being private. Catch up, Oovay. With the new boss of two minds on when I can and can't work, you're going to need to figure out how to take up the slack."

She grabbed a tray and loaded up a glass and one of Verfessa's private bottles. The second private room was empty, as usual. When she slipped into the first, she found Verfessa just getting comfortable in his chair.

"Attentive as always," Verfessa said.

"I try," she said, setting down his drink.

"Am I the only one you've been attentive to? Because attention is a lot like butter. You can't have too much of it, but if you don't spread it around, you'll really spoil what could be a good and proper meal."

"Mr. Verfessa, as much as I'd love to hear you stretch this turn of phrase until it screams, there are some things that need to be said, and I'd rather not spend too much time saying them."

He laughed and slapped the table. "Get to it, then."

"You want me to keep an eye on Madritz, right?"

"I do."

"Well, that's turning out to be really easy because she's taken a very keen interest in my life. Keen enough that she's willing to ruin it if I don't keep an eye on you."

"I can't say that surprises me. I'm an interesting fellow. What's her offer?"

"Her offer? She's holding my life hostage. Either I do what she wants and I get to keep earning enough money to live, or I don't and I get chased out of this cozy little hole I've dug out for myself."

"I certainly hope you're not here planning to negotiate a counteroffer out of me. I like you, but there's plenty of people I liked who spend their holidays telling very mean stories about the things I had to do when they left me without an option."

"I'm not that dumb. She'll make my life miserable if she doesn't get her way. I get the feeling you'll make my life *end* if you don't get *your* way."

He tipped his head side to side, considering the assessment. "I wouldn't say that'd be the first thing on the negotiating table. But it'd be there waiting if things got unpleasant enough." He fished a fat coin out of his pocket and started rolling the coin down along his fingers and back again. "So how is this going to go?"

"I'm here talking to you, aren't I?"

"And I appreciate that. I always enjoy our chats. But I am curious who else will be graced by your sparkling conversation and what you might discuss."

"I can't get around talking to Madritz. She's my boss and my landlord. I don't know what sort of questions she's going to have, but we've got to assume she's going to have a few about you, since she'd have to be a fool not to realize I'm talking to you right now." She rubbed her neck. "I'm reasonably sure she hasn't found a way to spy on this room, by the way."

"Oh, I'm more than reasonably sure about that. Remember, you're not the only one I've got in this place."

"As it stands right now, I don't have to keep much from her. I don't know much of anything about you."

"You'd be surprised how valuable what little you know about me could be to a woman like her. And what little you know about her could be to me. But before we get into it, we'll start where we ought to start. Did you happen to notice if she's got anyone watching her back?"

"She does. Sturdy fellow. Mercenary type. Leather armor. Nothing distinguishing about it. Cloth mask hiding his face."

"Did what you could see of his face ring any bells?"

"As a matter of fact, he did seem familiar. Couldn't quite place him, though. Just a big, intimidating fellow."

"No shortage of them around here. Doesn't narrow things down much." He drained half his cup. "Not to wander too far off the path we're on, but are you familiar with Robards stables?"

"Only that the stable hands come in here every now and then. Some of the more fragrant and heavily scarred people I'm willing to let through our doors."

"They're a little way out west of town. I know the fellows that keep those places stocked up. Mostly its oats and hay. Sometimes some dry mash. But lately? Venison and assorted offal. What do you suppose that means?"

"Either the horses have developed peculiar tastes, or they're keeping something a little more exotic in there."

"I agree. And seeing as how the meaty orders started coming through right around when Madritz showed up, I'm thinking there's a pretty clear answer to why someone would want to keep a meat-hungry steed a secret."

"That mercenary is a rider of some sort of Greater Mystic," Allie said. "And we've had at least three of those in the area in the last few months."

"All three after the Maskers, in one way or another," Verfessa said. "Does that narrow down the bell this face rung?"

She rubbed her eyes. "It's... what's his name... Questor. The griffin rider. The one that chased Fel back when you persuaded me to go after him. And that Velonia's got him following her all the way to my *home* means you're not the only one who might have 'kill the pesky barmaid' on the list of offers and counteroffers."

"I'm not saying that. But if you think that? I'd call that insightful rather than paranoid. Now, anyone with the skill and resources she plainly has should know I don't stick a knife in the back of everybody who comes to do business. You come with a good deal, and I'm happy to have you. You come with a bad deal or no deal at all but behave yourself, and I'll do the same. So the fact that she brought a heavy hitter means she's got plans she thinks'll go over very poorly if they're found out. That or going over poorly is part of the plan."

"As the woman in the center of this mess, that doesn't fill me with confidence."

"What we have here is two people staring at each other across the dance floor, waiting for each other to take the first step out and start the dance proper. Me? I don't like the music they're playing. Particularly not since she picked the tune."

"So what comes next?"

He laughed. "If you came in here expecting to walk away with orders, we both figured each other wrong."

"I don't want orders, but some advice would be nice."

"Oh, that's different." He took a sip. "We'll start with this. You don't want to kill her. First, on general principle. Take it from me. You get blood on your hands, even a single drop, and it starts leaving stains on everything you cherish most. But second, because she's just doing business. Even if you're doing it to protect yourself, there's nothing she's up to that'd justify violence in the eyes of the sort of people who dole out justice. And then there's the fact that she's ready for it. And the fact that there's plenty more people willing to do business if there's money in it, so they'll just send another."

"I wasn't really planning on killing anyone. But what are the other options?"

He rocked his chair a bit. "She's sharp, she's clever, but that's not why she is where she is. You're every bit as sharp and clever as her, and, no offense, you're not where she is. Not yet, anyway. She's where she is because of connections. That's where she gets her resources; that's where she gets her authority. And that's the only thing that gets her to back off."

"So I have to get her superiors to call her off?"

"It'd work."

"I don't like that idea."

"If I liked it, I'd have my crew working on it as we speak. It's where you have to hit her. You find a better way, you take it. But I'm keeping you from your rounds. I know things get rowdy when you're not there to keep order. And I am an investor in this place, even if I'm not so fond of the owner anymore. I don't cut off noses to spite faces. Tends to leave a lot of angry, misshapen faces around with axes to grind and bad senses of smell."

"You missed your calling, Mr. Verfessa," she said, heading for the door. "You should have been a poet."

Fel felt like a new man as he marched the streets. He owed part of that feeling to having had a hot bath for the first time in as far back as he could remember. The rest was owed to the reality that "as far back as he could remember" was approximately three hours. He should have known better than to trust his past self's assessment that he would soon recover from whatever had happened to his mind. Anyone stupid enough to get his brains scrambled shouldn't be trusted to know how long it will take to unscramble them. In truth, he probably should have been more concerned, but the anxiety that a sane person would feel after waking in a strange place simply wasn't there. Perhaps it was another side effect of whatever had done this to him. Perhaps he simply wasn't a sane person.

Instead of dissolving into a panicking wreck, he used his fresh eyes to take in Clickspring. There was a soothing familiarity to the place, even if nothing specific about it leaped out to him as home. The buildings had a shape that seemed right. Mostly low to the ground but promising the same deep and well-constructed basements of his own home. But much like his own head, it was strangely empty. During his walk to his appointment with his patron, which required handwritten directions from Mr. Wick like he was a child sent for a loaf of bread, he saw only one other person. There were no horses on the streets, no other pedestrians. Even the typical wildlife of a city setting was notably absent. No birds. Not even the droppings telling the tale of where they liked to perch.

His journey to the patron's house was a short one, mostly along the city's main street. If he wasn't afraid he'd lose his way if he wandered too far from the directions he was given, he would have liked to explore the city a little more. A dozen streets branched off the main thoroughfare. Most of them seemed to be under heavy construction, though just as was the case elsewhere, there was very little in the way of actual activity. Blocks of fresh-cut stone, excavated from the ground and waiting to be used to assemble the aboveground portion of a new home, stood in orderly piles with no sign of workers. The sound of swinging picks revealed a single crew chipping away at the rocky ground at the end of one of the streets.

He felt a shift on his back. Oiler was leaning toward one of the incomplete construction sites. All through the walk, it had been doing so, like a dog sniffing at a sausage dangling tantalizingly off the edge of a table.

"Easy, pal," he said, pulling the straps a little tighter. "You and I are sticking together until my head clears out. If I'm meeting with the one paying my way through an expensive town like this, I want the one thing that I recognize to be there with me. You're a big brass security blanket for the time being."

The street ended, splitting into two curving roads that ran perpendicular to it. The roads wrapped around what could only be the center of the city. It was a towering wall on a small hill. He couldn't tell what was behind it, but the soft squeak and clack of operating machinery suggested it was some manner of very large mechanism. He took the left fork until he found a relatively modest building that seemed to have been built into the wall itself in lieu of a gate, which was absent elsewhere. A gleaming placard, completely free of patina, proclaimed the place to be "The Lens Conservatory."

"Time for a meeting with the boss," Fel said.

He approached the door, which opened before he could knock. He'd expected to find a butler like Mr. Wick holding it open, but there was none. Instead, a set of complex linkages near the hinges indicated the door was operated remotely or automatically. Probably not the latter. If one wished to have a door that would open on its own when someone approached, one could simply not have a door at all.

"Ah. Mr. Masker. Punctual as always."

The voice startled him. It was tinny and unnatural and seemed to be coming from multiple directions at once.

"You'll find me in my office. Do hurry. We have much to discuss."

Toward the end of the statement, Fel finally spotted a delicate grill emerging from a long metal pipe tucked in the corner between the wall and ceiling. A soft blue light glowed behind the grill. That was the source of the voice. A bit like the innards of a music box, but presumably amplifying the voice of someone elsewhere in the house.

"Why are rich people always so strange?" he muttered almost silently, just in case the speaking contraption was a listening one as well.

The front door shut, confirming its remote control, and a door at the end of the hall opened. At least that would save him the trouble of asking which of the dozen or so doors visible from the entryway was the office. He paced down the hall toward it and tried to ignore the increasing sequence of nudges his mind was giving him. The anxiety that had thus far been held at bay for whatever reason was beginning to seep through. This was by any reasonable measure a wealthy person's home. It was small and discreet only in a relative sense. Certainly the wall dwarfed it, and most of the houses on the main street were larger, but it remained far in excess of the needs of anyone short of an elected official expecting to host committee meetings or a wealthy socialite hoping to impress his friends. In either case, it was standard procedure to fill every nook and cranny with signs of wealth and status. This Mr. Lens character had followed that procedure dutifully. Knickknacks, figurines, and paintings, anything that would cost a fortune to commission or collect, were arrayed with little regard to taste or style. They were there to be noticed, not to accentuate the home or convey meaning. That much was to be expected. But something else was not.

They were all new. Perfect, unblemished. Like they'd been completed that morning. There wasn't anything overtly wrong with it, but something deep in Fel's mind insisted that none of those things should look that pristine. Even when restored, something like that ballerina dancing box would have the hint of darkness in the crevices. One almost sought that. It was a sign of age, and it provided a visual contrast that made the details pop. Seeing these things perfect and untarnished made them look flat. Artificial. The depth and certainty of this knowledge combined with the fuzzy blur of the more specific memories surrounding it made him profoundly uncomfortable, less like he was suffering from amnesia and more like someone had gone through and censored his mind of offending knowledge.

Fel tried to push those thoughts back from whence they came and stepped through the open door. Immediately upon entering, he was struck by a new assault from his increasingly troublesome brain. This room felt awfully familiar. Not in the comforting, albeit eerie, way of the rest of the town. He felt a jolt of concern the instant he stepped inside, like some earlier version of him had been fixated on leaving such a room rather than entering it. For the life of him, he couldn't imagine why. There was nothing overtly frightening about the room itself. It was rather dim, most of the light coming from behind a strange wooden screen with gear-shaped holes that divided the room in half. This painted the rear wall with stationary, fuzzy-edged duplicates of the same shape. He squinted through the holes and saw only the vague silhouette of the man waiting on the other side.

"Something wrong, Mr. Masker?" Lens asked.

The voice was now free of the tinny distortion of the strange contraption but remained faintly concerning. He spoke in a perfectly calm, measured manner. Like the first read-through of a script before the actor attempted to layer in any emotion or performance.

"Having a little trouble thinking," he said, sliding Oiler to the floor and taking a seat in the only chair on his side of the screen.

"Still? That is unfortunate. I had warned you about those defensive mechanisms. Best that you keep to the primary task from now on."

"What can I say? I tend to let my mind wander. It's taking its sweet time wandering back this time."

"Very clever wordplay, Mr. Masker. But let us address the current focus of your patronage."

"Right. Right. Something about a clockwork diamond, correct?" he said.

"You've remembered that much. That is heartening."

"Mr. Wick reminded me."

"Ah. Then you will require a refresh?"

"If you're willing."

"Of course. The clockwork diamond was always intended to be the pride and joy of Clickspring. In a far more literal sense than usual, it is the crown jewel of our fine city. But despite the considerable skills of our artisans, we were forced to accept that the expertise did not exist within our staff to complete it to our desired level of functionality. The natural conclusion was that we should call upon the expertise of some of the region's finest contraptioneers. The Masker family already had an estate within the city's walls, so it was simple enough to call upon their favored son to return and complete the construction of the diamond."

"And that's me," Fel said.

"Quite so."

"What's the clockwork diamond do?" he asked.

"Presently, not nearly as much as it should."

He rolled his eyes. "Fine. What's it supposed to do?"

"If you step through the rear exit of my home, you will find the workshop with the schematics."

"Why aren't you telling me?"

"Because I don't know what it does or how it does it, Mr. Masker. Contrary to what you, in your diminished state, may believe, I am not the one who designed the contraption. I am merely the one financing and overseeing its construction."

"You're paying me to make a thing, but you don't know what the thing is?"

"It is grand, and it is one of only two in the world. That is enough."

"Yeah, that's definitely a rich person sort of thinking," Fel mumbled.

"I imagine you'll want some more time to recover before resuming work."

"I'd say so," he said.

He considered remarking that for both of their sakes, they'd better hope that this much-vaunted expertise was one of the things lurking behind his mental haze, but he thought better of it. If this person was the source of his money in what was plainly a very expensive town, pointing out he only had the vaguest notions about how contraptions worked right now was probably a poor financial decision.

"Maybe you can help speed things along. There are some things about this town that don't make much sense to me. Why is it so empty?"

"Rising hostilities have driven some of the less stalwart members of the town to better fortified locations. Though it is my hope that we will see this town rise to be the capital of the republic, it is quite recently founded. These things take time."

"Clickspring," Fel said. "Recently founded."

The two statements didn't make sense beside one another in his mind. Like "tiny mountain" or "slight pregnancy."

"Yes. I think we've come quite far in the seventeen years since our groundbreaking on the centennial of the republic."

Fel shut his eyes. The feeling of confusion and dismay was growing more intense by the moment. It would have been bad enough if he'd known why he felt so anxious, but he didn't. It was like someone he trusted was shouting a warning in another language. He didn't know what the trouble was, only that there was trouble. And there was a lot of it.

"I think I should go. I'm sorry to cut this short," Fel said, standing up and grabbing Oiler.

"You are a master contraptioneer. You are far too valuable to lose to over-work when you are ailing."

He paused. Not unlike the indication that Clickspring was new, the indication that Fel Masker was a master contraptioneer struck the ear wrong. But unlike the other non sequitur, this one was a pleasant little stroke to the ego. In the absence of sanity and reason, flattery was an acceptable balm for one's mental state. He wasn't too proud to admit he wouldn't mind another dose of it.

"I suppose I could grab the schematics and bring them home. Maybe looking them over will get the juices flowing. You know, since I'm a master, and that's the sort of thing that's as much intuition as anything else."

"The documents aren't precisely portable. But you are welcome to visit the workshop and look them over."

The door behind him opened. Elsewhere in the house, he heard a second, much larger door open. There was no sense asking why Lens used a complex, contraption-based parlor trick to run his house rather than having a servant or opening his own doors like a normal person. The wealthy found ways to one-up one another, and this was clearly his method of choice.

Fel stood and paced through the otherwise empty home. The second set of doors that had opened, a set of double doors, were directly opposite the entryway. He stepped through. It wasn't so much a room as a second foyer. Hooks lined the walls, hung with bags of equipment and assorted work gear: shoulder-length gloves with grease stains, long leather aprons, lanterns. Everything someone might need to tote around to work on something too large or too stationary to be brought into a workshop. The doors behind swung shut. The doors ahead opened to the courtyard beyond the wall.

Fel's eyes widened in awe.

There it was. The clockwork diamond. For a man who clearly valued contraptions in all their forms, there was no question this was the sort of thing Lens would pay any price to have in his collection. It was simply breathtaking. Carefully cut, shaped, and beveled sheets of glass or crystal formed the innumerable facets of its namesake. But the contraption made a true diamond seem simple and mundane in comparison. First was its size. The thing was massive. As tall as a mighty oak tree, and at its widest point, it reached at least as far as such a tree's branches. But more impressive was the motion. Most gems sparkled with the slightest motion, catching the light as it shifted through the impossibly intricate paths of refraction. This contraption was dizzying in its glittery, shimmering glory. Each facet was articulated, affixed to the end of a strut or linkage that was itself polished to a brilliant shine. The monument to complexity clicked and ticked to an internal rhythm, facets sinking shy of their neighbors, rotating in place, and pushing forward again. The facets formed rings, which rotated as whole, alternating the direction clockwise and counterclockwise. Beneath them, a secondary set of rings shifted, and when the crystal panels aligned, he could get the briefest of glimpses of further rings hidden deeper inside. There were even moments when the rings seemed to exchange facets between them, shifting diagonally or vertically.

Fel didn't know how long he'd been transfixed by the sight of it. Long enough that the sun had visibly shifted in the sky. He blinked his eyes. They burned as if he'd neglected to blink for all that time.

"What was... what was I..." he muttered, looking at his feet.

The Oiler pack, which he didn't recall dropping to the ground, was resting there. The contraption's serpentlike head was tucked into the pack, its eyes fixed on the same display as Fel. Finally, he shook from his near-trance sufficiently to question something.

He had only the most tenuous grip on most everything since he'd woken up. But for some reason he remembered quite a bit about Oiler and its quirks. It was designed, and dedicated, to repairing that which was broken. Fel didn't know for sure at the moment how it treated things that were incomplete, which the diamond supposedly was. But he very much suspected it should have done more than just stare for all that time. It had even stopped clicking at the puzzle box. The only indication that it could still move at all was the subtle, subdued shift and click of its claws, like someone doing calculations in their head. Oiler was, after however long it had been, still attempting to understand it.

Fel hauled the pack onto his back again and avoided looking directly at the clockwork diamond. The courtyard had three covered workshop stations. He made his way to the nearest of them. What he'd assumed was just one of three identical stations—something this big was bound to have multiple crews working on it at any given time if it needed to be completed or repaired—he discovered that the schematics in place were quite plainly only a subset of the total collection. And they were volumes deep, encompassed by six thick leather-bound books, at least triple the height and width of the kind of books on a normal library shelf. A seventh lay open. He swept his eyes across the page.

"Volume twenty-three, section seven hundred fifty-six: Tandem motion and cadence adjustment," he muttered. "The instructions to build this thing are a whole wing of a library."

He started to flip through the pages. The drawings weren't wholly incomprehensible. He knew he'd seen things like them before. When he reached the third page, one entirely filled with complex assembly instructions, some things began to dislodge his mind from its current state. It became clear to him why, even with instructions like this to work from, standard workers would struggle to assemble the thing. The procedures were written in a sort of shorthand. Common assemblies and standard types of cogs and pinions were called by names referencing their inventors, or their first usages. By far the most frequent shorthand was classifying a mechanism by its most common usage. One would have had to work with contraptions for a lifetime to have the context necessary to decode these instructions without stopping to research items every few sentences. He knew a handful of them, but he was certain his father would have known them all.

His father. It was a brief flash, something he snuck up on from behind rather than latching on to consciously, but suddenly he had an image of his father in his mind after being unable to remember much of anything else. That thought shook a few more free of the mist. Most were swallowed back again, but one was as undeniable as it was unsettling. The language he had been reading, the one every word of the instructions was written in, was not his own. It was one he could barely recognize, classified in his mind as "ancient" and "inscrutable." And yet he understood it. Every word.

The realization made his skin crawl, stabbing him in the pit of his stomach with the same creeping fear of someone in pitch-black darkness who has just heard the low rumble of a predator. Somehow, discovering a piece of this place had slid into position in his head at the same moment that some part of a forgotten history had asserted itself had served to wash away whatever was holding the concern over his situation at bay. He had to find out what was happening and why.

<h1 style="text-align:center">Chapter 9</h1>

Tome snapped the reins of the cart and tried to keep his eyes fixed on the gates of the city ahead. The ride had been long and slower than the trip to Fenfield. It was well past midnight, and he was fighting to stay awake. That, to his dismay, wasn't the main reason he was so faithfully watching the road ahead.

Parch bleated reproachfully. Until today, Tome had not known it was possible to bleat reproachfully, but he'd been enduring it since the moment he'd chosen to head back to the city rather than risk it all to follow Fel. The little unicorn's judgmental stare felt like it was jabbing Tome directly in the soul. He couldn't bear to make eye contact again.

"Have you determined how you will explain the current situation to Euphoria?" Wick asked.

"It has occupied my mind, yes."

"And what conclusion did you come to?"

"She's going to be angry. I'm hoping she directs most of her anger in constructive directions and not at... me. Particularly because it is the opposite of my fault that this happened to Fel."

"It is possible she will be angry at Fel, or herself, for not adequately preparing for or preventing this outcome."

"That's acceptable. As long as she's not mad at me." He glanced at the lantern, carefully avoiding the piercing blue eyes of the unicorn. "And I say that not out of cowardice. I say that out of concern for Fel. One way or another, I just know I'm the one who will be sent in to save him, and if she gets mad at me, it means I won't be able to learn any more or get any additional resources. So I hope to avoid her fury for Fel's sake. Cowardice is at best a secondary motivation."

"And, if I may inquire, have you planned for the possibility that you might be intercepted by agents of the Graves family and never have the opportunity to engage with Euphoria?"

Tome's eyes darted about until they fixed on what was undoubtedly the motivation for that question. Lattica was rapidly approaching from a side road.

Tome didn't know precisely what her plans were, but Lattica wasn't typically deployed for diplomatic reasons.

"Where is he?" she shouted when she was near enough to be heard.

"You are aware of where we were headed, yes?" Tome said.

"To Fenfield, like everyone told you not to."

"Well, I'm afraid Fel may have learned precisely why you'd recommended caution."

"He's sick?" she said.

"He never returned from the field."

"I was afraid of this. And you? How are you feeling?"

"No ill effects from the field, but I was much more cautious than Fel."

"A drunk boar is more cautious than Fel. Come on. We're seeing Euphoria." She turned her horse and guided him along a side street, notably heading in a different direction than he knew the Graves compound to be.

"Where are we going?"

"Euphoria fully expected this whole thing to go wrong, so she started the ball rolling on getting help in some other way. She's in the process as we speak."

"She expected Fel to get lost in the field?"

"No. Believe it or not she actually thought the two of you would wise up and come back empty-handed. I guess she never had to go on a mission with her brother, or she would have known better." Lattica shook her head. "I should have come along. Maybe I could have physically dragged him away from the field if he got too curious."

"Why didn't you?"

"Euphoria wanted me to, but the family wouldn't allow it. This isn't a Graves issue; it's a Masker one."

"The two families are related."

"By a single link in a single chain."

"And you're trying to forge a stronger allegiance."

"I'm not the one you should be trying to convince. I'm with you on this. As much as I can be. Technically I'm of the opinion you should have just let us handle it. But what's done is done, and just so you know, Euphoria has been busy."

They took another turn, now heading along a side road toward the north road out of the city.

"Where are we going?" he asked.

"Someplace no one outside of the Graves family has been. They thought they'd be letting Fel in. Like you said, at least he's got a blood connection to a Graves. Now it's going to be you. There's going to be a lot of angry old folks when this is said and done..."

As the sun began to rise, Allie trudged up the street to Masker's Antiquities. She'd gotten precious little sleep last night. Fear and doubt were no strangers to her, but the sheer volume of both had begun to tease at the frayed ends of her nerves to the point that a good night of rest wasn't really possible. Thus, she hadn't so much woken up early to run this little errand as abandoned attempting to get back to sleep once the sun peeked through the windows. She carried her lantern with her and hoped that Vivian Masker was at her place behind the counter despite it being well before the start of her business day. As she took the last few steps toward the door, voices croaked from the rooftops.

"Rat monkey thief?" cooed Judy the lesser harpy sweetly.

The others, previously snoozing with heads tucked under wings, perked up and added in their usual attempts at negotiation:

"Give me back that pie, or I swear I'll filth!" said Moody.

"Ow! That's my ear, you flying pig!" added Rudy.

"They're not so bad," remarked Toody.

Allie raised her eyebrows. "You four are starting to become real sweet-talkers, you know that?"

She tugged a bundle of cloth from her pocket and set down the lantern to unwrap the layers. All four harpies dropped down to the street and watched with obedient interest as she revealed her offering. Up close, she was able to see just how much more substantial they'd become in the last few months. She remembered them as scrawny and half-starved, but the daily doting they'd been extorting from the Maskers and others had put some meat on their bones.

"I know you prefer the bread and sweets, but money's been tight. It's just a bit of gristle and fat that I couldn't stomach from last night's dinner. I hope that'll do."

They hopped up to the pile and, one by one, pulled away strips of scrap.

"That'll teach ya!" piped Judy before dragging her share back to the rooftops.

The others gathered the rest, and she was permitted to approach the Maskers' shop unharrassed.

"All right. Not so picky about their cuts of meat. Good to know," she said.

She reached the door and tested it, but it was still braced from the inside. Leaning close and peering through the window revealed that while Vivian was not present, there was a smoldering lantern visible on a shelf. It wasn't the fancy one that stayed lit without fuel, and Vivian was far too frugal and sensible to leave an unattended flame burning all night in the shop. That, coupled with the open door and hatch to the lower level confirmed she was in the process of moving herself up to the shop and just happened to be down below at the moment. Allie shielded the window from the glare of the rising sun until she could spot a clock on the shelves. Still plenty of time before she was expected to arrive at The Fox and Log. She'd wait and hope Vivian showed up soon and was willing to chat.

Allie leaned against the wall and checked her lantern to see if the flame had gone still. It had not. Just as it hadn't in far too long. Her mind eagerly fell back into the rut it had dug itself, running through the different possibilities to fix her life and maybe extract a measure of revenge on Madritz for threatening to shake it to pieces. She made approximately zero progress in that regard before a merry clop of hooves drew her attention to a familiar, sleek two-person delivery carriage.

"Great minds think alike," Allie murmured.

"Morning, sweeties!" called Mariss from the seat of the carriage. She hopped down, draped a cloth across her forearm, and raised it up. "Come on. Come on," she prompted, tugging the checkered cloth from the top of a basket on the unused second seat.

Judy flitted down from the roof and landed on her arm.

"There you go," Mariss said, her voice dripping with honey as she pulled a bun from the basket and held it in a flat, open palm.

The lesser harpy plucked it from her hand and tipped back her head to shift it a bit more solidly into her grasp. She spread her wings to take off again.

"Uh, uh, uh," Mariss said. "What do you say?"

Judy dropped the bun back in her palm. "I'll have your guts for that," Judy said, with as much gratitude in her tone as the creature could manage.

"Good enough. Off you go," Mariss said.

The others came down, one at a time, and received their treats. The closest any of them came to saying thank you was Rudy, who crooned, "Serves you right!"

She dusted off her palm and folded the cloth into her apron. Allie paced up to her.

"Look at you. Got them doing tricks now, like a fairy-tale princess," Allie said.

"Oh!" Mariss said with a start. "You surprised me. Good morning! What brings you to the shop?"

She held up the lantern. "I have a lantern here that needs looking at. And you?"

"I try to bring them a little something now and then," she said, fetching the basket. "Is she in?"

"I think she's in the middle of something, but she should be along in a minute or two."

The pair was silent for a moment, simply standing and waiting.

"You want to start with the questions, or should I?" Allie said.

"Have you heard from him? About him?" Mariss said anxiously, gushing with worry now that she'd been given permission.

"Last I heard, he was meeting with his sister up north. But that was a while ago. I haven't heard anything bad, but I haven't heard anything good either."

"I hope he's all right," she said, her forehead creased with concern. "And what about you? How have you been? I've stopped by The Fox and Log a few times when I was sure you'd be there, and you weren't. Not feeling well? Do you need anything?"

"I have a new boss, and she's a problem," Allie said. "Money is going to be tight until I figure out how to deal with it."

"I can probably get my father to hire you at the bakery. Now that I'm doing more baking, I can't work the counter as well as I once did. I hate to say it, but in my part of town, the folks looking for work tend to come from wealthy families and aren't terribly accustomed to, er..."

"Working?" Allie said.

"More or less. We'd be happy to have someone who knows how to handle herself and an irate customer or two. Much like the employees, the customers in my part of town can be difficult."

"I appreciate the offer, Mariss, but I'm not interested in charity," Allie said.

"It'd be charity if I offered to just give you money. I'm offering you a job."

"Even so. I'd prefer to get through this on my own. Or as on my own as I can manage."

"It's your life to live," Mariss said.

Allie gave her a weary look. "But..."

"But you and I both know that Fel had a terrible way of not wanting people to help him, and we both know how much help he needed."

"Are you saying I have the same problem?"

"Yep!" Mariss said pleasantly. "I'm glad you're aware of it. Saves me the trouble of trying to find a way to word it so I don't hurt your feelings."

Allie simmered for a moment. The mere indication that Mariss's words would have hurt her feelings filled her with a bolt of irritation that, she was smart enough to realize, completely confirmed that notion. Best to keep quiet on the topic and avoid proving her right.

Fortunately, Vivian chose that moment to show up in the shop. She unbraced the door and let Allie and Mariss inside.

"Breakfast, courtesy of Divinity's Oven!" Mariss said, raising the basket.

"Thank you so much, as always," Vivian said.

She took the basket and set it down, then cast a quick glance at the lantern behind her. A second glance fixed on the lantern Allie was holding.

"Always nice to have a visit from you, Allie. What brings you here today?"

"You loaned me this old lantern here, and I've gotten a great bit of use out of it. But I've been having some trouble."

Vivian nodded.

"The flame has been a little lackluster lately, hasn't it?" Vivian said. "We're having similar trouble around here. The wick just isn't doing its job like it used to. I'd love to fix it, but Martin's got some rather important projects at present that require all we can spare in terms of replacement wicks. You'll just have to make do. Though if it's anything like the last time we had this problem, after a few days, things took care of themselves."

Allie nodded. Wick wasn't absent, simply too busy elsewhere. The message was both loud and clear and skillfully hidden. Allie wasn't sure she agreed that the subterfuge was called for, considering Mariss had to have been at least as trusted by the family as she was. Nevertheless, this was a shop with an open door. There was no telling who might overhear their secrets if she said them plain.

"And Fel? How is he?" Mariss said.

"Fel's fine," Vivian said. "By now he's met with his sister. You know the friction that those two have had, even if things have smoothed a bit since then. I'm sure the reunion has been rocky. We'll hear from him again soon enough."

There was something off about her tone. Allie's eyebrow shifted imperceptibly. Not so imperceptibly that it didn't earn a brief moment of eye contact from Vivian.

Mariss touched her chest with her hand and took a cleansing breath.

"That is a huge weight off. Thank you so much!" She turned and spotted the same large clock Allie had. "By the High, is that the time? I should really get going. An early start today. Mr. Royland is having his anniversary party, and we'll be supplying enough pastries to feed half the gentry all by ourselves. Have a wonderful day, both of you!"

Allie lingered while Mariss took her leave. While the baker wasn't nearly as naive as Allie had thought a few months ago, she was still quite eager to believe what she wanted to believe. She'd completely missed the crack in Vivian's veneer of certainty when discussing Fel. Before Allie had even turned back to face her, Vivian spoke again.

"You might want to take the lantern down to Martin. If you have a moment, that is," she said.

"You think he can fix it after all?"

Vivian looked down to consult her ledger for the day. "No. I suspect he cannot. But maybe you should see him regardless."

"I think I have a moment," Allie said.

She made her way down the stairs. Then down another flight, and another. She didn't encounter Mr. Masker until she reached the very lowest level. His workshop. He raised his head to see who was visiting him. The motion brought a wince of pain to his face, as though he'd not changed position in hours. The question of how someone could have been sitting still at one's workbench long enough to be cramped was answered by the haggard look on his face. He was beyond exhausted. It wasn't the look of someone who had worked long and hard and worn themselves out. It was the look of someone who, not unlike herself, had seemingly lost the capacity for sleep.

"Allie," he said.

"It's bad, isn't it?" Allie said.

Mr. Masker lacked his wife's capacity for hiding the contents of her mind when she spoke. His every concern was written across his face. He knew it and didn't bother lying to her. Almost from the first word, she wished he'd done her the mercy of holding back, if only a bit.

"He's missing, Allie," Martin said. "He's *still* missing. The device I made for him couldn't lead him as far as he needed it to. His sister couldn't persuade him not to go where he shouldn't go. Wick wasn't there to answer any questions he might have had. A thousand things had to go wrong for us to get this far. And they all have."

"Fel's a clever man. And strong. I'm sure whatever has happened, he can handle it."

"He can handle quite a bit," Martin said. "But Wick hasn't come back yet, which means there's no news, good or bad, about him. No motion at all."

"I see," Allie said solemnly. "How are the others? Tome? Parch? Euphoria?"

"They're fine. Fel went to the danger. The danger did not come to them."

She narrowed her eyes. "Tome's fine and you don't know where Fel is? Why isn't Tome looking for him?" she said sharply.

"The nature of the threat is..." He paused. "Tome made the right decision."

"And what are you doing? Besides torturing yourself."

He tapped the array of pages on his workbench. "The contraption I built for him, entirely of my own design, started to malfunction. It was why he had to make up his own mind about where to go. It's why he is where he is. I've been trying to work out what the flaw was with enough precision to work out how to fix it. There needs to be a way to lead him in the proper direction if he shows back up again."

"When he shows back up again," she corrected.

"Yes. Of course. But I can't find the exact nature of the flaw. I can find a plausible reason for it to behave as it had, but not a solid, concrete reason that I can act upon. And of course I can't. If my knowledge is incomplete enough to insert the flaw, what chance have I to discover the solution?"

He placed his palms on the workbench and peered down at the pages. "I allowed myself to believe I understood principles that had been lost for centuries. I allowed myself to believe I understood them well enough to wield them in novel ways. To build something critical to my child's safety. And now this."

"You can't beat yourself up about this, Mr. Masker."

"Oh? If not me, then who?" he asked. "I am the only one in the world with the skill to bungle things this badly. If I'd been a bit more of a fool, the blasted thing wouldn't have worked well enough to get him that far. If I'd been a bit wiser, it would have worked well enough to get him where he was supposed to go."

"You have an implausible life. That sort of thing is going to make finding plausible solutions difficult."

He nodded dully. He straightened up, a soft collection of complaints from his spine ringing out as he did so. "I'm sorry. I've been so lost in this. Where were my manners? Can I help you?"

Allie released a single, dry laugh. "Mr. Masker, you have enough to worry about. Now that I know Wick is still waiting for the good news before he delivers it, I'm satisfied. Let my problems be the furthest thing from your mind. I'll see you when all this blows over. I'm sure Fel will have a brand-new and very colorful tale to tell when it does."

"Thank you, Allie. Have a good day. You should probably hurry along. For all we know, this implausibility of ours is contagious."

"See you soon, Mr. Masker."

"See you, Allie."

She turned to climb the steps. Behind her, before she was too far to hear him, his voice murmured distantly.

"Implausible... Implausible."

Two hours of additional riding brought Tome and Lattica to their destination. It was an unassuming cabin, dug into a steep mountain slope in a sparsely wooded section of the region north of the city. The cabin wasn't the sort of place one would stumble upon, but neither was it terribly well hidden. There was a road leading directly to its door, the very road they'd been riding along all this way. The same road led to a logging encampment and what was evidently a very popular fishing spot. In Tome's estimation, it was the perfect way to keep something hidden, the precise midpoint of trying to tuck it away where no one would ever look and leaving it out in the open. Nothing about this place screamed secret stronghold. It wasn't hidden well enough. But the moment Lattica opened the door to let Tome and (to her dismay) Parch inside, that notion was banished from his head.

Two heavily armed men stood on either side of the entryway. The weapons they held were, to the best of Tome's knowledge, crossbows. But that was just a guess. They were certainly crossbow shaped, but the amount of machinery attached suggested they were some unholy evolution of the weapon that was at the very top of the nobility's "to be confiscated" list. He hadn't even seen them in the hands of the Bolivans or in the small assortment of contraband that the Maskers had added to their inventory. Tome endeavored to look as harmless as possible. He wasn't sure if Parch's presence was helping or hurting in that regard. The only other thing he carried was Wick's lantern, but they treated him as though he were wielding a battle-ax.

"At ease, you two," Lattica said. "He's a friend of the in-laws."

The words of support did little to ease the aggressive posture of the guards. Nor did the arrival of Euphoria.

"Men. I told you to expect this," she said sharply, placing herself between their weapons and Tome. She addressed him directly. "Where is Fel?"

"He went into Fenfield and didn't return."

She trembled with anger. "And you did? Without him?"

"If I'd gone after him, you never would have gotten the message of what happened to him," Tome said.

She tightened her fists and shut her eyes. It was the first time Tome could honestly say he saw anything of Fel in his sisters. The man had a temper, and from the look of it, a tiny shred of self-control was the only thing between him and an impressively similar amount of wrath from Euphoria. She composed herself.

"What can you tell me?" she asked.

"Not much more than I already have. He took Parch and a sample of Wick's flame with him. Parch came back with the flame. There was some minor evidence that Parch had been in a scuffle. That's all. No proof of any harm to Fel. No proof that he is safe either."

He took slow, deep breaths. Her eyes glistened with tears, but she didn't give the universe the satisfaction of making her truly cry.

"Follow me," she said.

"Where are we going?" Tome asked, pacing deeper into the cabin while Lattica and the guards stayed in the entryway.

"Where we should have gone first," she said.

He wasn't convinced he was any safer with Euphoria than he was with the men with the crossbows. The way forward turned out to be the way downward. Backed against a steep slope as it was, what appeared to be a relatively small cabin turned out to follow the Beffshire style of architecture and continued deeper into the heart of the mountain. It expanded into two successively larger floors chiseled out of the mountain, and finally ended in a door that sent a chill down Tome's spine. It was a perfect match for the doors in the Greater Lands Wall. The wall it was set into was comparatively fresh in its construction. The door itself was ancient. Bygone technology with a set of complex rings in its center.

The short journey had allowed a small slice of the pressure simmering within Euphoria to dissipate. She turned and gestured with her hand, motioning for Tome to hand over the lantern. She raised it to her face and glared directly at the stationary flame.

"How did this happen, Wick?" she asked.

"I do not know."

"You are a sentry lantern. Don't tell me you do not know."

"For the second time in my existence, I am ashamed to say I have been derelict in my duties. I have been working on a project with your father, and my dedication to advancing that project seized me."

"What is the project?"

"I do not believe your father would want you to know at this time. It could potentially endanger you."

She took another deep breath of the cool air through nostrils flared in anger. "If not for Fel's predicament, you'd better believe I'd be digging deeper into this. But first things first. Take a step back, please," she said. "And turn around. Tome, place yourself between Wick and the door. The Graves family needs to keep its secrets just as much as the Masker family needs to."

He did as he was told. A slow, deliberate sequence of rotating rings and shifting tiles signaled the entry of a complex Bygone Era unlocking code.

"That's enough. You can follow me," she said.

He turned to see a perfectly dark room ahead. He raised Wick's lantern. It was less of a room and more of a cell. Barely large enough for Euphoria, Tome, and Parch to enter, even with the door open. Heavy chains ran from the walls to a bust not unlike the one recovered from the Greater Lands but with visible signs of repair. Whoever repaired the bust lacked the finesse and nuance that Martin Masker applied to his projects. Replacement components were large and crude. Perched atop the bust, entirely intact and restored to a very high level of gloss and polish, was a mask. It wasn't the Student, nor was it the Warrior.

"The Diplomat..." Tome said.

"Correct. Because of the level of disrepair of our bust, the low quality of our repairs, and the uncertainty that future repairs would be possible if it were to further degrade, seeking council from the Diplomat is something the family only allows in the most dire of circumstances. Even if they'd known Fel was in danger while I was requesting a meeting with it, I don't believe they would have allowed it. We are here now because my father has demonstrated his ability to repair busts. Solving this problem was determined to be enough of a favor to the Maskers to warrant the eventual return favor of repairing and improving our bust. But I'll warn you now. Because of how poorly repaired this bust is, the messages that the mask is able to deliver are... not ideal."

"Why would anything be simple?" he asked.

"That should be emblazoned on the Masker family coat of arms," Euphoria said with weary resignation.

A single brass plate, one of the original pieces, hung down from the chest, dangling from a chain below the gap in the bust where it clearly was intended to reside.

"I will ask the questions. If you have something to say, whisper it to me and I will ask. We find it is better able to reply when the communication has a single focus. Wick, I'll ask you to observe closely. We may need you to repeat the contents of the conversation back to us."

"I will fulfill this service faithfully," Wick said.

"What value is there in asking a Diplomat for help in this instance?" Tome asked.

"The same value as asking a Student for help, as Father had been for quite some time. There is immeasurable wisdom and information locked within these masks. One need only sculpt one's thoughts into the proper form to unlock it," she explained. "Now let us begin."

She raised the plate and pressed it into place. It was a well-machined snap-fit. Once it was properly seated, a single glittering iris slid up into the empty eye.

"You seek guidance. Avoid conflict," said the mask.

The voice was almost inaudible. It sounded as though it was speaking from the end of a long pipe, resonating and rebounding on itself while a chorus of clicking and ticking did its level best to drown it out. Though only those five words were coherent, they were separated by long periods of soft clicking, making the end of a statement hard to determine. The overall effect was of some far away person transcribing a half-understood message, then speaking it aloud when enough of it was written down.

"Ambassador. In the past we have spoken of the disease that plagues Fenfield to the west. As before, we fear it may be the work of foreign agents. It has struck my own brother. He has entered the field and has not returned."

The clicking and ticking eventually produced the phrase: "Then, as before, the solution remains. Avoid the field. Illness does not pursue and has no agenda."

"The damage is done already. As you know, I have been hoping to broker a lasting partnership with my family of birth and my family by marriage. Because Fenfield lies within Graves territory, we fear the Maskers may blame the Graves family for what has befallen my brother and thus eliminate any chance of further partnership."

A long silence.

"Entering. Danger. Unwise. Motivation?" the mask uttered.

"It's starting," Euphoria said under her breath. "I'm surprised it took so long to drop to single words." She spoke up. "He was seeking a mask. The Student, specifically. It was in the possession of a foe who has repeatedly threatened the safety of the Graves and Masker families."

"Foe. Singular? Student. Danger? Limited. Warrior? Understandable. Student? Unwise."

"The question of whether it was wise to pursue the enemy into Fenfield is at this point irrelevant. The damage is done. And we feel that the best way forward is to find a way to liberate him from Fenfield without losing further members of our family or additional agents."

"Brother. Survival. Proof?"

"We don't know that he survived, but he is rather difficult to kill," Euphoria said steadily.

"Insufficient. Loss? Acceptable. Maskers? Truth. Establish. Clarify. Progress."

"This is not an acceptable loss. He is my brother!" she snapped. "It isn't even a loss. He is alive! I know it."

"Certainty? Impossible. Discuss. Debate. Moderate. Peace."

"You are suggesting I consider Fel lost and try to convince the family that it doesn't matter?"

"Matter? Yes. Sufficiently? No. War. Justified? No."

"He could be alive and you are suggesting he be sacrificed."

"Brother? Casualty. One. War? Casualties. Many. Peace. Preferable. Always. Unity. Preferable. Always."

"It isn't peace if it doesn't last. There is still a killer out there in possession of one of the masks. We need to rescue Fel. He's too important a soldier in the war that is already raging between whoever this rogue agent is and both of our families. And there's still the matter of whoever has been utilizing the flame without our say-so. I seek advice to properly counter the forces that oppose us."

"Peace. Lasting. Never. Freedom? Peace? Incompatible. Choice? War."

"Not this again."

"This? Yes. Again? No. Always."

She composed herself. "I will try to make this simple. Do you understand that the Student is no longer accounted for?"

"Yes."

"Do you agree that, in the wrong hands, the Student is a potential force for conflict?"

"Certainly."

"For this reason, was Fel correct in seeking the mask?"

"Yes."

"Then how do we achieve what he sought without befalling the same fate?"

"Sought. Mask? Safely? Impossible. Sought. Peace? Follow. Repeat. Fate? Ideal."

She shook her head and muttered to Tome. "From here it just becomes a loop." Euphoria tugged the plate from the chest of the bust. The iris dropped down.

"And that was supposed to be useful, was it?" Tome asked.

"It usually takes longer to get to that last bit," she said.

"Correct me if I'm wrong, but the Ambassador seemed to believe that the simple existence of choice made war inevitable," Tome said.

"Yes. I don't know if it is a function of the bust being in such poor repair, but despite profound insight that has helped to guide the Graves family to great success in both business and martial dealings, on certain topics the Ambassador begins to think in very simple, very extreme terms. You can follow the logic. If everyone thought and acted the same way, or didn't think or act at all, there would be no war. And the Ambassador exists to find peaceful resolution if at all possible. So that solution, once landed upon, is as far as the Ambassador ever wishes to go."

"Shouldn't the Ambassador be seeking solutions that are possible? That mask is a product of the Bygone Era. We've learned time and time again that contraptions that appear to think can usually only do precisely what they are designed to do." He glanced at Wick. "Although present company suggests that can change with time."

"The Ambassador hasn't spent more than a few hours 'awake' in total since I brought it here. I very much doubt it has learned any new tricks," Euphoria said.

"So why would it settle on 'people need to stop thinking for themselves' as a solution? It might as well just say 'snap your fingers and make the war go away.' There is no value in an impossible solution."

Euphoria tapped her fingers on her chin. "You are suggesting that the Ambassador considers eradicating free will to be not only an ideal solution but a possible one."

Tome's eyes unfocused, his mind suddenly churning through the trials and travails of the past year or so.

"The Bygone Era gave us the Greater Lands Wall. And I've seen, firsthand, what it does to the creatures it is intended to lock away. It is markedly similar to what the sufferers of the Haze described. I don't know how I didn't see it before."

"You didn't see it before because it doesn't make sense. We are very far from the wall, and unless I'm mistaken, the wall's effect is limited to creatures of the Greater Lands, not human beings."

"With every bit of investigation I do, I find that magic and contraptions are more similar to each other in operation and functionality than they are different. If I were able to write a spell that achieves what the Greater Lands Wall does, it would be a relatively simple matter to swap out the target of the enchantment."

"There isn't an equivalent to the Greater Lands Wall in Fenfield. It was a hunting ground. The plague didn't even show up until two years or so ago. Before that, people were in and out of that field without any ill effects whatsoever."

"Could there have been an excavation? Could someone have accidentally unearthed something? Activated something?"

She crossed her arms and considered the question. "I suppose I can't rule out the possibility. But one thing is certain. If it happened, it would have happened under Graves' supervision. I think it's time to take a trip to the archives."

Allie had worked through most of her shift. She would have liked to say that no one was any the wiser about her distracted state of mind, but a few of the regulars gave her tips considerably larger than she felt she'd earned. Charity. Why did it burn her so much to believe that people she'd wrung money out of all her career were now taking pity on her without even knowing what was wrong or why? Just another one of those wonderful ways her mind had to find a way to make her life more difficult.

Just when she'd gotten into the flow and felt as though she was actually earning the tips she was receiving, she heard the voice of her employer filtering down from an unexpected direction.

"Ms. Waverly, this way if you would," said Madritz. "Have Oovay take the floor. We need to discuss something."

Allie turned. On the rare occasion Sid would come to the tavern, he would "work" from the bar itself. Verfessa did his work from the back room. When Madritz started running things, Allie was certain that the little office that had come to be the dedicated break room for servers hoping to catch their breath—or for Oovay to doze off when he should be working—would be coopted for her purposes, and there simply wouldn't be any breaks. Such was not the case, it seemed. Madritz was addressing her from a stairwell behind the break room. The stairwell was effectively invisible to Allie because it was tucked away from the tavern floor, and it led up to a part of the tavern that hadn't existed before it was redone by Verfessa. Namely, it was "the perch."

She gave Oovay a shove and handed him the tray, then scurried up the steps. She only half remembered when Verfessa had announced his plan to include the perch. It was a rather small and very warm room directly above the office that provided access to something of a rooftop patio through one door and a narrow balcony over the main entryway on the other. Allie couldn't even remember his motivation for including it. Something about "addressing the crowds during festivals" for the balcony and "private entertaining" for the patio. In the months since they were added, neither had been used until now.

She reached the room. Both doors were open, providing a cross breeze that made the temperature almost tolerable to Allie. Madritz stood at a contrivance that looked to be the result of a bar and a desk having a child. It was entirely too tall to sit at, and entirely too covered with papers, books, and other stationary to drink at. For someone who Allie would have expected to have a focus on luxury, it was an impressively utilitarian standing desk that made the best possible use of the limited space in this jury-rigged office.

Despite the heat in the office, Madritz didn't have so much as a sheen of sweat at her temples. Allie had always joked that some people were too rich to sweat. There may have actually been some truth to it after all.

Madritz shifted some pages and held a stiff bit of creased parchment up. "Do you see this?" she gestured at a small pile of similar pages. "Do you see all of this? This is what it looks like when a noble tries to direct the daily operations of a business from afar."

She slapped down the page and folded it with the rest. "I know you became accustomed to running this tavern like it was your own, but that is not the way things are done." She tapped the pile. "Nor is this. You should count yourself lucky that you aren't so highly prized that someone with more money than sense decides they need to direct your every waking moment."

Allie didn't swat at the low-hanging fruit the comment provided. It was a struggle. Madritz continued.

"By now, you've had a chance to chat with both the Maskers and Verfessa," she said. "There was no sense having any of our morning meetings until then. Is there anything you'd like to share now?"

"I get the distinct impression what I'd *like* to do isn't really relevant anymore."

"True. Though the illusion of choice does help us get through the day, doesn't it?"

Madritz turned to the rooftop patio and tugged open the door of a small portable stove. Sid had picked the thing up, fully expecting to tuck it in the corner of the tavern and allow her and Oovay's predecessor to warm up sausages and the like for hungry patrons. Three hours after it had been installed, a drunk nearly burned the tavern down, and Sid had thought better of his idea. She'd wondered what had happened to it. Her boss stuffed the messages from the noble inside and lit a taper from the lantern in the office to ignite its flames.

"I'm waiting for an update, Waverly," Madritz said.

"I haven't learned anything you don't already know."

"Bold of you to assume you know what I do and don't know. And more to the point, I didn't ask you to make determinations about what I want to hear, I want to know what you've learned."

"Donovan Verfessa is wary of you, and Fel Masker is still away," she said simply.

"Is that all?" Madritz asked.

"I told you there wasn't anything interesting or worthwhile."

"Mmm." Madritz nodded. "Your judgment on that point is trustworthy. And I presume they asked similar questions of you. Your answers?"

"The Maskers have bigger things to worry about than you. They're impressed you managed to purchase stuff in town so quickly. And Verfessa believed me when I told him there wasn't anything about you he didn't already know."

"I don't appreciate your tone."

"I don't appreciate anything about this interaction," Allie said.

"Don't be short with me. I thought I'd made myself clear regarding what I expected of you, but it would behoove me to speak with greater clarity. You have earned the trust of some people who will never trust me. I want to know things about them. Your job, in addition to serving drinks and feeding heaps of roasted crickets to slack-jawed patrons, is to give me useful information about those people, their intentions, and their activities. If you are not giving me useful information, then you are not meeting expectations. And if you are not meeting expectations, then I see very little reason to permit you to live anything approaching the life to which you have become accustomed. Again, this is in your best interest, not mine. Victory for me is defined as stripping a valued ally from some individuals who depend upon that ally. This can be achieved through any number of means, none of which require your comfort or employment. You providing a service to me is the only way things work out well for you. So don't come back to me with nothing. And don't lie to me. Because you won't like how that turns out for you."

"I'll be more curious when the opportunity arises."

"See that you do." She fluttered her fingers. "Dismissed."

Allie trudged down the steps with her jaw tight. Anger and anxiety both flashed through her mind, but far more briefly than Velonia would have liked. There was something much more important in her mind now, and it was taking up much of the space that had previously been occupied by the less useful emotions. Madritz had finally become satisfied enough with her position of authority that she was certain Allie couldn't threaten it. And as always seemed to happen once someone let their guard down, their weakness gleamed like a lighthouse.

A plan was forming in Allie's mind. It wasn't the best plan. All the obvious avenues of attack were planned for by Velonia, so the best plans would probably fail. But a few weeks after the tavern had been redone with the occasional performance in mind, they'd had a magician perform there. Not a wizard, or a paper mage, or any of the real magical folks that could pull off feats like that legitimately. A run-of-the-mill charlatan who made his money convincing folks he could do those things if he wanted to but for some reason chose instead to expend his arcane skills on pointless, flashy bits of fluff and entertainment. Allie had struck up a conversation with him. He hadn't been willing to part with his secrets. She hadn't expected him to. But he had shared a piece of precious wisdom.

You don't need to fool someone by being clever. You can be as obvious as you choose to be. All you need to do is get them to dismiss that obvious trick as something far too foolish to work. Then you can do it right in front of them and they'll never see it. They'll be too busy trying to come up with a far cleverer solution that would never have worked in the first place.

She started to tick through the steps for this absurd plan to work.

"I'm going to need a lot of stale bread..." she murmured to herself.

CHAPTER 10

Fel sat at the table of an outdoor café, listening to the click of Oiler's puzzle box. He had a hot cup of tea and a sandwich that was a good deal fancier and a good deal less substantial than he would normally want to eat. But all things considered, this should have been heavenly. He'd discovered a rather large supply of silver coins in a small chest in his home. Despite the insistence of Mr. Wick that it was his own money, he'd felt a little uncomfortable filling his pockets. It had earned him an afternoon of absolute leisure. It should have been pleasant. It should have been relaxing. It should have been almost dismally normal. And it was. Yet somehow, that bothered him more than when it was foggy and obscured by amnesia.

He looked over a hand-lettered menu. It had typical things. Cucumber sandwiches. Sliced ham and cheese on crackers. Tiny food for people who weren't so much hungry as bored. He could read all the lines. And why shouldn't he be able to? But he was certain he couldn't when he'd first woken up here. And that was hardly the last piece of information to come filtering into his mind. He knew the names of the streets. He knew the names of the people. The waitress was named Venus. She'd lived here for three years. He was remembering what he'd forgotten. But it didn't feel like old information recovered. It felt like new information. Like it had been laid atop older memories and, in doing so, had buried them even deeper.

Fel shifted uncomfortably and tugged at his shirt. He'd grabbed something new out of his closet. It was exquisitely tailored, but it didn't feel right against his skin. Nothing felt right.

"Is everything to your satisfaction?" asked Venus, leaning low to get her face into his field of vision.

"Oh! Sorry, yeah. Everything's fine."

"Doesn't seem so. I had to ask you three times," she said brightly. "But I suppose one of the Maskers being back in town means you've got an important project on your plate. I don't know if I've gotten a chance to say it, sir, but it is an honor to have you back."

"It's nothing. Really. I had a job to do." He added under his breath, "Apparently."

"It's just that Clickspring doesn't seem whole without a Masker in the estate. Having you within the city's walls assures greatness is right around the corner."

"I do my best."

She paused. "Is it true that..." She shook her head. "No, no. It's terribly inappropriate to ask. Forget I said anything."

"If you knew me better, you'd know it's very hard to find something that I'd find inappropriate."

"Well, if you say so. I've wondered, it can't be true that you're not courting someone, but such is the rumor."

"It can't be true?" he said, puzzled.

"You're the most eligible bachelor in the republic! I don't know a single woman who wouldn't leap at the chance to become a part of the Masker clan. Most of the *married* women I know wouldn't think twice about trading up, so to speak."

"Really..." he said, his ego practically curling around the waitress's leg like an affection-starved cat.

"So is it true?" she asked again.

The eagerness in her eyes spoke volumes of what sort of future she saw for the two of them if he would only give the correct answer.

"As it so happens, I..."

He trailed off. Two thoughts clashed so powerfully in his mind that he could feel the tension like a coiled spring. The answer was yes, he was quite available. The answer was no, he had his heart set on someone else. Both answers came with rock-solid certainty. But the latter came with a flood of other memories. Long nights chatting and laughing. Sharp words and sharper aches as she helped him bandage wounds. A smile. A face.

"I'm sorry," he said quickly, fishing out a few coins too many and dropping them on the table. "I have to go."

"But you haven't finished your tea," she said.

He paused and looked at the table. One of the coins was different from the others. Copper instead of silver. He picked it up. It had a divot gouged into it. A flash of a face he'd seen emerge from his memories before struck him with almost dizzying intensity. An important face. Not family, but someone far too important to be gone without explanation. He pocketed the coin.

"I'm sorry. I have to go. I can't... I have to go," he stammered, nearly knocking down the table as he stood.

He hauled Oiler to his back and practically dashed back toward his home. No... The Masker Estate, not his home.

"This isn't real," he muttered to himself, his mind stirring. He glanced over his shoulder. "You're real, Oiler. And I'm real. But nothing else here fits. I mean, it does fit. It fits perfectly. It fits about as well as this pair of trousers. Tailored to precise measurements. There's a place in Clickspring for the Maskers. There's a place in Clickspring for the clockwork diamond. And there's a place in the *shape* of Fel Masker in Clickspring. But there is no place in Clickspring for Fel Masker."

He threaded his fingers through his hair. "But why can't I remember where I *do* belong? And why can I remember that the second house on that street belongs to Lucas Melchor, who owns the blacksmith shop but doesn't know how to smith at all? He hires people for that. Why do I know that three weeks ago a horse threw a shoe at that intersection? Why do I know every little thing about this town if it isn't real? Think. Think back to before."

He scoured his brain for some hint of anything that felt as solid and real as that flash of memory of... her. Her name never quite came out of the mists. And her face was already fading. It was no use. The truth wasn't getting any clearer to him. The only thing getting clearer was the lie.

"Fine... fine. What felt real after I woke up here but before the blasted clockwork diamond? Me." He patted the chain-filled pack. "You. And. And. That contraption."

He patted his pockets and found the heavy brass device. He pulled it out. The needle pointed roughly northeast. No matter how he turned it, it always settled back in the same direction. He nodded.

"I'm looking for a sign. This is it."

He held the contraption tight in his grip and marched in a straight line, directly in the heading indicated by the needle. It didn't quite align with the streets, meaning from time to time he had to weave one way or the other, but after two streets he'd run out of buildings and was faced with the sprawling fields beyond the city. Indeed, the route he was following was almost perfectly opposed to the city. The main street ran due west. Most of the city branched off that main street, and it didn't continue on the eastern side of the central courtyard. Viewed from overhead, the city was the shape of a keyhole, with the round central courtyard to the east, the fanning out of buildings around the main street to the west, and very little but farms and fields elsewhere.

As he walked away from the built-up portions of the city, more peculiarities started to assert themselves. The fields around it felt, for lack of a better word, young. It wasn't an assessment of the crops but of the land itself. There was a smell to it, a color to it. It felt like the peculiar and not-quite-right way a wealthy man's grounds started to look after he'd unleashed his gardeners upon them. He lacked the words to articulate it, even to himself, but the land was a little too flat, a little too springy. A little too new. It wasn't natural. It was planned. Sculpted. Constructed. And in a way that shouldn't be able to be done this thoroughly for a whole farm, let alone a whole region.

He came to a river, and a similar unnatural precision became clear. The river meandered well enough, but at some point not far from the city, it became arrow straight, like an aqueduct or an irrigation ditch. Except it was very obviously not manufactured. The bottom of the river was river stone and silt. The banks were moss and mud. It was in every way a real, proper river, except it was one that a surveyor couldn't have plotted out with such precision.

He paced forward, eyes on the contraption. He had to follow it. He had to see where it was leading him. He had to...

Fel didn't realize he'd stopped walking until he stopped hearing the crunch of grass beneath his feet. He didn't remember choosing to stop. He hadn't chosen to stop. Because choosing something implied there was some other option. And there simply wasn't. He could not move forward. There was nothing to move toward. He gazed at the field ahead, and even though he knew the land continued forward... he didn't see it. He didn't see the way the land turned to broken stone. He didn't see the smooth, carefully fit stones of a tall wall with no gates. He didn't see anything that lay before him. Because there was nothing to see.

He shut his eyes. Impressively, simmering anger and frustration managed to briefly push past the dulling effect that threw a wet blanket over his mind. He was so tired of grappling with contradictions inside his own head. He turned toward the farmland and the city in the distance. Instantly he was able to think more clearly. Where did he go from here? Instincts that he didn't truly trust told him that the city was where he belonged. His distrust of those instincts drove him to be contrary. But he couldn't. He simply lacked the capacity.

Fel looked down at the contraption in his hand. The needle still pointed behind him, to the northeast. It may as well have been pointing to the sky. Again, to his dismay, he needed to apply reason in a situation where he would much prefer to be applying force.

"I have a device that is leading me somewhere. I was looking for something. If I'm not really *from* Clickspring, then this device must have led me here. Maybe this was where I was heading. Or maybe Clickspring got in the way of me heading to my actual destination. Either way, there may be good to be done here. There could be something I can find that will lead me to whatever I was after. And if that's the case, there's only one man in this whole place that it would make sense if he was a part of it."

He glared at the city in the distance, a determined gleam in his eye. "It's time to talk to the boss again."

Martin climbed the stairs to the dining room with a pot of stew he'd just completed. He still hadn't had any sleep, but he felt strangely energized. If not for his hands shaking and the distracting sound of his belly complaining, he probably would still have been at the workbench. Enthusiasm at progress could only do so much to cut through the exhaustion, however. Nowhere was this more evident than when he slowly became aware that his daughter had been trying to get his attention, and he couldn't honestly tell for how long.

"Dad!" called Epiphany from the doorway.

He shook himself from his thoughts. "Fanny! You're home!" he said, nearly spilling the pot as he thumped it down to run to give her a hug. "It's been too long."

"It's good to see you too. Any word on Fel?" she said quickly. "Wick went quiet, and Mom said to discuss it with you."

"Wick went quiet because I told him to keep an eye on Tome and the others until the moment they had news about him. The next thing we hear from him will be assurance that he's safe or request for aid in how to rescue him."

"Or—"

"Those are the only things we'll be hearing," he said firmly. "But what of you? It shames a father to have more concern for one of his children than another, but I must be honest, I wasn't worried about you on our trip, so my mind was elsewhere."

He hastily filled a bowl and offered it to her. She waved it off and took a seat. He thumped into a chair of his own and ate for what might have been the first time in two days.

"You were right to put your focus where you did. Nothing worthy of mention on the trip. I sold quite near everything I intended to sell. And I even sold a few things I'd intended to bring back for the shop's shelves when I encountered someone willing to offer up a better price than I thought we'd get in town. So it has mostly been travel with an empty wagon for the last few days. Teya was, I'm surprised to say, *very* helpful. She developed quite the aptitude for spotting people who might be a problem and, er... *engaging* them."

"Did she attack them or intimidate them?"

"No. She just bounded over and tried to do business with them. I don't doubt she'd have bitten their fingers off if they got violent, but she figured out the same people likely to give me trouble were likely to want nothing to do with the strange little lizard lady I had with me. Other than that, she made herself as unassuming as possible to keep from fouling my other business."

"Where is she now?"

"Upstairs in the shop, trying to persuade Mom to put some of her fish-scale jewelry up for sale."

"A good trip, then. About time something went smoothly," Martin said.

"What about you? From the look and, forgive me, the smell, I'd say you've been distracted for a while. But your attitude seems a little more upbeat than I'd expect from someone who has been nothing but distraught."

"I've had a breakthrough. Or, at least, I believe that I have. The terrible state Fel is in right now owes itself in part to the shortcomings of the contraption I gave him. I raked myself over the coals trying to find how and why it had failed. And then it was something that Allie said during a visit that may have been the solution. I'd designed the contraption with a handful of assumptions in place. They didn't feel like assumptions at the time, because they were all things that in any sane instance could be taken for granted. But she pointed out that implausible things happen to the Maskers all the time. So I started to look at the assumptions I'd made. Two stood out to me, and both can be solved."

"What did you do wrong?"

"I assumed distance was immutable. That points A and B, once at a set distance would remain at a set distance. But we've learned from how Wick experienced the Greater Lands, and from how the Greater Lands appears to sprawl considerably farther than the enclosing wall would allow, that distance is *not* immutable."

"But Fel didn't head toward the Greater Lands, did he?"

"No, he didn't, but the point remains that distance can be altered, so I cannot make the assumption that it can't."

"And the second flaw?"

"I hadn't supposed that someone might attempt to stop the contraption from working. Either through some foreknowledge of its functionality or simply through an awareness of the visibility of the forces it was built to track and the ability to shield them. Now obviously I can't miraculously see through whatever veil may or may not have been raised to obscure the contraption's vision, especially since I don't know what it is. But I can alter the contraption to at least indicate that something may be obscuring it so that the behavior of the contraption wouldn't mislead Fel with its unpredictability. Now the changing-distance issue? I can't correct it without putting my hands on the contraption itself. But knowing when something is interfering? That should be simple enough. Fel would just need to open the casing and move two gears to bypass one of the internal mechanisms. It would make the device completely inert unless the target was close enough, simply indicating the last direction where it was detected. That would mean it would be worthless at a distance, and it would be terribly bothersome to reconfigure it with any frequency, but with some time in the workshop I could easily add a switch to—"

"Dad?" Epiphany said. "Eat, before you forget to do it again and just wander off to tinker with the idea."

"Right, yes. Of course," he said, shoveling more of the food into his mouth.

"You said Allie stopped by? Why, exactly?" Epiphany asked.

"She was worried about Fel. Very nice girl. And I imagine she was interested in discussing the matter of the new owner of the tavern. That's been troubling her. Did Wick not inform you during his updates?"

"I don't pry into local gossip when I give him my messages, and he didn't volunteer that information. By the High, how did someone manage to purchase The Fox and Log while I was gone?"

"A bit of a mystery. Your mother knows more about it. But I understand it has complicated Allie's life in a way that seems downright malicious."

Epiphany nodded and leaned back in her chair. "I think it is wise for the Maskers to familiarize ourselves with the new business owners in Beffshire. After I've given Mom a break at the counter, I think I'll pay a visit to The Fox and Log."

"I'm sure Allie would appreciate it."

The hatch above flew open with an enthusiastic shove. Bounding steps descended the stairs, and Teya burst into the dining room. She had necklaces dangling from both fists. The scales bent the light into a striking, iridescent sheen.

"Father of friend!" she crowed. "So good to return!" She trotted over. "A great trip! See many things! Meet many people. *Very very fishing!* News of Fel?" She paused and sniffed. "Your smell? Like hard work. Very very work smell. Good work? Bad work? We talk!"

"I'll catch you up. Father's got to get some sleep," Epiphany said.

"I'm fine."

"Look at your shirt."

He looked down. Only about half of the stew he'd been eating had actually made it to his mouth. A combination of too much enthusiasm and not enough coordination were to blame. The chances were very good that any attempts to cut gears or even take notes would probably produce borderline useless results.

"Perhaps a rest would not be unwise," he said.

"Have much good sleep!" Teya said. "More smelly work tomorrow!"

Tome followed closely behind Euphoria as they returned to her hometown. Approaching as they were from the north brought them to the Graves family's section of town from the opposite side. The buildings meant less to impress and more to serve utility purposes were clustered at the north end of their personal neighborhood. The buildings were stone, painted in similar shades to the fancier ones nearby, but there was no question of their purpose. Euphoria's home was built to invite people in. These buildings were built to keep people out.

Tome instinctively stepped toward the front door of a building marked with the Graves family crest but no other meaningful label. Euphoria subtly directed him to the alley beside it.

"This is the Graves family library?" Tome said.

"It is."

"Most of the cities I've visited that are cultured, or at least financially stable, enough to have a library tend to make it something of a visual centerpiece of the town."

"That's because half of the libraries in Shalia and Beffshire are private collections or parts of universities. In the former case, the library is merely a big heap of precious things that one could easily swap for jewels instead, for all the good the information within actually does anyone. In the latter case the books might get some use, but they still really only serve to attract people to the university."

"And this is different? It is a private collection, is it not?" he said.

She revealed a key chain and selected a key. The impatient unicorn trotting along with them started to lean its horn on the door, straining the latch.

"Would you get control over him, please?" she asked.

"I would if I could. The only person in the world who thinks he can control Parch is Fel, and he only thinks that because half the time he's asking the little creature to do something it was already planning to do."

"Leave it to Fel to find a way to irritate me from afar," she muttered.

Tome managed to compel the unicorn into a game of headbutts. It was a far more harrowing experience than Fel made it look. Ostensibly one was simply bumping or slapping the creature on the forehead whenever it reared up, but in practice the forehead was a very small target, and missing was a sure way to skewer one's hand on a broken horn or let that horn skewer some other part of the body of Parch's choosing. It did manage to keep the beast from interfering with the door, which got Euphoria back on topic.

"The Graves family library isn't what you think it is. We don't use this building for reference. What little reference material we have regarding contraptions is duplicated among the workshops of the three moderately competent fabricators and maintainers we've managed to find. This is a collection of family histories, diaries, and any material pertinent to Graves family business interests."

She unlocked the door, and they slipped inside.

"If the Ambassador was a difficult visit to arrange for me to attend, I can only imagine how difficult it was for you to persuade your family to allow me into this place, then. A house of secrets."

"I didn't persuade anyone to let you in," she said. "So we won't be discussing this. We particularly will not be discussing that we brought Wick in with us."

"You're sneaking us in?" he said.

She waved her hand around the darkened hallways they were marching through. "Does it look as though you have to sneak? This place has major activity once a month, when new entries are made. Most of the rest of the year, it is a musty little vault filled with forgotten pages. Every one of these doors requires a different key, and forcing any of the doors or locks will set off a string of alarm boxes that will bring the personal guards of half the family running."

"Even so. You have two full-time guards on the Ambassador but none in the repository of the family's history?"

She rolled her eyes. "It has been discussed, at length. The problem with letting the matriarchs and patriarchs of a family run things is the eventual tendency for things to be done a particular way because they always have, not because it's actually sound thinking or planning. This way. And try to keep the unicorn from making a mess."

They took a turn through the darkened hallways of the library, none of which were labeled. Wick's flame was the only light.

"We are operating under the assumption that Fel is still alive and is simply in the field somewhere. If he's lost and confused, we'll have to assume he would look for some sort of shelter. Fenfield was a private hunting ground that changed hands plenty of times over the years before the quarantine. The upper class who treat hunting as a delightful pastime rather than a way to get meat for their table aren't the sort to sleep in tents and drink from rivers. There are bound to be some manner of hunting lodges or other cabins within Fenfield."

"And we'll find that information here?"

"We have a better chance at finding it here than anywhere else. The last few owners of Fenfield are either dead, on the other side of Fenfield, unlikely to keep records, unlikely to share those records, or some combination of the four. But the Graves make their money in contraptioneering, and without someone as skilled as Father to repair broken contraptions, we've done extensive investigations of surrounding areas in search of caches and vaults. There will be plenty of detailed information about Fenfield. And if something was unearthed to cause the field to start suffering the Haze, it is almost certainly due to one of our investigations and thus will be on record."

"And what do we do with it once we find it? Is there any means of accessing the place safely?"

"I don't know. That's a separate problem to solve. But at least we'll know what to look for once we have the answer to that question."

She opened the relevant room. Some very fine shelves awaited them, filled with decidedly less fine books. Unlike the halls and rooms, the books and shelves were quite well labeled.

"Surveying is on that wall. The region should be on the second set of shelves from the left. Somewhere between the second and fifth shelves from the bottom. I'll check the sales records for the same region. We may have done some buying and selling with the previous owners. The records might give us a little more of an idea what we will find on the land."

"Are you theorizing there may have been some indication of this plague prior to when it was believed to have started?" he asked.

"You'd be surprised how obvious clues become in retrospect. Knowing the outcome has a way of doing that."

Tome paced over to the indicated shelf. Behind him, he heard the sound of a sparker as Euphoria lit a second lantern. He ran his fingers along the spines. A few plumes of dust rose up. He took a deep whiff. The combination of aging leather, cheap glue, and old paper was a love letter to his childhood. The Bygone Archive and similarly ancient libraries were valuable and precious places of pure knowledge. But this was the era of books he knew best. Assembled with the precise balance of cheapness and sturdiness. It filled him with an almost dizzying sense of nostalgia.

"This takes me back," he said.

"Right," she said distantly. "You're from that monastery on the west coast."

"The Gate of the Ancients," he said. "If I could remember one-tenth of the things that left my pen while I was growing up there and copying books, I would rule the world."

"Information is nice, but in isolation it can't really bring one to greatness," she said, flipping through some pages. "It takes resources, drive, and purpose as well."

"I have quite the quantity of both, I assure you."

"You must have a fair bit of drive to have made it all the way from the west coast to Beffshire."

"And a good deal farther. I've been to the Greater Lands twice, you'll recall."

"No shortage of resources either."

"One could always use more, but my partnership with the Maskers has given me a little something to work with."

"That just leaves the purpose."

He ran his fingers down the page. "I am a man of purpose."

"A fine thing to hear. And what might that purpose be?"

"I wish to build my skills in the mystic arts as substantially as I can, and earn with those skills a commiserate level of acclaim and respect."

"Rather a vague and self-serving purpose, isn't it?"

"I appear to be the only one willing to serve myself, and thus self-service seems quite permissible in my view. As for vague? I prefer the word 'flexible.'"

"It is refreshing to encounter someone with a level of introspection and self-awareness."

"It's refreshing to be appreciated."

He flipped through the pages of handwritten notes recording the details of surveyed land in excruciating detail, along with careful drawings of pieces of land. Every few pages the handwriting changed, some new clerk or scribe doing the job. It lacked a proper index, but the layout was obvious enough. A section of the map would be defined, then features of interest would be covered in detail. Because different people were doing the work, the length of each section varied tremendously. It made finding a specific piece of land a laborious exercise in flipping through the book and reading a few paragraphs to gain one's footing.

"This was clearly never meant to be read," Tome said.

"That's the thing about recordkeeping. It's important the information is present. Actually finding it is someone else's job." She flipped through a few more pages. "I thought surely it would be in this book. Are you finding anything?"

"It isn't forthcoming, but I'm only on my first book."

"This isn't right…"

"Is the index similarly convoluted in yours?"

"No. These are sales records. They are our bread and butter. It is taken very seriously. Most of the transactions are recorded to the hour. But there's nothing here about Fenfield."

"Couldn't it be that there's nothing to find?"

"We absolutely would have at least paid them for permission to check for antiques. It's too big of an area not to. There would have been an agreement. A list of how the earnings would be split. A list of things we found during the survey, if any. But it's not there. Nothing crossed out. No torn pages. It just isn't there."

"Curious," he said.

"Come here. You're an expert in books, right?"

"If such a thing exists, then I am most certainly one."

"Tell me if there's anything wrong with this book."

He set down the volume he'd been perusing and joined her on the other side of the room. "Let me see. 'Is there something wrong with this book?' is a broad question to ask someone who has spent so many years with his nose in one." He tugged up the ribbon from the binding to mark the page, then raised it and held it to the light. "The leather is quite poor. The book wouldn't stand more than a year or two of regular use as a day-to-day reference."

He sniffed the binding. "The glue is quite high quality."

"I wasn't asking for an appraisal. I was asking if there is anything strange."

"Give me a moment to work through it." He gave the first few pages a bend. "The paper is passable. Good ink."

He flipped through the pages, running his thumb down the stack to buzz through the full thickness. Midway through he stopped and tipped his head. He worked his way through a second time, then flipped it open, ending up roughly where the ribbon had marked. Then he flipped through pages one at a time.

"Something strange?" she asked.

"Perhaps," he said, deep in thought. "Are all these books from approximately the same time?"

"All the books on that level, yes."

He took a second book and similarly buzzed through the pages. He opened the book at random and rubbed one page against the next, then did the same on the questionable book.

"These pages are newer. The grain is different. It's subtle. But they're finer. The color should be different if that was the case, but it's a match... unless... Is there a magnifier about? There tends to be one in libraries, in my observation."

Euphoria marched to the door and opened a small cabinet to reveal a curved bit of glass. He held it up and inspected the page. It took three minutes of painstakingly working his way along the sheet, but he found a place where there was the faintest feathering and ringing, like a drop of water had fallen on the page and pushed some of the grime around.

"This was stained. This page was stained to match the color of the others. As was this one... and this one..." He tipped the book up and used the magnifier on the binding. "The entire signature of pages has been swapped out. I can't believe it. The labor involved. You'd have to soften the glue, remove the cover, snip the thread. The whole book would have to be essentially rebound. And everything formerly in that section of the book rewritten."

"With the exception of the transactions they didn't want to have a record of," she said. "And unlike tearing out a page or scratching out a line, you'd never know it was missing if you weren't looking for it."

He returned to the book he was working on. Now that he knew what to look for, he found that the survey book had been similarly altered. He looked to her. She knew what he'd found without a word.

"So what does this mean?" Tome asked.

"I don't imagine it means anything good. And there's no telling who could have done it, beyond that they likely had one of the keys. We already know there was a period of time that our flame was being used to send information elsewhere, and that even now there are bad messages coming through. Someone entirely loyal and trustworthy to the family could have done this, believing it was fully authorized by someone with a high rank. But it guarantees that there was something to hide. The Graves family, or some parasitic interloper, has some connection to Fenfield."

"You may have married your way into the only family with a greater density of major problems than the one you were born into."

"You can pick nits, or you can help solve the problem. Any ideas?"

The pair silently weighed their options. When the silence was broken, it was Wick who spoke up.

"The information still exists somewhere," he said.

"How can you be so sure?" Euphoria said. "We already know the information has been tampered with to hide it. Why wouldn't it have been destroyed?"

"The books were altered through a very complex and labor-intensive method. That suggests it was done by someone interested in preserving information," Wick said.

"Right," Euphoria said. "Because they could have simply destroyed the books. It would have made the discovery of the tampering with the records marginally more likely, but it would have achieved the same result. This probably was someone who didn't want to wreck the rest of the data. That suggests it's worth looking for the truth, but it doesn't really help us find it."

Realization dawned in Tome. "No... No, it does help us find it. Wick said it. Falsifying these books was a complex and labor-intensive process. Moreover, it was a specialized process. The books were effectively rebound. A bookbinder did this. A skilled one."

"And an unscrupulous one, because this is hardly the sort of job that one could have a legitimate reason for."

"Know anyone like that?" Tome asked.

"I don't. But I know someone who does."

"Excellent. Let's go!"

"It may not be so easy."

"I can't wait to learn why that might be."

"Thaddeus is the one who we'd contact if we needed someone with that sort of specialty. And he's been missing since his visit to Beffshire."

Tome shut his eyes tight and palmed his forehead. "That certainly sounds like someone cleaning up a loose end."

"Maybe, maybe not. There's a reason Thad was the one in charge of the bazaar. He was resourceful. Or, for our sake and his, I should say that he *is* resourceful. Let's have a look at his place in town. Maybe he kept a list of vendors."

Fel double-checked the hallway a third time before slinking into his bedroom and locking the door. The clashing thoughts of this place being his home and this place being some nefarious attempt at convincing him that it was his home had left him terribly stirred up. For the first time since he'd awoken here, he gave the manor more than a casual search, mostly timed when Mr. Wick was absent or otherwise indisposed, in case the butler was a spy of some kind. What he'd discovered had done little to set his mind at ease. The portions of the house he'd been living in—his bedroom, the dining room, the kitchen—were perfectly acceptable and precisely as one would imagine them. But when he ventured into the different wings of the house, places intended for guests and entertaining, he quickly found them lacking. They were sparsely decorated, mostly bare walls with an odd arrangement of furniture, like a table but no chairs or a bed frame with no bed.

It could have been as innocent as he'd only just moved back in after an extended absence, but there was just something so strange about the nature of the rooms. And in his exploration of the town, he got much the same feeling. A town building up from nothing wouldn't grow in this way. There was nothing natural about the way the buildings were popping up. Real cities grew up starting with the necessities. Neighborhoods naturally formed. This one was growing out from the center along a single road, like an icicle trickling down. Barely anyone lived here, yet it had stores and eateries and the sorts of things a town with a bustling trade would have. This was a city being built to some preexisting plan. Like they had the layout, the specifics, all ready to go and were simply trying to match it piece by piece without regard for anything else. It wasn't a real city. It was something meant to resemble a city. It was a set, assembled on stage to give just enough of the semblance of a city to allow the audience to accept the scene that was being played out.

What chilled him more than anything else was that each mystery and hard-fought-for answer he unraveled had to be held and focused upon, like a memory of a dream. The moment he let his focus wander, he could feel the curiosity and investigation start to slip away from him. If this was a show being put on for an audience, he didn't know what concerned him more: if he was part of the audience, or if he was part of the show.

A few things were certain, though. That clockwork diamond had a place in inflicting the unwanted thoughts upon him. The boss, Mr. Lens, had wanted to get him back to work on that thing, so he was absolutely not an ally in this. And that he hid himself behind that screen meant he had something to hide. The math was easy. If you have an enemy, and that enemy has a secret, then uncovering that secret will give you leverage over the enemy. Paying another visit on Lens's terms would just lead to more lies and manipulation. Paying a visit under Fel's terms might get some dirt. And the moment he started brainstorming how to infiltrate that facility around the clockwork, something curious happened. He felt prepared.

He set down the bundle of canvas he'd toted to his bedroom and unfurled it on his bed. For all the things that weren't present in this so-called town, tools and materials were in ready supply. A workshop within his own estate had provided various probes, cutters, priers, and other tools. It, like the rest of the house, had been set like a stage, with half-finished contraptions flanking the work bench as though they'd been set aside just the day before. But the tools, at least, were real. Rope and other gear, including grungy stuff that looked terribly out of place in the otherwise pristine city, had been available in the lowest level of the basement. He nodded as he ticked off the assorted things he somehow knew he would need, as though plotting a means to penetrate the defenses of something protected by complex contraptions was his stock and trade. Was he a thief? Was he some manner of specialized soldier? He didn't know. But if it came down to learning that he was a cad in real life, that was preferable to being whatever they wished to sculpt him into in this place.

He tore a few extra strips from the edge of the canvas and used them as ribbons to both tie the roll shut once he'd finished rebundling it and to fasten it to a makeshift sling he'd fashioned. All that remained was to wait until the cover of night. Until then, the gear and the sling would be stowed under his bed. He slid them deeper with the toe of his boot and pulled Oiler up from where he'd been pleasantly reconstructing a chair Fel had shattered. The plan had been to harvest some stiff wire to supplement the set of tools he'd scavenged, but it turned out to be a boon for keeping Oiler occupied. Sticking bits of splintered wood together and spritzing them with adhesive took a good deal longer and was clearly far more engaging, than clicking at the tiles of the puzzle box. So much so that the contraption hadn't yet noticed the missing wires, as it hadn't finished rebuilding the legs. There was a dash of mild protest from the contraption when it was taken away from the enjoyable task, but it eventually relinquished the leg and reeled into the pack when presented with its puzzle box again.

Fel marched to the door, opened it, and nearly fell backward. Mr. Wick was standing there, as though he'd been lurking silently and awaiting this chance to startle Fel.

"My apologies. I was just wondering if Sir had any wants or needs. Forgive me, but you've been rather difficult to serve of late."

"Sorry. I'm not used to this," Fel said.

"As you say," he said. "The question remains. Does Sir have any wants or needs that I can or should fulfill? A bite to eat? Some other refreshment?"

"Uh. Yeah. Let's go eat."

"What will you have, Sir?"

"Whatever you're having."

"The intention was for me to prepare Sir something."

"Too bad, because I'm the boss and I say I'm sick of eating alone, so I hope you brought your appetite."

Mr. Wick gently resisted all the way downstairs. He suggested that Fel might enjoy his meal more with some of the local socialites. He insisted he'd in fact already eaten. Fel was stubborn on the fact, and eventually Mr. Wick's dedication to serving Fel's every whim overruled his dedication to not rising above his social station. Two plates were set out, and a pair of pan-fried steaks with crispy broiled vegetables were arranged on them.

Before Mr. Wick could do so, Fel poured them both some wine.

"Loosen up, Wick. You look scared to death," Fel said, cutting into his steak.

"I am unaccustomed to this level of familiarity," he said.

"We're all learning to live with stuff we're unaccustomed to, I guess." He took a bite. "You make a darn good steak, Mr. Wick. What kind of meat is this?"

"Some manner of game animal, Sir. I must admit, I simply requested the butcher provide some steaks and chops."

Fel nodded. "Hey, Wick. Is that your first or last name?"

"Last, Sir."

"What's your first?"

"It simply wouldn't do for you to refer to me by my first name. Nor I yours."

"Uh-huh. Refresh my ailing memory. How long ago did I show back up in town?"

"A number of months ago, Sir."

"Which number?"

"That is... I am not entirely certain. Not more than six."

"Where do you live?"

"In a small residence adjoining the property."

"You from around here?"

"Yes, Sir."

"How long have you lived in Clickspring?"

"As long as I can remember, Sir."

Fel took a drink. "As long as you can remember."

"Yes, Sir."

"How old is the city?"

"Just less than eighteen years old, Sir."

"And you can't remember anything earlier than that?"

Mr. Wick paused. He looked away from Fel, his face scrunched up in the struggle of remembrance. "I... cannot, Sir."

"There's a lot of that going around. That didn't strike you as strange?"

"One doesn't think of one's past when there are things to be done in one's present."

"Sure. You have a wife?"

"I don't, Sir."

"A mother and father?"

"Everyone has a mother and a father."

"What are their names?"

Another telling silence. Fel watched his face closely. This wasn't the look of a man whose cover had been blown. This was the look of a man who, quite like Fel himself, discovered he had answers for some questions and no answers for others. Like the town, he had precisely what he needed to appear complete but nothing that actually contributed to that completion. And this revelation brought with it a dizzying confusion. Fel slid Mr. Wick's wineglass closer. He gratefully took it and drained half the glass.

"I don't feel terribly well, Sir," he said.

"Sorry about that. I just had to know who I was dealing with. And the fact that you don't really know who I'm dealing with actually makes me feel a little better. Can you make me a promise, Mr. Wick?"

"Of course, Sir."

"My head is a little messed up. I'm going to go to bed early, and I don't want to be disturbed by anyone. Maybe stick around for a couple of hours after sunset and watch my door. Just to keep me from being bothered?"

"Of course, Sir."

"Great." He hacked off another piece of the mystery steak. "Once again, darn good steak."

<h1 style="text-align:center">Chapter 11</h1>

If she wasn't so stubborn, Allie would have given up on this absurd little scheme two hours ago. It was taking far longer than she'd expected. The first part had been simple enough. Acquire a full sack of old rolls and cakes from Divinity's Oven. Mariss was a bit confused but more than willing to part with what would have otherwise been trash. The next part, which she wouldn't have predicted would be the most difficult part, involved getting and holding the attention of the lesser harpies. It had been simple enough to drop by Masker's Antiquities after dark and lob a bun up to the roof to get the attention of the irritatingly intelligent black birds. But once they'd each had one of the buns, one of their standard fees for leaving someone alone for a day or so, they simply retired to the roof again. That there might be a greater reward for something somewhere else was not something they were prepared to consider.

Determination and more than a few curse words had hammered the notion into their heads that they ought to follow her. Then came the struggle of repeatedly persuading them to stray farther and farther from their home turf. Two-thirds of the time devoted to this project had been spent getting them as far as The Fox and Log. Then began what should have been the hard part. She wasn't on the schedule for the late shift, so she shouldn't have even been at the tavern to start with. Madritz would have sent her home if she'd noticed Allie had come down. But the first thing anyone learns about their boss is when they arrive and when they leave. Madritz had gone home before Allie had even fetched the lesser harpies. Oovay didn't particularly care that she'd snuck in the back way. He was mostly just disappointed to discover she wasn't here to give him the last few hours off.

She grabbed the ladder out of the storeroom, hauled it outside, and made her way to the rooftop patio. The route to the patio through Madritz's office was, predictably, locked.

"All right, you little thieves. This should come naturally to you. You get this right, and I'll make sure your bellies are full for the next month. Got that?" she whispered to the phalanx of birds who sat on the edge of the roof and gazed at her curiously.

She opened the oven where Madritz had been disposing of all the messages she'd been receiving from her lord patron. The tray inside had a heap of ashes. She dumped them out and fetched a sheet of paper from her pocket.

"Watch me closely now," she muttered. "I know you know how to do this. You've done it on your own before. You just need to do it the right way." She slipped the page into the oven. "Watch me now," she said.

She pulled the page free, and quite theatrically, placed it in her other hand. "You see? You see that?"

She stuffed the page back into the oven and retreated to the corner of the roof. "Now you."

The harpies cocked their heads, almost in unison, and gazed at her as though she was halfway through a performance and they were waiting for the finale. She impatiently tapped her hand.

Toody hopped down from the handrail on the edge of the patio and bounced over to her. The bird hopped up to land on her hand.

"Cute, but no." She gently shook the creature off her hand.

Toody hopped back to the others. They had a brief discussion of croaks and cackles. Moody ventured over to the oven and pulled the page out. Allie nodded approvingly. Moving with the sort of care of a creature who had been swatted with shoes for stealing things far too many times to be willing to do it while being watched, he bobbed over and deposited the page on her hand.

"Brilliant!" she proclaimed, producing a piece of bun and tossing it to him in exchange.

"You rotten rat!" croaked Judy.

"Now we're going to do this again, but with a little more difficulty this time. Watch me, and..."

A flutter of wings burst from behind her. She turned to see that her students had flown the coop.

"Where are you going!?" she hissed.

Her answer came less than a minute later, when Judy arrived with a strip of paper torn from a cheap sign down the street. In short order, all four of them had returned with paper harvested from around the surrounding streets.

She covered her face. "This is going to be a problem..."

Fel dropped a short distance from the window to the ground. With Mr. Wick faithfully guarding the door to his bedroom against disturbance, there was no need to worry about him noticing the departure. And the sparsely populated town meant that at this late hour, he could take the main street and still not be at any risk of being spotted. As he drew nearer to the huge circular wall in the center of town, instincts and intuition started to call out to him. First and foremost was the intense desire to stay clear of the wall entirely. This wasn't some foreign will pressing upon him. This was just common sense letting him know that his last trip to the other side of that wall had scrambled his mind, adding a healthy dose of unfamiliar thoughts and pushing others deeper into the mists of his memory. There was no telling what would be left of his mind if he faced that diamond again.

He came to the entrance to Mr. Lens's conservatory. No lights burned in the windows. That meant not only that it wasn't in use at the moment but also that there were no guards walking the halls either. Whereas that would normally be excellent news for someone hoping to slip in undetected, Fel knew better. This was a very important place. It wouldn't be undefended. So if there wasn't a contingent of guards, that meant he'd be facing contraptions. Traps, alarms, perhaps things that were even worse. No matter. He was prepared.

Built into the wall as the entrance was, Fel was denied the safety of slipping into a back alley to do his work unseen. He had to hope that the empty streets remained empty long enough for him to get inside. He knelt beside the front door and went to work. The moment he pried the small metal plate from the wall beside the door, he felt as though his hands were moving on their own. If he'd been asked to fix this door, he would have been at a loss. But it took just one glance at the workings for him to be quite certain how to break the contraption that opened the door. Before he could, there was another step. This was a secure door. He'd encountered nothing that suggested a trap, so that left only one option. There had to be an alarm.

Fel slid Oiler's pack from his back and lay on the floor, blocking the view of the open contraption lest it start undoing his work. In the darkness he had no hope of actually seeing what he was looking for, so he worked by touch, easing his hand into the nest of linkages, springs, and gears, gently feeling for something out of place. He found a metal hook fed through a hole on one of the gears. A linkage above the hook led to a tilt wheel. He almost dislocated his shoulder getting his hand deep enough to determine one side was attached to a thin wire that was just barely slack. He tipped the wheel toward the wire, tugging the hook from the gear and ensuring whatever it was attached to wouldn't be triggered when the door opened. Thus disarmed, he yanked a ratchet pawl out of place and pressed some candle wax onto it to hold it there.

He climbed to his feet and pulled Oiler to his back. "Here goes nothing," he said.

Fel pulled at the door. It slid open with barely any force.

"No screeching alarm. So far so good."

He slipped inside. Only once he'd shut the door did he dare click his sparker and light a lantern. He allowed himself the tiniest ember of light to navigate by and crept forward like any errant step could bring the ceiling crashing down on his head. Every few strides he dropped to the ground and cast the light along the floor tiles, checking for sections that were a hair too high or too low. Twice he spotted a worrisome stretch of floor and hopped over it.

Two interior doors separated the entryway from the boss's office. Each had to be given the same treatment as the front door, with him disengaging both the opening mechanism and the alarm. He approached the door he'd been led through and grinned.

"Somebody's nervous," he murmured.

Nine full rows of tiles in front of the door were ever so subtly raised up. He was certain they hadn't been when he'd come here during the day for his first meeting. Pressure plates, primed and ready. Worse, now that he had reason to inspect them, he noted the ceiling tiles were spaced in a peculiar fashion. The gaps were just a shade too wide, and they aligned with the center of the tiles below rather than matching their layout. These weren't just alarm tiles. Something nasty would be dropping down from above if he activated them. A net if he was lucky. He suspected in reality it would be something sharp, heavy, or both.

He spied the edge of the floor. A tiny ledge along the wall, little more than a decorative stone molding, rose an inch or so above the raised tiles. It was certainly sturdy enough to support his weight. Combined with the wall sconces on either side of the door to support most of his weight, he could probably plant a boot on the molding and swing over enough to inspect the door. He reached out for the sconce, but stopped. He held the light over to it. A fine hinge ran along the bottom of the sconce. It too was a trigger for something.

"Somebody's *very* nervous," he amended.

He scratched his head. There was simply no way he was getting through that door. He would have to pry up and disable at least two tiles wide and six tiles deep just to get close enough to see what sort of locks, traps, and alarms the door might have.

Fel turned and backtracked to the previous door he'd opened. He leaned back through and assessed the thickness of the wall it was mounted in. Unlike the stone exterior wall, the interior was made from wood. He shut his eyes and envisioned the room when he was visiting with Lens, then paced toward the door until he was confident he was lined up with the adjoining room. He slid a prybar from his tool roll and slapped it on his palm.

"Lucky me, I'm not in a hurry."

Tome felt uncomfortably like a prowler as he huddled behind Euphoria and tried to keep Parch occupied. She sorted through a hefty ring of keys. Like everything within the Graves family, some seemingly random cousin in the expansive family tree was in charge of keeping the spare keys safe. As one would hope—in most circumstances, at least—he was solidly against offering them up for any reason. You couldn't very well call the keys safe if they were in the hands of someone who would hand them over to anyone who asked. But Euphoria was nothing if not persuasive, and after a lengthy discussion, she'd gotten the keys she was after.

"Why so many keys?" Tome asked after a fifth attempt had failed to open the door before them.

"This is the, um..." She paused. "We mostly call it the bunkhouse. The family members who spend most of their time as part of the traveling bazaar or otherwise out and about don't really have much use for a large, expensive home. So Thaddeus and others like him prefer to living in this manor. Each door has a different lock. I know that this is his door, but I don't know which key is his."

"So you live in a sprawling mansion while these folks, who clearly bring in a considerable amount of the wealth for the family, all pile into a single structure that's smaller?" Tome asked.

"I'm not interested in discussing it," she said.

"It is just that the line between employees and family members—"

"I'm not interested in discussing it," she repeated with precisely the same tone.

The seventh key was the winner. She shoved the door open and ushered him inside. Tome raised Wick's lantern. The place didn't strike Tome as the sort of living quarters befitting a valued part of a wealthy family. There were three rooms total. An open door led into a bedroom, a closed door presumably led to some sort of bathroom, and the rest of the dwelling was a single large room with a table, a single chair, and a potbellied stove with its pipe leading out of the wall. It might have been large enough to comfortably serve as a home for a single person, if not for Thaddeus's proclivities regarding storage. Cheap wooden crates had been stacked from floor to ceiling along every stretch of free wall space. A few more scattered crates were lined up at the base of each stack, revealing the contents that presumably filled all the others.

"Journals," Euphoria said, rummaging through one such crate. "Years and years worth of journals."

"You don't suppose he has some sort of an indexing system, do you?" Tome said. "With this much information, he's bound to have what we're after, but buried in decades of other information, it might take us months to find it."

Euphoria shook her head and thumbed through a journal. "This is from seventeen years ago. And this one is from six months ago. Side by side. If there's an order to this, it's not chronological."

"Do they at least have the same topic?"

"They all have the same topic. Sales records and associated observations," she said. "Probably every one of these crates could be said to fall under the same heading. It has been Thaddeus's life's work."

Parch hopped to the top of a half stack, then to the top of a full one. He stuck his head down and came up with a mouthful of the straw that was used to pack the crate. This, at least, freed up Tome to join in the search. He pulled up a thick book and flipped it open. He winced at the rush of lingering smokiness clinging to the pages.

"At least we know for certain it is Thaddeus's home," he said. "The man does love his badgerweed, doesn't he?"

"A side effect of keeping the flame nearby. Though I suppose it needn't have been badgerweed. I don't know why he chose such a horridly smelly thing to smoke," she said.

A soft click and crackle caused Tome and Euphoria to freeze. They turned to its source: the single closed door. Tome slowly set down Wick's lantern and fumbled for a spell. He readied it. Euphoria's hand went to her side, slipping into her purse to grasp what was no doubt a weapon hidden inside. A moment later, the door opened and out stepped... Thaddeus.

He breathed out a cloud of reeking badgerweed. And sighed pleasantly. "There's some value in having something memorable about you, when you're the sort of person someone only sees twice a year," Thaddeus said, puffing again at his pipe.

"Thaddeus!?" Euphoria said. "I didn't know you were in town! The family has been looking for you ever since—"

"I'm well aware. You not knowing I am in town is rather the point of hiding out," he said. "No telling who has plans for me."

"You're hiding in your own home?" Tome said. "That seems ill-advised."

"I waited until I was able to confirm it had already been checked and double-checked. People tend not to search a place they've already ruled out."

"But how were you hiding your comings and goings?" Euphoria said.

"A man needs to have some secrets." He puffed at the pipe. "It was killing me not to smoke this stuff while I was hiding. A bit of a giveaway to have fresh badgerweed wafting through the place. But now that I'm found out, may as well give in to the habit again. So. What brings you here? Besides a deep-seated desire to dig through my memoirs?"

Tome and Euphoria glanced at one another. Thaddeus raised his eyebrows.

"Something surreptitious, is it?" he said.

"I can't come up with a solid reason not to tell you," Tome said. "But it somehow seems unwise to share our recent findings."

He puffed again. "Mmm. That sort of thing, is it?"

Euphoria thumped down the book she'd been flipping through. "I'm through pussyfooting around. If you're in hiding because you're afraid you know too much, then we are most assuredly in the same boat. May as well share what's gotten us here. Fel came through, searching for the person who stole the mask. He became convinced the person was hiding in Fenfield, and against everyone's advice, he went there. He hasn't returned."

Thaddeus puffed the pipe again and spun his chair away from the table to take a seat. "That's unfortunate. My condolences," he said.

"We aren't ready for condolences yet," Euphoria said. "We're here because we sought information on Fenfield in the archives, and it was not only missing but carefully removed. The sort of removal that would require specialized expertise."

"You're looking for Greft Brannon," Thaddeus said quickly. "Forger and bookbinder. We used him primarily for his binding services."

"Yes, precisely. Where can we find him?" she said.

"Morrai Cemetery, in the family plot."

Her joy dropped to concern. "He's dead?"

"Buried six days ago. His carriage went off the edge of a narrow road farther north in the mountains. Curious circumstances, but I wouldn't have called them suspicious until now."

"This is someone covering their tracks," Tome said.

"Almost certainly. And evidence that I was wise to make myself scarce," Thaddeus said.

"Then the trail is cut off," Euphoria said.

"Yes and no." Thaddeus stood. "As it so happens, I haven't been idle in my exile. Follow me."

"You've been investigating the same thing?" Tome said.

"No. Or at least, I wouldn't have thought so. My investigation was into something that was quite opposite. Not information that was vanishing but information that was appearing." He hefted a crate from the top of one of the piles and pulled a few books from the crate beneath it. "My concern was the security of our flame. Moreover, the apparent delivery of messages with no known origin point. I didn't know if someone had simply acquired a persistent flame that had escaped our notice or if some member of the family was working at odds with the rest of the clan in secret. Forgive me, Euphoria, but you were quite high on my list of people to worry about."

"For what possible reason?"

"You were the bit of connective tissue between the Maskers and the Graves family. Just as the vanishing of the Bolivans and the Maskers would leave the entirety of the contraption market to the Graves clan, a similar disappearance of the Maskers' competition would leave them in an excellent position. You are a servant of two masters."

"The family still doubts my devotion?" Euphoria said. "After years of cutting myself off from my own flesh and blood to focus on the Graves family, at the first indication of deceit, I am placed under scrutiny?"

"A leopard cannot change its stripes. That goes for you as well as us."

"Leopards have spots, not stripes," Tome said.

Thaddeus dismissed the correction. "Regardless, I've found no evidence to link you to anything that's been going awry. Whoever has been doing this has been quite cautious. With one very notable exception." He pulled out a stack of pages tied with red thread. "Do you know about the mine vault?" he asked.

"It doesn't sound familiar," Euphoria said.

"It isn't so much a secret as an obsolete part of our business. Years ago, before the construction of the family library was finished, we still had quite a bit of information that we wanted to keep safe. This is back when I was a boy. An old vault, supposedly the first one found and cleared by the Graves family, was found to be an ideal place to store documents. Cold, dry, remote, easily secured. Everything had been moved out and safely stowed in the new building when the library opened its doors. But my investigations turned up two messages that indicated something was to be stored there. Messages I couldn't associate with any known sender. They were likely from the individual responsible for *all* the mysterious messages. I managed to make my way there, and I found these." He dropped the bundle of pages on the table.

"What are they?" she asked.

"I haven't severed the thread," Thaddeus said.

"By the High, why not?" Euphoria asked. "Why would you investigate and then ignore the fruits of the investigation?"

Tome squinted at the thread. "I believe I know the answer."

He pressed his fingers down beneath the thread, revealing that a portion of the thread was glued to a sheet of paper wrapped around the rest of the bundle.

"I had thought that outer sheath of paper was something intended to make tampering clear, but when I was able to pry a bit of it up, I saw writing that reminded me quite a bit of the sort of things our paper mage friend works on. I thought for certain were I to disrupt it, the pages would have been destroyed."

Tome poked at the page. "A pocket knife? Something with a narrow blade," he said.

"I haven't anything of the sort in the house," Thaddeus said.

Euphoria removed what looked like a moderately oversized knife grip from her purse. She depressed a small button, and a stiletto blade snapped out with enough force to threaten to yank it from her hand.

"You know, your sister prefers a set of brass knuckles," Tome said.

"I prefer to only strike someone once," Euphoria said, handing it over.

He slipped the blade along beneath the sheath, then twisted it up and sliced through both the sheath and the string. The loop of paper fell slack. Tome pulled it free and held it up.

"A very rough spell... I'd almost left enough of it intact to activate. I expected it to be shorter."

"Would it have incinerated the pages?" Thaddeus asked as he and Euphoria pulled the pages from the stack and started spreading them on the table.

Tome muttered under his breath. "Flame... targeted... isolated... flesh. No, no it wouldn't have incinerated the pages. It would have incinerated you."

"Ah. All the more fortunate I chose discretion," he said.

Tome continued looking over it. "Have you encountered paper magic being used anywhere else? It seems most people I talk to have never heard of it, or certainly don't know any magic themselves."

"If it wasn't for my dealings with you, I never would have known to suspect it."

"And I imagine it made you suspect I had a part in this," Tome said.

"The thought had crossed my mind. But I've got a bit of an eye for handwriting, and that didn't strike me as something from you, even at a glance."

"It isn't even something from a paper mage. Not a trained one, anyway. This phrasing—again, sloppy. This looks like... how can I explain it... if you were to give someone a sample of a spell that would technically activate but was horribly simplified to make each of the elements easier to understand, this is what you'd get. The kind of thing a tutor would work up. A toy version of a spell."

"And yet it could incinerate someone?" Thaddeus said.

"Normally I would say no. But this paper, and this ink. To put it simply, this was made by someone with access to Greater Mystics. The stuff vibrates with power. You could probably jot down a shopping list in the appropriate structure and activate the spell to cause the goods to simply appear. This is a spell crafted by someone with more resources than know-how, at least with regard to paper magic. The words were written by a complete novice working by rote. But this spell would have been easily as potent as the best of mine on the strength of the materials alone. What was it protecting?"

Euphoria and Thad flipped through the pages.

"They're all the... what do you call them, signatures? The groups of pages?" Euphoria said.

"Right, yes," Tome said.

"Taken from different things in the archive," she said.

"There are notes attached to each one. Indicating what order they should be stored in. This one specifically requests that space be left for two other additions before 'protection is applied,'" Thaddeus said.

"It seems like random records... I... No, here. This is an entry mentioning Fenfield," Euphoria said. "Materials. Several tons of stone. Tools. Contracts for masons."

"I have something here as well. A survey report. Dated almost five years ago," Thaddeus said.

"Anything notable?" Tome asked.

"It would take a man with expertise to tell you that. There seems to be a remark here about a vein of some odd mineral. I couldn't even begin to pronounce it."

He handed the page over. Tome mumbled a bit.

"I believe that would be... phonetically, pray-sid-ill-ah-ped-ite. Praesidila-pedite. That would translate to... shield stone... stone. It includes the word stone twice, two forms. I get the feeling this was not written by an expert on the topic either," Tome said.

"There's a lot to go through," Thaddeus said. "I see a number of requests for big game and fees paid to trappers. This will take some time. But it begs the question. Why is it here? Hidden away as it was, why hide it at all? Why not just destroy it?"

"Because information must never be destroyed," Wick said.

Thaddeus flinched, his pipe falling out of his mouth. He scrambled to fish it up. "I must be losing my touch," he said. "There was a time I never would have missed that the flame was stationary. Of course, I also never would have assumed you would bring the Masker flame with you to do an investigation into the Graves family."

"It was supposed to be an investigation into the safety of my brother," Euphoria said. "What do you mean, Wick?"

"Information must never be destroyed. It is a core tenet," Wick said.

"For a sentry flame, perhaps. But it is hardly a universal opinion," Tome said.

"It would explain this behavior, would it not? Hiding information rather than destroying it. Taking care to retain all of the information in the books they were taken from?" Wick said.

"I suppose so. Then the person responsible is similarly reverent of informa-tion," Tome said. "Let's see what else this information can teach us."

Allie blinked blearily. Several hours had passed, and she'd learned a few things about the lesser harpies. They were smart. Very smart. They clearly under-stood more spoken words than they let on. Or at least more than she'd given them credit for. They picked things up quickly. Too quickly, in fact. Once they worked out they'd be getting treats for doing something properly, they'd become phenomenally eager to get the payoff, often jumping to the entirely wrong conclusions about Allie's endgame. It took three tries to convince them she wasn't trying to teach them to gather up every scrap of paper in the world. When it became clear it was only the one in the oven that got a treat, they started packing the oven full of scraps. Once that was trained away, there came the issue of competition. The one who delivered the page from the oven got a treat, so they started fighting over the page. Rewarding all of them for getting the page worked, and from there things went more smoothly. They learned to open the door. They learned to do it only when she wasn't watching. They even learned to fetch the pages without getting hurt while the oven was lit, and to do it quickly enough that the page wasn't so much as singed. Now was the last step.

"Come on. Come on. You've figured it out this far," she muttered, eyes fixed on the sky.

She'd gotten them to deliver her the page as far as two streets away. But if she didn't get to sleep, she wouldn't be functional for tomorrow's day of work, so it was time for graduation. She'd gone all the way home and now sat with a bag of stale buns hoping for them to show up so she could give them the rest of the bag and head to sleep.

She heard the flutter of wings. Then, the page dropped in front of her, drifting down to the ground. All four of the lesser harpies plopped down, glancing back and forth between her sack and her face.

"Wonderful. Brilliant. Excellent work! One last trick. I know you can do it," she said.

She sprinkled some treats on the ground and picked up the page. When they were through bickering over the biggest crumbs and were once again watching her, she waved the page to get their attention and slipped it under the door.

They watched intently. She produced another page and dropped it on the ground. The birds scrambled over each other to grab it, and the first one to reach it slid it under the door.

"Perfection!" she said.

She upended the bag. They gleefully attacked the meal.

"Just remember what you learned. And I promise I'll keep the treats coming." She paused. "Once a day. I don't want to wake up to a heap of pages under my door. Got that?"

Two of them stuffed a heroic amount of bread into their beaks to fly away. Another stood guard over the pile. Judy hopped up and gazed up at her.

"Smelly monkey rat," the harpy stated with honor and reverence.

"It's a pleasure working with you, too," she said, turning to slip into her home.

Fel gave a final shove. The wood panel that made up the interior wall of the boss's office creaked free of its nails and dropped to the floor. He froze as he discovered that light came pouring through the opening he'd made. He braced himself for an assault or for a voice to call for guards. Nothing of the sort came. With the utmost of caution, he poked his head out of the hole.

Sure enough, he'd broken through to Lens's side of the full room partition. The lantern was lit, but the chair was empty.

"He leaves the lantern burning all night. That's not even flaunting one's wealth. That's pure thick-headed stupidity," he said.

Fel dragged Oiler through the hole and kept the contraption on his back to keep him from causing mischief, even if repairing a broken wall ought to be considered the opposite. He scanned the "office." There wasn't much to see. No, that wasn't accurate. There was virtually nothing to see. Aside from the lantern set on a small table in the back corner, there was a chair with a dusty, cushioned back slumped to one side and a desk of sorts attached to the partition. That was all. No switches. No chest filled with incriminating evidence. Nothing else. Most confounding of all, there wasn't even a door.

"Surely the partition isn't hinged," he said.

He gave it a shove. It didn't budge. Not only wasn't it a disguised door, it was quite clearly fastened to the wall on both sides.

"I don't understand," Fel rumbled. "How does he enter and exit?"

He stood on the chair and checked the ceiling. No hatch. Likewise for the floor and the walls he hadn't smashed his way through. Solid. Finally he lifted the lantern, as if somehow it concealed the secrets to entering and leaving without the use of a crowbar. The only thing different about it was the smooth copper disk it had been sitting on. Fel tried tapping or twisting the disk, but it was quite stationary.

Fel set the lantern down, set Oiler on the floor, and flopped into the chair. A plume of dust erupted from the seat, adding insult to injury after an evening of sneaking and smashing his way through the place had turned up less than nothing. Oiler started maneuvering the plank to reinstall it. Fel didn't bother to put a stop to it. He needed some time to think and recover, and when all was said, there would be something therapeutic about bashing another hole through this place. As his simmering frustration crept steadily closer to a boil, he set his eyes on the one interesting thing in the room: the lantern. Something was off about it. Something important. He tipped it one way, then the other.

"The flame isn't moving," he muttered.

The realization cut through him. This was a sentry lantern. The contraption burst from his memory, and as seemed to be the case whenever the fog parted to allow some older lesson through, it brought a few other thoughts. He remembered why this room had seemed familiar the first time he was in it. It wasn't because he'd had multiple meetings with Lens in the capacity of being a patron. It was because he'd encountered Lens before this. Before all of this. He'd had what felt like a clash with Lens in a room just like this but under very different circumstances. But most importantly, he knew that when a sentry lantern's flame was stationary, it was occupied. He was being watched. He was as good as caught.

He fixed his eyes on the lantern, then gave Oiler an encouraging nudge.

"Go ahead," he said. "Fix up the hole. If there's no other way in or out, then who's going to come get me? The least I can do is give them the fun of bashing their way through to get me."

Oiler happily indulged in the reconstruction of the damaged wall. Fel gave his ailing mind a chance to work through the riddle thus far. He wasn't getting any ideas. More notions than anything else. Normally when he started to poke and prod at a problem, he could feel the pieces start to click together, the things that fit finding the edges of other things that fit to give him some semblance of a whole picture. This was quite the opposite. Things were bouncing off each other, revealing more and more of what he thought had fit tumbling out of position. He scoured the shadowy remnants of whatever memories were being pushed aside by his time here. It all kept leading him back to the same image. The indistinct shadow of Lens, mocking him from the other side of the screen. Fel fixated on it. He stood from the chair and squinted at it.

Then came the click. The realization that something was familiar. He shifted the chair, positioned the pillow as it had been, and unfocused his eyes. The silhouette of the chair was the same. Precisely the same. He'd had a conversation with Lens, and this was all that he could make out, backlit by the lantern. He turned and sat in the chair again and focused on the shadow it cast on the screen. He could see the shape of his shoulder. His head. It would have been impossible to know without knowing the precise shape of the chair, but there was no way a normal-size human was seated in this chair, casting the shadow he'd had a conversation with. The chair had been empty.

He turned, eyes fixed on the lantern with an intensity that burned as hot as its flame.

"It's you," he said. "It's always been you. That's why there's no way in here. You don't need doors to come and go. There's a mucking sentry lantern calling the shots in this place."

A moment of silence passed. Then another. Long enough for him to begin to doubt his assertion. He roughly grasped the lantern and popped it open. He licked two grimy fingers to pinch out the flame.

"Don't," stated the sentry lantern, calmly. "It would cause more harm than good to leave this place without leadership, and it would be terribly troublesome to send someone to relight the lantern."

"I want answers. What is this about?" Fel demanded.

"There really is no point in giving you answers. If things go according to plan, they won't linger in your mind long enough to do you any good. And if things don't go according to plan, having those answers in your head would be a liability for future plans."

"You're not giving me much motivation to keep you burning."

"Would you like motivation?" the sentry lantern asked.

A soft sequence of clicks and rattles signaled the activation of some manner of contraptions hidden in the ceiling and floor.

"Until I decide to deactivate them, canisters filled with some very nasty poisons are now held shut only by my will. If my will is removed, the room floods with an impressively potent cocktail of toxins."

"How do I know you're not bluffing?"

"You could snuff the flame. That will provide you with a definitive answer, though it will be the last thing you learn."

Fel rumbled with anger but set the lantern down again. "I met you before," he said. "I don't remember it exactly. But I remember finding my way into the room and finding it empty, save for a lantern, just like now. Wherever that was, whenever that was. It was you then, wasn't it? How many times has 'Lens' escaped, when in reality you were sitting right there watching people search for a man who never existed?"

"Never existed? Hardly. Though I am disappointed that you have held on to that memory. I'd overestimated my capacity to modify the workings of the clockwork diamond. Or perhaps the workers who assembled it thus far failed to follow my instructions properly. Or perhaps it is you."

"You don't try to mess with Fel Masker's head," Fel said. "It's not so easy to twist up my brains."

"If you have a special resistance to the clockwork diamond, it isn't because you are Fel Masker, it is because you are simply *a* Masker. The clockwork diamond was initially designed, in part, by the Masker clan. It would make perfect sense to design it so its influence excluded the designers, so that if its behavior was dangerous, those capable of fixing the flaws would remain capable. No matter. That it's affected you at all is evidence that it will eventually do its job. That's really what all this is about. Learning about its capabilities. Testing them. Adapting and trying again. Once you've been sculpted into the person I require, you will correct any minor flaws such that this inconvenience will not persist into the next stage."

"You honestly expect me to make changes and fixes to that monstrous contraption in there? If you know anything about the Maskers, you know you grabbed the wrong one for this little scheme."

"Oh, trust me, Fel. Attempts were made to acquire your father. Attempts were made to acquire his resources, his texts. Even now, such attempts are underway. The best I was able to manage was to acquire the fruits of his labor. And even that has helped streamline this enterprise enormously."

The statement knocked another memory loose in his head. He shifted the lantern aside to look at the disk again, then crouched and crammed his pry bar into the wooden side panel of the table. He wrenched the wood aside to reveal a glimpse of what was behind it. A complex, articulated contraption.

"Coupler..." Fel said, the word tumbling straight from his memories to his mouth.

"I wouldn't touch it or attempt any further demolition," Lens said. "Unless you would like to feel the sting of venoms taken from seven different mystics."

"So it works with, what, the heat of your flame?" Fel asked.

"How it operates is irrelevant to my plans for you."

"The point is, if you were able to get this to work, and get it to work with all the rest of these contraptions, then what do you need me for? Get someone else to fix that contraption in the middle and never have to worry about bringing in the one person in this world who might be able to defeat you."

"That you are the one person in the world who might be able to defeat me is an excellent reason to use you as the primary test subject. Once this all works on you, there will be no other obstacles. I couldn't *believe* my luck when I discovered you were coming here of your own accord. And let us not forget that your father has attempted to teach you. Despite the resistance of your mind, you have absorbed more under his tutelage than most other people in this world will even know about contraptions. Enough, for example, to know that you are using the improper terminology. A contraption is a complete assembly, capable of producing its designed effect. What is the name for a portion of a contraption, only able to bring about a portion of its effect?"

Fel shut his eyes and found he was able to dredge up the answer. "A mechanism."

"Because of its size and complexity, because of the potency of its partial effect, the clockwork diamond appears to be a contraption. But it is merely a mechanism. And just as you cannot use a tool to repair itself, the effects of the clockwork diamond cannot facilitate its completion. This cloudy manipulation of your mind can render you willing to perform the tasks I require, but it cannot render you capable. The pieces that are missing cannot be willed into existence. The corrections to the flaws must come from without, as they do not exist within."

"And if I'm too dumb to figure out what needs fixing?"

"I am confident some ingrained intuition will provide you with the insight I require. And if not? I will pursue your father, or I will acquire a reference. The solution will be found."

"Why? What are you doing? What is so important that you'd cross the world and... time?"

"Again. My plan does not require you to be thusly enlightened, and so you shall not be."

Fel trembled with fury. He considered smashing the lantern. Yes, it would bring the lethal failsafe raining down upon him, but it would also give him the brief satisfaction of inconveniencing Lens and delaying whatever plan he was executing. But given the lengths he'd gone to in order to bring things to this point, it was a near certainty that Lens would stop at nothing to get his father in here. Even as the influence of the diamond fought to blot out his clear memories of his family, he knew he couldn't bring the wrath of this twisted sentry lantern upon them. No, he'd have to solve this problem on his own.

"So what happens now? Do I tear a hole through this whole mess to get back out, then pretend I never discovered any of this?"

"You need not pretend. When you sleep, the diamond will do its work. You will awaken with fragments too sparse to connect. And to depart? As it happens, while you were correct in asserting there was no hatch to gain entrance to this place, that was not always so."

The soft click of traps disengaging was quickly followed by the crackle of the rear wall shifting. Panels that were solid when he checked them a moment ago wobbled as though unsupported. Fel kicked the weakened wall, and the boards clattered down as though they'd been little more than balanced on end. Beyond it was a section of stone that had been pivoted on mechanisms similar to those that operated the doors. Just as Fel had supposed with the room he'd come through to get this far, the room revealed by the hatch was one of the workshops in the diamond's courtyard.

"The courtyard. The only way out through the courtyard is past the diamond." Fel turned to the lantern. "You want me to go out there and get another dose straight from the source to make sure I don't remember any of this."

"As I said, you have a reliable intuition."

"I'm not going that way. I'll bash my way back through, if it is all the same to you."

Again he heard the clicks of traps activating.

"It is not the same to me. You will enter the courtyard and take your medicine, or guards will be summoned who will drag you through. Make any move that I consider to be contrary to my goals, you'll be killed and we will progress through your family and its holdings until I have what I need."

Fel gritted his teeth, but there was no way around it. He stepped through the hatch. Instantly the pressure of the diamond's influence grew stronger. It was still hidden from him by the walls of the workshop, but he could hear its clicking and whirring. The sounds were hypnotic. They drummed on the edge of his mind like tiny hammers, trying to chip their way through. The hatch shut, leaving him and Oiler now trapped and in near total darkness. The only way out of here that didn't involve bashing through a stone wall involved exposing himself to the full force of the diamond's influence. He could march out there and face it, and wake up some time later with some scattered patchwork of memories that suited Lens's whims, or he could stay here and wait for the same fate to fall upon him more slowly.

He'd learned so much. And he was about to lose it all. Who knew if the version of Fel that woke up tomorrow would have the cleverness or will to rediscover it? He scanned the dim workshop around him. Plenty of tools. Plenty of reference material. He could tear out a page and write what he'd learned, but there was no chance they wouldn't be searching him on his way out. Still, it was worth a try. He grabbed the largest of the books in the workshop and started to work through it, seeking a page with enough space to record a message. As he flipped through, he saw things that set even his desperation aside. Designs. Schematics. These weren't parts of the diamond. The forms were familiar to him in a sharp, anxious sort of way. Something he'd faced before. Something that had nearly ended him.

Fel's hands started to shake. His time was running out. He could already feel the edges of his focus unraveling as the diamond tried to iron out the wrinkles his investigation had raised. He tore a page from the book and grabbed a hammer.

"I'm sorry about this, buddy," he said, turning to Oiler. "I promise I'll make it right later..."

CHAPTER 12

Tome finished reading through the last page of the heap of material that had been split off for him from the cache Thaddeus had found. Though the pile of information wasn't massive, it was sparse, and much of it was written in coded language. That meant that uncovering the meaning of any given bit of information regarding Fenfield often required checking and double-checking with Thaddeus and Euphoria for clarification. He noted the information relevant to their search and looked up to the others.

Looking up revealed that a few things had changed since he'd begun work on this final bit. The sun had come up, for starters. Thaddeus had dozed off, seated on one crate and slumped over the other that had been serving as a makeshift table. Euphoria had been working from the only real table and chair and had managed to hold off the clutches of exhaustion while Tome finished his work.

"Anything?" Euphoria said.

"A few more dates, that's all," he said.

"Anything earlier or later?"

"One date, six months later. And the delivery instructions were included."

She nodded and wiped her eyes. She made a note. "That's significant. Thaddeus! The job is done!"

The older man snorted awake. "Mmmh. Yes. Ah... Anything definitive?"

Euphoria flipped through the summary she'd assembled. "Here is what we've learned. Starting several years ago, and completely unrecorded in the day-to-day operations of the Graves family business, money and resources were redirected to Fenfield. Based upon the tools and materials sent there in the early days, it was a mining operation that was set up. But there was also some manner of operation involving exotic animals, including a *very* large fee paid to a trapper from the coast. Then, at a point three months after the disease appeared, all business stopped. No more flow of money. No more flow of workers. No more flow of tools. Nothing."

"Whatever business it was worked almost precisely at break even," Thaddeus added. "After an initial outflow of money to begin this mysterious enterprise, there was a significant inflow due to sales of nebulously defined 'byproducts' to even more nebulously defined 'investors.' This balanced the books, and after that, the enterprise became almost entirely self-contained and ceased creating regular additions to the archives. Hence the huge gaps and sparse information."

"It ended after the disease appeared. And not immediately after, I should emphasize," Tome said. "This certainly has the appearance of someone doing something they shouldn't and unearthing something they wish they hadn't in the process."

"I don't think the timeline works," Euphoria said. "Yes, it ended after the disease appeared, but it was also before the quarantine started. If that operation was the source of the disease, it should have ended precisely when the quarantine started, shouldn't it?"

"I'm more inclined to imagine they wised up and shut down before they were forced to," Thaddeus said.

"Possible," Euphoria said. "Regarding what we thought we were after in this, the answer is yes, there are three hunting lodges in Fenfield, but none of them are near enough to the center of the quarantine area to be useful to Fel. But let's not overlook the delivery instructions. In the last three confirmed shipments of materials to the place, one of which was *after* the appearance of the disease, instructions included a very precise route for delivering goods. All goods were to be sent to Ossaw first, and then sent 'as directly as possible' to the center of Fenfield. The second one actually specifies 'as the harpy flies' regarding just how direct the route should be."

"That's telling," Thaddeus said. "It's fair to assume they knew about the disease before anyone else did, but they were able to continue working until at least three months after everyone else discovered it. Given how thoroughly it effects people, they couldn't very well do that unless they were able to find a safe way to work."

"Do we really believe that something as simple as 'coming in from a specific route' would be enough to ward off the effects of the disease?" Tome asked.

"I think you are going to find out," Euphoria said.

Tome winced. "Are we going to consider this enough evidence to move forward? Enough new information to risk my life?"

"This information, plus your intuition and wisdom? Absolutely," Euphoria said.

He raised an eyebrow. "You do score some points for flattery."

"My brother is a survivor. You are a thinker. Those two traits are enough to get through virtually anything. I'm asking you to go find him and bring him back. If you can make sure the person or thing responsible for leading him into that field doesn't get the chance to do it to him or anyone else ever again, all the better. I'll make sure you have whatever you need. Make a list."

"I don't imagine there's anything else I need that I don't already have. Besides sleep."

"Ossaw is twelve hours away, and the trip back to Fenfield is another four. You can sleep on the way. I'll set you up with a driver and another driver to handle your cart. They'll get you as far as the city and turn back; you'll continue to Fenfield. It's been days already. This can't wait any longer."

"Right. Yes. I understand," Tome said.

"And, Wick, you go and tell Dad what we've learned. Tell him what our plans are," she said.

"If you don't mind, I'd prefer you left the Graves business out of it," Thaddeus said.

Euphoria gave him a firm glance.

"I still have my own family to look after," Thaddeus said. "Unless you've missed it, that's what all this has been about for me. Fel is a good man, and I want to see him survive, but even if he comes back holding up the spoils of war like a conquering hero, there remains the issue of who is responsible for the Graves involvement when it certainly wasn't generally known family business. Before we have answers and a course of action planned out, too much information spread too far could warn those responsible into hiding their tracks better and us losing the trail forever."

She sighed. "Don't hold anything back that will endanger Fel, but... use discretion."

"I will endeavor to oblige," Wick said.

The flame flicked to motion again for the first time since Fel's disappearance. Euphoria dusted off her hands.

"Let's get you on the road. And, Thaddeus, when he is gone, you and I should have a word."

"I'll find a way to arrange a safe meeting."

Tome straightened up and kneaded his aching neck. "Remind me never to get involved in business of any kind at a high level. It seems to be more trouble than it is worth."

Fel rolled out of bed and reluctantly staggered to the bathroom to freshen up. While he splashed water on his face to try to chase away the dregs of sleep, he tugged the sash to summon his manservant. While he waited for Mr. Wick's arrival, he leaned forward and tugged at his eyelids. His eyes were bloodshot, and there were dark rings around them.

"Why am I so exhausted? I must have been at it for a few hours too long last night," he said.

Despite his mind feeling sluggish and muddy from a bad night's sleep, he found the planned events of the day laid out for him at the front of his mind in a way that seemed far sharper and more accessible than he was accustomed to.

"Breakfast," he muttered. "Then to the smith for some iron rod. Brass rod, too. Running low on that stuff. To the archivist for the next volume of reference. Then a meeting with Lens."

"Sir?" Mr. Wick said, knocking on the door.

He opened the door to find his butler looking just as worn out as he did. "Mr. Wick? Late night? You look like death," he said.

"I waited outside Sir's room last night, as requested, to keep anyone from potentially disturbing you. I must have nodded off, as I woke up there just an hour ago."

"Oof. Listen, my friend. If I ask you to do something like that again, you tell me that's not your job." He patted him on the back. "I don't want you using yourself up before we get this city on its feet. That said, I must have needed the rest, because I can barely keep my eyes open despite your vigil."

He yawned and reached down beside the bed to pull up Oiler's pack. The contraption quickly held out its puzzle box. He scrambled it and tossed it over his shoulder for Oiler to solve again.

"Forgive me. I didn't have Sir's agenda for the day before you went to bed."

Fel tapped his head. "It's all right here. Bright as day. Guess even if I could have used a few hours more, I still got enough to keep me sharp."

A breakfast of a single very large poached egg with some toasted bread and butter got him ready for the day, and his daily visit to the smith for supplies went smoothly. Indeed, everything was going smoothly today. It was like Lens said. When everyone plays their part, the world works like clockwork.

He missed a step as the thought passed through his mind. For some reason the instant he thought of Lens, his mood soured. He paused to consider why, but no answer was forthcoming. No sense puzzling over errant thoughts. He'd reached Clickspring's Archive.

"Hello," Fel said, marching in through the door.

The archivist, an older and exceedingly excitable man, nearly jumped out of his skin as Fel appeared.

"I'd only just disabled the traps and alarms. I *do* wish you wouldn't enter unannounced."

"That's what 'hello' was for. I need the brass etching reference, and the one on mystic infusions," Fel said.

The man nodded. "I'll have a look through the index."

He tottered off, leaving Fel to observe the main room of the archive. Fel must have been in this place a hundred times since he'd returned to Clickspring a few months ago, but it still felt new. Brand new. Like he'd never set foot inside before. It really was a wondrous place. The walls were covered with books, but it also housed all manner of mystical and mechanical marvels that were considered crucial to the city's operation. He spun a complex orrery and watched it click through its dance. Locked inside a case on one wall was a strange curved and carved bone. A flute, he imagined. Only the High knew why such things were "crucial to the operation of the city," but it wasn't his place to ponder over such things. He had a job to do.

"I have the etching reference. We are still waiting for the infusion," the archivist said, emerging with a book.

"A pleasure as always," Fel said, accepting the thick book. "Let me know when it arrives."

"You shall be the first to know, Mr. Masker."

Fel hurried out the door. So much more to do. He ticked through his mental agenda again. Next up, before the day's proper work, was a meeting with Lens. He paused and gazed up the street.

"Morning meeting with Lens," he said. "To discuss the day's work. And then this evening, I have another meeting to plan out the next day's work. Nothing happens between those two meetings but sleep. If I've had the evening meeting I can skip a morning meeting. He'll be happy that I've gotten a quicker start on the day."

He took a few steps closer to the clockwork diamond's wall, but the same sourness tugged at his stomach. He suddenly had no interest in going into the courtyard where he'd been doing all his work for months. He stopped again.

"No, no. I love my work." He took a few more strides, but the sourness intensified. He paused again. "I came here specifically to do this. It is important work, and only I can do it. I need to get this done, and as quickly as possible."

This time he managed only one more step before he had to stop again, turning his head aside. "Why does it feel like I'm paying lip service to some meaningless prayer..." He turned. "Forget it, if I'm not in the right state of mind to work at the courtyard, I can work just as well in my own shop. It's just some linkages, a few struts, and a bunch of engraving today."

The instant his back was to the clockwork diamond, he felt an odd sense of relief that lasted him all the way to the front door of his home. He slipped inside.

"Mr. Wick!" he called.

"Did Sir forget something?" his butler called, hurrying from a side hallway.

"No. I just needed a change of scenery, I guess. I feel as though I'll get more done working in the basement. If L... if he sends someone to check on me, let him know I'm down there and I'd rather not be disturbed."

"Of course, Sir."

Fel brought the materials down to his workshop. The place was in very good order, which stood to reason. He really didn't use his personal workshop terribly often. The bulk of the reference volumes were there along with some of the more specialized tools. Some unfinished tinkering sat on either side of the workbench. But for what he was doing today, it wouldn't take much more effort to work in this space than the courtyard workshops. He laid out the materials and got to work laying out a gear. Twenty minutes and six attempts later, he was still laying out the gear. It wasn't a lack of knowledge that slowed him. He knew just how to do what was asked of him. It was a simple procedure. But every time he actually tried to do it, the muscle memory just wasn't there. It felt like regardless of which hand he tried to use, he was using the wrong hand. Things that should have been afterthoughts had to be done slowly and deliberately, like he was a novice with all of the theory but none of the application figured out.

He was on the verge of throwing his scribing tool across the room when a welcome distraction came in the form of a rattling puzzle box beside him. He turned to find Oiler holding up its toy.

"Right. All right," he said, taking the box.

A few of the tiles were difficult to move, but he left them where they were and shifted the rest. "At least someone is getting something done today," he said, presenting the toy. "Maybe I should have just slept in. My hands feel so..."

He'd glanced at his hands to make the observation, and for the first time saw just how chewed up they were. His knuckles were bruised. Pink patches of skin marked fresh scars that had been scrubbed clean of their scabs just a bit too early. Thick calluses had cracked skin with stubborn grime ground into them. This wasn't the result of a single bad night. These were hands that one earned through months of hard labor. Years even. He was a Masker, a contraptioneer. Metal shards had a way of rubbing one's hands raw, but these were the long, slow effects of wielding an ax, a shovel, or a club. He opened his hand and spotted a thick splinter that he didn't even feel, lodged as it was in one of the tougher patches of his hand. He found a tweezer in his tool kit and pulled it free.

"What was I doing last night?"

He leaned forward to get some better light and spotted three more splinters. The last one was stubborn, smaller than the rest, and only seeming to make its presence known when he'd decided it was gone and tested the patch of skin by pressing it. Again there was a rattle of the puzzle box. This time the distraction was not nearly as welcome. Fel snatched the box and looked at it.

"The least you could do is actually finish before you hand it over," he grumbled.

A single tile remained out of place. It was one of the same tiles he'd had difficulty moving, which in retrospect probably explained why Oiler had solved it again so quickly. Moving some tiles caused other tiles to move, and one could only jumble so many of them without the stuck ones coming into play. He nudged at the stuck tile, trying to shake it loose of whatever was gumming it up. No luck. It was wedged tight.

He sighed and rummaged around for his smaller tools. This was something oilers never seemed capable of grasping. They could fix almost anything that needed fixing. But if it had to be disassembled to fix it? That always tripped them up. Once he had the thing in pieces, Oiler would happily reassemble it, but if it was whole and still malfunctioning? There was nothing to be done.

This task, it seemed, his hands were fully willing to cooperate with. He popped one of the faces off the puzzle cube and rattled it, sending the complex workings spilling out onto the table. The wheels and tiles hadn't even finished rattling before Oiler began gathering them and aligning them in preparation for the eagerly anticipated reassembly. Fel knew there were more pieces that should have tumbled out after having a face removed. He turned it up and held it under the light.

"You've got something jammed in there."

He grabbed the tweezers and caught the edge of the dull, nonmetallic mass jamming the works. A good hard yank finally pulled it free and sent a scattering of internal components sprinkling to the workbench and the floor. Oiler grabbed them with the enthusiasm of a pigeon cleaning up scattered crumbs. Fel set down the rest of the puzzle box and inspected the blockage. It was a tightly wadded bit of paper.

Fel felt an odd, burning tingle in the back of his head, something like recognition but combined with anxiety. He unfurled the page. A short, desperate message had been scrawled on the page, growing more labored and illegible as it went.

Don't trust Lens.
Find a way out.
Find and destroy...

A final line degenerated into scribbles. But what worried him was the penmanship on the first line. He pulled a clean page from one of his journals and grabbed a pen.

"Don't trust Lens," he said, tracing out the words as he went.

He compared them to the page. A match. This was written in his own handwriting. The realization struck him like a hammer. He felt dizzy. With shaking hands, he flipped the page over. This had been torn from one of the reference books in the main courtyard. A partial schematic of a gauntlet mechanism filled the opposite side of the torn page.

Fel drummed his fingers on the workbench. "Either you and I have a very skilled and very creative person playing the best prank of all time on us, or we have a problem." He tapped the page. "It wouldn't be so difficult to copy my writing. Especially as bad as it gets after the first words. But how would someone get it into your puzzle box? You never let go of that thing. And you've had it since..." He squinted his eyes. "Since..."

The answer simply wasn't there. He knew he'd given the box to Oiler. He knew Oiler was a handful without it. But he didn't remember where he'd gotten it or when. As he struggled to pick that information out of his mind, he found nothing but hazy half memories and vast gaps. There were plenty of facts clogging his head, but he could only clearly remember what had happened since he woke up.

"Mr. Wick!" he shouted.

His butler arrived with his usual speed. "Yes, Sir."

"Have I been sick?"

"I wouldn't say Sir has been sick. There *has* been some trouble with Sir's memory."

Fel took a breath of relief. "Right. All right. That explains a lot. When did that start?"

"Yesterday morning."

"... Yesterday morning. Not this morning?"

"No. Sir was having trouble remembering things yesterday morning. It was quite the vocal concern. This morning, such was not the case. Is something wrong?"

He eyed the message again. "No. No, I think I have it handled. That'll be all for now."

"As Sir wishes."

He thumped the table again. "Wait! When was the last time you cleaned the workshop here?"

"Not yet this week. Would Sir like me to clean it this evening?"

"No. No. Just wondering. Now that will be all."

Mr. Wick paced away. Fel placed his palms on the workbench and lowered his head, eyes shut.

"I came back here a few months ago. I am a master contraptioneer. Working on contraptions is my passion."

He recited the essential truths that were set quite rigidly in his mind. But none of them felt true. He opened his eyes and looked at the tools arrayed before him. A master contraptioneer wouldn't struggle with the finer points of fabrication as he had. Though if there was something working on his memory, it could easily be fouling his dexterity. He scanned across the tools carefully placed along the backboard of his workbench. He knew all of them by name. Of course he did. That knowledge felt real. He plucked a graver from the set. It was ruthlessly sharp, as it needed to be. It was a key part of finishing any contraption, engraving the runes and designs. If the profile of the graver was dulled at all, it would show in the final contraption.

He opened the drawers on the front of the workbench. Everything that needed to be there was there. Files. A sharpening stone. Oil for the stone. Fel paused. He snatched the sharpening stone up and held it to the light.

"Perfect. Pristine. Not a drop of oil. Not a smear of filings. I've never used this sharpening stone." He pulled the drawer open again. "Or this one. Or this one. I'm a passionate contraptioneer who has never used his own workshop."

He looked up, eying the incomplete contraptions on either side of his workbench. "But if I've never used this workshop, then how did these get here?

None of it's real. None of it. So what do I do now?" He snatched up the page. "According to a version of me who seemed to know more than I do, don't trust Lens, find a way out, and find and destroy something. That's what I do."

He grabbed one of the mallets from the bench and tested its heft against his other hand. "I feel better already."

After not nearly enough sleep, Allie found herself once again at The Fox and Log, on the way up the steps after being summoned like a dog to her daily meeting with Velonia. The woman was nothing if not a creature of habit, as when Allie arrived in the little office she'd set up for herself, Madritz was once again going through her messages for the day. Allie recognized the high-quality paper and the glimpse of the watermark. More messages from the lord. Madritz noticed Allie's gaze.

"Two," Madritz said. "Two messages from the man today. A man who needs to wait a full week for a reply. Two full weeks from when he sent it, assuming I answer immediately, and he can't even keep himself to a single message per day."

She stepped out onto the rooftop patio and opened the oven. It was already lit and sizzling. "This one? I addressed six days ago. It was obsolete almost before he sent it." She stuffed it in the oven. "And this one, a pointless addendum to the list in the first one."

The second joined the first in the oven. She stepped inside.

"If ever you find yourself in a position of authority, Miss Waverly, I entreat you to learn the whole lesson that he only seems capable of learning half of. Hire good people and let them do their jobs."

"I'm flattered you'd even suggest I might someday have the chance to make a decision like that," Allie said, not terribly dedicated to making the statement sound genuine.

"Don't be so sure you won't. Because I live by my own lessons. I may not have hired you, but I've maintained your services, haven't I? And despite multiple opportunities to attempt to free yourself of me, you've begrudgingly but adequately done what I've asked of you. To the limits of your access and ability, at least."

"I imagine you're looking for an update?"

"Quite so."

"I don't have anything new to report. I haven't seen Verfessa since last time."

"Mmm. Anything about the Maskers?"

"Fel is still somewhere up north, and I don't think there's been any news of him."

"And that's all?"

"That's all there is to tell. I suppose you'll mess with my hours again as punishment for not getting you something juicier?"

"No, heavens no. I want honesty out of you. You could have lied and made up something you thought I'd want to hear, and you didn't. That's further evidence you're a worthwhile employee."

Allie kept her eyes trained on Miss Madritz, but out of the corner of her eye, she saw a pudgy black form hop quietly up to the oven.

"You may think I operate exclusively out of malice and spite, but there's no money in that. It's inefficient. I do what it takes to get people to do the work I need from them. To that end, I'm satisfied you are capable of following orders even when you don't like them. That's good. I'm also quite certain if I leave you without suitably challenging work and don't provide sufficient financial motivation, you might get up to mischief. So, the time has come to challenge you."

The oven swung open at the gentle urging of a beak. A second lesser harpy hopped up and snatched at the pages. It wasn't the stealthiest of maneuvers. Allie spoke up to cover the noise.

"I'm worried what you might consider suitably challenging, though I wouldn't mind finding out what you'd call sufficient financial motivation."

"I'll begin by telling you what I know. It doesn't matter how I know, just be aware that I speak with certainty, and attempting to claim fault in my information won't be doing you any favors. First, Donovan Verfessa is in the business of selling forbidden contraptions. Second, the Maskers are also in that business and partnered with Verfessa. Despite the efforts of a somewhat less effective agent, no evidence has been found to confirm this in a way that would bring official, legitimate consequences. This could only have been achieved if contraband was hidden elsewhere. In huge volumes. Volumes that could only have been moved and stored by Donovan Verfessa's people."

Two pages slipped free of the oven. The harpy carrying it took to the air. The second one shut the oven and followed.

"I don't believe you work for the Maskers in any official sense. Likewise for Verfessa. But you are certainly friendly with both. That positions you quite well to perform a task for me. I am going to tell you the name of a book. You will repeat it back to me and memorize it. I won't be writing it down, and you won't be repeating it to anyone else." Madritz gestured at what she didn't know was now an empty oven. "As you can see, I take security seriously."

"I see that," Allie said with a carefully neutral expression.

"The book is Professor Milton Governor's *Treatise on the Infusion of Alloys with Mystic Properties*. Repeat it."

"Professor Milton Governor's *Treatise on the Infusion of Alloys with Mystic Properties*."

"Very good. That is the translated title, but if Martin Masker is as thorough as I've been led to believe, it will have been indexed by that name. My request is a simple one. Acquire for me that book. You may do so by bringing it to me personally. You may do it by learning the location and finding evidence of its storage there, such that an assayer, who will be in town in two days, will be able to locate it in a search and confiscate it. You can provide a location and a means to enter and it will be stolen by a capable agent."

"If an assayer confiscates it, you won't get it."

"I am not asking for strategic advice, I am giving you instructions. Do as you have been told."

"And the financial motivation?"

She laughed wryly. "If I am satisfied by your performance, and only if I am satisfied, then your rent for this month will return to its normal level, and you will be given a degree more leeway in setting your own hours."

"That's not so much a reward as putting things back the way they were."

"That's the nice thing about making the lives of your employees materially worse. Simply loosening the straps suddenly serves as a gift."

"Does that mean if I fail, it's the same volatile hours and expensive rent?"

"Oh, heavens no. The straps can always get tighter. Now off with you. The doors open soon, and I expect our patrons to be happy."

Allie entertained a number of snarky replies, but she'd pushed her luck far enough. She trudged back downstairs. There were plenty of things to do before the tavern opened for business. She had to check the stock of the most popular booze. There were the mugs to see to. If there weren't enough clean ones for the first half of the day, they'd fall behind once the real crowd showed up. But most important of all, there was a debt to be repaid. She opened up the fresh sack of roasted crickets and transferred a double scoop into a basket. She worked her way to the back door, making sure to stay under the overhang, as going any farther risked Madritz catching a glimpse of her if she ventured onto the patio. Before the door had shut behind her, the flutter of black wings brought one of her henchbirds to the stone before her.

"Rotten thieving sneak," said Judy with a regal waggle of her head.

Allie dumped the entire basket of crickets on the ground. The lesser harpy snatched one up and gulped it down, sampling the merchandise. Satisfied, she raised her voice.

"I'll stomp your rotten heads," she croaked.

Two more harpies fluttered down. Presumably the third hadn't returned from delivering the ill-gotten goods.

"When I get a good look at those notes, if they're as good as I hope they are, you'll be getting something much better. Even if I have to buy it from a butcher shop or Divinity's Oven myself."

"Rat pile," Judy proclaimed before gorging on the mound of roasted insects.

Allie slipped back inside and grabbed a fresh apron, ready to work through the real chores of the day. As she tied it in place, the flame in the lantern she'd been toting back and forth from work for days fluttered, then became still. She locked her eyes on it.

"Spit it out," she whispered.

"I wish I had better news," Wick said.

"He's not dead," she barked, cutting off any claims to the contrary before they could be voiced.

"We have no reason to believe that he is dead. But he is still missing. Tome and Euphoria are confident they have found a way to approach and attempt a rescue."

"How long will it take?"

"Tome should be arriving at Fenfield in a few hours. No telling how long it will take to determine if he is successful."

"Good. All right. That's hope. That's enough for now," she said.

"Are you well?"

"My struggles are a drop in the bucket compared to what Fel and the Maskers are going through. Never mind how I'm doing. Just focus on getting Fel out of his mess."

"I will. Good luck to you."

"Just go!" she snapped.

The flame wavered again; Wick had gone. Allie shut her eyes and allowed herself a moment to clench her fists and her teeth and endure a moment of rage at the confluence of tragedy sweeping across herself and everyone she cared about. The moment passed. There was plenty of work to do. She had to just trust that those things beyond her control were being handled. Her own corner of the world needed tending to.

In Masker's Antiquities, the flow of customers was just beginning to pick up. Handling the shop by herself during Epiphany's absence had settled firmly into Vivian's mind, such that she felt derelict in her duties whenever she marched down the stairs to have a meal even though her daughter was more than capable of taking over now. If circumstances were different, she probably would have remained in the shop. The wave of antiques had nearly been sold through. It had brought a brand-new set of clientele who weren't terribly interested in the more impressive contraptions that were normally on sale. Meanwhile, with the dwindling antiques, the contraptions were beginning to return to the shelves, and word had spread among those collectors that fresh stock was appearing. Thus, for this brief window in time, both contraption collectors and antique hunters were filling the shop in record numbers. It wouldn't last long. The least of the problems with Fel's absence was a lack of new stock, but the fact remained that until he was back to work fetching fresh inventory, they certainly wouldn't be getting any new antiques. It was best to strike while the iron was hot. But she had more obligations than simply keeping the shop running. And just as she felt a dereliction of duty when not taking sales, she'd been terribly remiss in another of her roles.

She reached the dining room and found Martin. His expression was distant, his arms folded. Wick's lantern sat on the table before him, flame flickering.

"Nothing new?" Vivian said.

"Nothing new," Martin confirmed.

She sat at the table beside him. "I'm sure there's something you could be doing right now to take your mind off it," she said.

"There's nothing I could possibly be doing right now that has any value to anyone," he said. "I have worked out how to adjust the mask-tracking contraption, but that doesn't have any value until Fel is back, and if it points toward the plagued field, the disease will need a cure or a defense first. I don't know anything about disease. Despite access to the archive within the Greater Lands Wall, an archive that contains no fewer than seventeen books about exotic and common diseases, according to the index we copied, I don't have any of them. Of course I don't. I focused on contraptioneering and history. Two things that are meaningless right now. And even if I had the cure, the only thing we could do is send information to Tome and hope he has the cleverness and resources to use that information."

"You didn't know this moment would come. No one could have anticipated it. You can't sit here and punish yourself for not predicting the future."

"One doesn't need clairvoyance to see that something like this would eventually happen," he said. "You remember how I was when I was younger."

"At least as danger prone as Fel. Like father like son."

"That's not an excuse; that's an indictment. We knew things like this awaited him, and we still crafted him into the man he is. We didn't just allow him to go off and do things like this, we encouraged him, and we allowed these things to become not only possible but necessary. I can go down there and I can tinker with my pointless toys. I can unlock old secrets or make new innovations and discoveries. But why would I seek such things if not to make the world better for our children? And this? This is not a better world."

"Martin, what's done is done. The past is past. It is set in stone. We can only see what it has taught us and move forward. I became a part of this family, and when I did, I took on the burden of keeping an ancient and crucial part of our history alive and the honor of raising two wonderful daughters and one wonderful son. It hasn't always been easy. It hasn't *ever* been easy. But we've always done it, and we've done it together. You've seen the world in your travels, and you've experienced antiquity through your work. My place has been behind the counter of our shop. I may not have seen as much of our land firsthand, but I have seen more of its people than you can imagine. People from all over the world. And I have seen the people of this city. I have seen the wealthy, and I have seen the poor. None of them have lived without tragedy. None of them have lived lives free of mistakes or regrets. Myself included. I've seen mothers who spent more time with their little ones, who spent the years I spent working the shop caring for and doting upon their children in a way I had neither the time nor the capacity to do. But again. What's done is done. And I am proud of what we've done together. Because I know that through it all we've never done anything short of our best. Until now, that's always been enough. And if times require more of us, then we will do more. Because we always have. We will get better. It is who we are. We can do no less."

She stood. "There are very few things in this world that are certain. So we should hold tight to every piece of certainty we can find. And right now, I am certain that sitting here and simmering in regret won't do anyone any good. Take the time if you need it. But get back to work. Because you are brilliant, and you are dedicated, and right now we need those things infinitely more than we need you to punish yourself. So get yourself straightened out and be strong because sometime soon I'm going to need a shoulder to lean on again, and I can't have you curled up feeling sorry for yourself when I do."

Martin stood and threw his arms around her. "You know something? I need to remember, whenever it feels like I'm the unluckiest man alive, I need only take one look at you and realize there's never been anyone luckier than me. Because I found you."

"Finally, you're starting to sound sensible again," she said.

Claws scrabbled on the stairs, and Teya dashed through the room. "Need more music things," she explained, hurrying through. "Fel sister, sell so good!"

The kobold continued down toward the inventory levels. Martin watched her go.

"Has she been... troublesome up there?" he asked.

"She spends her time fiddling with necklaces out of sight behind the counter. Evidently she's gotten rather protective of Epiphany, ever since she saw the sort of rough customers she had to do business with on the road," Vivian explained. "But it's hard to keep her from lending a hand. To that end... just as the rest of us are struggling with the feeling of helplessness over Fel's absence, Teya seems to feel that service to the family is the least she can do until there's a clear way to help him. Mind you, if you *do* find a way to help Fel, I don't think we'll be able to keep her from charging off to find him."

"Music boxes coming for shelf!" Teya chirped, dashing through the room with two such contraptions held high.

"She does seem happiest when she has something to do," Martin said.

"A perfect fit for this family," Vivian agreed.

In the hours that followed his discovery of the unnatural happenings around him, Fel's world had become terribly small. It was a tricky thing to pick fact from fiction when one had very little evidence to separate one from the other. He took a walk, circling the town. All who saw him offered a polite smile at the least. He saw respect and reverence in their eyes for the most part. Anyone he spoke to knew him by name and reputation. It took a few minutes for him to realize that simply noticing something like that was evidence that it was not typical. A man doesn't walk down the street noting how those around him look upon him unless it is different from what he's used to, no more than a man fixates on how his shoes feel unless they're new or on the verge of wearing through.

What did this mean? Was he a pariah in whatever amounted to "real life"? Or simply someone beneath notice? Whoever he was now, he was the sort who no one came chasing after when he didn't show up for work, because despite having a full agenda set in his mind for the day that had been completely neglected, he continued on his way, unharrassed.

Slowly he came to recognize two distinct types of memories in his head. The first, and by far the most prevalent were things he knew but did not feel. The names of the streets, the names of his neighbors. All the pointless, trivial elements of his own history. Even some important things fell into this category. He knew he had a father, a man more skilled in contraptioneering than he was. He could recite these things effortlessly, but it felt like he was telling someone else's anecdote, giving a report on a historical figure, not recounting his own life. The second type of memory was deeper, interwoven into the very fabric of his mind. He had no doubt they were real, but at the same time they didn't amount to anything. He could conjure the features of a face that he knew belonged to a friend, but he didn't know her name. He could remember the salty crunch of his favorite snack, the addictive frustration of a game of chance, the laughter and joy of his last night out. Some of the things that should have been the most precious to him fell into this category. His mother? He had one. He could see her eyes. And sisters, two. But he couldn't dredge up their names. Even if they slipped through his fingers as he tried to grasp them, he found himself dwelling on these thoughts. Everything else felt like it was crafted from paper, flimsy and false.

He'd changed into a ratty set of clothes that rang all the same bells as these thoughts. Mr. Wick had cleaned and mended them, but even looking as respectable and kempt as they likely ever had, the outfit was by a wide margin the lowliest he'd seen in town. But it fit him like a glove, shaped by his body rather than the skill of a tailor. Likewise, he kept the company of Oiler, who was the only semblance of a living thing that seemed to bridge the gap between fleeting flashes of a real life and towering volumes of imagined identity. He'd also found a familiar contraption, a compass-like device, stuffed in one of the pockets of Oiler's pack. It was one of those deep, tactile memories, one that had been papered over with something new, a notion that he should be ignoring it. And so he didn't. He followed the compass to the edge of town and sat on an unfinished section of wall, gazing off in the direction it pointed. Something in him, something he trusted, told him there was no sense following it any farther than this, that some dead end awaited him if he did. But he didn't know what else to do. If nothing else, there was someone tinkering in his thoughts who didn't want him to pay the thing any mind, so he would keep an eye on it out of sheer spite.

Spiting someone he couldn't even identify—that felt like one of those deep memories too. He got the feeling the real Fel wasn't perhaps the stablest or most reasonable of fellows. But considering what must have happened to him to get him this far, that seemed an appropriate way to be.

As the day crawled on, very little happened. He had no epiphanies... though the mere thought of that word seemed to spark something. After a trip back into town just long enough to grab some food to bring back to his spot on the wall, the first notable event happened. Someone was on their way into town. A brief flash of a face, a young studious man with an infuriating level of intellectualism in his expression, surged to the front of his mind. He saw everything about him, and even the details of a ridiculous little cart. Then, just as quickly as they'd showed themselves, the images fizzled away.

"All right," he said. "So I was expecting someone."

He shielded his eyes and peered at the figures approaching. This certainly wasn't the annoying intellectual of his memory. Three heavily loaded carts were rumbling along the road. The first was strapped with a cloth cover, obscuring its contents. The others carried ore. It glittered with a sheen that he didn't recognize. Too metallic to be crystal, to crystalline to be metal. Angular gems with a silvery-white, highly reflective, perfectly opaque surface.

It wasn't until they were a good deal closer that he realized there was something far more notable than an unfamiliar mineral about this miniature caravan.

"Are those... unicorns?" he muttered.

Sure enough, strapped to the carts like common pack animals were three majestic, mystical beasts. Their hides caught the light with a pearlescent sheen. Everything about their appearance sang of magic and beauty. Their demeanor was another thing entirely. These beasts moved in a subdued, defeated trudge. It might have been the size of their load, carts that when heavily loaded should have required two or four great draft horses to move. But there was more to it than that. Just as there was a heavy cloud resting atop most of his mind, these beasts were being muted. He could feel it.

Fel hopped off the wall and trotted toward them. The three drivers noticed his approach one by one. They were the first humans he'd encountered in this place that didn't seem happy to see him. They didn't seem unhappy to see him either. Their expressions were as blank and sullen as the unicorns'.

"Hey, fellows!" Fel called when they were in earshot. "Been a while since I remember someone coming in from out of town. Where are you coming from?"

They didn't answer. He let them get a bit closer and tried again.

"I say, where are you boys coming from?" he called.

Still no answer. Though they had certainly heard him. They all dully shifted their eyes to watch him.

"Don't speak the language, I take it?" he said.

He prepared to try the other language he knew, the one half of the texts and reference materials were written in. He stopped when he realized the words simply weren't there. He could draw meaning from the writing, but there was no link to spoken language. Another paper-thin facade inserted itself into his mind.

"Never mind. Something tells me you boys aren't much for conversation anyway."

He slowed a bit to keep pace with the wagons and lifted a fist-size sample of the ore from one of them. As before, they either didn't notice or didn't care that he'd done anything. He pocketed the ore and lingered, watching the strange trio roll on, but a gleam on the side of one of their heads caught his eye, stirring the clouds of his memories. He trotted a bit faster to catch up to the driver and gazed up for a better look.

All three men wore an identical silver earring in their right ears. He didn't know where he'd seen it before, but he knew that it was very important. With that little nugget tucked away in his mind, he held his ground and watched the procession. Fel had expected it to lead directly into the clockwork diamond's courtyard, but it didn't. In fact, it never even entered the built-up portion of the town. Fel moved only as much as he needed to in order to keep them in view. The three wagons continued on along the outside of town around to the north and entered a small, isolated warehouse a short distance from the city. It wasn't really big enough to contain all three carts, but there was no mystery to that. This was Clickspring. People built down, not up. He made a mental note of that location. He'd be paying it a visit soon enough.

Chapter 13

Against all odds, despite knowing what he was getting himself into, Tome had indeed managed to get a full ten hours of sleep during the ride to Ossaw. Exhaustion was a remarkable thing. He almost missed being stretched to the limit, because it had made his mind dull enough to keep him from fixating on the task ahead. That was long gone. From the moment he'd climbed into the Masker family cart and snapped the reins to head toward Fenfield again, his mind had been sharpened to a needle of focus. Every sense available to him, both mundane and mystical, was turned inward, waiting for the earliest indication of the strange pressure the disease would place on his mind.

Almost worse than the fear of what lay before him was the utter lack of regard for it displayed by his two companions on this journey. Parch alternated between standing on the seat beside him, standing on the horse's back, and clambering onto the top of the cart. The unicorn was either manic and prancing or lazily reclining, not a care in the world. Wick had been with him for almost the entire time. Only brief trips to check on the Maskers in Beffshire interrupted his vigil with Tome. And when he spoke, it was with the cool detachment of a hardened soldier before a march.

"Is the area beginning to look familiar?" Wick asked.

"It is a forest. It looks like a forest," Tome said rigidly.

"We are very close to the quarantined section of the field."

"I know, Wick. I know we are close."

"It should look familiar."

"I was on the other side, and I never got particularly close," Tome snapped. "It might look familiar to Fel if he were here, but let's hope not, because he most likely caught whatever it is this field is trying to give people, let's not forget."

"Have you detected any evidence of that illness?"

"If I had, we wouldn't be continuing forward. I want to find Fel as much as any of us, but there's nothing to be gained by simply succumbing to the same fate. And, once again, I genuinely do not understand how approaching from a specific direction could alter the likelihood of being infected."

"If the disease is of supernatural origin, it need not adhere to behaviors that govern natural diseases," Wick said.

"Which means there may be no way to protect oneself," Tome said.

They rattled along the rough ground for a few more moments. Tome couldn't tell if he had begun to feel something or if his mind was playing tricks on him. He may have claimed he would turn back at the first hint of the sensation, but he dared not turn back before. He had to be certain it wasn't his nerves.

"You were gone for a long time," Tome said.

"An indiscretion that may have led directly to this tragic turn of events," Wick said.

"You've known Fel longer than I have. Something tells me he wouldn't have listened to reason even if you'd been around. But what had held your attention so thoroughly?"

"Mr. Masker completed an operational set of arms for the bust. I was building my familiarity with their operation and had begun transcribing books."

"Books? Plural?"

"I completed fifteen of them."

Tome whistled. "Fifteen. The monastery could have used someone like you. That's an achievement and the beginning of something big, if you truly can rescue the contents of the Telestressa Archives."

"It seems a cursed enterprise. Perhaps the knowledge itself is cursed. First wiped from the world by war. Then endangering friends and family members through the overeager attempt to restore it."

"Stop. Stop that right now. I don't want to hear about 'forbidden knowledge' or 'cursed wisdom.' You can feel bad for what you might perceive as abandoning your post. You're not perfect. No one is. But I can tell you, in the same position? I still might not have come up for air. Watching the wisdom of the ages issue forth from my pen? Snatching whole books from oblivion? Important, necessary work. And if this happening has put you off doing that job, then that is the real tragedy."

"Are you suggesting that information is more important than Fel's life?"

"It would be a horrid thing to suggest, but pragmatically...?"

He let the statement dangle in the air. Before Wick could press him to elaborate, Parch's demeanor changed markedly. The little lesser unicorn huddled behind Tome as though sheltering from a storm. Tome returned his focus to feeling for the effects of the illness. Still he felt nothing. But in his sharpening of his senses, he spotted something. Wick observed it at the same moment.

"A stone marker," the sentry lantern stated.

"I see it."

Almost squarely in the center of the route they were traveling, an arrow of stones pointed forward.

"Fel came through here," Tome said quietly.

"This is a good sign," Wick said.

"Is it? Fel probably got sick and vanished. Retracing his footsteps isn't something I'm keen to do."

"Fel vanished. By the very nature of that act, we do not know if he got sick or not. We have wisely operated under that assumption out of caution. But is it not equally possible that he found something and investigated and has simply not completed his investigation?" Wick said.

"I wouldn't place the balance at equal," he said. "Go tell the Maskers we've found a mark left by Fel. I'll wait until you get back before we move forward."

"A wise course of action," Wick said.

The flame fluttered. Tome gazed at the stones ahead and started to pore over the rest of the forest before him. The way forward was free of trees. They could easily continue onward without deviating, just as they had since they left Ossaw. That hardly seemed like a coincidence.

"The Maskers have been informed. They wish you luck and urge caution and speed in equal measure. Teya, who was present, added that you should 'be brave, very very.' I concur."

"You really are making those trips more quickly," he said.

"A consequence of other activities that can be discussed at a later time."

He lightly snapped the reins, bringing the horse to a slow walk. "If you see anything relevant, say so," Tome said.

"Ahead. A sparkle of metal. Slightly to the left," Wick said.

"Where?"

"Five yards forward along the side of the path."

It still took a few more seconds of slow progress forward before Tome spotted what Wick had indicated. It was a short length of chain, coupled together at a buckle or latch.

"Is that... that looks like a contraption," he said.

"That is my assessment as well," Wick said. "Recently repaired."

"How recently?"

"I am not an expert on such things."

"Fel breaks things; Oiler fixes things. We already know they got at least this far…"

They continued on. The ground was sloping upward slightly. Not enough to make the horse struggle, but enough to hide what lay ahead behind the peak of the gentle hill. It felt like fate was purposely drawing out the suspense. They inched closer to the peak. Tome's heart thumped in his chest. Finally, they started to crest it. As they did, Tome squinted. Something was wrong. His eyes were suddenly telling him two contradictory things simultaneously.

It was supernatural, it was dizzying, and it was more than enough to convince him he'd been hit with the first symptom of the illness. Tome turned aside, shielding his eyes.

"That's it. That's it, we're turning back," he said.

"Wait," Wick insisted.

"Wick, if I succumb, this is over," Tome insisted.

"You saw something impossible, correct?"

"Yes."

"Would you describe it as a wall, approximately fifteen feet tall, enclosing a space not much larger than the city square of Beffshire, yet simultaneously seeming to enclose something larger than the whole city and the surrounding fields, composed of dense, lush forest and sprawling rocky ground?"

"Yes. And that doesn't make any sense."

"I see it too. And additionally, some distance away, a second wall concealing a second disproportionate interior."

"So?"

"I am not susceptible to disease, and my mind is not like yours. If I am seeing it, it is real."

"You said yourself if it's a mystical disease, it needn't follow the rules. That goes for who it can infect. We're going."

"The effects of the disease make fleeing difficult. You want nothing more than to flee right now. If the disease had you in its grips, you would be fighting the urge to flee and you are not. Just continue forward until we are below the level of the wall. I beg of you. When it hides the view, you can assess if your mind is whole and intact."

Tome growled and shielded his eyes. The horse, with its much simpler mind, seemed content to simply look to the ground, as though an uncomfortable glare had shone upon it and it need only avert its gaze. They rumbled down the hill toward the wall. Gradually the view was hidden by the wall, and sanity once again reigned. Tome's mind still worked at the riddle it had been presented with, and his heart still raced with concern that he was in the grips of some otherworldly disease, but things seemed to have settled somewhat. And with the shock gone, there was room for reason. Against all odds, there was a familiarity with both the bizarre sight and the wall ahead. In the case of the mind-bending visual, it was present in miniature when he crossed the threshold of the Greater Lands Wall. A piece of land entirely too large to have been enclosed by a wall that was nevertheless quite happily contained by it. It was simply much more pronounced in this case due to the second point. The wall itself also appeared to be the Greater Lands Wall in miniature. It wasn't as tall as the one to the south, and unlike the real thing, the view over the top suggested it wasn't thick enough to house any hidden chambers and hallways. But the layout of the stones, the overall artistry and architecture was a perfect imitation.

There was only one other significant difference between this wall and the true one. This one was new. Time and the elements had not yet had a chance to round the sharp corners or smooth away the chisel marks. He swept his eyes along the wall and tried to take in what it could all mean. In doing so, he noticed that the trees to the south obscured what looked like a second wall, identical to the first in scale. There were two separate circular walls. He closed his eyes and tried to envision them from above. They were close, but not quite touching. Like a slightly disconnected figure eight.

"What is going on?" he muttered.

He tugged the reins with the intention of guiding his horse toward this second wall for a closer look. The moment the horse started to veer off the straight line they'd traveled since Ossaw, a worrisome fogginess started to tease at Tome's mind. He hastily corrected. Once realigned on the path, his mind cleared.

"So that confirms it," he said. "The path is protecting us. Comforting, though it does rather limit our options regarding exploration. Or, to put it more bluntly, this is a spectacular way to force someone into the jaws of a trap."

"A limited scope of travel limits the scope of attack. We must merely be vigilant," Wick said.

They approached the wall straight ahead. Another significant difference from the Greater Lands Wall presented itself in the form of a gate. It was remarkably well integrated into the form of the wall, made from stone and matching the design, but a wide, flat recess into the ground in front of the wall suggested where it would be lowered in the style of a drawbridge, and the staggered pattern of the wall's bricks aligned on either side of the door, marking two clear seams. Tome brought the cart to a stop just shy of the edge of the depression and carefully climbed down. Ahead, the very chain that seemed to be responsible for either providing or marking the edge of the safe pathway emerged from the dirt and latched on to the wall. This, at least, gave Tome a visual indication of how far he could venture on either side of the door. He had perhaps a yard on either side. Parch, on the other hand, had as much room as he wanted, as the little unicorn happily bounded back and forth across the chain with no sign of trouble.

"It's not a disease," Tome mused. "It's the influence of the wall. The symptoms are identical to what the Greater Mystics experience when they attempt to cross the wall to the Greater Lands. And as with the Greater Lands Wall, Lesser Mystics are unaffected. But something about this wall effects humans. That is profoundly concerning."

"As I recall, Teya was able to navigate a walled area even prior to acquiring her earring by using Parch as a guide. It may be advisable to leash Parch as a contingency against the effects of the wall," Wick suggested.

"Not the worst idea I've heard. Parch! Come here, I need you!" Tome shouted.

The unicorn wasn't the most obedient of creatures for people that he liked, and Tome was rather low on that list. Thus, rather than obligingly trotting over to have a makeshift leash thrown around his neck, Parch instead bounded up the wall and stared down at Tome from the safe vantage.

"Now is not the time, Parch!" Tome barked. "We're trying to find Fel, remember?"

He made ready to reach a bit deeper into his vocabulary for some appropriate profanity when he realized there was a new sound. A distant chatter, filtering through the wall. After another moment, one of the bricks in the wall shuddered and started to grind inward. It clicked and then slid aside a few inches to provide a view through the gate.

Tome took a few steps back and readied a flame spell. If this place had any link to the Greater Lands, there were very few friendly creatures he would expect to find lurking within. Better safe than sorry. He inched closer.

"Hello?" he said. "I warn you, if you mean me harm, I can dish it out to you in kind."

A small, round, positively demented face appeared in the gap. It was gray green, with a pointed nose and teeth that were so needle-sharp and haphazardly pointed that they looked like they were attempting to escape the mouth they were protruding from.

"Wha'd'ya want!" bellowed the thing. "Yer a little late or a lot early. The shipment went out already."

Its voice and attitude were equally grating, and Tome realized that it must have been rather diminutive. Despite the stone opening being roughly at eye level for him, the thing on the other side was plainly holding on to the edge with knobby-knuckled fingers. It had to haul itself up to speak or get a decent look at him, and every such motion produced the soft jangle of a chain.

Tome weighed his options. Clearly this thing had mistaken him for someone else. The question was, did he risk attempting to tease out enough information to play this unknown role, or did he appeal to the thing's reason?

"Out with it! I ain't got all day!" it squawked.

Reason, he suspected, would not be the winning method.

"There was a problem with the shipment," Tome said.

"Like dreck there was a problem with it. Two carts of shield stone and one cart of misk-ell-any-us. Ya got what ya were after!"

"Ooy," bellowed a low voice from somewhere farther beyond the wall. "Who are you hooting at?"

The creature at the door looked awkwardly over his shoulder. "I'm talkin' to the humans!"

"But there's nothing there," remarked the unseen voice.

"How many times I gotta tell you, I got the chains, I can see the stuff what you can't see, on account of the wall!"

"... You what?"

"I got a job to do, ya thick oaf! Just—yah!"

The narrow fingers lost their grip, and he vanished from the gap amid much jangling and griping. The low voice laughed.

"We'll see how ya laugh when I tell the boss ya were distractin' me from my very important job!" The manic creature scrambled up to peer out again. "Listen. I'm lettin' you in so's I don't gotta dangle to work out what yer yammerin' about. But if ya do somethin' I don't like, Chuckles back there'll make paste out of ya."

The door rattled in place and started to descend. Tome dashed clear, just in case the already-belligerent creature decided to drop it and crush him. The edge lowered down, and once again, Tome was treated to the utterly baffling view. The effect was somewhat diminished at this perspective. Though he could see from the curvature of the wall that it couldn't possibly have concealed the vista he was now seeing, he could at least convince himself he was looking through a window to some other world rather than a scale-defying countryside.

If he could set aside the issue of size, the fields set out before him weren't immediately unusual. The flora was lusher and more vibrant than the field, with leafier and more temperate trees than the pines that dominated the forest outside the wall. The fauna, on the other hand, was something else entirely. The acerbic creature at the door was some manner of goblin. Potbellied, dressed in rags, and with spindly limbs and a face that seemed capable only of emotions with the prefix "fiendish." A chain ran from his neck to a loop installed in the wall. The last two links and the collar around the goblin's neck were silver. The previously unseen speaker was a nine-foot-tall minotaur, eyes hidden beneath a dusty mop of hair settled down over a bovine snoot. He was armed with some manner of savage club that looked like someone had taken six double-sided ax-heads and arranged them into a bladed ball at the end of a stick. He scratched a bare belly with a three-fingered hand and swished an ox-tail at a cloud of flies around the makeshift loincloth that served as his only clothing. Despite his size and overwhelming physical strength, something about the way he carried himself came across as affable.

"Now what's yer problem!?" barked the goblin.

Tome stepped forward cautiously. As seemingly pleasant as the minotaur looked, Tome wasn't going to trust him not to put that club to use if instructed to. Better to linger near the door where escape was at least possible.

"The issue, good sir," Tome said, "was with the aforementioned miscellaneous shipment. The quality left something to be desired."

The goblin waved a finger at him, generally encompassing his entire outfit. "Yer a wizzid."

"A paper mage," Tome corrected. "And a rather skilled one, so behave yourself."

The goblin waved a hand dismissively. "A wizzid's a wizzid. Hey, Chuckles. Don't tell this one here yer name. He's a wizzid. They do stuff with names."

"I'm not afraid. Name's Thurb," said the minotaur.

"Oh, sure. Ya ain't afraid now. But when this one here decides we ain't doin' what he wants, paff, yer a toad." He jabbed himself in the chest with his thumb. "And I eat toads."

The goblin turned back to Tome. "And as for ya, ya can't come and tell us we didn't make the misk-ell-any-us right, because yer the ones that taught us how to make it. So if it ain't right, ya taught us wrong."

"Then a degree of retraining will be necessary, because I was most dissatisfied."

"I ain't gonna bring ya in here to look over all our stuff just because…" The goblin trailed off as his beady eyes fixed on Wick's lantern hanging on the cart. "Cripes! He's got the boss with 'im," he hissed under his breath. "Thurb, you take this here wizzid wherever he wants to go. Sorry, boss! Didn't see ya there! Ya been gone for weeks. I didn't think ya was comin' back."

Tome didn't pause long enough to question his good fortune. He had a way inside now. That was enough. He hurried to the cart and snapped the reins. Parch hopped down, startling the goblin, who muttered something unrepeatable before pulling a lever to haul the gate shut. With Parch trotting along beside the cart, Tome followed Thurb down a marked path heading toward the center of the strange field.

"Where am I taking you?" the minotaur asked. "It's a little hard to focus over by Chrimp. That's the goblin at the door. If you turn me into a toad, turn him into a littler one, so he can't eat me."

"I'll take it under advisement. You'll be taking us to the facilities where you make the items besides…" He paused to recall the listed contents of the wagons. "Shield stone."

"We make them in tents. Not facilities. That fine?"

"I'm sure it will be sufficient."

"This way, then."

"I should add, for the duration of this trip, I will be the spokesman for 'the boss,'" Tome said, giving a pointed glance at Wick.

"Wise, as it is unclear to me why I have earned that designation in their eyes," replied Wick, presumably such that only Tome could hear.

"Suits me," said Thurb.

The lumbering creature got close to address Tome secretively. That he had to stoop to do so despite Tome's place in the driver's seat of a cart underscored just how enormous the beast was. That he "whispered" louder than most people spoke, and on the side of the cart where Wick's lantern hung, underscored his lackluster intelligence.

"We don't much like the boss around here," Thurb whispered.

"I'm sorry to hear that," Tome said, eyes watering at the scent of the creature's breath.

Thurb shrugged. "It's just the way it is. When you're locked up somewhere, you don't like the one who has the key. Unless he's coming to let you out." He scratched his head. "Are you coming to let us out?"

"It had not been my immediate intention."

The minotaur shrugged again. "Worth asking."

"You say the boss hasn't visited in weeks, yes?"

"Did I say 'visited'? He didn't really visit, so much. He was always here. Or there. Around, I suppose. Then a few weeks ago that changed. All the places the boss was, he wasn't. That's when they put Chrimp in the chains and took him over to where the nothing starts. And it's when the elf showed up."

Tome's fingers tightened on the reins. "The elf?"

"Yeah. One of the hunter ones. Rangers? Rangers. Came over wearing a silly mask. The boss loved it. Don't know much else. I spent most of my time over where the nothing starts back then, too. The boss didn't tell you all this?"

"The boss is rather taciturn unless he has specific instructions. Hence my role as his spokesman."

"That means he doesn't talk much, right?"

"Correct."

He thunked his head with a thick digit. "Fancy words can't fool me."

"Do you recall the elf's name?"

"He's the only elf in the whole place. He's the elf."

"Sensible," Tome said.

He didn't know why he'd even bothered to ask. He'd come here in search of Fel. Fel had come here in search of Mevrelle. It only stood to reason that he would have found him here.

"Have any humans been through here?" Tome asked.

"What, are you kidding? All the time. Three came and picked up the wagons this morning."

"Have any unexpected humans come through?"

"No. But along with when everything else changed a few weeks ago, the humans mostly don't come through this side. They come through the other side now."

"Of course," Tome said. "May I say, you are being very helpful. I didn't expect you to be so talkative."

Another shrug. "There aren't too many people who can or will talk. Just Chrimp back there, and he's not so fun to talk to. The humans when they come through, and they're pretty dull. And... that's about it. All the rest don't talk or won't. Too busy."

"How long have you been here?"

He scratched his head. "A year? Seems like a year. Could be two. Who counts?"

"And how did you get here?"

For the first time, Tome saw the hint of threat in his expression. Thick lips peeled back into a sneer, and he huffed breath from his snout.

"Her," he rumbled. "If you're so new you haven't met her yet, don't worry. You will. Everyone does..."

The last few days had set new records of difficulty for Allie when it came to keeping her mind on her work. Today was easily the worst of all. The giddy thrill of a completely harebrained scheme to steal incriminating evidence from Velonia actually working combined with the doubt of how she'd pulled it off. She'd had the lesser harpies tuck the stolen pages under her door at home. Madritz had access to her home. As far as she knew, the woman had never entered while Allie was away, but there was no reason she couldn't. Should she have found a different place?

Presently the most pressing concern she had was the tightly shut door on Verfessa's room at the back of the tavern. She'd received her ultimatum. Now she found herself in the unenviable position of having to issue a matching one to him. She prepared her tray with his drink of choice and, for the sake of her nerves, included one for herself. She slipped inside. As always, he had a look of pleasant contentment on his face. The lack of one on hers was evident to him the moment she stepped inside.

"I take it things have not been progressing as you would prefer," Verfessa said.

She thumped down his glass and filled it. "I'm not going to sugarcoat it. She knows a lot about your business. More than I think you realize. She's given me orders to acquire a certain book or tell her where it is. I have two days, or else things get tighter for me."

"A book?" Verfessa said. "I would have expected one of the more valuable contraptions."

"It's a book. I can tell you the title if you want, but something tells me you're not going to hand it over or tell me the address, so what's the point?"

"Best that you don't. More stress than it's worth. If it turns out she is right and it's something I have, that raises all sorts of questions of how she found out. Then there'll be the urge to add some security to keep it safe, which'll just tip her off where it is. I feel for you though." He laughed. "You're in a tight spot."

"I'm glad one of us can laugh about it," she said.

"Anything else worthy of note?" he asked.

"She's been getting regular communications from whatever lord has been helping her get permission to do business here. Burns them when she's through."

"A good sign she doesn't like the idea of someone seeing them."

"That's been my thought as well."

"That been putting any plans in your head?"

"Best that you don't know that either, I think."

He laughed again. "Let me set your expectations. Someone like this? They're not going to be doing business out in the open. There probably won't be codes. At least not in the way that a military or such would use. But they won't be laying their plans out plain. Lots of weasel words. You do enough dirty business, you're always expecting that noose to draw tight. The minute you do something you shouldn't with money and influence that isn't yours, you're sticking your head in a noose. There's no two ways around that. I've got my head in one, the Maskers have got their head in one. You've got your head in one."

"I didn't do any 'dirty business,'" Allie said.

"Funny thing about nooses, most often someone puts one around your neck for you. But the point is, we all have one. The best thing you can do is get your head back out of there. Try to get yourself clear, snip that rope, and hope for the best. But that means getting out of the life, and once you're in it long enough, it gets to feel cozy. So the other option is putting plenty of slack on that rope. So if someone grabs a hold of it, you can get a fair distance away without it going tight. They're going to hide things with context, with innuendo. Anything they can to add a couple of inches to that rope collar to keep it from getting too snug before they can wriggle away."

"Lovely."

"Tight spot," he repeated after a sip of his drink. "This is a test. A test of loyalty. Tricky thing about loyalty tests. You set them up right, and it's always one or the other. Can't be a servant of two masters. If you don't side with someone, you sided against them. Simple as that. You try to please both, you please neither. You try to please neither, you'll succeed. And you pick either side, you failed the test on the other."

"Are you telling me this is a test from your end as well?"

"I don't mean to be tugging on this rope around your neck, Allie. But if something comes down on me and mine because of something you said or did?" He shook his head and swirled the drink. "I like you. And I trust you. I wouldn't be drinking your drink if I didn't. But there's a lot of people I liked and trusted that don't show their faces in Beffshire anymore. Some by their choice. Some by mine. Now if what she's threatening is going to hit you in the pocket, don't forget you know a fellow who pays well for good work."

"My head's in enough nooses already. I'm not eager to stick it in another."

"Then you'll do what you need to do, she'll do what she needs to do, and I'll do what I need to do. And we'll all see where we are in a few days."

He raised his glass. "Here's hoping that the right rope gets pulled."

She raised her own. "I'll drink to that."

In the Masker household, Martin was still furiously scribbling notes minutes after Wick had finished updating them on what had happened thus far. Epiphany was with him, eyes staring into the now-flickering flame as she struggled to grapple with what she had been told. Teya joined them, an uncharacteristically serious look on an expression normally defined by raw enthusiasm.

"There is a second, smaller Greater Lands in a private hunting ground in Shalia. And it is the source of the plague that forced a quarantine..." Epiphany muttered.

"It may be a second link to the same Greater Lands. Or perhaps something else entirely," Martin said. "They've only just penetrated the wall. But it answers why the detector failed. Sure enough, distance was not constant. The wall and its influence naturally would have produced faulty behavior. Now that the detector is within such a place, it may well function properly again, but that's not the important thing. The important thing, the only important thing, is that the elf is likely there, which means Fel is likely there. They are on the cusp of finding him. I am certain of it."

"I go? I find?" Teya tapped her ear. "Greater Lands Wall? Not matter. Earring. More destiny, maybe?"

"The circumstances aren't ideal," Epiphany said. "And you are a *long* way away to be the one doing the rescuing."

"There are no ideal circumstances for what he's been sent to do. But we excel in adverse circumstances. That said, I do agree that this is best left to Tome. It will take you weeks to reach him. Tome should have him rescued by then. There's been mention of shield stone. Do you know what that is?" Martin said.

"I can't say I do," Epiphany said.

Teya shrugged.

"Follow, follow!" he said quickly, marching down the stairs toward his workshop.

Epiphany traipsed after him, trying to keep up both physically and with his running mouth. Teya scampered along behind the pair.

"Bygone Era components are uncommonly strong. Some are nearly indestructible. I have been able to reproduce a considerable amount of the more basic effects of contraptions thanks to the reference materials. But the durability and some of the more impressive results rely upon materials that are not available to me. Shield stone is most certainly the one associated with the durability. There was never any indication where it came from. I'd assumed there might be some in the Greater Lands, but without a firm indication of its location, it would have been absurd to send anyone to seek it. And much as I am intrigued by the possibilities of what I might achieve with access to it, I don't really have much need for that level of durability. But if there is a source as nearby as Shalia? One that we needn't risk our lives for?"

"It remains to be seen what level of risk is involved, Dad," Epiphany said.

"Greater Lands? Many good fighters. Little Greater Lands? Probably still some," Teya agreed.

"Right, yes. Certainly. But if it is available..."

They reached the workshop, and Martin grabbed a book from the shelf. Epiphany looked over the room she'd not seen since before she left for her most recent trade journey. Thus, it was the first time she had seen the stack of handwritten books that had been produced. They had been gathered up neatly, which underscored the amount of work it must have taken to write them out.

She leafed through the pages as her father flipped through some of his own journals. Teya gazed up at the shelves of half-finished contraptions and released a sound of something between awe and irritation. Despite working with the Maskers for a while, it seemed the ingrained distrust of contraptions ran deep in Greater Lands creatures. For many of the same reasons, Epiphany wanted to feel repelled by these books. Their creation directly contributed to the situation Fel was in. But one look at them, the ancient language, the skillfully rendered images on the pages, was all it took to change her mind. These books were a piece of antiquity. She didn't have the same reverence for this knowledge as her father—few people could—but she was not immune to the potential each one of these books held. Not just for the family but also for the world. It wasn't more important than her brother. But it was important. And once Fel was back, safe and sound...

"Here!" Martin said. "I was right. Shield stone. It is used in a treatment applied to individual components or whole contraptions. It is meant to be applied as the last stage of a contraption's finishing process. That stands to reason. Etching the runes and sigils before hardening the components would make things far simpler. It seems very high temperatures and an enclosed chamber are necessary... I'm not certain what this attached contraption is, but it shouldn't be difficult to work out..."

"How much shield stone would be needed to harden a contraption?" Epiphany asked.

"Let me see... Fragments. Fractions of an ounce for something of the size we'd stock on our shelves. It is a very efficient process. Something they refined right until the very end of the Bygone Era."

"... A fraction of an ounce?" she said. "You're sure?"

"That's what the notes I took indicate. Why?"

"Because Wick indicated that two wagons full of the stuff were being delivered, and the implication was that it was part of some larger sequence of shipments."

"Very much stone..." Teya said, clearly understanding the ramifications.

"What in the world could be using so much of a substance that is so efficient to use?" Epiphany asked.

Martin looked up from his notes. "What indeed..."

Tome had to marvel at how quickly the novelty of having a conversation with a minotaur could wear thin. The journey into the miniature Greater Lands had been a slow one. The raw distance was actually quite short, but thanks to the steepness of the path, it required them to turn back and forth along switchback trails, which probably quadrupled the distance and taxed the horse with an incline the entire time. The minotaur had filled the journey with what could charitably be called conversation.

"And then a left. And then two rights. And then a left. And then straight ahead twice. Very important. You don't go straight ahead twice, and you'll end up falling in a spike pit or triggering a trap door that sends you back to the right-left-stairs-right-stairs-left-ladder part."

Tome shook his head. "I'm sorry, how much longer does this go on?"

Thurb flicked his fingers a few times. "Two-hundred-eighty-nine more steps."

"And where precisely is this labyrinth?"

"Back in the Greater Lands."

"I really don't see how this is of any value to me," he said.

"You say that now. But I could tell you the names of seven people who really would have loved to hear all this. One of them had a real funny-shaped skull. I miss that skull…"

Tome gave him a worried look. "Why do you miss the skull?"

"I had this really fancy stick. I think a wizard left it. Gnarled and stronger than it should be. I tied the three skulls I liked best to it and kept it in the middle with me. There was the long lizardy skull, the little round skull, and then his skull, which was more tall than round or long. They went together real well."

"You didn't eat the former owners of these skulls, did you?"

"No. Meat doesn't sit well. I've tried it. Oats. Oats are good food. They have good oats here. They grow them over there, by the lake. Matter of fact, I'm going to go have some. This is as far as I take you. Any closer and I'll be dealing with her, and I don't like dealing with her. If you need me, just go back the way we came. Straight, left, straight, right, left, straight."

"Won't I need an escort?" he asked.

The words fell upon deaf ears, as the hulking beast had already crouched to launch himself into his full stride. Within three bounding steps, he reached a speed that Tome was comfortable defining as utterly terrifying. He very much doubted he would be able to stay ahead of such a beast even on horseback. In retrospect, perhaps being a less than sparkling conversationalist was the lesser of two evils, considering what he might be inclined to do if he were ill-tempered.

He turned back to the road they'd been heading along. The tents where the miscellaneous goods were made were just visible around the edge of a thicket of trees where the steep slope leveled off. He snapped the reins and drew closer. He had expected to see perhaps three or four tents, but the farther along the road he traveled, the more that became visible. By the time he reached the edge of the encampment, there were dozens of them, with a massive central tent dwarfing the rest. They weren't fully enclosed, at least not presently. One wall of each tent, the wall facing the road, had been rolled up and tied to offer light and ventilation. This also provided a glimpse of the creatures within.

Kobolds. Hundreds of them. Other creatures he couldn't quite identify milled among them, but he guessed them a satyr and a dryad. But the overwhelming majority of the workers were kobolds. Visually they were quite like Teya, some a bit larger, some a bit smaller. Few wore even a scrap of clothes. But their dispositions couldn't have been further from the manic enthusiasm of the gray-blue creature who had shared their home for weeks. They worked with their heads down, ears hanging low. Their motions were sure, precise, but subdued. They worked steadily but not quickly. And they were silent. Not a chitter or croak, not a squawk or titter. No laughter or words of any language he could recognize. The things even seemed to be working to a rhythm, synchronized from tent to tent. They were glassy-eyed, either incredibly focused or under the control of some other force.

As for the tasks at hand, they varied from tent to tent with very little rhyme or reason. This one assembled clothing. That one hammered out silverware. Here a trio of them worked together to stitch a saddle. One tent was working hard to assemble a whole wagon. They were producing the trappings of a city. A human city, as none of the things they produced were at a proper scale for the creatures producing them. Farther from the road, a few stone huts belched smoke and rang with the blows of hammers. Smithing was going on. And smelting. It was an entire industry. Enough to keep a city thriving... or an army on its feet. A pair of kobolds hobbled by, toting a sword far larger than anything a kobold or even a human would reasonably handle.

The large tent in the center loomed closer. He could see inside now. And what he saw was the crumb of information that slowly traced out the answers to a thousand questions. The closest his mind could come to assigning a name to the thing was "siren." It had the very basic shape of the mystic he'd seen illustrated in a few books. But it was by no means a close match. Sometimes poor memory, a too-brief glimpse, exaggerated accounts, and degraded descriptions with repeated retellings could sculpt a creature into something unrecognizable when it reached the page. Having seen many mystics firsthand after reading about them, he'd become something of an expert at retracing the origins of a faulty description. This didn't match any he'd seen before. This was a creature that failed to match its historic depiction not because the depiction was inaccurate but because the creature was.

In the books, stories, and songs, sirens were beasts of haunting beauty, something akin to more elegant and pristine harpies. Typically they had the face and perhaps some additional anatomy of a beautiful woman. This creature had a far lower proportion of humanity. A mildly human-shaped torso, though still fully feathered and with wings rather than arms, bore an avian head with a dash more wisdom in its eyes. The torso sat atop a much larger bird body. It looked like someone had heard stories about centaurs and assumed a human torso where a larger beast's head should be was common enough in the wild kingdom that a bird would be a fine fit. The result was a being with two pairs of wings, a hilariously bottom-heavy hawk-type body, and not a trace of dignity.

Tome knew his own fate and the whims of mystic creatures too well to let his guard down. Sirens had the power to compel and lure their targets. Even if this misshapen creature looked disarming, it was plainly a force to be reckoned with. Talons large enough to flay him clutched a carved wooden perch. The claws of alternating talons clacked against it, digging into well-worn divots with a soft thock. The tempo perfectly matched the rhythm at which the kobolds were working. If those things were slaves, she was their master.

He stopped the horse and put his mind to work.

"I refuse to come all this way and find a way to escape one source of mind control, only to fall victim to another." He pulled at the reins. "Come on, Wick, Parch. Let's get to a safer distance. We need to plan."

The planning process was swift enough. The answer came from either legend or antiquity, depending on the true insight of the author of the book Tome chose to reference. He hoped it was antiquity, because that tended to be a shade more reliable than legend. Though he doubted his present situation would have been predicted by either.

Tome fastened a strip of cloth tightly over his ears, blocking out all but the thump of his heart and his breathing, both of which were a good deal faster than he would like.

"Give it a try," he said, his voice a bassy thrum in his ears.

"I presume you can still hear me?" Wick said.

The flame's voice, not a sound in the proper sense, was unaffected by the hearing protection. It rang clear in his mind.

Tome asked, "And you are confident you will be unaffected by the siren's wiles?"

"I am. And more to the point, even if I am compelled by her, I am incapable of doing anything but observing and speaking. I cannot be made a threat to you."

"Excellent. Let's find out if we can get some answers."

Just to be safe, Tome tied his horse to a tent post. He didn't want to think about what would happen if the siren decided to work her magic on the horse. Though it was wishful thinking, he also tied Parch to the post. The unicorn watched with disinterest as he did so, as if to underscore just how ineffectual a leash would be if the creature got it in his mind to wander off.

With Wick in hand, he approached the siren. She turned her predatory eyes toward them as they drew near, watching with interest, but not malice.

"There is a soft, lilting tone at the edge of hearing," Wick said. "In addition, a gentle and idle melody is wavering in harmony."

"There are two singers?" Tome said quietly.

"No. Both voices belong to the siren."

"Fascinating…"

When they were near enough, the creature spoke. Wick relayed the message.

"An emissary of the flame?"

"In a manner of speaking," Tome said. "I will be acting as a spokesman of the flame."

"The flame has a voice. It can speak."

"But I will be speaking for him. And I do not want to be questioned. Though he does not speak, he hears everything you say. That is why I have brought him."

The siren glanced to the lantern. "The flame you carry is not the flame I serve."

Tome froze briefly. He hadn't planned for this eventuality. But as with all bluffs, until one is certain one has truly been found out, the only way forward is to live the lie. "A bold claim. You would risk his wrath in denying his identity?"

"I do not fear his wrath. His whims depend upon me. But it is so tiresome. I welcome the company. Please. Come closer." Wick interjected. "The word 'closer' was uttered with a particularly clear and wavering tone, harmonizing both voices."

For the sake of appearances, Tome took a step closer. Best to allow the beast to believe it was in control, the better to avoid learning what drastic measures it might take when it learned that it wasn't.

"Do you know of Fel Masker?" he asked.

"I do not. It sounds like the name of a man. There are only three men I see, and only briefly. I suppose he may be one of them."

"How long have these men been coming through?"

"Many months."

"He is not one of them."

"And by what name are you known?"

"That is not important."

"Names are very important. Mine is Two-Voice."

"Those at the door were concerned about speaking their names to a wizard," he said.

"I have no concerns about wizards. Wizards must act with will. And will is mine to sculpt."

"You say you are necessary for the flame's whims. You are confident you cannot be replaced?"

"I am tasked with keeping the mystics working. There are no other creatures with the means to compel an army of this size. Without me, free minds. And free minds lead inevitably to free bodies. The flame cannot abide that."

"If you hold such power in service of the flame, and feel no fear of reprisal, then why do you serve him?"

"Because it suits me." Again, Wick interjected. "These final words were spoken with a particular edge to them."

Tome grinned. So, he was not the only one bluffing.

"While it may suit you to serve the flame, it may not, for much longer, suit him to be served by you. We are most displeased by the recent fruits of the kobolds' labors."

"I do not craft the recipes. I merely ensure they are followed. Turn your accusatory tone elsewhere."

"Unless you can illustrate your value, your useful service may be at an end."

"My value." Wick interjected briefly. "She is most cross." He continued. "All that surrounds us is proof of my value. Every creature in this place is here because of me. My voices alone have the capacity to lure mystics across that blasted wall. Every Greater Mystic that walks, swims, or flies outside the Greater Lands does so because I have willed it so. Even these walls were built by labor that followed my cloying call. Even the flickering, glimmering toys that twist the world around them and imitate my own power were built by hands dancing to my tune. My value is not to be questioned."

"If you are so capable, then surely you will be able to provide a more expedient route to the second wall, as the man I seek must surely—"

"She interrupts you," Wick said. "Enough. I grow weary of your presence. I know you are not who you claim to be, because there is a reason the flame I serve no longer has a place within these walls. And I have no doubt that quite soon, you shall learn it as well. Off with you."

"I am not through with—"

"Off with you," Wick added. "Her intonation is quite pointed and melodious."

"Very well," Tome said. "I shall seek proper cooperation elsewhere."

"There is a minor commotion behind us. Parch has grown impatient," Wick said.

Tome turned. Parch was trotting along toward the south. He was dragging half a tent behind him. The kobolds formerly sheltered by the tent continued working as though they were unaware of the change. Tome quickly made his way to the cart and unfastened the horse from his own pole. It was clear that they would have no more help from the siren. And that meant if they were going to find Fel or any more answers, they were going to have to search for them. Given Parch's tendency to follow Fel, the direction the unicorn was heading was as good as any. When they were far enough from Two-Voice to be relatively certain she wouldn't impose her will upon them, Tome uncovered his ears.

"That was less elucidating than I would have liked," he said.

"Some information is better than none," Wick said.

"The question now is, which will happen first? Will we find Fel? Or will we find out what her little ominous statement about why the flame doesn't come here anymore meant?"

"Based upon past experience, the less pleasant truth will reveal itself before the more desirable one."

"Truer words were never spoken, Wick."

Chapter 14

Fel struggled with the burden of carrying two packs on his back as he approached his goal. It had taken an hour or so to gather up the tools he felt he would need, a process that felt terribly familiar, as though he'd had to do precisely that quite recently. With Oiler weighing down one shoulder and his gear weighing down the other, he'd set out for the storehouse he'd seen the carts vanish into. From the looks of the tracks, the carts hadn't left yet, and there didn't seem to be a second exit for them to have slipped out. There were no guards, at least no visible ones. Two lanterns burned, but their flames danced. Not sentry lanterns. If this place was protected, and he couldn't imagine it wasn't, then it had contraptions. Locks, alarms, and traps.

Yet another wave of familiarity bothered him as he inspected the doors and walls for things that could give him away or end him. Either this entire enterprise was something he did often enough for it to feel commonplace, or he'd recently made a habit of it. He tried to rely upon the instinct and ignore the very real threat he was likely in. That felt even more familiar.

The only legitimate way in was a pair of large barn doors on the front of the otherwise entirely stone building. They were massive, far stouter than he could hope to bash his way through, and secured with a complex lock that seemed inadvisable to tamper with. But at this distance, it was doubly clear that this was merely the top level of a deeper structure. And structures dug into the ground required ventilation. He found the first shaft a short distance away. It had been capped with a heavy brass cage, which had been affixed with an alarm. It was no simple task to remove the cap and disable the alarm, but it was far easier than trying the front door.

Oiler eyed the disabled trap as Fel tied a rope to his gear bag to dangle it below him.

"Don't get ahead of me," Fel said. "You can fix it, but you have to wait until we're in the shaft first."

He tied the gear bag to his belt and lowered it into the vent, then braced the sides of his boots against either side of the shaft. It was a tight fit. Someone with a fear of tight spaces would have been screaming at the very thought of slipping inside even if they knew where it led, which he didn't. He didn't give either of those things a second thought. This was where he wanted to go, so down he went.

A space as tight as this meant there was no fear of falling. All he had to do was spread his legs and arms and he could turn a fall into a controlled slide. Climbing back up would be an ordeal but manageable. Not that he had any plans to do that. The nice thing about places built to keep people out was that they were seldom also built to keep people in. He would be leaving through the doors, when the time came.

Above, the light dimmed as Oiler dragged the cover in place and started repairing both it and the alarm from the inside. The distraction would keep the contraption out of trouble while Fel descended. And descend he did. This wasn't merely a few floors carved out of the earth. He lowered into pitch blackness for two minutes before the constant breath of wind from above started to tug toward an outlet within the warehouse... or whatever this place was.

A rare bit of fortune smiled upon him, as the outlet was nearly flush against the ventilation shaft. He hadn't relished the thought of crawling through a similarly narrow horizontal tube to find a way out. The maniacal dedication to security continued here, as there was once again an alarm. A clipped trigger wire pinned to the stone to keep it from retracting took care of that. He planted both boots against the cage and heaved. No motion. Now came the complex process of applying a pry bar in a space that permitted zero leverage.

Progress was slow enough that the jangling mass of chains had clattered its way down to him by the time he got the cage off.

"You are not built with stealth in mind," he hissed at the contraption.

He gave the pry bar a yank. The cage jerked forward far more than he'd intended, completely breaking free of its mountings. It fell away, and he clenched his teeth, bracing for the cacophonous sound of a metal cage striking a stone floor. Seconds passed. It never came. He peered through the hole. The dim light of distant torches didn't penetrate far into the darkness, but his darkness-adjusted eyes could see well enough to know there was no ground below the sheer face of the wall he was emerging from. A yawning chasm, at least five yards wide, separated the wall from the stone walkway across from it. The walkway was clearly constructed. It was perfectly smooth and even had a wood and chain railing to keep people from tumbling into the void. But the chasm itself? Fel hesitated to call it natural, because the wall was perfectly vertical and so flawless it was practically polished. But at the same time, mining something out like that was the work of generations.

He gazed back across the void at the walkway he'd have to make his way to. It was one of several, though only the one even with him and the two above it had any form of light. They all had a slight incline, indicating they might in fact be a singular walkway spiraling up the outside of a monolithic structure. This looked less like something had been chiseled into preexisting stone and more like a tower had been constructed underground. Dimly visible below him was an arch leading off the natural wall and leading to the structure.

"Is the whole center section suspended by arches installed on the natural walls? What sort of a lunatic builds something like that?" he mused.

Oiler peered out through the opening, gazing down after the fallen cage.

"You won't be fixing that one. Sorry," Fel said. "Any chance you could lend a hand here?"

The contraption looked him in the eye. Without looking away, it raised one of its claws and pivoted the thumb up to match the position of the other fingers, producing something that looked quite like a grappling hook. It hooked the claw over the edge of the opening and cast the other claw out across the chasm. The rattling chain slid from the pack, rendering it progressively baggier, but before it ran out of slack, it was able to grasp the support post for the chain railing protecting the edge of the walkway.

Fel tested the tension Oiler was able to create. "Much obliged, Oiler. Always a handy one, aren't you?"

A harrowing shimmy brought him safely to the walkway, and finally the real search could begin. For all the security precautions to this point, the makers of this place clearly didn't expect anyone to make it this far. From here, doorways were wide open. Thick layers of dust with no footprints attested to the lack of patrols. Though there were lantern hooks and sconces at regular intervals, only the handful nearest to him were lit. Thin metal pipes ran between them. More contraptions. He inspected them and found that it was likely just a mechanism for lighting and extinguishing lanterns. He followed the illuminated stretch of walkway in the direction he knew the proper entrance must lie. His mind kept a running tally of the mistakes he was making. He was leaving footprints. He was moving exclusively in the light where he could easily be spotted. This had begun as an attempt at a flawless infiltration, but that had fallen away the moment the vent cage did. With no way to reaffix it, there was now a subtle but impossible to hide bit of evidence that he'd entered. That was all the excuse he needed to dispense with the caution and replace it with speed.

He followed the walkway far enough to be certain the bridge, which attached one level up, connected to a tunnel that led all the way to the surface. When the time came to leave, he'd be doing so in a hurry. His theory about the walkway serving as a ramp to other levels proved accurate, which unfortunately meant reaching the bridge would require at least one full trip around the place, circling around into the unlit walkway behind. He didn't relish that, and carrying his own light wasn't like leaving footprints. Footprints let people know he *had been* there. Carrying a light in the darkness told them precisely where he *was*. Better to slip inside and see what could be found within the level he had reached.

He peered through one of the open doorways. Unlike the walkway, none of the interior lanterns were lit, but lights in the walkway hung low over each doorway, casting a fair amount of light inside. The light fell upon the figure of a robed person with their back to the doorway. He pulled back and pressed to the wall. In the brief instant he'd seen the form, there had been no motion. He hadn't been seen. But alas, after managing to be an asset for so long, Oiler had finally decided it was time once again to be a handful. The contraption shifted and squirmed on his back, jangling its chains softly.

"No, no, no," Fel whispered, holding tight to the straps.

Oiler ignored the pleas and reached back to easily yank the straps from Fel's grip. They slid down his arms, and Oiler thumped to the ground. Before Fel could snatch it up again, the contraption clamored through the doorway. Fel braced himself, ready for a shout. None came. Instead, the soft click and smooth slide of mechanical components meeting and assembling started to ring out from within. Fel hazarded a glance through the doorway. The robed figure was still motionless. At first Fel couldn't see where Oiler had gotten off to, but then he spotted the pack sitting at the figure's feet. Oiler was reaching up, fiddling with something.

"Fine," Fel grumbled. "If we're throwing caution to the wind, let's at least get a good look."

He pulled his lantern and sparker from his gear and lit as dim a flame as he could manage. He crept around the figure and got his first look at its front. It was no human. No living thing, even. Though it wore a robe and boots, this was plainly a contraption. The clothes were the only attempt to conceal this fact. The rest of the figure was minimal, a skeleton of linkages and struts. It felt strange to use the word "simple" to describe what likely took several thousand pieces to assemble, but it lacked the artfulness and flare of most contraptions.

Even high-quality tools were curved and shaped into something with beauty as well as purpose. This had nothing it did not require. Oiler was happily slotting components into place in the chest, teasing small bars, axles, and hooks into position in order to complete the connection from the chest to the mechanisms that would drive the arms. The parts had been laid out on a high rolling table. This was an assembly station, where a worker was meant to do exactly what Oiler was doing. Fel raised the light of the lantern ever so slightly and found similar stations on either side, each at a similar level of completion.

Though the thing was a marvel, Fel found his eyes drawn to its head. The largest unfinished section of its assembly was the neck. Though the head was held in place by some clearly temporary clamps and positioning apparatus, there was a large empty space awaiting a subassembly that didn't seem to be present among the assortment of parts. And then there was the face itself. Separated from the rest of the head by a visible seam, it was a mask, exceedingly simple to the point of appearing unfinished. There were slits marking the positions of the eyes, nose, and mouth, but the facial features were blocky and angular. It was the minimum amount of work necessary to make something identifiable as a face, and not nearly the work necessary to make something work as even a component of a contraption.

He paced along the row of assembly tables. All the figures were missing the same component in the neck, and each had a similarly simple mask. Pacing deeper into the floor revealed additional rows of figures, each at a significantly earlier stage of its assembly. By his estimation there were enough stations and components for about fifty such figures. That was, assuming the missing component could be found and included.

Beyond the fifth row of assembly stations, the floor was mostly empty, as though whatever industry this represented was still in the process of ramping up. But now that he was nearer to the center, he found that a spiral staircase was visible in what he assumed was the very center of the facility. And if he listened closely, he could hear the sounds of labor, and the distinctive aroma of large animals suggested the unicorns that had hauled the carts were present in the floor above as well.

He squinted back toward the front row of inert automata. Oiler finished up and merrily moved over to the next to begin assembly. At the very least, Fel could trust the contraption to keep itself busy for a while. He crept up the stairs far enough to see that the next level was almost fully lit. Inching just far enough to peer over the edge of the floor revealed a harrowing sight.

If the floor below was still building to its full potential, this one was in full swing. Large machinery populated the side of the floor farthest from the wide bridge leading to the surface. Smelting furnaces, currently cold, filled the area. Hoppers of coal and the same sparkling mineral that had heaped the wagons alternated between them. Closer to the bridge, the unicorns stood, motionless and subdued, still hitched to their wagons. One of the loads of mineral had been emptied. Two of the drivers were grunting their way through unloading the second. Their shirts were off, and they were glistening with sweat. The third driver was hammering at something. As anxious as it made Fel to be so near to people who could notice him and raise an alarm, right now the far more alarming thing was the row of workstations that filled the remaining space on the floor.

The stations were not unlike those on the floor below, though a multiple of their size. Each station had six tables filled with carefully aligned parts surrounding a slightly raised platform. On the platform of each station was a single mechanical figure that could still technically be called human-shaped. Though the mechanisms at each station weren't quite shaped like any human *he* had ever met. The things stood seven feet tall and were built broad enough to give them an almost square silhouette. Silvery metal traced out a mesh in the shapes that would have been a human musculature, though the space behind was largely empty. He assumed this was due to their current level of assembly. There were a lot of parts remaining to be assembled. That said, beneath it all were skeletons of mechanisms that seemed at least as complete as the figures below, minus the notable neck component. Their masks were the same basic shape as those below. They were even the same size, making them seem oddly small compared to the frames. If these things had a function, they could probably perform it already. Like a wagon stripped to its frame and axles, the functionality of motion was completed. What remained was the utility. And if those heaps of parts were any indication, these things were meant for significant utility. He would have almost preferred the mystery of working out what that utility was meant to be, but the answer was readily available.

Behind the assembly stations were tool stations, though these tools were not meant for human hands. Picks and shovels scaled for the mechanical marvels stood ready for use. And behind those? Swords, shields. Also scaled for the unfinished automata.

Fel was shaken from the awe and wonder of the sight by something refreshingly crude. The grumbling complaints of overworked laborers.

"Blast it! I almost snagged the rotten jewelry again," barked one of the shovelers, fiddling with his ear.

"You're not used to it yet?" said his partner.

"No, I'm not used to a lousy bit of metal dangling from my ear while I'm trying to work," he snapped. "And why are we the ones who are supposed to do this anyway? Those lizard things dig the stuff up. They load it onto the wagon. Why do we have to unload it?"

"Don't complain. This is the best I've been paid in my life. I'll do whatever they ask."

"The boss hides his face. Those people in that town are creepy. I mean, a big fat guy who I *know* used to be here every day to build those things and unload stuff is suddenly a blacksmith? Says he doesn't even recognize me? Bunch of liars trying to act crazy to get out of the hard work and make *us* do it. And in the other place, all those monsters just working? I think it's shady."

"Of course it's shady! You don't pay this kind of money for people driving wagons and slinging shovels for something that's on the up and up. So you keep your head down, you keep your eyes open, and you do the job until it looks like the hammer is about to drop."

"Will you two stop your complaining?" remarked the third man in frustration. "At least all you need to do is shovel. I had to be the one who said I knew my way around tools, and they've got me putting this... thing together. Now that the other workers decided to play 'city' and stop doing assembly."

"You're not putting it together. You're just laying out the parts for the real workers when they come back. And you get paid extra to do it," remarked a shoveler.

"I have to stick this part onto this part and hammer down the rivet, and I have to do it for everything in this pile. That's putting things together. I should have stuck with guard duty. At least that let me boot around a couple of critters now and then."

"I hope the hammer drops soon. No sense making heaps of money when you can't spend your time anywhere but surrounded by a bunch of addle-headed smilers or droopy-eyed monsters," said the other shoveler.

"I just wish they didn't make us sleep over on the monster side."

Fel slipped down again and ran through what he'd seen and learned. Something was certainly going on here. These men were a bigger part of it than anyone else he'd met, he could tell. But he could also tell that they didn't know what they were doing or why they were doing it. Simply hired grunts. He'd get no answers from them. That note he'd written to himself mentioned finding and destroying things. These hulking automata were undoubtedly what he'd been referring to. The gauntlets on them were a match for the diagram on the opposite side of the page. But the sheen on their metal was familiar. They were proper, treated, high-quality contraptions. Just about the only thing that would be able to reliably damage them would be similarly high-quality contraptions, and he very much doubted he would have the time or opportunity to find something sturdy and heavy enough to bash them to fragments. And there remained the question of why something that was clearly not complete, and couldn't be completed, would need to be destroyed in the first place.

Unless they *could* be completed.

The trays below had lacked the missing components: the neck and a proper mask. When Oiler had moved on without adding it, that confirmed it. But there were plenty more parts in these trays and tables on the upper level. He climbed up again and scanned them as best he could from his vantage. At first he thought it was an impossible task. He couldn't get a clear look at the tops of the tables, and they were a half a floor away besides. Considering he didn't know what he was looking for beyond its shape and purpose, it wasn't as though it would leap out at him if he saw it. Until it did.

Not to give himself too much credit, it wasn't as though he'd reasoned that a given item on the tray was the component he was looking for. He'd simply swept his eyes far enough to see a particularly well-lit section of the assembly area, clearly some sort of a primary workstation. And positioned above it, as the masterpieces from which new pieces would need to be crafted, were two items. A mask, far more ornate and finished than the rest he'd seen, and a hinged cylinder just the right size to fill the gap he'd seen in the vicinity of the neck. His mind supplied the word "coupler." He didn't know why he knew that's what it was called. But he was just as certain of that fact as he was of his own name. And what's more, the mask beside it wasn't merely a mask. It was the Student, another name that surged up with certainty despite the surrounding memories remaining blotted out by the fog of his mind.

These were old memories. Real ones. The ones buried under clouds and haze by whatever reality had been concocted for him. And they were important enough that they were able to break through.

He had a target. By hook or by crook, he had to get those two items. He didn't know what he would do with them once he had them, but after groping around in the dark and in confusion for so long, he didn't care. This was a direction, and it was all he needed.

Well, that and a plan. He had to think.

Allie toted a particularly heavy sack toward her door. Despite claims to the contrary, she hadn't been permitted to work her entire shift. Velonia, through Oovay, had informed her that she would be given a few extra hours this evening and suggested she use them for "personally fulfilling activities." She couldn't very well be asked to be Madritz's personal errand girl if she wasn't given the time to run the errands, after all.

As she approached her door, she heard the well-timed flutter of wings and couldn't stifle a grin.

"So help me," she said without looking. "I'm actually starting to look forward to when you fellows show up."

"Stinking boot-biter," remarked one of her little crew of avian imps.

She looked up and saw the four lesser harpies arrayed on the rooftop across from her door, peering down into the alley.

"Give me two minutes to check the goods and get situated. Then we'll settle up," she said.

A soft murmuring among the harpies concluded with "Monkey," which seemed to play a number of roles in their mangled little language.

Allie opened her door slowly and slipped inside. There on the floor, as requested, were two pieces of very high-quality paper. One was lightly singed in one corner. The other was a bit sooty but otherwise fully intact. The messages were brief, but for the sake of her helpers, reading them could wait. She removed her own meal from the bag, a meat pie that she knew from experience would be rather underwhelming, and stepped into the alley.

"When I picked up my supper, I asked around at the vendors to see what sort of foods they have the biggest problem with certain creatures making off with. And there was one big answer." She rummaged around in the bag. "And I quote: 'I swear to the High, there is nothing those things wouldn't do for fresh eggs.'"

She removed an egg from the bag and held it up. The effect it had on the lesser harpies was immediate. Eyes widened. Heads turned. A brief and intense negotiation among them erupted with a splash of posturing and a flirtation with violence. Finally Judy flitted down and landed at Allie's feet. She lowered the egg. The harpy tipped her head and plucked it from Allie's hand. Another tip and shift of the beak skillfully cracked the egg, dumping its contents down the bird's throat with a chef's aplomb. It then crunched the shell and gulped it down. Allie produced a second egg, then a third, and a fourth and each time was treated to the same level of skill and satisfaction as the other birds accepted their payment.

"That's it. You did good. Now run along. I don't want to make it a habit of spoiling you, and I certainly don't want to make it a habit of needing your services."

The flock turned and looked at one another. Judy once again stepped forward as spokesbird for the group.

"A smelly, rotten thief you are," she said politely. "Good gracious. A smelly thief. Egg monkey."

The others nodded.

"I'll take that in the spirit it was intended. At least you got the word 'good' in there," she said.

They took off, satisfied that the transaction had been mutually beneficial. She retired to her home and stoked the flames enough to heat the pie.

"Allie," came Wick's voice from her lantern.

"I must be getting a little too comfortable with you," Allie said, tending to the fire. "I don't even jump when my lantern talks to me anymore. Any good news?"

"Fel has not been found. But progress has been made."

"Do you need my help with anything?"

"Not to my knowledge."

"Then you can skip the rest of the update. Save some stories for Fel to tell when he gets back."

"As you wish. Do you have any messages for me?" Wick said.

"No. My problems are my own to deal with."

"Then I shall be on my way."

She stared at the crackling fire. "Wait," she said quickly.

"Have you thought of something?"

It would be a few minutes before the food was ready to eat. She pulled out her chair and sat before the pages.

"Forgive me but I need someone to talk my thoughts out to again. Are you busy?"

"Tome is currently following a unicorn away from a kobold work camp, and the Maskers are variously concluding a lengthy price negotiation and researching uses for a rare mineral. There are no pressing needs for me at present."

"Kobold work camp?" She flattened the two stolen pages. "These are going to be some good stories. I'm going to have to get him to tell them early in the night before he's had too many."

She held the pages flat in the light of Wick's lantern and read the messages aloud.

On the subject of Gem. I'm pleased contact has been made so quickly. This remains important to me, as you know. But you should know that timeliness is second to discretion. Gem is sensitive and delicate. Please provide a full summary of the ways you've ensured discretion.

She flipped to the next page.

At the risk of belaboring the point, Gem fully occupies my mind, and I cannot rest until I am satisfied. By now the requested aid has been passed along. The way forward should be clear for you. Do what you must to smooth things as much as necessary, but Gem is everything.

Each of the pages was signed with the flourish of a signature. Lord Katritz. Ally drummed her fingers on the table.

"Katritz and Madritz. It's like fate is mocking me by applying such similar names to the people most dedicated to ruining my life," she said.

"What, if it is not too bold of me to ask, is Gem?" Wick asked.

"I was warned they'd be using weasel words to keep from saying anything that'd bite them if someone found out. 'Gem' must be what they're calling this little project that is burning my cozy little corner of the world to the ground and seeking to ruin a lot of others. Madritz was right, though. The lord says a whole lot of nothing. It was a long shot, but I was hoping there would be something in here that would lead me up the chain or answer why they're doing what they're doing. No such luck."

"So, a dead end?"

She crossed her arms and leaned back in her chair. "Not necessarily. I'm digging. And sure, I'm digging a hole looking for something. But when it all comes down to it, when you dig a hole, there's one thing you're absolutely certain to find. Dirt. And dirt is useful. You just need to know where to spread it." She shook her head. "I'm starting to sound like Verfessa. The point is, thanks for sticking around, but you can run along. I have some plans to make."

"I wish you luck."

"For once, this isn't something that'll take luck. Magic is magic. Contraption-eering is contraptioneering. But there's a force in this world that puts both of them to shame." She folded the pages and slipped them into her apron. "Gossip. And something tells me a *lot* of important folks get their gossip while picking up their expensive pastries in the morning. I'll have to pay Mariss a visit."

Euphoria Graves had a place in her family that was far more akin to someone running a massive, multicity business enterprise than simply an in-law. This was because the Graves family effectively was a business enterprise masquerading as a family. But that didn't change matters. Her husband, Jonathan, was still away and would be away for weeks more. That left her with all her own decisions to make and obligations to see to, plus any of his local ones that couldn't wait. Still, the family wouldn't have allowed her to marry in if she wasn't the sort who could make several dozen sales routes and inventory decisions and still have time to plan a fancy soiree. And the extracurricular tasks presently added to her agenda were taxing, but not nearly so taxing as finding the favorite desserts and wines of three dozen important local leaders to curry their favor.

She signed off on a final major decision and handed the missives to a courier to deliver them. The instant they were out of her hands, she informed her staff that she had personal matters to address for the rest of the evening and took her leave.

As with many other things that really ought to have no place in business, covering her footsteps and finding secret places to meet were skills she'd honed needle-sharp in her time as a Graves. It was child's play to meet Thaddeus in a windy little mountain shack where neither of them would be disturbed. She opened the door to find him seated at a table with a modest but inviting meal before him. Two plates, two glasses.

"You're partial to Leer Valley Vineyards, are you not?" he said, holding up a bottle as she took a seat.

"When I feel compelled to indulge," she said.

"I've locked myself away from everyone and everything for weeks. I am most certainly interested in a bit of indulgence. And some assertions are best made with the benefit of intoxication." He filled both of their glasses. "Nothing about Fel yet?"

"Unless Tome had simply found him standing in the middle of the road, I wouldn't have expected him by now regardless. But we can discuss that later. I get the impression we're here to talk about unpleasant accusations."

"Quite so." He sawed at a cut of meat that was considerably lower quality than the wine. "There has been evidence of this for quite some time. And nothing I have seen has done anything but highlight it. The family has been having troubles with the flame. First, people inexplicably got their hands on it and held so firmly to it that there was no simple way to determine when they acquired it. Information that should have been unique to our family, unique fruits of our surveillance, fell into the hands of rivals. Even when this problem seemed solved, messages started to appear with unknown origins and written in our own codes. Old codes. Some of the original ones. And now we find out about thefts of information that require an intimate knowledge of our archives and a reverence for that information that forbids its destruction. Every fragment of this information points in the same direction."

"Piotor Graves," she said.

"He's always been a little touched in the head, and no one in the family has greater latitude to operate without supervision."

"It was my understanding that his interest in research and secrecy were so maniacal that the greatest challenge in dealing with him was getting him to divulge that information even to the rest of the family. That's not the recipe for a schemer."

"It's not a recipe for stability, either. Grappling with the riddles of antiquity in complete isolation for decades? Never speaking to someone except through a flame for all that time? I did my research. No one has seen him face to face since the fire that chased him out of his old cabin. No one. I'm not saying there have been no meetings. I'm not saying he hasn't attended a wedding. I'm saying human eyes have not settled upon him since that day."

"That can't be so," she said.

"That, Euphoria, is precisely how it has gone unnoticed. Everyone is of the opinion that someone *must* have seen him. Granted, *they* haven't dealt with him, but someone else *must* be keeping track. Each runner who brings him his supplies simply dead-drops it, never catching a glimpse but always assuming one of the other runners has spoken to him. The man is a ghost. I'd suggest that someone had simply gotten ahold of his lantern some years ago and posed as him, except that the codes and knowledge he has aren't the kinds of things someone finds written in a journal. They aren't even the sorts of things one can coax out in an interrogation. And two of the couriers I tracked down do claim to have heard him give instructions verbally after they dropped off a shipment. So this is Piotor. And I believe he has gone rogue."

"To what end?" she asked.

"To what end indeed," he said. "If we take the curious activities as a whole, and combine them with the activities that are not curious, we get a picture of a man with his own agenda, but one that is not strictly aligned against the rest of the family. Not my family, that is. Far more of the jagged end of his schemes has been shown to point toward the Maskers."

Euphoria gazed into her wineglass, contemplative.

"Piotor is the secret-keeper of the family," she said. "The researcher. He has not so subtly become one of the anchors and pivots that makes the family's current operations possible. Worse, unlike the other powerful members of the family, he holds a position no one aspires to. Anyone else, if there was a sign of weakness, there would be someone eager to see them unseated. And that person could be an ally. There will be no allies in a quest to bring Piotor to task. No one has the skill or desire to become the new researcher and archivist. It is going to take more than compelling evidence to get other members of the family to act against him. It is going to take a solution to the problem that would be posed by his absence. Employing a scoundrel is distasteful, but it is acceptable if he remains useful."

"I'll be working on the former. That leaves you to work on the latter. When we are through here, I'll be heading to his old burned-out manor. It's been decades since the fire. It won't be guarded anymore. It will be the very opposite of a fresh trail to follow, but my instinct tells me if Piotor went wrong, he went wrong that day."

"Sound reasoning," she said. "I'll have to remain here to see to family business and finish the situation regarding Fel. Are you certain you'll be able to handle this?"

He erupted with a mirthless laugh. "How *could* I be? But the job needs to be done. I've already asked far too many questions to be safe until I have enough answers to finish things."

"I'll provide whatever aid I can."

"Expect a message or two. I imagine I'll need all the help I can get. And if you get word of my death? I'd recommend heading back home to Beffshire. Any path that leads to me will lead to you."

"I don't scurry with my tail between my legs. This is a matter of both the Graves and Masker families. It concerns me more than anyone." She raised her glass. "But you'd be doing me a tremendous favor if you'd get to the bottom of it before anyone tries to kill either of us. I'm terribly busy at the moment, and assassination attempts are a distraction I don't need."

"For you, Euphoria? Anything," he said, raising his glass as well.

Fel held his ground in the underground facility as two of the surly trio of workers finally took their leave. His plan had been to wait for them all to leave before he did anything else, but the one hammering at the subassemblies had sent the others on their way. He wouldn't be able to leave until he'd finished, and that would take an hour or more. That didn't bode well for anything that required both speed and solitude.

Fortunately, complete stealth was already impossible, and that meant that "solitude" was negotiable. That was the benefit of a lousy plan. Sweeping changes to it were just as likely to succeed.

He crept closer to the increasingly frustrated worker as he tried and failed to get a rivet to set properly four times in a row.

"How does anyone build anything?" the man barked. "This is pointless! Worthless! It's not worth the extra money!"

"You're supposed to position it over the anvil," Fel said.

At the sound of the unexpected voice, the man turned and swung his hammer. Fel stepped aside, planted a foot behind one of the worker's feet, and simply tugged him toward it. The man awkwardly stumbled backward and struck the ground hard. Fel flipped him to his belly, wrenched his arm behind his back, and had him bound before he could recover.

"I'm a little too good at that," Fel remarked. "I'm really starting to question what sort of a man I am when no one is toying with me."

"Let me go! You don't know who you're dealing with!" the man barked.

Fel hauled him up and thumped him down with his back against the legs of one of the half-constructed hulks.

"You're right. I *don't* know who I'm dealing with. But lucky for both of us, you're going to help me fix that. We'll start with this. Where are we? My mind is telling me we're in Clickspring. But my gut is telling me not to trust it. Time to break the stalemate."

"To blazes with you," the man spat.

"'To blazes.' Fancy talk from someone who doesn't know how to peen over a rivet. That one even *I* can figure out."

"You won't get a word out of me," the man said. "They told me not to talk, so I'm not talking."

"Uh-huh," Fel said. "They told you not to talk. Did they give you an 'or else'? Because I know what *I've* got planned if you don't get chatty." He grabbed the hammer the man had been using and hefted it. "And I'm the one who is actually here to make good on the threats."

The worker looked at him defiantly. "You think you're safe here? Look, I can't explain it, but they know things. If I talk, they'll know. They probably already know what you've done."

"Oh. Then I'd better work fast," he said.

Fel shoved him aside, allowing the man to thump to the ground again. He reached up and grabbed a heavy block of metal from the work surface above.

"See, here's how it's done. You put the anvil under the thing you want to peen over," Fel said, sliding the block beneath the man's head like a pillow. "You make sure it's centered in the little divot. Then you raise the hammer up and—"

He hoisted the heavy hammer. The instant there was even the hint of motion down again, the man yelped.

"I'll talk!"

"Smart! So, where are we?"

"We're in Fenfield! They built these walls, and there's more room in them than out of them."

"That doesn't make sense."

"I know it! But that's what it is. They did something. Contraptions or magic or something. It pulled big hunks of land up out of the ground and spread it around. I don't know how it fits, but it does. Lots of ore and stuff came up with it. And then there were all these deep holes like this."

"And who do you work for?"

"He calls himself Mr. Lens. I don't know what he looks like. He just hides behind a screen or something."

"So we have the same boss. The man likes to keep some pretty curious plates spinning. And who am I?"

"What do you mean, who are you? How should I know who you are? You came wandering in a couple of days ago, empty-headed like most of the newcomers. Had a pushy little goat thing with you that needed to be taught a lesson."

Fel shrugged. "It was worth a try. What are these things, and why are you building them?"

"I don't know what they are. And I'm mostly not even the one who builds them. Workers from the city were doing it. But they completely changed overnight a couple of days ago, and now I'm supposed to get them set up until the old workers get back to it. Don't ask me. It's another Lens thing."

Fel glared at him. It was becoming clear that either Lens kept all his workers in varying degrees of darkness, or this man hoped he would believe such was the case. Either way, it didn't appear answers about identities and agendas would be as forthcoming as he'd hoped. The thought of going so far as to effectively kidnap a man to puzzle out the motivation behind his ailing mind and curious surroundings only to be left with all the same questions was beyond frustrating.

"What about this?" Fel asked, snatching the earring from the man's ear roughly enough to cause him to grunt in pain. "What difference does wearing a piece of jewelry make that you three all wear them despite the shoveler complaining?"

The man blinked at him, the combination of fear and defiance sliding gradually to a neutral, vacant expression.

"Answer me!" Fel said, brandishing the hammer while he shook the earring. "What's it for?"

No answer. The man's eyes didn't even seem focused, like he'd ceased to see Fel and was simply looking through him.

"Don't make me make a mess," Fel growled.

He hoisted the hammer high and brought it down, stopping it so close to the man's face that the rush of air tousled the man's hair. His prisoner didn't even flinch. Fel stood and turned the silver earring over in his hand. Somewhat unpleasantly, the man's ear was irritated and not fully healed from when it had been pierced. This earring was fairly new. Fel wasn't a great judge of things, but he would be surprised if the piercing was more than a month old. He didn't know what that meant. He didn't know what any of this meant. But he didn't need to understand the purpose of the earring to know it had a purpose.

"So... the people of this town. They've changed at least once. Some from workers to just random people in a city. And my mind is being tugged and rearranged. I pull this from your ear and you just go blank. Like there isn't a role for you to play, so you don't play a role at all. And this earring was keeping that at bay."

The thing felt warm in his hand. Warmer than the air around him. Warmer than the man's body heat. And it had a weight that transcended its physical size. It wasn't heavy, but he was more aware of the gentle pressure in his palm than he was of the hefty hammer in the other hand. More important than all of that was the effect on his mind. The dull haze clinging to his brain parted ever so slightly, specifically around his recollection regarding the earring itself. He saw a face. An elf. He heard the name Mevrelle. And he saw a mask.

Fel raised his head and looked to the main assembly station he'd eyed up earlier. It was the same mask. He looked at the earring again. His lips curled in disgust.

"This is going to be gross," he grumbled.

He dropped the hammer and wiped the post of the earring on his shirt. After a steadying breath, he jabbed it through his earlobe. The white-hot sting of pain flooded his mind. The wave of intensity burned away the fog that had clouded his thoughts. The memories thrust upon him remained, but they were a thin and flimsy veneer of lies, like a story told by a toddler that everyone accepts just to humor the child. He was Fel Masker. His parents were Vivian and Martin, his sisters Euphoria and Epiphany. Everything was there, intact and whole. Straight up to the moment he'd damaged the chain surrounding Fenfield. He remembered his will being forced from him, walking like a mindless husk around the edge of one stone wall and through the gate of another. He remembered Parch trotting along with him and being driven away by the very man at his feet.

Fel gave him a kick to the ribs. "That's for trying to kill my unicorn," he said to a man who absolutely couldn't hear him.

With his fury sated, he marched over to the main assembly table and stopped himself an instant before he could pull the mask and coupler from their places on the shelf. Instead, he felt beneath them. The ever so subtle hint of motion confirmed they were sitting atop a pressure plate. It was very precisely fitted into the workbench itself. That was a problem. Every single pressure plate Fel had ever defeated had been installed in a heavy stone floor. The tricks to defeating them mostly depended upon that solid mounting. Built into something else, the risk of motion as he levered something or tweaked it could easily activate the plate. The walls and ceiling around the thing showed no signs of traps. This was an alarm.

His options at this point were limited. He could attempt to disarm the alarm. Success meant he could get the mask and coupler that this whole mission had, in part, been about acquiring. Failure meant the person who had captured him would be aware of where he was and what he was up to. He could also wait and have to grapple with whoever came to check up on the man tied at his feet.

"All right. Let's sweep this all together into a pile. I have Oiler, some decent gear, the mask, and the coupler. Plus the wagon and the greater unicorn. I don't know where Tome or Parch are. I have to destroy not only these automata but also their ability to make them, or we're liable to have trouble in the near future. And if I had to make a guess, I have maybe an hour or two before I have visitors looking to do work or do battle."

He turned the facts about in his head. "Things have been worse," he said with a shrug.

Chapter 15

"The Greater Lands in miniature," Tome mused, gazing at the fields that spread around him.

After far too long following Parch in a roughly southerly trot, he decided whatever instinct guided the little creature didn't take distance into consideration. For all he knew they would be walking for days before they reached whatever Parch was after. It seemed sensible to take a moment to get a lay of the land from a better vantage. Among the many things about this oddity of a place that differentiated it from the land that should have been here was the sheer variety of plant life. Following Parch had taken him a stretch thick with huge, stout trees. It put him unpleasantly in mind of the place he'd been held prisoner when he ventured to the Greater Lands last time, but at least the trees were quite tall and very easy to climb. And Parch was more than willing to delay his slow trek to climb a tree with Tome.

The paper mage held tight to a branch that stuck straight up from the one he stood on and shielded his eyes from the setting sun. It was a mind-bending sight to behold from this vantage. A wall that shouldn't have been able to contain more than a street in an average city was enough to encompass all this, so even a small forest would have been a supernatural achievement to find here. This was much more. He saw many lush fields with the telltale straight lines and square patches of farms. He saw sandy, dry stretches of desert, and in the distance he could even make out what seemed to be the snow and ice of a mountainside or tundra. Such variety shouldn't exist so close together. The place was at once impossibly large and laughably compact.

Even at this height, the farthest wall was hidden behind the horizon, and Tome tried to avoid looking past the sections of wall that were near enough to see. The human mind wasn't well-suited to the task of unraveling the visual riddle of what lay behind the wall. His eyes alternated between two scenes: the view of Fenfield from this height as though the Greater Lands simulacrum wasn't even there, and the tiny portion of Fenfield directly against the wall duplicated as many times as was necessary to cover the required visual space. It was a dizzying experience, and dizziness was quite near the bottom of the list of sensations one wants to experience while at the top of a tree.

The most valuable lessons learned from climbing this high were that they would have at least two days of travel ahead of them if they continued in the direction Parch was leading, and that there was a major landmark not so far away. A comparatively small wall wrapped around a small stone courtyard. The center of that courtyard held a marvelous mechanical contraption. Working out the scale of it from this distance was difficult. Doubly so considering how flexible the very concept of scale seemed to be at the moment. But if he were to estimate, he guessed it was about twenty feet tall and equally wide. A mechanical gem with dancing, rotating facets. In other words, a clockwork diamond.

"It'll take a long time to search this place if we don't get help," Tome said. "But I can think of no better place to start than with that diamond."

"Upon that we are in complete agreement," Wick said. "And I would suggest we move quickly."

"I hadn't intended to dillydally," Tome said.

"I mean in a very immediate sense. I recognize you are avoiding looking in the direction we came from, but something has asserted itself which makes the extreme state of exposure you find yourself in highly undesirable."

Tome squinted and scanned the sky behind him. It didn't take him long to spot what Wick had been indicating. It wasn't a feature of the land or wall but something above it. A muddy-yellow monstrosity gliding on bat-like wings cut sleekly through the air. It was a wyvern, different from a dragon in ways that mattered chiefly to pedants. It was large, it could breathe fire, and it was heading toward them. That was all that mattered.

He didn't waste time or breath on questioning how his luck could have turned so sharply. He dashed along the branch toward the trunk of the tree and set about working his way toward the ground. That the tree was easy to climb didn't mean it was swift to climb, and Tome was learning what many a cat had failed to—climbing down a tree was an entirely different skill from climbing up one.

Parch bounded from branch to branch, effortlessly descending the tree until he was able to wriggle beneath a thick root that arched up from the ground. Wick jangled from Tome's pack as the wizard tried to keep panic from fouling his grip.

"The wyvern is still quite distant, but it is covering distance quickly."

"That isn't helpful, Wick."

"Would it motivate you to learn that, at your present rate, you will reach the ground shortly before its arrival?"

"Will I reach *shelter* before its arrival?"

"I am not able to identify suitable shelter from my present vantage."

"Then it doesn't motivate me!"

Desperation set in as the sound of the wyvern's wings reached his ears. He abandoned climbing and shoved away from the trunk of the tree, plummeting to a branch. His boots slipped when they struck it, sending him tumbling to the ground below with enough force to knock the wind from him. Fear of being roasted to a cinder proved sufficient to hoist him from the ground and send him stumbling toward where he'd left the cart. It wasn't there. The horse had the good sense to make itself scarce at the hint of a predator's approach.

A shadow swept over the land. Tome reached into his pocket and slipped a page free. He would have preferred a less dire situation to see if his spells would work as intended in this strange place, but fate had other plans for him. He tore the page and dodged aside. A swirl of blue light resolved itself into a flawless duplicate of him running in the original direction.

Above, a crackle and shaft of flame. It traced a brilliant line of destruction along the ground, searing the landscape around the illusory duplicate. Even at this distance, the heat was painful in its intensity. When the fire died down and his illusion continued running unaffected, Tome heard the wings flap vigorously, and the shadow passed over again.

Ahead, two shorter, stouter trees had grown together, providing a crevice between them that he might be able to wedge himself into. Hiding under something flammable when pursued by a fire-breather didn't strike him as a sound tactical decision, but it was the best option by virtue of being the only one. His hands fumbled in his bag. The time he'd taken to prepare for this trip had given him the opportunity to produce some much more potent, entirely new spells. A spell the size of a small pamphlet slid from his bag. He'd filled in the final touches just minutes before reaching the tree. It was fresh. It was complex. In any other situation, he would be certain of its capacity to rise to the challenge.

He dove into the crevice and turned. A neat tear activated the spell. The rest of the pages flashed away, consumed by a cold white flame. With each page that vanished, a flickering membrane resolved itself between his body and the wyvern. The beast touched down, turning a swoop to a sprint. The final page raised the final layer of the shield. Tome shielded his face with his arms and prayed to whatever powers might listen.

The monster struck the shield with its jaws opened wide, ready to pluck Tome out of his hiding space. When its teeth met the shield, the sound was like a crystal wind chime. A thousand tinkling notes rang out at once. A brilliant flash of violet light colored the crevice around him. He ventured a glance. The dragon's jaws were locked around the shield, giving Tome a horrifying view down the monster's throat, lit by the glow of great radiant cracks in the mystic shield. The cracks spread and forked. The muscles of the wyvern's jaws bulged and struggled. The shield was holding, but it wouldn't last much longer.

He fumbled for another spell, knowing full well it wouldn't do him any good. No spell available to him would reach the dragon with the shield in place, and the time between when it fell and when he died would be measured in a single heartbeat. But if he was going to die, he'd do it with a spell in his hand.

The shield began to fail. One by one the membranes shattered, producing a clap of energy each time. Another noise split through the rhythmic bursts of magic. The wyvern flinched and reeled back, pulling away a few seconds before the shield entirely failed. Tome heard the noise again. Without the clashing of the magic, he was able to recognize it. It was the hiss of an arrow. The wyvern reeled aside again, two shafts bristling from between scales on the side of its chest. Wings sent dust and debris from the forest floor into the air. The wyvern lurched skyward. And just like that, the threat was gone.

Tome hauled himself from the crevice. Little shards of shield were still fizzling away on the ground. "It took me twenty-seven hours to write that spell. Plus seventy-five duots of high-quality paper and ink. And it lasted through a single bite."

"It saved your life," Wick observed.

"... I suppose there is that."

Motion near the base of the tree drew his attention. He produced the page for an ice spell and held it ready, eyes sweeping for what had caught his attention. It took three full seconds before he realized that there was indeed a form standing in full view, dressed in clothing so expertly matched to their surroundings that he may as well have been invisible.

It was Mevrelle.

Tome grasped the edges of the page, ready to tear. An arrow hissed past him, slicing through the center of the spell and streaking past his sleeve close enough to jostle the fabric. The damage to the spell rendered it inert.

"Peace!" shouted Mevrelle.

"You call that peace? You shot at me!"

"If I wanted you dead, there would be an arrow sticking out of your eye. If I wanted you dead, I wouldn't have assaulted the wyvern. Peace."

"Considering how many times you've tried to kill me or my friends, saving my life once doesn't even bring you to neutral, let alone trustworthy."

"You came here looking for answers. I can give them."

"I came here looking for Fel." Tome felt as though underscoring the intention to take care of Mevrelle once and for all could wait until a moment when he didn't have a bow and arrow ready to skewer him.

"Then you need from me precisely what I need from you. I can tell you where Fel is. I can tell you how to reach him." He pointed. "I have a shelter in that direction. If we reach it before the wyvern decides two arrows aren't enough to give up a meal, I am sure I can convince you of the wisdom of a truce."

Tome took his eyes from Mevrelle just long enough to spot the tracks left by the horse and cart. They headed in roughly the same direction as the elf was pointing.

"I won't endure so much as the *appearance* of treachery. I am no match for you in battle, but with my magic and your bow, the bout between us won't last more than a single attack. Anyone can land a single attack if they're prepared." He narrowed his eyes. "And I am quite prepared."

"Then follow." Mevrelle marched between two trees and onward into the forest.

"I think, for the moment, he can be trusted," Wick said.

"You, of all people, I'd expect to be more cautious," Tome whispered in response.

"He's turned his back to you. Either he has no respect for your capacity to attack him even from an undefended side, or he considers the reward of your cooperation greater than the risk of your attack. I believe he genuinely needs your help."

"That's quite the tactical analysis," Tome said.

"Recent collaboration has provided me with a greater tactical insight."

Tome narrowed his eyes. "We'll be talking about that later. For now, just keep your eyes open."

"I shall happily fulfill this service."

Fel dusted off his hands. He'd been busy investigating and improvising. To his dismay, though not to his surprise, the results of the investigation had greatly increased the amount of improvisation he needed to do. Six of the floors of the facility he was in were accessible, and in any other situation, he would have been beside himself with joy to discover what they contained. Only the top two floors were dedicated to assembly and storage of these strange automata. The next two were filled to the brim with raw materials and prepared components. This place was Martin Masker's dream, an assembly of Bygone Era tools of every stripe, and enough sheet stock, rod stock, and assorted gears and fasteners to build whatever a contraptioneer's heart desired. The remaining two floors contained more mundane supplies: rope, timber, standard shovels and hammers, coal, water, and a great deal of the glittering ore the men had been delivering. The spiraling walkway ended there, rather abruptly, as though farther downward construction had been planned but they simply hadn't gotten around to it.

His first order of business had been to swap every piece of equipment in his bag of gear with a higher-quality version from the materials available. Second, he loaded an assortment of the most useful and most valuable materials into the unicorn's wagon, including a few sacks of the mysterious ore that may or may not have been called "shield stone," if recent memories could be trusted. He strapped one of the completed automata from the second level into the seat of the cart as well. The unicorn seemed about as blank-minded as its former driver. Fortune shined upon him when he discovered that it was perfectly obedient to spoken commands. And not just standard pack animal commands. Things like "hop" or "keep going" or "until I say stop" worked. He wondered how. Out of curiosity and a dash of concern, he tried the same commands on the man. He remained inert and blank-faced. A bit of searching turned up a taming contraption as part of the unicorn's gear. That was a relief. The thought of any unaccounted-for humans simply becoming perfectly obedient husks made his skin crawl. As a final act, he stripped one of the robes from the other automata and pulled it over him. Anything to add a level of disguise and protection was better than nothing.

Thus equipped, he'd shifted his focus to a plan that was about as clever as he ever imagined he would be. It helped that it was less a plan and more a prank he'd used to scare his sister while they were growing up. Back then it had nearly burned down the house, which in this instance was an asset rather than a liability. The current iteration of the prank involved splitting a barrel and placing the halves end to end just inside the double door at the surface.

Then he'd taken some sheet stock and formed a metal trough above it. A bit of time with his sparker got the coal smoldering nicely, charring the door and making the entryway unbearably hot. Then it was a simple matter of completely ignoring the fact that there was an alarm on the two items remaining to be taken.

"All right, Oiler. Let's get moving!" he said.

Oiler had been just as busy, but even so, only about twelve of the fifty automata had been completed to the contraption's satisfaction. Getting Oiler to abandon such a rewarding task took a great deal of coaxing, but once Fel had hauled it to the bridge and tossed it into the back of the wagon, it settled down.

The unicorn was lined up on the bridge. Despite the heavy load, the majestic creature barely showed any struggle keeping steady on the inclined bridge. Fel marched over and grabbed the mask and coupler. Almost before they were lifted from the plates, a horrid whistling alarm blared out.

"I'm glad I didn't waste my time trying to disarm that," he said, climbing into the driver's seat of the wagon.

He set his eyes upon the orange glow of burning coal at the top of the incline. In his mind, he traced the path back to the city.

"A place like this? Five guards will be on their way. At least," he reasoned. "Fast horses. Didn't see any shacks or anything between here and the city. They'll have to ride all the way from there to here. At full speed, not more than ten minutes, not less than five."

He counted off the time, picturing the whole trip from the bizarre false Clickspring to this underground fort. What he knew was that just a few minutes felt like an hour. The anticipation was agonizing. But the moment came. He heard the mechanisms for the heavy doors begin to activate.

"Run! Fast! Go!" Fel barked.

The unicorn leaned against the load and quickly brought it to a trot, then a sprint along the incline of the bridge and onward into the tunnel. Ahead, the glow of burning coal had been joined by a slit of fading daylight between the two doors. The purposefully precarious coal trough collapsed, dumping the burning coal into the barrel of water. A hissing burst of steam filled the tunnel and billowed out through the doors.

"Faster! Faster!" he urged.

The unicorn continued charging toward the hissing, spitting cacophony even as the shouts of arriving guards started to compete with the startling sound.

"Fire!" shouted one man.

"What is that?" shouted another.

"Back off. Something's happened."

Fel raced toward the cloud of steam, a grin widening on his face.

"And... jump!"

Outside the door, the captain of the guard shouted for his men to keep clear of the door. If a fire was raging below, they couldn't risk entering. The smoke rushing up through the entrance would leave them helpless before they even reached the facility below. The dim realization that this was not simply smoke, but steam, came an instant before a startling mass parted the clouds.

A unicorn leaped out of the tunnel. The wagon dragging behind it struck something hidden in the vapor. Water, bits of broken barrel, and smoldering coal exploded from either side, plowed apart by the heavy wagon. By the time the chaos of the moment settled enough for rational thought to return, the wagon was thundering down the road.

"You, you. Clear the tunnel. You, you're with me. Follow that wagon," he instructed.

The chief guard climbed onto his horse. He and his partner gave chase. It was astonishing, and more than a little unnerving, that the unicorn was able to keep ahead even while dragging the wagon. The driver must have known the trouble he would be in if caught, because he drove recklessly. The wagon barely stayed on the road. Bits of ore and stolen equipment scattered from the back of the wagon, rendering the road behind even more treacherous.

Minutes passed. The unicorn's sprint reduced to a run, but the guard's horse was nearing exhaustion as well. The second wave of guards were on the road ahead. Two held their ground. Two more took up positions on either side and raised crossbows. The charging thief didn't slow. Those blocking the path were barely able to dodge the wagon. Bolts hissed through the air. One struck the driver on the shoulder. He didn't even flinch.

"Impossible..." the chief uttered.

They were closer to the city now. The road was wider. He spurred his horse for all it was worth, pulling aside the wagon. The driver's hands weren't even on the reins. He charged farther forward and brought his horse beside the unicorn, barking angry commands at it as he tugged and pulled at the gear. The creature obeyed, slowing its sprint and eventually stopping.

The other guards had already arrived by the time the chief had dismounted his steed and scrambled into the driver's seat, crossbow in one hand.

"I don't know who you are, but if you so much as move, this next bolt will go in your eye. There will be no shrugging that one off!"

The driver wisely chose to comply. The guard reached up and tore back the hood, ready to rain fury upon the thief who dared to defy him. When the rough cloth was pulled away, it revealed a faceless, incomplete head wrought of brass and wood. This was no man. It was merely a man-shaped piece of inert contraptioneering.

The chief turned, his confusion and anger mirrored on the faces of the other men. His eyes fixed on the road behind them, irregularly scattered with stolen goods. All along the roadside, fields and farms stretched into the distance. He hadn't seen anyone jump from the wagon during the pursuit. But during those first few moments after the wagon emerged from the doorway, anything could have happened. And that was assuming there had ever been a driver at all.

"Go to the others. I want you to begin a search starting from the doors and fanning outward. I am going to have to talk to Mr. Lens and see what should be done."

Tome stood beside a crackling fire, arms crossed and waiting. Along the way to Mevrelle's shelter, he'd managed to find where the horse had dragged the cart. Having his equipment and a means of escape at his disposal made the prospect of listening to what the elf had to say slightly more palatable. Mevrelle emerged from a well-built improvised shelter. He'd insisted on taking whatever steps were necessary to "care for" his bow before they could start their conversation. That he hadn't uttered so much as a single word along the way suggested the elf wasn't entirely pleased with this arrangement either, despite being responsible for it.

"Are you going to explain yourself, or was this all an elaborate means to get me in position for a trap?"

"I have survived this far because I have learned that the proper things must be done in the proper time. Preparation. Discipline. It keeps one alive. I am satisfied that we have not been followed and that we are not observed. My equipment is maintained and cared for. Now is the time for talk."

"Good. Because I have questions."

"Save them. I'll tell you what you need to know. If you want to waste your breath on trivia beyond that, you can do so after. I was brought here after our clash. The Student mask, combined with the spells cast upon me, was just barely able to make the trip survivable. Agents of a being that calls itself Lens ensured that I came to this place, which is a product of his machinations. Through the influence of the contraptions within its center and within the wall, the same twisted influence that shaped the world as a whole was conjured again in a reduced capacity. This wall contains a makeshift Greater Lands, populated by whatever Greater Mystics could be coaxed across the wall from the true Greater Lands by the siren. It is at once a prison and a work camp. I know not what the food and materials are used for, but I can only assume they are meant for the contents of the second wall. I do not know what it holds, but I know that humans are taken there while Greater Mystics are taken here."

"If this is a prison, why are you allowed to run free?"

"I am not free. They have taken the Student from me, and without it or any other suitable contraptions to overcome its influence, I remain at the mercy of the clockwork diamond's influence beyond these walls. This is as much a prison as the Greater Lands. It is simply smaller, and flawed."

"Flawed."

Mevrelle pointed viciously in the direction Tome knew the clockwork diamond could be found.

"That hideous perversion of magic in the center of this place has a different influence. A weaker one but more nuanced. I shouldn't be able to think of it, to conceive it. But I can. Indeed, under its influence, I find myself even able to think of and dwell upon the proper clockwork diamond that has held my people prisoner since the Bygone Era. It is not so flawed that I can escape this place or reach the diamond myself. When I approach the center walls or the outer ones, I am robbed of the will to press on. But where the new diamond falls short of the power of the original, it achieves devious works the original cannot. The Greater Lands Wall and the real, original clockwork diamond exert their influence over the minds of those within in only one way. To wipe the knowledge of and desire for the outside world from the minds of those within. But this one? Three times our captors have sent people through the wall to do something to the diamond. And each time, the behavior of those within has adjusted. New wisdom entered their minds. New desires drove their actions. I believe it is, in part, why I am permitted 'freedom.' It is a test. With each adjustment, they will try to shave away that will. And when they succeed, they will know they can dominate even the strongest of minds."

"This is... a tremendous amount of information," Tome said, diplomatically choosing to leave the word "dubious" out of his description. "You say your freedom is in part a test?"

"Initially they needed me for something else. Something they've since acquired to their satisfaction. It is why the flame can no longer be found within this wall, within the false Greater Lands. It is what you need to find your friend Fel, and it is what I need to restore proper freedom to my thoughts. The earring."

"The silver earring. The one that allows Teya to exist beyond the Greater Lands Wall," Tome said.

"It was intended for my people," he spat, briefly letting anger resurface. "I am no wizard. I was given a poor imitation of the earring's spell to link me to the masks. My purpose was to acquire a sentry lantern so that more earrings could be made. I nearly succeeded. If not for the influence of the Warrior mask, fate would have held a far greater victory for me. But Lens has great wisdom and powerful mystics available to him. Combined with the residue of the spell upon me, what little I knew of that spell, and the mystics present both within these walls and elsewhere, the enchantment to create the earrings was re-created. Five earrings were made, and two chain links. Lens, the voice from the flame, provided his own essence to fuel the spells."

Tome shut his eyes tight. "Lens is a sentry flame. He is somehow responsible for all of this. And he offered himself up as raw material for the earrings?"

"Correct."

"How is that possible? You made a single earring using Wick, and it nearly killed him. It took weeks to recover. There simply hasn't been time to create five since your arrival without destroying a handful of sentry flames in the process."

"Lens has a far deeper reserve of power. The chain links were flawed, good for approaching the wall but not crossing it. The first three earrings worked perfectly and seemed not to diminish him in the slightest. Only after the fourth did he decide that no further earrings should be made until he had recovered. A period of six months, by his determination."

"And yet there is a fifth."

"We created four silver earrings. Which meant we had access to four silver earrings, and with them, the freedom to act without the influence of the walls or the diamonds. Two of the mystics here held firm to the silver earrings they had created and decided there was value in being rid of Lens and his influence. Making the earrings until Lens was destroyed seemed the best way to eliminate a foe and arm ourselves against whoever would replace him. Alas, only a single additional earring was created before Lens's guards killed one of the mystics involved. But the damage was done. All flames within this wall that had been lit from Lens were extinguished, for fear that they might be used to further weaken him."

"It sounds to me like I should be careful to keep Wick away from you."

"If it was that simple, you would be dead and I would have taken Wick for myself. Lens killed one of the mystics who made the earrings, and he took his own wisdom with him when he left. We might be able to injure him, but we cannot make another earring."

"So what is this all about? What would you have me do?" Tome asked.

"You are able to think clearly here because this wall and this diamond were made to influence the minds of Greater Lands beings. That means that you will be able to enter the central wall of this place and access the diamond. You go there, find a way to damage or end the diamond's influence, and that will allow us to leave this place. And in the field outside this place, there is a second prison with its own wall and its own diamond. The other prison is where the humans are kept. That they needed earrings *proves* that it has its own diamond, its own influence. You free me, I cross the wall to the place where our minds are free and yours are enslaved, I acquire earrings, I locate Fel. We defeat our mutual enemy."

"You are asking me to break your chains and trust you to use your freedom to break mine?"

"I am informing you of the only possible way you or Fel will ever be free again."

"I have a way out. There is a path into and out of this place for humans."

"Every few days, three humans enter this place to pick up loads of ore and goods. They wear three of the earrings. They would not be wearing them if they weren't necessary to permit humans to enter and leave the other prison."

"Then Fel can't be free without the earrings in that prison, but I can be free without the earrings in this one."

"For now..." Mevrelle said ominously.

"Do you know something else you aren't telling me?"

"The clockwork diamond in the center of this place has been changed again and again, each time exerting greater control. It is merely a contraption. What can be done to one can be done to another."

"Then that would be a problem for you and the other creatures of the Greater Lands, should someone find their way to the heart of the Greater Lands again."

Mevrelle shut his eyes and shook his head. "Of course. You aren't aware. How could you be?"

"Of what?"

"By now you must realize that the wall does not enclose the Greater Lands. It merely separates the Greater Lands from your own lands. From within the Greater Lands, it appears the wall encloses your lands. From within your lands, it appears the wall encloses the Greater Lands. There is a clockwork diamond at the center of our land. Why wouldn't there be one in the center of yours? Hidden from you by its own influence just as ours is hidden from us?"

"Why would there be? The wall exists to keep the dangers of the Greater Lands sequestered, regardless of the relative appearance. You are the ones who cannot cross the wall. We can. There is nothing limiting our perception."

"This place has a diamond. The other wall must have a diamond. The Greater Lands has a diamond. And your lands look precisely the same from our point of view as ours looks from yours. Your land must have a diamond. And if these diamonds can be changed to alter your behavior, then that one can as well."

Tome was silent. There was logic to what Mevrelle said. There was no evidence, but he'd seen with his own eyes how the nature of the Greater Lands concealed itself from all but the strongest, or weakest, minds. It wasn't certain. It wasn't likely. But it was possible that Mevrelle was right, and some unseen wall tucked somewhere in the world held a diamond doing the same dark service as the one toying with the minds of these beasts.

Mevrelle continued as though he could see the pieces falling into place in Tome's mind. "If you allow Lens to perfect the spells and mechanisms he is tinkering with, someday soon you may find your whole world has become a prison," he said.

"Can you get me to the clockwork diamond safely?"

"I can."

"Then I'll investigate it for you. But I make no promises. It is a contraption, and I am a wizard. I've learned a thing or two in my time with the Maskers, but the operation of these contraptions remains a mystery. Now let's go. Quickly. Before I change my mind."

Fel pressed his back against a low wall in a field of wheat some distance from Clickspring. He listened closely and tried to control his breathing. Two guards were on the other side of the wall. They'd lingered in the nearby field for most of an hour, led there by his footprints. But he'd managed to find some dry, well-packed ground to cut across, and thus they'd lost track of him. He heard the crunch of dust beneath their boots as they marched along the wall. They stopped walking. A heart-stopping moment of silent contemplation passed and the guards paced away, finally giving up on the search to retrace their steps.

He breathed a sigh of relief and let his muscles relax for the first time since he'd jumped from the wagon during the chaotic burst from the doorway. So long as he moved slowly and with more care, he could be anywhere in "Clickspring" by the time a fresh set of eyes came to investigate his trail. He'd gotten away. That was more than he'd been expecting to achieve—it seemed like everything in his life these days was a long shot, but it wasn't everything he needed to do.

He checked his gear bag. The coupler and the Student mask were each still inside. The items he'd been sent to acquire were safely in his possession. And he had the silver earring, which should allow him to escape this place's influence, assuming the wall wasn't well enough guarded to keep him from leaving. But Mevrelle had yet to be found, Tome and Parch were still missing, and he'd learned of some heinous new scheme being run by the Graves family flame itself. One that involved an army of automata and a city of kidnapped Shalians who had been brainwashed into believing they were the residents of an ancient city. He couldn't in good conscience leave these people at the whims of Mr. Lens. And he didn't have the slightest clue how to defeat him.

He gave himself a few more minutes in the shelter of the wall, just to be doubly sure that he wouldn't be spotted, then began his trek through the fields. Along the way, he plucked some mostly ripe vegetables. If he'd been thinking, he would have waited until after a big hearty meal before abandoning his honored place in this false city.

A short walk took him to a small hill not far from the edge of the developed portion of the city. A heap of cut stone had been piled there, a temporary stockpile for whenever the next dividing wall between farms would need to be built. The river was a short distance away. He had a good vantage on the city. He didn't have a plan, and it didn't seem likely he'd come up with one that would make an assault on Mr. Lens anything short of suicide. From his vantage, he saw the cart he'd stolen slowly making its way into the city. For some reason, the sight made him smile.

"They're going to investigate. As though I left some sort of clue," Fel said. "There's something satisfying about knowing that I'm a huge pain in the backside for a person who deserves it."

Tome stepped down from the cart and peered up at the wall before him. The journey to the central wall was a surprisingly short one. It was all the more surprising given Mevrelle's insistence on leading the way on foot. He may have been a good deal faster than Tome, but the pace he set was half what the horse could have managed comfortably. No matter. The elf had been an asset. Four times they were threatened, and four times Mevrelle's arrows either injured or ended the beasts. It was telling that only one of the near-attacks came from what Tome would have considered a proper threat in a place that pretended at being the Greater Lands. A dire wolf, something closer to the size of a bear than its mundane namesake, had charged them. An arrow to the side was barely enough to persuade it to retreat. The other three attacks came from a mountain lion, a bear, and an elk. Evidently the task of populating this place with purloined Greater Mystics was more trouble than it was worth, and a handful of more traditional threats had been included to fill things out.

He turned his mind back to the task at hand. Reaching the wall was the easy part. Now he had the riddle of how to get past it without being turned to dust by a Bygone Era trap, or at least an imitation of one. The gate on the central wall certainly had an earnest attempt at the complex locking mechanisms on the real Greater Lands Wall, albeit with a greatly reduced complexity. Tome wasn't willing to bet that the simpler form meant it would be any easier to open or any less deadly if he triggered a trap.

Mevrelle would be of no help. The effects of the wall were quite apparent. He'd ceased to lead the way a dozen paces back and now stood with his head turned aside as though enduring the glare of a setting sun. Tome peered down at Parch, who looked evenly back at him and flicked an ear.

"We're going to have to do the rope thing, aren't we?" he said. "Are you going to make it difficult?"

Parch continued staring at him expectantly. Tome muddled his way through fashioning a rope harness with a long, dangling free end. Astoundingly, Parch allowed him to slip it on. The tricky part came in coaxing him to actually scale the wall, but the unicorn chose to do so after only a few minutes of making Tome look foolish for arguing with a nonverbal creature. The freshly built nature of the wall meant the edges of the blocks were sharper and better defined. The wall may as well have been a staircase for how easily Parch climbed it. Once he was at the top, he locked his little legs and anchored himself for the much more laborious climb by Tome. If he'd known his adventures as a paper mage would involve so much climbing, he would have taken the time to learn proper technique. Fortunately the wall was shorter than its Greater Lands equivalent, so he made it to the top without too many near-plummets.

The top of the wall was crenelated and lacked any obvious triggers for traps. That stood to reason. There was a kingdom-size ring of land filled with dangerous creatures separating any outsiders from the clockwork diamond, and the locals mostly didn't even have the ability to observe that it existed. Anyone who could survive all of that probably wouldn't blink at an extra trap or two.

He gazed down at the diamond. It had looked dazzling in its complexity from afar, but up close the finer points of its operation became visible, adding an order of magnitude more detail and motion.

"What in the world do they expect me to do about this thing?" he muttered.

He freed Parch from the harness and fastened it to one of the crenellations, then dropped a second rope down the inside. While Parch trotted happily along the top of the wall, Tome lowered himself down and tried to work out a plan of attack.

The clattering, shifting, glittering contraption dominated the courtyard, but everything else about the place actually stank of neglect. Weeds grew thick through the cobblestones of the courtyard. Standing water had pooled in the western quarter. Two workbenches had been set up, one on either side of the entry gate, but they had only the most basic of tools or reference books.

He approached the contraption, venturing as near as he dared without getting caught in the swing of its many panels and struts. At that distance, even though this contraption's effect was intended for Greater Lands creatures, he could feel some shadow of it. It was a cold tingle in the back of his mind. And it seemed to pulse or oscillate at times. Like everything else about the clockwork contraption, the oscillations came at regular intervals. He crossed his arms and observed. In time, he realized the oscillations came when a sweeping arm near the bottom of the contraption moved across shiny sections of a ring set into a sheltered portion of the ground. He knelt down and watched closely. Wheels at the bottom of the arm rattled and bounced across the metal ring. Smooth sections produced no oscillations. Engraved sections produced oscillations. And there were very faint seams between sections.

Tome tried to put what he was seeing into a context that he understood backward and forward. Paper magic worked, in part, but assembling elements of a spell in different ways to produce different effects. If the clockwork diamond could be made to produce different effects, then it stood to reason there needed to be some means to exchange the different elements.

He knelt down and reached under, after the arm had finished sweeping by the nearest section. It lifted effortlessly out of place.

"Fascinating…" he mused, turning the piece about in his hand. "Could it be as simple as working out what 'spell' one wishes the diamond to cast and etching it on a plate like this?"

Judging by the speed the arm was moving, he had two or three minutes before the plate would have to be back in place. Time enough to see if he could make sense of any of the patterns in the plate. The maker of this plate, and all the others, had neglected to include any sort of notation to indicate what purpose it served. Still. Language was language, and he'd yet to encounter one that didn't at least feature some aspects he could wrap his mind around.

The clicking rhythm of the contraption continued. He kept a half-hearted count of the tempo, the better to estimate when his time was running out. There was still plenty of time left, more than a minute, but something compelled him to glance in the direction of the gap created by the removal of the plate.

There was a second arm.

He noticed it an instant before the wheels dancing along the previous plate dropped down into the gap. For a quarter second, the amount of time it took for the wheels to pass the results of his tampering, chaos reigned. A ripple tore through the courtyard, like the world itself was a spring that had been drawn back and released, rebounding in a wave of distortion. Cobbles shifted and cracked. His mind filled with a terrible shriek, like the workings of his own brain were briefly attempting to do a dozen things at once. He dropped to his knees and grasped his chest. His heart felt like it was trying to hammer its way out of his chest. The moment passed, wheels clicking up onto the next plate and continuing as though nothing had happened. Tome was not so swift to recover. He fumbled for the dropped plate with trembling fingers and nudged it into place. He refused to take his eyes off it until the first arm rolled over it again and failed to produce the quake in reality itself that the tampering had produced.

He checked his surroundings once more, awed by the damage done to the solid stone. Parch was still atop the wall. One of the crenellations near him had broken away. The unicorn glared at Tome as though he fully understood that the near-disaster was his fault.

"This is beyond me," he said, when he was able to find his voice. "There's nothing I can do here."

He paced to the rope and prepared to climb, but his hands were shaking, and he wasn't entirely comfortable trusting where the rope had been anchored to support his weight. Fortunately, the inside of the door had a clear, simple release. He opened the gate and stumbled out. The damage caused by his mistake hadn't been limited to the courtyard. For a few hundred yards in every direction, the ground was churned up and fault-ridden, with minor damage to the surrounding trees stretching farther still. The sky was filled with birds and other winged beasts shaken from the ground by the sudden tremor. Half of Tome's gear was scattered on the ground. The horse had dragged it to the very edge of the damaged ground, probably in a panicked sprint that he was surprised didn't end in a broken cart or broken leg. Mevrelle was on his feet, but from the looks of him, he'd been thrown to the ground and had only just now arisen. Tome marched toward him. The moment he was far enough from the central wall to be seen, the elf fixed him in his gaze and readied his bow.

"What did you do?" he hissed. "You could have killed me."

"I tried to remove a part of the contraption. Something powerful enough to twist the land is powerful enough to destroy it. I can't do anything about that contraption. It will take someone with specific instructions or far deeper knowledge of contraptions."

"Fel Masker," Mevrelle rumbled.

Tome waved his hands. "No! I've seen the man work—you don't want him anywhere near that contraption. Martin might be able to do something with this, in time. But he's weeks away, and I am not comfortable leaving something like this in control of anyone with vile aims for that long. We need another way."

He glanced at the sky. Most of the airborne creatures had returned to the ground, but one of them was still in the air. Tome briefly feared it was the dragon, but its odd shape soon gave its true nature away. Two-Voice was coming. His rattled mind was struck with inspiration.

"Listen. I think I have a plan," Tome said, grabbing a loop of fabric from the dumped gear from the cart. "Unless you're confident you can resist the siren, I'd suggest you make yourself scarce. I'm going to try a bluff. If it works, we'll have an option."

Mevrelle sneered and looked to the sky. He gave Tome a savage look but retreated. It was clearly fear of falling under Two-Voice's influence that motivated his departure rather than confidence in Tome's plan.

The paper mage tied the hearing protection in place and held Wick firmly. "Are you ready for this, Wick?"

"I am infinitely more comfortable dealing with the siren than with Mevrelle. The scars of elven magic remain the only pain I've ever felt, and I am not eager to risk them again."

Two-Voice approached. Tome did his very best to look like a man in control of his situation. Wick relayed her messages as quickly as possible.

"My work requires calm and silence to be most effective. Whatever you think you were doing here, know that I will be sure that you answer for it when the master returns," Two-Voice said.

"Just the creature I was hoping to see. You are mixed blood. You can resist the influence of the clockwork diamond, can you not?"

"I am, and I can."

"Then I require you to carry a message on my behalf to the other wall. Or better yet, a package."

"I will not. I have my purpose here, and I shall fulfill it. I am here only to demand you cease to interfere."

"If you perform this purpose out of loyalty, I urge you to rethink that, because any loyalty to the creator of this place and the person who runs it is profoundly misplaced. The reasons are endless, but I will highlight a few." He indicated the devastation around them. "That contraption? It enforces its will on the creatures within these walls. Right now you are needed to fill the shortcomings. But I've seen the contraption. It is a single adjustment away from doing precisely your job. You'll soon be useless."

"I have value. This is my domain."

"Nothing lasts long after its usefulness. Right now, you are an asset. But when they finish their work? You will be surplus to requirements, a liability. But that is, honestly, the least of your concerns. This? The destruction you see here? The devastation that reached even you? This is what awaits you. First, the work you've been facilitating will instead be handled by the contraption. Then, when that work is complete and no longer necessary?" He snapped his fingers. "Rubble. A loose end tied up."

"You speak madness."

"I speak truth. Look around you! I tried to shut the contraption down and this is what happened. It defended itself."

"Lies."

"Either I am telling the truth, and you are arguing with the man who is trying to save you; or I am lying, and I personally caused this level of devastation on the off chance you might believe my lies. In either case, you really feel as though arguing with me is wise?"

The siren's expression faltered slightly. "Why? If they can use that thing to work art at my level, why use me at all?"

"You've dealt with the flame. Did it strike you as a patient being? You are a stepping-stone to reach his goals quickly and with minimal dirt on his hands. When you're used up, he won't tuck you away somewhere. What sane man would? A creature capable of controlling legions with the power of her voice? You're too dangerous to be allowed to live. Same goes for the rest of the creatures here. You are tools, and you are about to be disposed of once the new tools, the ones of his design, come along."

"And if this is true, why do you defend us?"

"Maybe I don't like wholesale murder. Maybe I have a code of morals and ethics."

"Doubtful."

He crossed his arms. "Maybe I happen to have a score to settle with Lens, and anything that leads to his failure is a reasonable price to pay."

She nodded. "This I believe."

"Then deliver a package for me. Fly it past the other wall."

"I cannot. It is true, this wall and the other hold no sway over me. But Mr. Lens does." She spread the wings on the lower portion of her strange body. A long scar could be seen beneath one of them. "May years ago. After such a fine time singing sailors into the sea, a ship with a deaf crew got the better of me. They took a rib. In the hands of a wizard, it was fashioned into a talisman. By the will of the creature who wields it, I feel pain. And should they will it, I die. I have been commanded to stay within these walls and do as I am told. Without the flame to observe, I have some freedom. But were they to see me in the air over their city, I would be killed."

"I see... But you can fly close?"

"I would risk flying as far as the nearest wall."

Tome kicked at one of the fallen bags of gear. A bit of tugging and rummaging turned up a metal smoking pipe.

"That should be close enough. We'll just need a way to get a message the rest of the way from there. Let's get this done. Quickly. Who knows how much longer before they decide to be done with you."

Chapter 16

Allie finished preparing The Fox and Log for the day's business. The doors would open soon, but she'd yet to hear Velonia's voice calling for her. Until now, Madritz had seemed to take great joy in making certain Allie knew that the debriefings and any other little pointless interruption she might have took precedence over her normal day-to-day activities. If she didn't hear her boss milling about and muttering from time to time, Allie would have suspected she wasn't present. That seemed like it was the only way to get through the daily prep without an interruption these days. The first patrons began to arrive. They were a thin stream of people composed of hopeless drinkers who saw no issue with combating the hangover of the previous night's excesses by pouring more booze on top of it, and lonely folks who simply had nowhere else to be. Several of them arrived before Oovay did, which said as much about his work ethic as it did about their social lives.

"Oovay! You picked a job that opens later in the day than most, and you still can't make it here on time," she said.

He let the observation slide off him. "Is the prep all done?"

"Yes."

"Anything I need to know?"

"Nothing you shouldn't already know." She paused. "Oh! And listen, there's been some gossip going around. I'm frankly sick of hearing it, so if you hear someone talking about Lord Katritz dallying about with someone named Gem, do us all a favor and stomp on it. How a man spends his time and money is none of our business. Even if his money comes out of our pockets in the form of tribute."

Oovay raised his eyebrows. He nodded vaguely, more to acknowledge that he'd received the instructions than that he had any intent to follow them. She filled a few extra baskets of crickets—the first few patrons had a habit of making a breakfast of the table snacks—and waited. Within seconds, she heard Oovay muttering something in a bit of a stage whisper. The word "Gem" was repeated six times. Five minutes later, half the conversations in the tavern circled around the word. Allie grinned.

Sometime later, Velonia made a rare appearance on the floor of the tavern. She lingered in the corner, near the stairs that led up to her little office. Allie made sure to wipe the grin off her face while her boss was in a position to notice it. It was no simple task. After the way this woman had willfully twisted Allie's life into knots, seeing her squirm was a delicious experience. Madritz and Allie caught eyes from across the room. Her boss motioned up the stairs with her head. It would seem the time had come for her daily meeting.

She hurried up the stairs to find Velonia pacing about. The office was even more fastidiously clean than usual, and the air stank of burnt paper.

"The book," Madritz snapped. "Do you have it?"

"Not yet, ma'am," Allie said. "I believe I'll know where it is by this evening."

"This evening... I would have expected you to work more efficiently than this."

"I can only do my best," Allie said.

"That would be an acceptable excuse for you, but presently your 'best' reflects upon me, so it will need to be improved."

"I'll work harder," Allie said. "Though things have gotten terribly distracting down there, what with so many people muttering about this Gem business."

"So I've noticed," Madritz rumbled.

"I wonder if word has reached Lord Katritz yet."

"Gossip is gossip. It is an occupational hazard for those in positions of power, though I still don't know how it overtook the entire *city* so quickly."

"Sometimes being small and unimportant enough to be ignored is a blessing, huh? Still. It must be embarrassing and frustrating. And I don't imagine it's all true, but gossip does sprout from a seed as often as not. I'd be very cross with whoever let that seed tumble into the dirt if I were Lord Katritz."

Madritz's look could have withered an orchard. "Keep your mind on your work, Waverly. Do whatever it takes to get me that book or the location where it can be found. I want it by this evening, or there will be consequences. If that means you need to run along and work your sources, do it. If that means plying your wiles within these walls, so be it. But get. The job. Done."

"Yes, ma'am," Allie said.

She did her best to affect a scurry as she descended the stairs. It was a delicious but inadvisable decision to add that little jab about the consequences for being the leak. There wasn't very much Madritz could do to stop the chatter around town. And eventually the gossip would get as far as the lord himself, especially considering how many of the local elite got their morning treats at Divinity's Oven, where Mariss was dutifully chatting people up about this mysterious "Gem" business. Allie very much doubted it would take much more than a week. Then another week for his fury to reach Madritz. Two weeks was plenty of time for an increasingly desperate Madritz to cause irreparable damage to Allie if she had solid evidence to suggest Allie herself was responsible for knocking down the house of cards she'd built for herself. If Allie was going to remain afloat, she was going to need to complete the assignment given to her. She'd need to get Madritz the book. Fortunately, she had a plan for that as well.

Fel lingered at the edge of the field. It had not been the most restful of nights, though it had at least been educational. He'd learned that the false Clickspring had twelve guards in total, and two chiefs. They worked in shifts and with a mechanical level of efficiency. The searches were precise to the point of feeling like they were drills from a manual, which made sense. Everyone in this city had been harvested by the so-called plague. These weren't really town guards. Maybe some of them were, but certainly not all of them. And none of them were trained to be the sort of guards Clickspring had. These were normal townsfolk who had been rewritten by the clockwork diamond's influence, precisely as they had attempted to rewrite him into a more useful version of himself. Thus, these people were running through knowledge forced into their heads. They performed it with the precision of a book because, in a very real way, the information had come directly from that book. It hadn't been learned; it had been inserted. They didn't know it well enough to stray from it in the useful ways that an actual soldier or worker would. On the plus side, that made them predictable. On the minus side, it must have been a very good book, because the gaps in their searches were diabolical to slip through. He had to sleep sparingly and keep shifting his hiding place. Once he had the hang of it, he dared venture a bit closer to the city. Now he observed it and milled over what he needed to do and how he needed to do it.

It was tempting to imagine that the guards doing constant sweeps around the city looking for him would leave the city itself undefended, but that was a dangerous line of thinking. His real foe was Lens, and Lens could be watching from nearly any light source. He had at least one persistent lantern in the city, and considering the handful Fel now knew housed him outside this place, there was no telling how many of them there were in total. It wasn't as simple as just snuffing the flame. What he needed was wholesale destruction, something he typically excelled at. But nothing of this scale. The whole city was a part of Lens's scheme, and at his best, Fel didn't think he could bring a whole city down. Worse, the people in the city weren't a willing part of it. They would play the role they were given, probably right up to the point of death, but they didn't deserve it. He'd seen things from their perspective. There was very little choice in their actions.

As much logic as he applied to the situation, it changed nothing. Something had to be done, and the sooner it was done the better chance he'd have to do it before plans were made against him.

He held a makeshift grappling hook in one hand and a coiled rope in the other.

"I make a sprint for the wall, I scale it, and I get inside. The earring should keep the diamond from stirring up my brains. Once I'm inside"—he shrugged—"no sense wasting time planning for that, because I'm certainly not going to make it that far."

He crouched, eyes on the distant patrol of guards between him and the center of the city. It was going to be a long run, and he wasn't the fastest thing on two feet. It would have to be perfectly timed if he was going to make it. He counted to himself, muscles tense, ready for what might end up being the last thing he'd ever do.

A half-muffled bleat from mere inches from where he was standing nearly caused his heart to burst from his chest. He turned, brandishing the grappling hook, and found himself staring at Parch, who had a metal pipe in his mouth.

"Parch?" he hissed. "Perfect timing as always."

The unicorn dropped the pipe and pranced happily about, pleased to be united with the only human whose company he actually enjoyed.

"Shh, shh, shh," he urged, plucking up the pipe and wiping it on his shirt.

He took a puff. Doing so brought a voice to his ears that was midsentence, so eager was Wick to speak to him.

"—truly astounding to find you in such good health. Are you of sound mind as well? A great deal of information has been found regarding the so-called plague and—"

"Wick, you're a sound for sore ears, and I'm going to let you fill me in on everything I missed. You might start with how long it's been since I wandered off, because I think I lost track. But let me start, just to save you some time and to give me a chance to say some words to someone that might actually answer, unlike Oiler, and isn't under the influence of the diamond, unlike everyone else here."

"Of course."

"The clockwork diamond had me convinced I was one of my own ancestors back before the fall of the Bygone Era. Mr. Lens, who is also the Graves flame, was trying to get me to work on the clockwork diamond. He was hoping I'd figure out a few things about how to get it to do its job better, but I couldn't. He also dumped a whole ancient language into my head. There's a place in those fields over there where they're building some slightly simpler versions of that thing the Warrior tried to use to kill us. I got the Student and the coupler back, but considering how much time they had it and how many contraptions are about, I wouldn't put it past them to have figured out how to copy the coupler by now, though I couldn't find any duplicates. There's also about fifty less sturdy-looking automata. Don't know what those are for. And the guards of this place are all looking for me. I'm trying to figure out a way to destroy this whole place without killing any of the people, and I've come up empty on that." He tipped his head back and squinted his eyes. "I think that about covers it. Oh! No. Also I have a butler here, and he's named after you. I think that was on purpose to try to help me dismiss any lingering memories I might have. Now that covers it."

"I admire your terseness. I shall endeavor to match it."

"Right. You do that. And as soon as you're done, head back and tell Allie and my folks that I'm all right."

"Shouldn't we focus on making a plan to get you to safety and thwart your enemies?"

"Right now I'm most concerned about setting their minds at ease. And if I'm honest, a few extra minutes to think will probably be called for."

"As you wish."

A few hours had passed, and the ball of gossip had been rolling along nicely. What had started as "some business with Gem" had evolved into a series of second- and thirdhand anecdotes recounting everything from assassinations to jewel thefts to romantic trysts with varying levels of graphic detail. The trysts were by far the most popular stories, which was hardly a surprise.

She'd just overheard one that would make a sailor blush when she saw that the time had come for her second meeting of the day. Verfessa's door was shut tight. She loaded a tray and slipped inside.

He was midchuckle as she slipped through the door.

"Something funny?" she asked.

"Lord Katritz's Gem. I assume this is your doing?" he said.

"What the lord gets up to in his spare time is hardly any of my business," she said.

"Remind me never to get on your bad side," he said. "I wish I could be there when the word of this hits him. The man's face will work its way through every shade of red and end up blue before he's through yelling. Glorious. It must feel good to dump a handful of thistles into the bed of the man who is at the root of your struggles, but you don't really expect this to stick to him, do you?"

"He's not the one I'm interested in," she said. "The lord can go on lording for all I care. I just want his lapdog to scurry off."

"It won't stick to her, either. That's the nice part of being so slimy. Stuff like this slides right off. A fun story is a fun story, but even if the general public will repeat it and add their color, all but the thickest of them know it's easy enough to make up a story like that."

"Who says I made it up?" Allie said. "There is a situation involving the lord and something he's calling Gem."

"You have proof of that?" he said.

She tugged one of the letters from her apron and slapped it on the table. He flipped it open. His eyes flicked between the page and Allie. He held it up to the light of his candle.

"It's his signature. It's his watermark." He set the page down. "There is no way in this world or any other that someone like Madritz could have gotten as far as she has and still have been empty-headed enough to let something like this slip through her fingers."

"Oh, she took all necessary precautions. But I've got low friends in high places."

He tapped the page on the table thoughtfully. "There is nothing here that will do much damage to the lord. But it's an information breach, and it is addressed directly to Madritz. Assuming Gem is a codeword, hearing that bandied about will make it abundantly clear to him where the leak happened. And if there's any doubt, you have the actual leak to hand over." He handed it back to her. "Inspired work. This will lose Madritz her patron, and if he's as petty as I've heard, that'll just be the start of it. She'll be out of both of our hair and probably looking to start over in a whole new kingdom before this is through. It's just a matter of time."

"That's the problem," she said.

"At least ten days, probably closer to two weeks, and all that while with an increasingly unstable employer to deal with. She'll know full well what's coming for her. And either she'll be looking to get while the getting is good—best case for either of us, as it chases her out early—or else she'll be looking for a win, a big one, to get her back in the lord's graces in a hurry."

"Right now, that win is the book I'm supposed to be getting," Allie said. "And considering she's mostly after making sure I stop helping you and the Maskers, and presumably you and the Maskers stop being so successful, I can think of a few things a desperate person might do to make that happen in a hurry."

"So you're eager to give the attack dog a nice thick steak before it takes its share out of your hide." He drummed his fingers on the table. "That's a tough position. I can't just hand over the book. And I can't just let someone waltz in and take it. There's the issue of it making me look weak, for starters. Madritz isn't the only one with a taste for fresh blood, and I don't want to be springing any leaks and giving any other meat eaters any ideas. There's also the personal pride of a job well done. The Maskers are trusting me—and paying me—to keep their things safe, and what would it say about me if I let one of their books walk away? I'll tell you what. It would tell the Maskers they shouldn't trust Verfessa anymore, which is just the sort of thing Madritz wants to happen. I'm not so sure that isn't the whole point of asking for the book. Setting me up to seem like I let the Maskers down."

Allie rubbed her neck and glanced aside.

"Got an idea you're not too keen on?" he said with a knowing grin.

"What if it's not you who loses the book? What if you hand it back over to the Maskers, and it gets taken from them? Now you haven't broken or botched any promises, she gets the book, and I earn some favor from her."

"I know you're not just suggesting I foist the book on the Maskers and let them take the hit instead of me."

"You let me worry about what happens afterward. If you get the request from the Maskers to hand it over, are you ready to do it?"

"Wouldn't be much of a safekeeper if I refused to part with it when the time came."

"Then expect a request to come through soon." She topped his drink off and turned for the door.

"Don't forget your prize," he said, sliding the page across the table.

"Oh, you can keep it. I have a spare," she said.

He laughed again and pocketed the page. "I'll say it again. Don't let me ever get on your bad side."

Tome scribbled some final notes on the back of a botched spell sheet. It had been a short but intense planning session, relayed through Wick, putting the combined intuition and insight of the Maskers and himself together. The resulting plan was ambitious to the point of implausibility, but it wasn't entirely unachievable. Between Fel and Tome, the paper mage's part in it was the least immediately dangerous but arguably the most important. Fel had to risk his life. Tome had to persuade some very hostile creatures to play a part. All the while, Martin had to take what little they'd learned about the clockwork diamond and come up with a way to take it out of the equation. They had their tasks cut out for them.

He looked to the lantern. Wick was present.

"Time to see how well I've learned the art of diplomacy," he said, pulling his hearing protection back into place.

"I am confident your skills in that regard exceed Fel's."

"Fel is the opposite of a diplomat. He makes friends easily, but if we needed someone who could guarantee there would be a brawl by the end of the day, he's the one we'd send."

For the sake of privacy and safety, he'd conducted the planning phase within the central wall, right beside the diamond. Mevrelle couldn't access him there, and while Two-Voice probably could, the siren didn't seem eager to venture too near to the thing that had torn up the countryside. But the time had come to leave the shelter of the wall.

He opened the gate and stepped out. Two-Voice shifted uneasily. She sat on the ground, but the nature of her anatomy made flat ground less than ideal to rest on. She fidgeted for lack of a perch.

"Well?" the siren said, through Wick.

Tome looked about. "I notice Mevrelle is not present."

"The elf fears the lure of my voice. Speak your piece."

"Direct. I like that. You know that we need your help. And I trust you believe me when I say that my goal is to minimize the amount of bloodshed. What I want is as much freedom and safety as can be managed."

"Freedom," Two-Voice said. "Freedom is not the goal of a siren. Control is the goal of a siren."

"Do you want to continue to be a prisoner?"

She tipped her head and fluffed her plumage. "It depends upon how comfortable the cell is."

Tome pointed at a fault produced by his tinkering with the diamond.

"The very moment Mr. Lens has no more need for you, that's the fate of your cell. Torn asunder. And that's assuming they don't simply use the enchantment to end you directly."

"She is murmuring melodically," Wick explained. "And now she speaks clearly again. I will not risk my own life. I do not do battle. And I do not act against my masters while they hold the bone that could end my life."

"I wouldn't dream of asking you to endanger yourself without something in return. The nature of alliance is compromise."

"The nature of alliance with me is proof that I will not be killed. Then, and only then, does my voice turn to your aim."

"Fine. We guarantee your safety."

"And for that, what do you require?"

"There are two walls. The wall surrounding this place and the wall surrounding the place with my friend. Within this wall, I can think clearly. Within the other wall, Greater Lands creatures can think clearly. You are of mixed blood, unaffected by either wall. Your role in this is to act as a bridge. Use the strength of your voice to compel creatures to cross the walls."

"No combat?"

"No combat."

She considered this for a long moment. "Prove to me that they will not strike me down, and you have the strength of my voice."

"Excellent," Tome said. "Now I just have to find a way to make sure everyone else will play their role."

"Until such a time comes, I must return to my perch and to the task that the flame requires of me. Failure is not tolerated."

"It so happens I have business there as well."

She raised her beak and turned aside. "Then you have a long walk ahead of you."

Two-Voice spread her wings and took to the sky. Tome gazed at the stretch of ground between him and the workers. The bird could cover it in minutes. It would take him hours, and yet he knew that all this was taking place within something that from the outside was barely larger than the courtyard behind him. The laws of time and space had been distorted in the precise way that maximized the amount of walking he would have to do.

"Wick," he muttered. "One of these days I'll need to figure out why heroism and inconvenience are so tightly aligned."

Allie would have preferred to spend her time in The Fox and Log, but given Madritz's desperation and the necessity of keeping her wrath at bay, she'd determined it was wiser to depart and see about the book she was after. She marched directly to the Masker house, since there wasn't very much reason to be sneaky about her intentions anymore. There were only two reasonable ways for her to get access to the book that Madritz wanted, so it wouldn't take a network of spies to determine where she was headed.

Both Epiphany and Vivian were in the shop when Allie arrived. Vivian was with a customer, Epiphany was marking something down in a ledger. Allie could tell by the very air in the shop that there had been good news. At the sight of her, Epiphany snapped the ledger shut and motioned her toward the stairs.

"Call me if you need me, Mom," Epiphany said quickly. She led Allie downstairs. Before the hatch was even shut behind them, she spoke up. "Have you heard?"

"I haven't seen the light go still in my lantern since I found out they were on Fel's trail," Allie said.

"They found him. Wick's in touch with him. We're not out of the woods yet. He's still got his original mission to worry about, and a fair bit besides. But he's in touch and healthy."

"As if there was ever any doubt," Allie said, her tone of relief underscoring just how much doubt there had actually been, even if she didn't want to admit it.

"The end is in sight. We just need to see this through. Dad and Teya are downstairs working on it. But I don't suppose that's why you came here."

"Don't get me wrong, I'm pleased as punch to know things are looking up. But you're right. I sort of have my own problems. I hate to add them to yours…"

Epiphany waved off the looming apology. "No need to apologize. Forgive me for the assumption, but I get the notion your problems are going to be smaller and easier to fix than his."

"They tend to stay in the city, at least," Allie said. "Though the ease of fixing this one really has more to do with you than with me. I need one of your books."

"Doing research, are you?"

"No. My new boss who has been making my life miserable is hoping to lean on me to lean on you to get a book that Verfessa is holding for you. Her boss, Lord Katritz, is about to be breathing down her neck."

"This sounds to me like something she'd prefer you weren't so forthcoming with."

"I *could* care less about her preference, but it would take some effort."

"What's this I've been hearing about Lord Katritz and someone named Gem, by the way?"

Allie laughed. "Same rules as usual when it comes to gossip. You should only believe about half of that, and the tricky part is figuring out which half. When it all blows over, I'll be happy to tell you the ins and outs, but right now me knowing the truth is a bit of a secret."

"Understood. So. A book. Which one?"

"Professor Milton Governor's *Treatise on the Infusion of Alloys with Mystic Properties*. I think they said that's the translated title."

Epiphany crossed her arms. "And the intention is to hand it over to her?"

"That's what I'd prefer. Both to curry her favor and also to keep her from doing something unfortunate to try to get it on her own. Like I said, she's going to be desperate soon."

She clicked her tongue and glanced aside, mind churning a bit. "That book is rather difficult, if not impossible, to replace. You'll have to discuss that with Dad directly. He won't be keen on giving up something that precious."

"I wouldn't ask if it wasn't important. And I'll take every precaution I can to make sure nothing happens to it. But, I'll be honest, that'll be mostly up to Velonia. Considering the lengths she's going to just to get her hands on it, I don't think she is going to risk anything happening to it."

"That means it'll be hard to get it back from her. But there's no sense discussing it with me. Dad's down in his shop. Teya's been running about, helping him with things. You're welcome to head down there. But if they're in the middle of something..."

"It's fine. I'm in no rush. I'll just linger in the corner until there's room for my little problem."

"Good luck to you, then. I'll be upstairs."

Epiphany hurried back to the shop. Allie descended the stairs until she heard Teya's excited chatter.

"And that is all! You say, they hear. Do what you need. Very very!" Teya crowed.

"You're certain? That seems disarmingly simple," Martin said.

"Very simple. Yes. Hard? Not all things." She turned. "Allie! Nice lady, gives drinks. Friend of Fel! Welcome!"

"Hello. Don't let me interrupt," Allie said.

"Oh, I'm through with Teya's insight, if what she says is true," Martin said. "And if you're concerned about distracting me, don't be. I'm told when I get my mind set on something, dislodging it is the greater challenge."

"I have a pretty big favor to ask."

"Our resources are a bit stretched at the moment," he said, flipping through pages of notes. "But if it is in our power, the family owes you a great deal."

"A book. Professor Milton Governor's *Treatise on the Infusion of Alloys with Mystic Properties*," she said.

"Ah! It so happens I have precisely that book in my collection. It is presently in storage, but if you need to borrow it, you are welcome to it."

"That's the problem. It might be a little more than borrowing. My boss has been after me to acquire that book."

"I didn't realize Sid was interested in the manufacturing methods of the Bygone Era."

"Sid isn't the owner of The Fox and Log anymore," she said slowly.

"Oh?" He looked up for a moment. "Yes, now that you mention it, I remember someone saying something to that effect. As I said, the trick isn't distracting me, it's getting my attention. Who is your current employer with the interest in mystic infusion of materials?"

"Velonia Madritz. But she's working on behalf of Lord Katritz, and I have my doubts that he really cares about that stuff either. It's more about driving a wedge between your family and Verfessa's team."

"Lord Katritz, through a businesswoman, purchased a tavern to put you in a position to request a book that was being stored by Verfessa? That seems terribly roundabout."

"No argument here, but it is what it is. The whole thing should be cleared up in a couple of weeks, but I need to keep her happy that long. My job hangs in the balance at the very least."

"Mmm..." He flipped through some more pages. "I do not believe that book is, strictly speaking, one of a kind. And it may as well be. The chances of us ever locating another copy are vanishingly slim. When do you need it?"

"Ideally by tomorrow morning."

He found something in the book he was referencing and jotted it down. "Fel and Tome cannot move forward... or at least Fel can't, until I find the answer to this problem. It will take me an hour or so, assuming things go well. In a moment, Wick will need to deliver Teya's advice to Tome for his part. After that, we have until I solve the problem before Wick needs to contact the others again. From there, he will be with them until the job is done. Wick, it's established your memory is swift and, in effect, flawless. Do you feel as though you could faithfully retain the entirety of a book after viewing its pages, rather than by burning its pages?"

"So long as I am given time enough to fully observe each page, yes. Doubtless," Wick said.

"And how much time will you require?"

"Two or three seconds per page."

Martin shut his eyes and tipped his head back. "As I recall, that is a rather thick book. You'd best get moving. Allie, take Epiphany with you, see Verfessa, and request the book. Take the time to memorize it, and it is yours to do with as you please. The information in the book is what interests me. The book itself, while valuable, means little to me."

"Thank you, Mr. Masker. You're a lifesaver."

"For the sake of a disquieting number of people, I hope you are correct. But you are welcome. Please move quickly. As much as I would love to indulge you, when the time comes if you aren't through, Wick will need to move along, and I cannot allow you to give up the book without recording its contents."

"You need help? For move fast and safe?" Teya said eagerly.

"This is my town, Teya. I think I can handle it. But thank you," Allie said.

"You need help, call! Ask! I give." Teya slapped her on the leg. "Fel? Least worst friend. You? Fel's least worst friend. You to me? Less worst friend."

"I'm honored. But I have to go."

"Good luck and victory!" Teya said.

"Here's hoping," Allie said, hurrying up the stairs.

Things happened swiftly after that. Epiphany agreed to accompany Allie almost before she was finished explaining. They hurried as quickly as they could, with a lantern housing Wick in hand, to The Fox and Log, where Allie was pleased to find Verfessa was in his "office." In a rare achievement, Allie's appearance with Epiphany by her side seemed to put a genuine look of surprise on Verfessa's face.

"Two visits in one day from my favorite barmaid. And joined by my second favorite shopkeeper." He glanced at Epiphany. "Forgive me, but there is your mother to consider."

Epiphany shrugged. "She's my favorite, too."

"To what do I owe the honor of this meeting of the minds?" he said.

"She's here to formally give permission to hand over the book to me. But time is of the essence. Martin won't give it up until we've had an hour or so alone with it."

"Doing what, exactly?" he asked.

"Dad wants to make sure he has a thing or two copied from within," Epiphany said.

"I'll send word to have the book fetched. You'll have it soon."

"Soon isn't soon enough," Allie said. "There isn't enough time to explain why there isn't enough time to explain, but I need the book immediately. Just tell me where I can find it, and we'll get it ourselves."

"Cutting close to a deadline is a sign of poor planning," Verfessa said.

"An awful lot of people are bending an awful lot of their rules to get me this far," Allie said.

"And you're hoping to add my name to that list?" Verfessa said.

"I'll owe you a favor."

"You're damned right you will," Verfessa said with a laugh that lacked his usual level of avuncular charm. "Do you know how a fellow keeps a whole network of storage houses secret inside the walls of a city like this? I'll tell you how you don't do it. By having people come and go at all hours of the day. You break routine, you raise eyebrows."

"I wouldn't be asking if it wasn't important. It's this or I face the wrath of Madritz."

"You're asking me to break my own rules, the rules that keep my investments safe. So yes, you'll owe me a favor. And I need you to understand just how heavy a burden that is. I get value for my favors. You're talking about owing me something in exchange for shaving some time off an errand to keep your current employer from putting the spurs to you harder than she already is. Are you sure you want that?"

Allie didn't allow herself the time to rethink things. "Yes," she said.

He put out a hand. She shook it.

"Argent Avenue. Three doors from the intersection. Around back. Just you. Pack a bottle of booze. Something cheap. Make sure it's a bag big enough to hide the book. You're delivering the booze. That's the reason you're there.

Compliment the fella lingering in the alley on his boots. Show him the bottle, and tell him it's for the inventory clerk. He'll let you in. The book will be on the top of the third shelf. You have your time with it, take your notes, and walk out with the book in your bag. You touch anything else while you're in there, and we're going to have a problem."

"I'm not nearly that stupid, sir."

"I wouldn't be letting you in if I thought you were, but I learned a long time ago, sometimes you say things that don't need to be said because a few wasted words are a better deal than a big misunderstanding. Once this thing blows over, we'll discuss what it'll take to make us even."

"Thank you, Mr. Verfessa. I really appreciate this. You've—"

He raised a hand to silence her. "Save it for when we settle up. You might feel differently then."

Chapter 17

Fel slipped through the narrow space between two shops. He'd been moving into position with as much care and stealth as he could manage. The sweeps by the guards had been getting steadily closer to his hiding spots closer to the edge of town. He'd barely avoided them last time, which made the shift to a hiding place closer to the center of the city the lesser of two evils. Or so he'd thought. Having Parch with him was a bit of a handful. The unicorn wasn't the ideal creature to have tagging along when silence was called for. He made up for it by having sensitive enough hearing and a sharp enough sense of smell to serve as an early warning of approaching guards. But he also didn't differentiate between guards and other types of humans. Worse, his way of dealing with the issue of a looming threat was to bound up to the top of the nearest climbable edifice. If the guards ever got the bright idea to look up when they heard a strange sound, Parch would be found, and Fel would quickly follow.

He puffed on the pipe and waited to see if Wick had shown back up. Fel dearly hoped this was the last time he'd have to depend upon a pipe rather than a lantern to stay in contact. He wasn't fond of smoking, he wasn't fond of not being able to tell at a glance if Wick was around, and the smell of smoke was at least as much of a threat to revealing him as the glow of a lantern. Or, at least, it should have been. Three times since the pipe had been delivered, search parties had passed by near enough that they must have been able to smell the pipe, but they didn't so much as look in his direction. Again, it must have been the unnatural way they earned their roles as guards. Whoever had crafted the new contents for their heads hadn't included the scent of smoke as a warning sign, so it had no place in their actions.

Another puff produced nothing but silence in his head. Parch lingered beside him, the previous sweep having just passed. For the moment he was as safe from being discovered as he was likely to get. This allowed him to turn his mind fully to the tasks laid out before him. The doorway barely visible at the nearest intersection was his first target. It was the office of the archivist. Somehow he had to get inside and grab a few key items. Back when his mind wasn't entirely his own, he'd spent a few minutes in the place, but it never would have occurred to him at that time to try to spot traps and security concerns. The only thing that visit had taught him was where the items could be found once he was inside. It made the job faster but not any easier.

He shut his eyes and muttered to himself. "There didn't seem to be a back door. Makes sense if it's a mini stronghold. But disabling an alarm or trap on the front door of a city street without being spotted—not looking forward to..."

Fel trailed off. A studious older man marched past where he was hiding, heading for the very doorway he was scrutinizing. His arms were heavy with wooden cases, no doubt items from the archive that he was returning to their places. Fel narrowed his eyes, his mind suddenly awash with a new plan that was a good deal less safe, but much faster and more certain than defeating the traps himself. It would set things in motion that he couldn't stop, though. If his father needed more time, then he would be in a tight spot. Then again, he was already in a tight spot. And given how rigid the schedules were, if he missed this opportunity, it wouldn't come up again for another full day. He did not like his chances of avoiding the guards for that long.

"Time to make a mistake," he resolved.

He secured all his gear as best he could, including Oiler, who had been very well behaved thanks to the near total absence of things that required repair in this place. He judged the distance between him and the archivist. When the time was right, he dashed from cover.

The jangle and jostle of multiple bags of heavy equipment was impossible to silence. As was the clippy-clop of a unicorn happily charging along beside him. But in a few moments, discovery would become inevitable. He just had to make it that far. The archivist fiddled with the cases, attempting to unlock his door without putting them down. He gave up and set them down just as Fel's thundering approach reached his ears.

He turned and a heartbeat later was slammed against the door by Fel's full bulk. Fel pinned a hand over the man's mouth and gave a swift glance to ensure they hadn't yet been spotted. The half-deserted nature of this place worked in his favor. They were still alone.

"Sorry, buddy," he said. "I'm going to need you to open that door. As the local contraptioneer, I need to make some withdrawals."

The man released a startled yelp, muffled by Fel's grimy mitt. After the initial jolt of fear passed, he mumbled something else. Fel couldn't make that out either, but it was delivered with a look of brave defiance that conveyed the message clearly enough.

"Look, you're doing the job. I understand it. I'd say I respect it, but right now it's literally the only thing you can do, so it's not really virtue. More necessity. Either way, it doesn't change anything. I need to get in there. Fast. So either you open it up and disable the traps, or I use your body like a battering ram to bust the door open and then heave your carcass along ahead of me to trigger all the traps. No matter what, this ends with me getting what I need. But only one way ends with you still alive."

Another defiant murmur. Fel growled. He could feel the time running out, the next patrol marching ever closer. The evidence was really starting to mount that he wasn't as good at bluffing as he liked to tell himself at the grum table. The solution? Don't bluff.

With one arm still wrapped around behind the man's head to cover his mouth, Fel grasped the man's hand and muscled it up to the contraption locking the door.

"Last chance. Either you enter the right combination, or I take a wild guess with your hand and we see what sort of excitement that causes."

The man's hand trembled in his grasp. Fel pushed it forward to nudge against the first tile in the combination. The merest hint of motion in what must have been the wrong direction finally broke the man's resolve. He quickly performed the combination, and the door clicked open. Fel shoved him through and shut it behind them once Parch had clopped through. He released the man, trusting that some combination of his self-preservation and the thick door between them and the street would keep shouts from alerting anyone.

A foyer or coatroom of sorts separated the front entrance from the rest of the building. Fel had robbed enough ruins of the Bygone Era to know this was effectively an execution chamber, riddled with traps to make sure people who got this far didn't get any farther.

"Keep going. I know there's more than one trap or alarm to worry about," Fel said.

"I don't understand. When I heard that Fel Masker had somehow become an enemy of Clickspring, I didn't believe it. You are an honored part of our community. A contraptioneer of the highest order."

"Yeah, yeah. What can I say? Times change," he said.

Fel inched the front door open again to check that he'd not been seen, then swiftly grabbed the packages the man had been carrying to keep their presence from tipping anyone off that something had happened. The archivist jingled a key chain with shaking hands and inserted keys into well-hidden keyholes, one by one, until the door to the rest of the building opened without alarm or attack.

Fel shoved the archivist through and hurried to the item he knew he was after. "Parch, put a hole in this guy if he does anything unfortunate."

Parch looked vaguely in the man's direction. There was no chance the unicorn understood or planned to obey the order, but the archivist didn't know that.

"Wh-why do you have a lesser unicorn with you?" the archivist asked.

"That's a longer story than I have time to tell."

Fel found the wire cage that held what he'd initially thought was some kind of arcane flute. He now knew it to be the rib of a siren. A quick inspection revealed that the case, too, had an alarm attached. It was a simple matter to disable it.

"I don't know what you are up to, but you aren't going to get away with it," the archivist said.

"Let's hope for both our sakes that you're wrong." He took another puff of the pipe. "While I'm waiting, is there any part of this place that contains something you've never actually looked at?"

"I am the archivist! It is my profession to keep and organize these goods," the man asserted.

Regardless of his words, the man's eyes betrayed him, glancing in the direction of a bookcase that had a telltale layer of dust absent from most of the other items on display.

"It's a good thing your job isn't to hide things," Fel said, plucking a book from the shelf.

The book was blank, as was the next one. He went to the start of the row and grabbed the first book. It was mostly blank, but the first third or so contained a sequence of short entries with the same basic format. A name, an occupation, a second name, and a second occupation. He read through three or four pages of them before he came to the one that made the purpose of this book clear.

"Does the name Gus Mallory mean anything to you?" he said.

The man blinked and shut his eyes. "I... it does seem familiar."

"Does the name Terrance Plover mean anything to you?"

"That is my name, sir."

He held up the book. "Not until a couple of months ago. Before that, you were Gus Mallory, a big-game hunter and, apparently, a poacher, because you made your way to Fenfield, got your mind mixed up by the 'Clickspring' wall, and got a new identity as Terrance Plover, archivist."

"That's... That's absurd," the archivist said.

"Absurd or not, this is a list of everyone in town. And knowing there was a whole row dedicated to that information makes me think the man in charge was preparing for a much bigger population." He stuffed the book into one of his overfilled bags. "At least this'll help me make sure I've got everyone, once the time comes to clear things out." He puffed the pipe.

"Fel? Where are you right now?" came Wick's voice in his head.

"I'm in the archivist's place," he said.

"Yes, I know you're in the—" the archivist began.

Fel waved off the comment.

"I was under the impression you weren't meant to move forward with any stage of the plan until Martin provided the solution to the clockwork diamond issue," Wick said.

"An opportunity presented itself. Did he figure it out?"

"Not yet. A few more minutes."

"Have you spoken to Tome yet?"

"I intended to visit him next."

"Let him know I have the rib." He held it up. "It looks like this."

"Noted. I hope to return shortly with the remaining information. Be safe."

"Not up to me, but I'll do my best," Fel said.

The vague sense of Wick's presence faded.

"You... you have a sentry flame at your disposal?" the archivist said.

"Yep," Fel said, fetching the book again. "See, unlike you, I didn't get a new name or a new job. I just got a little more prestige when I got here. I've got loads of contraptions and knowledge."

He held up the page which listed him as Fel Masker – Novice Contraptioneer → Fel Masker – Expert Contraptioneer.

"Just goes to show, the only difference between a novice and an expert is what people are willing to call you."

The lantern in Allie's hand went still again.

"My apologies for the departure," Wick said. "My services are in high demand. Let us continue."

"It's fine. Just be quick if you can," Allie said.

She didn't feel comfortable standing in one of Verfessa's storage caches. The items on the shelves had mostly been stored in sacks, the better to keep a casual observer from recognizing that they were contraband. Indeed, if Allie didn't know what this place was, she could easily have assumed it was little more than the spare inventory for the textile shop on the other side of the heavy door on the west side of the room. But she did know what this place was, and thus her imagination was awash with thoughts of what sort of precious and forbidden treasures were lurking inside those sacks. Exotic spirits. Precious artifacts. The skulls of his enemies. She didn't know what worried her more: that he didn't trust her in here and her very presence was making him rethink the amount of faith he'd put in her, or the thought that he did trust her in here and that he might have similarly illegal plans for her now that she owed him a favor.

Every few seconds, Wick prompted her to turn a page. Three quarters of the book had been memorized before he'd gone to check with the others. A few more minutes and she could get out of this place.

"You appear to be tense," Wick observed.

"Just read. Don't worry about me."

"Turn the page. You'll find that observing a page requires the least of my capacities. Turn the page. I am quite capable of conversation while doing so. Turn the page."

"I live in a tiny home barely upwind from a tannery. I work more than any one person should at a tavern. And I've gotten myself neck deep with a criminal enterprise and a corrupt businesswoman serving an even more corrupt noble just so I can stay in the lousy job and keep living in the lousy home." She turned the page.

"Such are your desires, and the actions necessary to serve those desires."

She turned the page again. "My desires are stupid. I could have just quit. Or I could have asked for help faster. I ended up needing help from both Verfessa and the Maskers, after deciding from the start I wanted to solve this problem myself. Being stubborn and proud is only an asset when you actually have something to be proud of. I'm fighting to preserve a life that's barely worth living."

"Your life is worth living because you are the one who is living it. You sought help when you needed it, and because of who you are, there were those willing and able to provide that help. You have made mistakes. Turn the page. You have had instances of poor judgment. Perfection is not a necessary component of a life well-lived. Turn the page. Perfection is, in point of fact, unachievable.

And even if it were achievable, it would lack the flavor of trial and error. Turn the page. And most importantly, it would lack the education that comes with discovery. You will survive this because of who you are, and in surviving it, you will become the sort of person who will survive what comes next. Do not dwell on the past. There lies only regret. Turn the page."

"You seem to be speaking from experience."

"Experience is effectively all I have. You are human, and with your humanity comes a gift you often lament. You can forget. I cannot. History is present, sharp and bright as the day it happened. Mistakes are not dulled by time. Failures are not softened by age. Hold precious your ability not only to learn from your mistakes but to forget the pain of them as well. Turn the page."

She flipped the page to discover that they had reached the end of the contents. The last few pages were blank, earmarked for notes that had never been taken.

"Ah. And so we are through," Wick said.

"You're sure you can remember all that?" she said.

"As I have said, I lack the capacity to forget. The book is yours to do with what you please. Forgive my haste, but I should return to the others. When last I left Martin, he was on the verge of a breakthrough."

"Go. You gave me more time than I deserve. Thank you."

"It was a service I was happy to provide. Good luck to you."

The light flickered. Wick was gone. Allie dropped the book into the bag and slipped out. The fellow who let her in nodded to her and checked the bag. Satisfied she was carrying only one item, he slipped inside after she moved on, no doubt to check that nothing else was missing. Verfessa's organization wasn't one built on trust, nor should it be. She found herself fighting the urge to quicken to a sprint. The weight of the book was a constant reminder of a half-dozen things she wanted to be done with. She reached The Fox and Log but found that Madritz was absent. Oovay said she had taken her leave and specifically informed him that she would not return until the morning. Faced with the option of either keeping the book on her person and returning to her shift or heading home and stowing it there, she decided she couldn't justify the chance of having it stolen. She hurried home, all the way doing the mental arithmetic of how much favor this would curry with Madritz and if it would be enough to carry her through to the woman's inevitable dismissal in a few weeks.

She reached her door. It was shut tight, braced from the inside.

"Why is..." she murmured.

Confusion wasn't given much time to linger. A figure appeared at the mouth of the alley, the imposing form of Madritz's seldom-seen bodyguard. Then the grind of a brace rattled the door and it opened. Madritz stood before her, the woman's expression cold and detached.

"Miss Waverly. Please. Come inside."

"To my own home? I should hope so. What's this about?" she said.

Madritz stepped aside. Allie considered making a break for it, but with the bodyguard positioned as he was, she was already trapped. It was better to slip inside where she at least could grab something a bit more formidable to make a violent escape if it became necessary.

"This may be your home, but it is my property," Madritz said.

"That's all well and good, but if you're going to be coming and going, you should be paying a share of the rent."

Madritz stood and shut the door. "You know something, Allie. I don't think it would surprise you to know that The Fox and Log is the first tavern I've owned. I pride myself in knowing the value of any given enterprise and exploiting that value to the utmost degree. But I'll admit I'd overlooked one of the key elements that, I suspect, you were keenly aware of. A tavern is a massive crossroads of information. Seldom reliable, but it is a wide net, and like any wide net, it's bound to catch at least a bit of what you're after along with a great deal else. Over the past few days, I've listened to the gossip about Lord Katritz. And I noticed a pattern that I've seen elsewhere but never so pronounced as it is here."

She paced to Allie's fireplace and lit a taper from a lantern that wasn't in the house when she left. Madritz must have brought it herself.

"Rumors circulate. Then people travel to someplace new, some counterpart to The Fox and Log out along the roads of Thayne. The story is repeated, with juicy little additions and alterations. And the story heads off in every direction as the travelers continue their trips. People heading north tell the story to people heading south, and it ends up, in a twisted form, back where it started. Ripples, bouncing from shore to shore. I've seen four waves of the story bounce back. And I have to say... it seems to me, based on how the story has changed, that all I've been seeing is echoes of stories that started here."

She fanned the flames a bit. "Obviously I can't be certain that's true. Not without proof. But someday soon, sooner than I'd like, I'll have to answer some questions from my patron. There's a word that's held firm in every variation of the story. Gem. Now the rumors will be an embarrassment but ultimately meaningless. But the presence of that word will let him know how the rumor started. It will reflect poorly on me. And I asked myself, who has something to gain from a poor reaction to me specifically?"

She looked up from the fire. "You have the book?"

"I do. But I'm starting to wonder if I shouldn't hold on to it until I'm convinced you don't have any sinister plans for me," Allie said.

Madritz was quiet for a moment. "There is only one way that anyone could have the information that found its way into the outside world. Written messages, which have a very short chain of custody. It begins with Lord Katritz, passes to a series of trusted messengers, and ends with me. Now me? I'm more than willing to embrace the messengers as the weak link in the chain. In order for him to keep his foolishly abundant sequence of messages coming and going, he employs twenty personal couriers. All it takes is one with a little too much curiosity. But here's the problem. Those messages are sealed. And the messenger lacks the signet ring. Were one to arrive with a broken seal, it would be my obligation to report such a breach back to the lord. And so it comes back to me. Either I allowed a message to fall into the wrong hands, or I neglected to address that it had happened elsewhere." She looked Allie in the eye. "Please, sit."

"I prefer to stand."

Madritz shrugged. "As you wish. Now, I've faced attacks like this before. If there is a gap in an argument, I will slip through it. And I have got to imagine that anyone clever enough to bring something like this about would have to be aware that I would have precisely that sort of expertise. Thus it would only make sense to keep hold of solid, incontrovertible evidence that could conveniently turn up during an investigation." She released a short, sharp whistle. "I don't know how you did it, but you got your hands on one of my letters."

"The letters that you burn daily?" she said, her tone as dubious as she could manage.

"I searched your home. I found nothing. I searched The Fox and Log. I found nothing. Now, the very reason I placed you so firmly under my thumb was because you have friends in some very useful places. You could have passed that letter to anyone for safekeeping. But if I were you, I wouldn't trust that sort of thing to just anyone. Verfessa? He's an opportunist. I wouldn't give it to him. He'd spend it on something that would favor him rather than protect you. The Maskers? Perhaps. But you and me? Cut from the same cloth. And something that valuable? I wouldn't let it leave my side."

The door opened. Her bodyguard, summoned by the whistle, stepped inside. Allie reached for a heavy wine bottle from the shelf, but the guard anticipated the move and slammed her against the wall. He pulled the bag from her hand and tossed it to Madritz. While he continued searching and Allie continued to struggle, she retrieved the book and flipped through the pages.

"Don't bother screaming. The building is empty. I had the other tenants sent away for the day to give me an opportunity to search their homes as well." She snapped the book shut. "This is the actual book. Whole. Intact. Well done."

Without another word, she tossed it into the flames, which remained suspiciously steady as the book was consumed. After finding four different weapons, hidden to one degree or another, the bodyguard finally pulled a folded page in Allie's apron free. He forced her to the floor and kept her there with a boot, handing the slip to Madritz. She unfolded it and shook her head.

"Astounding. I distinctly recall placing this in the stove to burn away. And I kept my eye on you the entire time." She shook her head, staring down at Allie. "It is such a shame you chose contrariness and rebellion. Someone with your resourcefulness and skill could have gone a long way in service of me."

"And it's a shame you decided that corruption and greed are a proper way of life. You might have ended up being worthwhile instead of destined for a shallow grave," Allie spat.

Madritz raised her eyebrows. "Really now? Hollow threats? Those are beneath you."

"Not a threat," Allie said as the bodyguard hauled her to her feet, hands behind her back. "A warning. Maybe if you head out of town now, you can stay ahead of it for a few days. You don't know the kind of people you're messing with."

"I've done my research," Madritz said, fetching a rope and preparing it for her bodyguard. "I know all about Verfessa. I know all about the Maskers. I know all about the pathetic, worthless city guard in Beffshire. I'm far too visible in this town already, and too closely connected to the lords, for Verfessa to raise a blade against me for someone as meaningless as you. The only member of the Masker family stupid and violent enough to attempt to strike me down is a long way away, likely never to return. And no one else cares enough about you to lift a finger."

Velonia took a poker and pushed the cover of the book out of the flames, such that it wouldn't burn completely away. The bodyguard finished binding Allie's hands and legs. He pulled a sack over her head.

"Take her out to the stable," Madritz said. "And from there, take what's left out to the woods. Make sure there's enough of her left to be identified. Between the theft of a Maskers' book from Verfessa's stronghold, its destruction, and the death of someone known to be working both sides, even if they don't feel compelled to clash, it will certainly look like one. That should cast enough light on the Maskers and Verfessa's organization to complicate their lives too much to continue to be such a blasted thorn in everyone's sides."

Allie shrieked until a gag was tied over the bag on her head. She heard the flutter of a page, no doubt the stolen letter finally being burned as Madritz had intended. She was hauled outside and tossed into the back of a cart of some kind. No amount of struggling would break her bonds, and the bodyguard had found all her blades.

Panic pushed at the edge of her mind, but she didn't let it take over. Once she let that happen, that was the end. No more chance for an idea that might save her. She fought to keep her breath steady and fixed her mind on the one sense that would do her any good. Her sense of hearing. She heard and felt the cobblestones of the street. She felt the turns. Drew a picture in her mind of where she was going. She didn't know what good it would do her, but something was better than nothing. When she heard the sounds of people, she kicked and thumped at the cart as best she could. Alas, one of the things she liked best about this part of the city was the tendency for people to look the other way and mind their own business. Half of her neighbors may well have spotted her being loaded into the cart and still ignored it. Sticking your nose into such things was a great way to have it cut off.

The rumble of cobbles gave way to the worn-smooth grind of the main road through the gate. The north gate. Once they were clear of the town, any hope of rescue would be gone. But one sound, almost lost among the rest, had simmered just beneath the din of the city almost since she was pulled from her home. Now that they were past the wall, it remained, still quiet, but dominating her senses for what it represented. Her one, slim glimmer of hope hung upon the flap of wings and the soft croak and chatter of crow-like caws.

"Just so you know," Fel said, munching on some dried fruit and tea that the archivist had kept in his office, "the real Clickspring houses usually had more windows."

Oiler contentedly did some maintenance on an old chair, and Parch periodically tried to eat parts of another chair. Fel had been lingering by the only window facing the street, peering through a narrow gap in the shutters to keep an eye on the guards' patrols. The sun was beginning to slide from the sky.

"This is the real Clickspring," said the archivist.

"The real Clickspring is an island," Fel said. "I've been there. It's been abandoned for hundreds of years. The only thing that lives there is a dragon with a real bad temper."

"This is the real Clickspring."

"Quite the compelling argument you've put together." Fel grabbed a pair of strange lenses mounted on a stick. "Are these opera glasses?"

"They are."

"Do you have an opera house in this town?"

"Not yet."

"Then why do you have them?"

"They are part of the archive."

"You're the archivist, right?"

"Yes."

"Then shouldn't you be able to tell me why they are in the archive?"

"I... They are..."

"They look good on the shelf. That's why. This is set dressing for a fake city. That shelf was looking a little thin, so the one in charge added them to the shelf because it was an easy artifact from the Bygone Era to polish up. This is fake. It's all fake. And it might be comfortable, but don't get too lazy, because it's not going to last much longer."

"What are you implying?"

"Quiet for a minute. Something's wrong. The patrol is already a few minutes late, and I don't see them anywhere."

"Shouldn't that make you happy? As a person with obvious ill will toward the city, the absence of the guards should be a boon."

"These people can't think for themselves. If they're late, it means something happened to pull them off their training. And if that thing is some tip-off of where to find me, we're going to have trouble."

He puffed the pipe.

"Fel," Wick said. "Your father has given me a procedure for you. I have informed Tome. He is already commencing with his side of the plan. It will take some time. They have to leave via the far side of the Lesser Greater Lands and circle around the outside of the wall in order to avoid traveling for a half day at least."

Fel stood and slapped the archivist on the back. "Good news, buddy. You're not a hostage anymore. I have better things to do. But do yourself a favor. If someone gives you a chance to get out of here, don't put up a fight."

He approached the door. The archivist, in a demonstration of better judgment than Fel would have had in his place, stayed in his chair and didn't try to do anything violent while Fel was checking the street. Fel made ready to sprint toward the central wall and put their plans into motion, but something occurred to him. He doubled back long enough to grab the opera glasses.

"A thief, too?"

"As far as I'm concerned, this place is just a fancy vault, and I make my living cleaning those out. You should be happy this is the only thing I'm taking."

He slipped into the street. It remained all but deserted, the barest bit of activity farther toward the edge of town. Whether the people had been instructed to stay indoors or the little artificial schedule they lived their lives by didn't have any entries for this time of day didn't matter in the slightest to him. He'd take every bit of good fortune he could get.

Rather than attempting to bust through the front door, Fel's plan was to take the direct approach. Scale the wall around the clockwork diamond, do whatever his father told him to, and disable or avoid any traps along the way. He didn't even care about alarms. If things went right, they wouldn't have time to do anything about what he was planning. If things didn't go right, an extra alarm wouldn't make much of a difference.

Two minutes of running took him, huffing and puffing, to the base of the wall. He twirled his improvised grappling hook and started to scale. Parch clattered up the wall with little difficulty and met him at the top. Once there, he stopped long enough to raise the opera glasses and scan the city from this, the tallest point in it. He'd expected the fading light to make it difficult to spot anyone on the move, but the opposite was true. A line consisting of half of the town guard and a handful of townsfolk was headed directly for the same facility Fel had infiltrated not so long ago. The man at the head of the line, judging by his fancier helmet, was the chief of the guard. He was holding aloft a lantern that singled him out quite easily against the dim countryside.

A half-dozen questions ranging from why they were headed to that place to why they wouldn't defend the most obvious target bounced off Fel's mind. He didn't have the luxury of time to ponder such things. He just made a mental note that he'd have to fight through, at best, half of them once it became clear what he was doing. That would simplify matters.

He pulled up the rope he'd climbed and stopped short of the inner edge of the wall. The entire inner ring of floor tiles had the suspicious look of raised pressure plates. The crenellations similarly seemed unnecessarily precarious. He took a small wooden stick from his gear, stood clear of any major gaps, and tested one of the tiles. A breath of wind and the whistle of blades caused his hair to flutter, and the stick fell into three pieces. This wouldn't be a simple trap to avoid. It was sensitive enough to make sabotaging it near suicidal. And worst of all, the moment it activated, the lanterns casting their gleam on the dazzling display of the diamond at the center suddenly went still.

"Fel Masker," boomed Lens's voice.

"A little busy. We can chat when I'm finished wrecking your plans."

Fel reached out with the only other wooden pole in his kit and shoved at a spike at the top of one of the inner crenellations. No trap activated. He'd seen this sort of structure a thousand times when working his way through ruins. It was a bit of exposed support. In a real Bygone ruin, it would be strong enough to still be standing even if the wall had rotted away around it. Here, he suspected it wasn't quite so reliable.

"You of all people should see the promise of what I am attempting here," Lens said. "You who has seen the greatness of the Bygone age, even in ruin. You who has visited the true Clickspring. You who has seen what was taken from us by time and foolishness."

Fel folded the rope over to double its thickness and carefully cast a loop of it over the spike.

"Building a pretend kingdom and playing with the people inside like puppets doesn't appeal to me," he said.

"You're a contraptioneer at heart. A contraptioneer by breeding. You understand the concept of a prototype."

"See, I already don't like where this is going." He fastened the free end of the rope to the hook as well.

"The world you were born to is a remnant of what it once was. Small-minded people, afraid to embrace the wisdom of the past. Squabbling over pointless things. It's a place of war and greed and meaningless strife. I seek to end that."

"With kidnappings?"

"By returning the old wisdom to the world in the only way that will guarantee small minds will accept it. By removing the choice to reject it. Imagine a world of peace. Unburdened by doubt and confusion. A world once again guided by the brilliant creations of the Bygone age. The greatest mistakes of the last few hundred years erased and forgotten. The clock turned back to a golden era."

"You can't turn back the clock."

"Look around you! For all the people here but you, I have turned back the clock. Memories rewritten. And soon, history rewritten as well. The lost archives of Telestressa raised from the ashes. Just as your father seeks to do. But while he does so slowly and timidly, I strike forward boldly, uninhibited."

"Funny thing about Dad. He doesn't like brainwashing people."

He spun the grappling hook up to speed and sent it flying. It clattered against the top of the rotating clockwork diamond. After a few skipping, clinking bounces, the tines of the hook caught the edge of a panel and the doubled rope started to reel in.

"You don't think the diamond can be so easily disabled, do you? I spared no expense and no effort salvaging what it would take to build it to as near to Bygone specifications as possible."

"I'm counting on it," Fel said.

The rotation pulled the slack out of the ropes. They drew taut and began to creak. A row of the traps activated simultaneously as the stones of the inner wall shifted and crackled. Finally a whole section of the wall pulled away, dragging the innards of the traps with it. They spun, jammed, and went still.

"You will fail, Fel Masker."

"I'm happy with how it's going so far."

"You will fail because fate has spoken. A long-awaited piece of information, the last piece I needed, has finally reached me. A long-planned machination has borne fruit, a book from your own father's stolen collection consumed in my flames. Irrevocably given to me."

"It's amazing you get anything done at all with all the talking you do."

"Then let actions convince you of the truth of my words. Before you waste your time with the diamond, turn your eyes to the assembly facility once more."

Fel wanted to ignore the request, but his eyes betrayed him, flicking toward the distant stone building barely visible in the evening light. A string of steady green embers flowed from the doorway. They moved nearly as fast as a horse at full gallop, but in a tight, unnatural formation.

"Your father is a brilliant man, and his ingenuity and insight are still key to what I seek to do. But in his zeal to create a new solution, he failed to take the time to see if his ideas could be better served by other forgotten techniques. The coupler was inspired. But the trick of its functionality can be separated from its mechanism. A single line from a single page of Professor

Milton Governor's *Treatise on the Infusion of Alloys with Mystic Properties* was all that was missing from the procedure I was seeking."

Fel jumped past the disabled traps, even as Oiler made an ultimately pointless attempt to repair them. A bit of the wall gave way beneath his feet, leading to a graceless plummet the last two yards, but he scrambled to his hands and knees and made his way to the base of the clockwork diamond.

"Make it quick, Wick," he said. "I don't know what those things are, but they'll be here soon."

"You know what they are," Lens said. "You encountered them in the facility. The larger ones were not complete. But many of the smaller ones, I believe thanks to Oiler, were completed."

"They were missing masks and couplers. That's not complete. Wick, speak up," Fel said.

"I am attempting to concoct a summarized articulation," Wick said. "Your father is quite verbose."

"They no longer require a coupler, and though the ancient design called for one, these were never intended to wear a mask," said Lens.

"Then how are they moving?" Fel hissed.

"I have taken direct control of them."

"Sentry flames can only be in one place at a time! You can't be a dozen automata and here mocking me."

"If you would like to discuss how I have achieved my desired effect, I invite you to discontinue your attempted sabotage. I will be happy to share my methods with you. You and your family still have a place in my plans, though some modification of both my plans and your minds will still be necessary."

"Wick!" Fel urged.

"If the northern end of the courtyard is to be considered twelve o'clock on the face of a clock, an engraved plate featuring a cross shape and two diamond shapes as the initial symbols should be located just past the two o'clock position. Wait until the first arm sweeps past it and remove it, exchanging it with the plate in the four o'clock position."

"Good, good. Keep it up," he shouted, rushing to do as he was told.

Martin lingered behind the counter of the shop with Vivian and Epiphany. The family had gathered in the shop to remain near Wick's currently flickering lantern. When the news came of his success or failure, they wanted to be together. Even Teya—who normally could be convinced to remain in the lower levels of the Masker household for the sake of not worrying the customers, stood just out of sight behind the counter.

Wick's speed at switching from flame to flame had grown much faster over the last few months, but it still took some time, and given the rapid rate at which things would need to be done on Fel's end, once Fel started manipulating the clockwork diamond, there wouldn't be time for Wick to come back and seek guidance or clarification. Despite this, Martin held a book under his arm with copious notes. Just because something was impossible didn't mean he shouldn't prepare for it.

Presently the shop was free of customers, leaving the entire family to wait in silence for Wick to speak up. The tension was steadily growing unbearable. It was a welcome chance at release when someone across the street paused to squint at the display in the window. Vivian automatically ticked through the sequence of actions that preceded a customer interaction. She smoothed down her dress, opened her ledger to the relevant page, and reached up to turn a particularly attractive Bygone figurine toward the doorway to better show it off. But before the customer could even set foot into the street to approach the door, a quartet of black forms slammed into the windows, rattling and scratching against them.

"Monkey! Egg monkey!" screeched Moody the lesser harpy.

"Precious egg monkey!" added Judy between hammering pecks at the glass.

"I'll kill you, you thieving rat!" croaked Rudy.

"Rat thief monkey egg thief!" cried Toody.

Vivian's expression became stern. She stalked to the doorway and threw it open. "Really now. You know better than this. You've had your treats and thus the door is to be kept clear of your antics!" she chastised.

In a flurry of black feathers, the lesser harpies burst inside the shop and huddled in the center of the floor. They had never dared enter the shop, and from the way they kept their heads low and glanced desperately about, ready for a thrown boot or swung broom, they knew the danger of doing so. But still they continued their chaotic chatter.

"Egg monkey! Thief! Kill!"

"Kill it! Kill it before it gets away!"

"Mine! That's mine, monkey egg. Rat thief!"

"Go, go, go!"

"This is entirely new behavior," Martin said. "I don't recall 'egg' figuring so prominently in their vocabulary."

Teya emerged from behind the counter, causing the lesser harpies to skitter back toward the open door. "What you say, friends?" Teya asked. "And why? Why you say this?"

"Egg monkey!"

"Precious egg monkey!"

"Thief! Rat thief!"

"Family!"

"Family," Martin repeated.

"Didn't... didn't Allie say she bribed them with eggs recently?" Epiphany said.

At the sound of Allie's name, the harpies exploded in renewed urgency.

"Monkey egg!"

"Family!"

"Allie!"

"Kill the thief!"

"Dad, this means something," Epiphany said. "This is important."

"We go! We follow!" Teya said, hopping up and down.

"Do we have any contraptions that would help in a fight?" Epiphany asked, grabbing her coat.

"I sent the best of them with Fel, but I think I can find something."

"Go! Fast fast! I get arrows. We go!" Teya crowed, leaping down the hatch ahead of Martin.

Fel had been working as quickly and precisely as he could as the minutes ticked by. All the while, Lens had been calmly attempting to convince him of the wisdom of his own scheme. Fel clicked a plate down again a moment before the arm swept over it. Aside from a bit of a change to the way it was rattling, there was no clear indication he'd done anything at all.

"All right. Any more steps?"

"No. That is the final aspect of the reconfiguration."

"Are we sure I did this right? I'd expect there to be some sign I was monkeying around with it," Fel said.

"Martin claims the effects the diamond has inflicted upon both the land and the minds of the people will be reversed, but to give you time to escape, he's had to ensure that the reversal is iterative. The change will be more apparent as time goes on."

"That's all well and good, except it means I'll have to defend it," Fel said. "Otherwise they'll just be able to fix it."

"That is correct, to a point," Wick said. "The motion of the diamond should begin to accelerate, and thus the iterative changes will come more swiftly. Once the speed of rotation is high enough, no further changes can be made without causing catastrophic failure."

"How much time will pass between when they can't fix it and when everything starts falling apart?"

"Everything will already be falling apart by the time it is irreversible, but Martin estimates it will take seven minutes between the changes becoming irreversible and the complete elimination of the diamond's effects."

"We're way more than seven minutes away from the outer wall."

"The outer wall will be much closer at that time."

Fel rubbed his face. A rhythmic clatter was ringing out from the main door to the courtyard. Whatever Lens had put together to defeat him, it had arrived.

"Oh, good. A distraction. That'll keep me from fretting about if this plan will kill me or not. Now I just have to focus on defeating whatever is being thrown at me by the sentry lantern who wants to rule the world."

The door opened. Spindly automata marched in. They still had the framework indicating a head and neck would need to be installed, but a flame stood roughly stationary in the place of a face. There were twelve of them in total. They moved in what at first seemed like perfect unison. When they reached their intended position and stood at attention, Fel realized that they moved in a quick but discernible wave, each one's motion offset from the one before it by a fraction of a second. The motion of the flame matched the offset, a brief flicker and dance of flame barely perceptible before it snapped back to stationary again. Lens wasn't controlling them all at once. He was controlling them one at a time, but so rapidly it seemed as though they were independent.

"I am not attempting to rule the world," Lens said, his voice seeming to sweep around Fel, moving from flame to flame. "If global domination was my aim, I would already have it. I have influence within all the most powerful organizations. All three kingdoms seek my advice through some means or another. I control communication; I control trade. This world is mine for the taking. But I do not want this world. I want the world that was taken from us when the Bygone Era ended. And you still have a place in that world. So please do not force me to destroy you. A Masker is a difficult thing to replace."

A horn rang out from somewhere in the city, followed by the subdued shout of what he imagined must be the shouts of the guards who had remained in the city.

"What is happening?" Lens said.

Fel grinned. "The cavalry has arrived. See, this is the problem with making loads of enemies and trying to enslave them. You end up assembling your own rebel army." He puffed the cigar. "Wick, tell Tome it seems like his side of the plan is rolling in."

"So I shall," Wick said.

Fel clamped the pipe hard in his teeth and widened his stance as the automata spread around the diamond. "Oiler, if ever you felt like breaking your rule about weapons and repairing things, now's the time. Parch? Here's hoping you're feeling violent."

For the sake of not testing Oiler's pacifistic tendencies, Fel pulled his second grappling hook from his gear. It wasn't overtly a weapon and thus ideally wouldn't compel Oiler to disarm him. Alas, the automata were entirely unarmed as well, so Oiler wasn't likely to be a help or a hindrance.

The things moved forward in a wave. Three targeted Fel; nine targeted the ring of plates. Fel dropped low and rushed forward, ramming his shoulder into the midsection of the nearest contraption. It felt roughly like he'd slammed himself into a wrought-iron gate. The blow was enough to knock the thing from its feet but came close to fracturing Fel's shoulder. He stumbled upright and felt an icy metallic hand grip his wrist. He curled his arm in, thumped his shoulder to the thing's chest, and bent sharply at the waist, flipping the thing over him and bringing it down hard atop the fallen one. The third contraption grabbed his belt and hauled him back, but the clank of bone on metal sent the thing stumbling as Parch rammed full force into its leg.

Two more of the contraptions peeled off from those assessing the plates. Fel tied a hasty loop into the end of his rope. The first of them reached him, and he snared the thing's arm in the loop. A desperate toss hooked the other end of the grappler into one of the outer rings of the rotating diamond. It was dragged backward and reeled inward, screeching across the semicircle of would-be repair contraptions, clattering them to the ground.

The tangled automaton became something of a slow-motion wrecking ball, screeching along the ground at a gradually increasing rate, forcing the others to dodge and reposition each time. It became clear that one mind split across a dozen bodies, even a phenomenally quick mind, gave Fel the tiniest bit of edge. Lens was thinking for a dozen. Fel barely thought at all.

He retreated to just outside the reach of the spinning contraption and re-assessed. Five of the things were still attempting to reach the plates. Lens knew the functionality of the clockwork diamond well enough that it wasn't enough to remove a plate from its tampered position. It had to swap places with the proper plate, and each had to be done before the sweeping arm reached either plate. Failing to do so was the equivalent of attempting to defuse a bomb and simply tossing it in a campfire instead. Discounting the ensnared automaton, the remaining six were coordinating themselves for an attack. Rather than moving as one, Lens had learned from his mistake, reducing the mental effort by focusing on only two of them. They moved faster and more precisely. Not massively, but notably. Enough that both were able to get ahold of Fel before he could disable either one. He was strong enough to just barely topple one of them. Two were too much for him.

"You put up a valiant effort. But it will be for naught," Lens said, inching his many bodies into position to undo Fel's changes.

One of them delivered a blow to Fel's chest. The wet, sickening snap of a broken rib caused him to double over.

"That should help you to behave," Lens said.

The rotation of the diamond had accelerated to the point that the entangled automaton was elevated far enough off the ground for the others to duck beneath it. Parch attempted to ram one of them, but it turned and swung a backhand. The unicorn dodged, but the near attack was enough to make it think twice about a follow-up.

Fel's sabotage had started to assert itself. Each revolution was producing a tangible tremor. Some of the stones of the courtyard had started to rise up, crowded out of their position. And the entire courtyard had a slope toward its center. Most importantly, though, the entangled automaton had been badly damaged by its repeated impacts, and its flame had been extinguished, leaving it fully motionless. This meant two things. That the flame was just as fragile as a natural one, and that suddenly the dangling automaton had become very interesting to Oiler. The repair contraption reached up, reeling out its chain arm. It caught hold of the dangling leg. When its arm started to reel out, it clamped its other claw into the stone of the courtyard's floor. The rope started to wrap tight. The tension in Oiler's chains began to build. Something was going to give. Two of the automata guarding Fel turned to deal with the situation. They didn't do so quickly enough. Oiler, rather than allowing the swinging contraption to break further, released it. Oiler's arm snapped back with remarkable force, and the dangler did the same. Three automata reaching for plates were slammed by their swinging counterpart. The force knocked one of them into the rotating arm, causing a brief but intense tremor as the diamond's work was disrupted. For a moment, all the various bodies Lens was controlling were either damaged, entangled, or off-balance. Parch, ever the opportunist, struck by driving his horn through the back of the knee of one that was holding Fel.

He wrenched his arm free. A bolt of pain from his broken rib robbed him of some strength, but he brushed it aside. What came next was going to hurt a whole lot more regardless. He slapped his palm down onto the burning plate at the base of where the neck should be. A hiss of smoke and a sizzle of seared skin snuffed the flame. The automaton fell limp. Another grabbed Fel's upper arm. He took a hearty drag on the pipe in his mouth and slammed it against the recently extinguished metal plate. A new flame slowly sparked into being.

"Oh. A body," Wick said calmly as his flame took hold on the automaton.

"I could use some help, Wick!" Fel said, pulling a hammer from his bag and smashing at the flailing arm of one of Lens's bodies.

Wick staggered to his feet. "Forgive me. I am unaccustomed to legs."

Two of the automata attempted to grasp plates and were scattered to bits by the rotating arms. Each cycle of the rotating diamond was now subtly but visibly faster than the last. Fel pulled Oiler to his back and groaned at the pain in his side.

"Wick, If I'm going to make it out of here alive, I'm going to need you to do what you can to stop these things."

"I will do my best, Fel."

"Parch! Let's go!" Fel shouted.

The unicorn got one last ram into the calf of an automaton and galloped after Fel. He passed through the open gate of the courtyard and got a proper look at what was happening to the city of Lens's creation now that the diamond had been sabotaged. Great ridges of cracked ground were rising up, like a tablecloth bunching up. Elsewhere deep faults split streets. And swarming everywhere, moving with manic but strangely coordinated motion, were kobolds. Hundreds of them. Some were leading frightened and confused humans. Others had taken a more direct route, hauling them up and toting them away. Six of them spotted him and charged toward him.

"Fel the human?" chattered one.

"Friend of Teya?" chittered the next.

"Who is friend of Kazel?"

"That's right," he said.

One of the automata burst from behind him. Four of the kobolds screeched and threw themselves at the thing, teeth and claws rending it to shreds of twisted metal. The other two helped him forward, leading him along the path they'd taken through the decaying city to reach him.

"By the High, I love kobolds," he huffed, struggling to keep his feet. "Creatures after my own heart."

The rattling cart reached its destination, a stable a short distance from the city. Allie heard her captor deliver a gruff order.

"Leave. Don't return for an hour. You heard nothing, you saw nothing."

Heavy boots scurried away. The horse leading the cart snorted and nickered. It refused to continue forward. Allie knew precisely why. Even she could smell the heavy, unsettling aroma of a large, vicious animal. The bodyguard grabbed her and hauled her out. She was carried roughly inside and thrown down. The scent that stirred ancient survival instincts to flee was now joined by the equally distressing sounds of a massive predator. The gag and sack over her head were pulled away. She blinked her eyes in the dim light of an enclosed stable. A griffin, complete with a heavy saddle and a curious metallic headpiece glared at her with its piercing gaze. The bodyguard, and now without any doubt the same griffin rider who had threatened the Maskers once before, looked down upon her with a combination of faint disgust and boredom.

"If you feel the need to scream, go ahead. They slaughter pigs a short distance down the road. No one will even notice a little extra screeching in a given day."

She kept her silence, for now. He paced away from her, toward the griffin. As he did, he shook his head.

"Madritz told me to bring you here before doing a poor job of hiding you in the woods," he said, almost conversationally. "I'm sure she assumed I'd slice pieces off of you to feed the griffin. Everyone assumes riding a meat eater means they'll devour the fallen. I really don't have any interest in this thing developing a taste for human flesh."

He slashed open a bag and revealed a whole hog. He tossed it into the pen with the griffin. It put its beak to work.

"You still have to die. Because killing whoever needed killing is one of the things I was paid to do. But my employer doesn't get to tell me what to do with my mount."

"You don't have to do this," Allie said.

"I do. There's a contract. Mercenaries get work based on reputation. Do what you're told, or you'll never see another duot."

"And you know who I work for."

"You work for Madritz. And you've done a piss-poor job of it if it's come to this. But if you're talking about Verfessa or the Maskers, I'm aware of the big happy family they've put together."

"Then you know that you're not going to survive this."

"They got the better of me once. That doesn't happen twice." He narrowed his eyes. "To that end..." He turned to the griffin and clicked a command. "I already know that no one sent any heavies after you. At least not fast enough to do you any good. I would have seen them. But Verfessa sends someone who is decidedly not a heavy from time to time."

The griffin raised its fierce head and sampled the air.

"Everyone knows to fear a griffin's sharp eyes. But they neglect the sense of smell. Perhaps not as powerful as a hound."

The creature released a low avian screech and angled its head to a dark place in the corner of the roof. Questor raised his lantern and stalked forward. As the flickering flame's glow pierced the darkness, a small form dashed across one of the planks separating the stable from the loft. Questor clicked another command. The griffin charged forward and thumped the support post. The figure was knocked free and narrowly avoided being scissored in half by the snapping beak of the griffin. It was Davie. From the way he limped as he darted from the stable, the fall hadn't done him any good, and without his speed, it would be suicide to try to face the man or the beast.

"Verfessa gave me a new respect for gnomes as assassins, but that sort of thing only works well when you aren't expecting it. It does mean I'll have to work a bit faster. People know where I am." He knelt beside Allie and drew a stout blade. "I'll make it quick. No sense letting you suffer. That costs extra, and they didn't cough up for it."

In the distance, she heard a commotion of cackling and cawing. A shaky smile came to her face. "I don't wish death on anyone," Allie rumbled. "But your fate is sealed. I only hope I linger long enough to see it."

"Sorry to disappoint you, but you won't."

He raised the blade. She braced for its bite. The shutter on the window rattled and was yanked open. He turned to assess the threat. His reward was a face full of lesser harpy talons. He swatted at them and fought to his feet. They scraped and clawed at his hands, at his arms, and if not for his skilled defense, they would have made a meal of his eyes. The knife fell from his grip. Allie rolled herself to the fallen weapon. He clicked a command. The griffin screeched. The sound was terrifying at a primal level and convinced the lesser harpies to retreat.

Allie fumbled with the knife, her hands still bound behind her back. Desperation was no friend of precision, and working blind was difficult enough as it was. She felt the sting of the blade on her fingers and her forearm twice before she aligned it properly to work at the ropes. She'd barely nicked the binding when he grabbed her and pulled her up.

"That's enough of that," he roared.

Questor wrenched the knife from her fumbling grip. The griffin planted itself in the doorway, its mere presence more than enough to keep the harpies from returning. Strong though he was, he needed a moment to wrestle Allie into a position where the knife could do its work, and in that moment an inhuman battle cry filled the air. The distinctive sound of an arrow biting into the side of the stable came next. Then the hiss of a second arrow streaking through the window and narrowly missing him.

The mercenary growled and threw her down. He turned to assess the threat, raising a crossbow from his back. Teya appeared in the window, either too frenzied or too brave to be frightened away by the griffin. A bolt from his crossbow nearly lodged itself in her skull, and she vanished again.

"Congratulations," he rumbled, drawing back the crossbow for another bolt. "A bunch of your friends just decided to die for you."

He clicked a command to the griffin, and both man and beast stepped from the stable. Allie fought with her damaged bonds. Between the warm blood from her self-inflicted injuries slicking her wrists and the extra slack from nicking the rope, she was able to slip her hands free. Untying the ropes around her ankles proved very difficult with bloody fingers, but she got it done and stumbled toward the doorway.

It was a sight to behold. In the fading light of evening, Teya and the lesser harpies were combining their manic efforts to keep the griffin busy. Questor was shielding his eyes from a spray of sparks erupting from a contraption brandished by Epiphany Masker. He pulled down the goggles meant to shield his eyes during flight and charged toward the shopkeeper-turned-rescuer.

Total chaos swallowed the stables. Teya scrambled up a tree. The harpies took to the air. The griffin followed, shaking the branches with the force of its wings as it took flight. Allie tried to tackle Questor to the ground, but he was too strong and she was too light to properly knock him down. Staggering him was enough to foul his aim, keeping Epiphany from catching a crossbow bolt to the liver.

Allie retreated before he could bury the knife in his other hand in her chest. He'd only just steadied himself on his feet when he cried and reached for his ankle. The half-seen form of Davie could be seen dashing for cover after taking a stab at his ankle. Allie made ready to try once more to knock Questor to the ground, but a shouted warning from Epiphany convinced her to keep her distance.

A moment later, something shrieked through the air between Epiphany and Questor, and he was slammed painfully into the wall of the stable. He struggled but couldn't seem to pull himself free. It took Allie a moment to realize he was pinned to the wall by a net that had been launched from a contraption in Epiphany's hand.

Allie yanked the crossbow from his hand. Epiphany approached and pulled the knife from the other. He continued to struggle, but the net held firm. The two women stood before him. What should have followed was a triumphant, taunting victory speech. Instead, the only vocalization was a chattering warning in Teya's native tongue. The flailing kobold hurled her compact form at the two women. Despite her size, she proved quite capable of forcing both humans back.

"What was that all about?" Allie asked.

"Rotten egg monkey thief!" came an angry cry.

They turned in time to see four black blurs whisk by. Two darted through the door to the left of the wall Questor was pinned to. Two darted through the window to his right. A heartbeat later, the griffin in pursuit of them split the difference, colliding full force with Questor. Allie and Epiphany covered their heads as splintering wood and the screech of the griffin filled the air. When the dust settled, Questor, the griffin, and the stable were no more.

Teya, Epiphany, and Allie brushed away the splinters that had pelted them during the collision. They blinked at the still settling debris. Davie limped up to them.

"You ladies need to learn a thing or two about collateral damage," he muttered.

Wings fluttered. Four lesser harpies landed on the branch of the tree where Teya had sought refuge.

"Egg?" crooned Judy.

"Yeah. Yeah, I think you four have earned a baker's dozen." Allie winced in pain. "After I get patched up."

Fel and the kobolds scrambled over a mound of earth and slid down the opposite side. The tremors of the diamond's rotation had become a constant, rumbling quake, and the truth of what was happening to the land enclosed by the wall became abundantly clear. Sections of the countryside descended into the earth, leaving faults that then slammed shut. Whole streets were swallowed by the churning ground. It was as the disgruntled man he'd tied up in the facility had said. This land wasn't created by the contraptions. It was drawn up from below. And now that the diamond was undoing its work, the land was returning it from whence it came, along with everything that had been built out of it or atop it. The outer wall was visibly receding toward the center, drawing closer to them at easily twice the speed they were approaching it.

In the moments that he could spare from the desperate sprint for safety, Fel saw the Greater Lands creatures that had been lured past the wall, and the residents of the false city. The brainwashing was reverting just as quickly as the land, leaving people with the sudden awareness that they'd been held prisoner for months or years. For those who weren't yet shaken from their enchantment, most reacted to the destruction of the city from the inside out in precisely the same way as their liberated associates—by dashing away from the center of the catastrophe. Only the absolute most subjugated needed to be helped along by the kobolds. As Fel had learned, four of the creatures were more than capable of hauling a human over whatever terrain they needed to, whether the human wanted them to or not. One such quartet scrambled over the crumbling remnants of a building with the archivist slung between them.

The wall lurched closer. Until this moment, Fel had been faintly aware that the wall was a part of the contraption. Its unnatural role in this twisted land was now an acute reality. Not content to simply buckle, crumble, and churn into the land like the rest of the false Clickspring, huge sections of it were dislodging and drifting toward the center as if drawn by an invisible force stronger than gravity. The clusters of blocks left wide gaps in the wall. Kobolds and humans dashed through them by the dozen before the ragged ends came together, rendering the wall briefly whole before a new section tore away.

The end was in sight. The one section of the wall that seemed unwilling to bend to the whims of the failing enchantment was the main gate. It and the section of road leading from it remained intact and steady. A rush of evacuating kobolds and humans flooded onto it and dashed for the gate. Search parties started to bunch up as the land beneath them slammed together and contracted. As near as he could tell, Fel and his helpers were bringing up the rear.

Fel's lungs burned and his rib throbbed. Now he was near enough that he could see Tome through the open gate, shouting orders and waving evacuees to safety. The world beyond the gate was rock solid and intact, but reaching it was a literal uphill struggle. The land was slumping down beneath them. It had contracted so much that the outer wall of the clockwork diamond had caught up to them. It was just as close behind as the exit was in front. The clicking and whirring of the clockwork diamond had accelerated to a high-pitched whine. But the sound that worried Fel was the clattering of metal. He focused on the gate, unwilling to waste the time it would take to check what was pursuing him. Barely five yards from the gate, it made its presence known.

Something hooked one of Fel's bags. He was pulled back. When he rolled to his back, he caught a metal boot on his chest. Three of the automata had reached him, with the top half of a fourth dangling from the grip of one of them. Judging from the scattered metal parts on the churning path behind them, they were the only ones left.

"I could not stop them all," uttered Wick from the flame on the dismembered contraption.

One of the automata raised Fel from the ground and held him up. With only three bodies to control, Lens's reflexes were considerably faster. The remaining two swatted kobolds aside when they tried to render aid.

"I had a place for you. I had a role for you," Lens said. "But if you would do this to the prototype, you must be removed before the final plan can take shape."

"Everyone back!" Tome shouted from the gate. "I'll handle this!"

Metal fingers closed around Fel's throat. He dangled from the grip. It took both of his hands wrapped around the arm to keep from having his neck snapped. A heavy book thumped to the ground beside him, arcane blue flame consuming it. The air twinkled in front of Fel's fading vision. Then, the sound of tearing metal. He dropped to the ground. The blood started flowing again, his vision returned, and he was treated to the glittering outlines of hands. They drifted through the air, matching Tome's motions and effortlessly tearing through the metal of the automata. The kobolds were emboldened by the clash with the automata, scrambled forward, and hauled Fel out through the gate. Three more swipes with the glittering hands left the contraptions bent and shattered mounds of worthless metal.

The whine of the spinning clockwork diamond was well below the surface now, and what little remained of the wall of its courtyard was barely two yards from the outer wall, which from the outside seemed entirely intact. The whine switched to a grinding roar. Bits of stone and structure rained down upon it. Finally the last of the courtyard wall slumped in. The whine failed, shards of crystalline panel erupted upward, and stillness finally reigned. Where once had been a massive, sprawling region of farms and city wrapped in a wall, now was a mound of unrecognizable rubble. The outer wall may as well have been erected to close off a trash heap.

Fel caught his breath and took a look around from his place on the ground. A legion of a hundred or more kobolds stood with bewildered or terrified humans interspersed among them. He spotted two of the unicorns, still strapped to carts. A third unicorn was milling about. Parch stood atop the gate of the now-fallen Clickspring. Fel peered at Tome.

"That was quite a show," he said.

"Thanks."

"If you can do that, why would you ever do anything else?"

"That spell took three weeks of work and more money in supplies than I care to account for. And it gave me eleven seconds of distance manipulation."

"Ah. Still. Those might be my favorite eleven seconds ever." He pulled his pack to his lap. "I have... ow... I have the Student mask. That bone thing you had me steal. Some gear. The coupler. ... Ouch. A broken rib or two. And this book. I'm pretty sure it has the names of all the people who were captured here. Let's get a head count. See who we saved and who we lost."

He flopped back. "But first... if you've got a healing spell... that'd help."

Wick, now speaking from the lantern by Tome's side, chimed in. "It appears that the danger has passed. Shall I inform your family?"

"Yes. Please. Maybe leave out some of the more exciting parts. I need some stories to tell. Plus I'll need some time to figure out how to sugarcoat them." He groaned and placed his hand on his side. "Good job, everyone. We survived. Now let's go home."

Epilogue

Two Weeks Later...

Allie paced down the street. After so much time carrying one of Wick's lanterns with her, she'd grown accustomed to having a light with her as she walked the city after closing at The Fox and Log. Now, even though she was quite familiar with the stretch of street leading up to Masker's Antiquities, it felt off to see it lit only by the moon.

Ambitious and optimistic as she was, even Vivian Masker didn't imagine that she'd get any business this late at night, so the shop was mostly dark when she arrived. But she'd been asked to stop by, and sure enough, a faint glow from an upper shelf let her know that Wick was keeping an eye on things. She probably didn't even need to knock, but she approached the door to do so anyway. Before she could put her knuckles to the door, she heard a voice from above her.

"Hey! Thanks for stopping by. Up here."

She looked up. It was Fel. For some reason, he was on the roof.

"What are you doing up there?"

"Keeping busy. The folks aren't letting me do any heavy lifting or vault dives for a while. There's a ladder in the alley. Come on up."

"Do I have to? This feels a little like a child inviting me to his tree house."

"My tree house was much more impressive than this. We built a hoist out of the old dumbwaiter."

She muttered under her breath and marched alongside the shop. A short, somewhat precarious climb brought her to the roof, where the fruits of Fel's labors became clear to her.

A sturdy, comfortable little shelter had been erected. It was about the size of a chicken coop and outfitted very much like one as well. Little perches were assembled inside, as were spots for both food and water.

"What do you think? Is it going to take convincing to get the lesser harpies to move in?"

"I'm surprised they haven't invaded already," she said.

She stepped up to him and slapped him on the back. He winced.

"Still healing up?" she said.

"Turns out Tome doesn't quite know how to fix a broken rib with his magic. Guess I know why he hasn't just taken a job as a healer. If you end up with something he doesn't know how to treat, he just lets you tough it out."

"I think that's what healers do, too."

"At least healers throw some words you don't understand at you first," Fel rumbled. "It could be another month before I can take deep breaths without seeing stars. But I don't want to be on the mend when I hit The Fox and Log for the first time. One too many congratulatory drinks and I'll probably wake up with two busted ribs instead of one."

"You could have at least come down and said hello."

"We've been talking nonstop through Wick."

"Not even nearly the same. But as long as we're talking about that, the last thing we talked about before I handed the lantern back to your folks, you were still waiting to find out if you'd rescued everyone."

"Twenty-nine out of thirty-two, still," Fel said, taking a seat and wiping some sawdust from his face. He filled a tankard from a quarter keg of ale beside him and offered it up.

"No, thanks," she said.

He took a sip. "One of them is definitely dead. They found him this morning, according to Euphoria. Stabbed. Probably right around when we wrecked the diamond. Not more than a few days after. He was... not fresh when they found his remains. It was the missing guy with the earring. The other two? I don't think we're going to find them. They were two of the first ones who went missing back before they even realized there was 'a plague.' For all I know they were dead before I even got there. Or they got crushed when we monkeyed with the diamond." He rubbed his eyes. "It's going to be fun not knowing which."

"You saved a bunch of people that the locals thought were gone forever. Take the win instead of dwelling on the loss."

"Yeah... And hey, we didn't lose any kobolds."

"What's going to happen to them?" she asked.

"Good question. The people of Shalia are not thrilled at the thought of a legion of Greater Mystics lurking in a field nearby. Of course, they already thought the same field was killing people with a plague, so six of one, half a dozen of the other. It's just irritating that it doesn't seem to make a difference to them that more than two dozen of their people made it out of Fenfield alive because of the residents of the Lesser Greater Lands. For now, the place stays put, and the creatures stay in it. If only because the alternative involves finding a way to move the whole lot of them back to the Greater Lands. And the Lesser Greater Lands is way bigger than False Clickspring was. Putting it back to normal will be a much bigger deal."

"So the creatures there are still prisoners?" she said.

He rubbed his head. "Yes and no? They can't leave. They only way they got out in the first place was the siren ordering them across the wall of the Lesser Greater Lands and into the wall of False Clickspring. Two-Voice's abilities were potent enough to overrule the diamonds for a minute or two, and then the diamond in False Clickspring took over and it didn't care about kobolds so they were free within those walls."

"Complicated."

"Yeah, it hurts my head. But Two-Voice isn't there anymore. I guess she was part of a trapper's collection, and he took custody of her again since Lens isn't around to keep paying his fees for her usage. I didn't feel great about that, but I felt even less great about having a creature who can control other creatures floating around half a day from my sister. And without her, the rest of the creatures can think straight, more or less."

"The diamond doesn't mess with their minds?"

"It does, but not nearly in the same way. They're just, sort of... mellow without Two-Voice. Though you'll never guess who's going to be fixing that."

"Your dad isn't heading up there, is he?"

He laughed. "No. That would make sense. He's too busy messing with the lump of shield stone I brought back with me."

"Who then?"

"Teya," he said. "Dad's been teaching her how to strip out the plates that are doing the mind-messing, and she is itching to head up to visit the other kobolds."

"All things considered, mission accomplished, then?"

"I got the mask back. I got the coupler back. Saved a bunch of people. But the elf is lost in the shuffle."

"What do you mean he's lost in the shuffle?" she said sharply.

"The last anyone saw of him was when Tome had a brief, uneasy truce with him. Best we can figure, he's still in the Lesser Greater Lands somewhere. He didn't follow into False Clickspring, which is good for him, since False Clickspring doesn't exist anymore. Plus, now we know for certain that the Graves family flame itself is somehow the mastermind of half the disasters in my life. Supposedly the Graves extinguished all their lanterns, but who knows if they're sticking to it. Euphoria has something lit from Wick, so the Graves can still talk to Beffshire, but that's it. It has completely cost them their edge in trade, having to depend upon the same messengers as everyone else. Someone is going to decide having a demented would-be world conqueror eavesdropping on and manipulating their communications is worth it if they can get back to one-upping the competition."

He covered his face. "Things are just a different kind of mess, only now I have a busted rib. But I'm running my mouth. How about you?"

She shrugged. "Same. Look at this."

She held out her hand. A thick white scar, still a bit sensitive, ran across the back of the knuckles on her left hand.

"Wow. You got yourself good. That's from when you cut yourself free from the griffin rider's ropes?"

"Yep. A little deeper and I wouldn't be able to bend my finger anymore. I got lucky. It should heal fine. Eventually."

"What's going on with this Madritz lady?"

"Still haven't heard from her. She made herself scarce after her bodyguard got smashed, remember? At least I think she did. Someone else might have done it for her. All I know is she's gone and has been since that day. And guess what that means about where I live and where I work?"

"They both belong to Verfessa?"

"They both belong to Verfessa," she said with a nod. "A man who, might I add, I still owe a favor. I can understand how he ended up with the tavern. He was part owner already. But I don't know how he ended up owning the building I live in."

"You sure you don't want this?" he said, tapping the keg.

She squinted at him. "Hand me a cup."

He grabbed her a tankard. She filled it herself and sat beside him. The drank in silence for a few seconds.

"I'm sorry, Allie," he said.

"For?"

"This mess we're both in."

"Oh, come off it," she said irritably.

"Your life wouldn't be half as complicated if it wasn't for me."

"You don't get to take credit for things that are my fault," Allie said.

A few more seconds of silence.

"Did I tell you the first thing that tipped me off that things weren't right, back when I was in 'Clickspring'?"

"Was it that people were actually giving you respect for being a contraption-eer?"

He laughed. "No. They made that feel like it was natural. But I started trying to remember some things. It was getting uncomfortable. I paid for some food, and that coin you gave me came tumbling out." He dug in his pocket. "This one here. I looked at it, and there was your face. My family? They were there when I thought back to them. They had a place in my memories, and I could imagine them being elsewhere. But there was you. Unaccounted for in the life they built for me, and yet I couldn't imagine you not being there. That's what shook their grip enough for me to start looking elsewhere. You saved me."

She smiled at him. "You sure know how to make a girl feel special."

"Hey now. What was that about me not taking credit for things that are your fault? Anyhow, I got you something. This was in the works even before I left, but it sort of got lost in the madness until now." He nudged open a crate and pulled out a smaller one from within.

"I'm already not happy how big this present is."

"Just open it."

She muttered under her breath and pulled the lid from the smaller box. Inside, smelling of fresh leather, was a pair of boots. They were the same size, and the same basic design, as the ones she wore every day. But they were exquisitely made. Gorgeous, sturdy. Practical. Precisely what she would have bought for herself if she had the money.

"Courtesy of Reynard, next door to the antiquity shop,"

"Gotta love a man who listens," she asserted quietly.

She reached around him and hugged him with one arm, leaning against him and sipping her ale with the other. He felt tense, rigid. She grinned. *The man fights hordes of thinking mechanisms and destroys whole cities, and all it takes is a half a hug to make him tense. Unless...*

"I found the bad rib, didn't I?" she said.

"It's fine," he groaned.

She moved her arm to his hip. He relaxed a bit.

"So why build the coop now?" she asked.

"Judy and the crew saved my behind. Now they saved yours. A fellow can only hand over so many yeast buns before a proper reward is called for."

"So does that mean you're going to build me a house? I saved your butt a few times, let's not forget."

He laughed. "You find me a place to build one, and I'll think about it. Why? Not too keen on having Verfessa as landlord?"

"That and I'm starting to think room for two might be nice."

He smirked and put his arm around her. "Yeah. That might be nice..."

They sat in comfortable silence for a few moments.

"Smitten," Fel said.

"What's that?"

"Tome says the word I'm looking for is 'smitten.' He says I'm smitten with you."

"You were talking this over with him?" she said.

"Just looking for the right word. I'm not convinced he's right, though." He pulled her a little tighter. "I think probably the word I was looking for is 'love.'"

She released a breath, and for the first time since she was a child, she felt her cheeks burn with a blush.

"It's about time," she said. "That elephant was overstaying its welcome."

Euphoria flipped through the last few pages of the day's business. Perhaps it was her years of living in Beffshire and struggling to put food on the table with their earnings from the shop, but she considered the Graves family finances to be in very good shape. The rest of the family was less enthusiastic. They were merely successful now, rather than dominant. It would take time to adjust, but she was confident the loss of the flame as a tool could be compensated for. Who knew, perhaps it would accelerate the timetable for properly partnering with the Maskers.

She doused the light and yawned. It was time for bed. But a routine was a routine. She could never get to sleep without checking her mailbox. Wealthy neighborhoods were comically "proper" places. People left calling cards at all hours, fully expecting to have their visit repaid at the earliest opportunity. She flipped the box open and found only a single envelope. There was no address. No name but hers. And it was heavy and misshapen, like someone had stuffed something besides a letter inside.

She stepped back into her house and opened it. A short, folded note was inside, and a signet ring crusted with soot. She turned it over. It was an old Graves family signet. Specifically, it was Piotor Graves's signet. She flipped open the note.

Euphoria,

I would suggest you destroy this message when you are through and find a good place to hide the ring. You'll need that signet as proof when the time comes. I found the site of the old fire, the one that chased Piotor farther north. It took more than a week of digging and searching, but I found a small section of the foundation of the collapsed manor that hadn't been found after the initial tragedy. It was rotten, decayed. Untouched for decades. Inside, I found remains. Human remains. Dead for decades. Charred black. And that ring was on the finger. Piotor is dead. Burned in the fire that consumed his manor. And yet through the flame his codes have been used as recently as weeks ago. Answers only Piotor could know were given as recently as months ago.

I do not have the answer. I cannot know the answer. But something sinister has happened, and is happening. Be safe. Be careful.

This isn't over yet.

FROM JOSEPH R. LALLO

Thank you for reading! If you liked this story, or perhaps if you found it lacking, I'd love to hear from you. For free stories and important updates, join my newsletter at: www.bookofdeacon.com

Discover other titles by Joseph R. Lallo:
The Book of Deacon Series

An epic fantasy series spanning six main novels and assorted spin-offs and prequels. Follow the journey of Myranda Celeste and the rest of the Chosen as they fight to save their world from a terrible war and its aftermath.

The Big Sigma Series

A sci-fi action adventure series with six novels. Trevor "Lex" Alexander is a former hover-racer who finds his world turned upside down when he becomes embroiled in the schemes of mega-corporations, criminal syndicates, and a mad engineer with a quirky AI.

The Free-Wrench Series

Take to the skies in this six novel steampunk series about airships in an era of steam, brass, and excitement. Nita Graus joins the Wind Breaker crew, a group of smugglers in a constant clash with the twisted and nefarious fug folk who run the world from their place in the toxic mists that blanket the land.

The Shards of Shadow Series

An ongoing Urban Fantasy series following the trials and tribulations of a photographer named Alan who unwittingly becomes entangled in the dark machinations of the shadowy shades thanks to Blot, one of their weakest agents. These exciting stories take place in modern day Philadelphia and shed light on the supernatural invasion that could tip the balance of power for the entire world.

The Greater Lands Saga

An epic fantasy adventure in a world where magic and supernatural contraptions coexist. Fel Masker is an explorer and adventurer, tasked with securing mysterious, arcane devices for his family to repair and sell. Rivalries with other contraptioneering families are heating up, and soon the lost history of the world may return with a vengeance.

www.ingramcontent.com/pod-product-compliance
Lightning Source LLC
Chambersburg PA
CBHW052026220726